For Sandi

Kindest regards. This
is the country where I grew
up. Enjoy the adventure.

Joseph L. Dorris
Smoky Hawk, Colorado
July 2017

SHEEPEATER
TO CRY FOR A VISION

Joseph L. Dorris

JOSEPH DORRIS

iUniverse, Inc.
New York   Bloomington

Sheepeater

iUniverse books may be ordered through booksellers or by contacting:

iUniverse
1663 Liberty Drive
Bloomington, IN 47403
www.iuniverse.com
1-800-Authors (1-800-288-4677)

*Because of the dynamic nature of the Internet, any Web addresses or links contained in
this book may have changed since publication and may no longer be valid. The views
expressed in this work are solely those of the author and do not necessarily reflect the
views of the publisher, and the publisher hereby disclaims any responsibility for them.*

ISBN: 978-0-595-50915-7 (pbk)
ISBN: 978-0-595-50545-6 (cloth)
ISBN: 978-0-595-61694-7 (ebk)

Printed in the United States of America

iUniverse rev. date: 02/6/09

For my wife, Susan, and our three children,
Scott, Timothy, and Krystle.

SHEEPEATER
TO CRY FOR A VISION

JOSEPH DORRIS

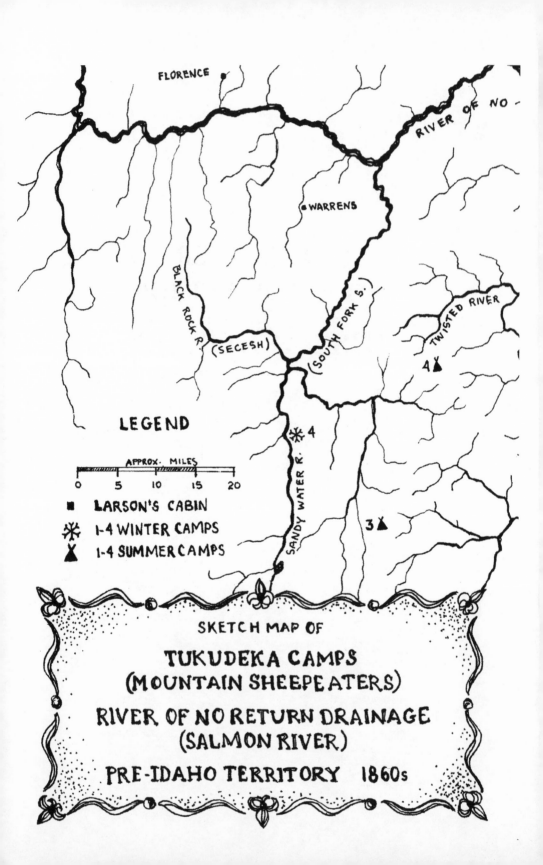

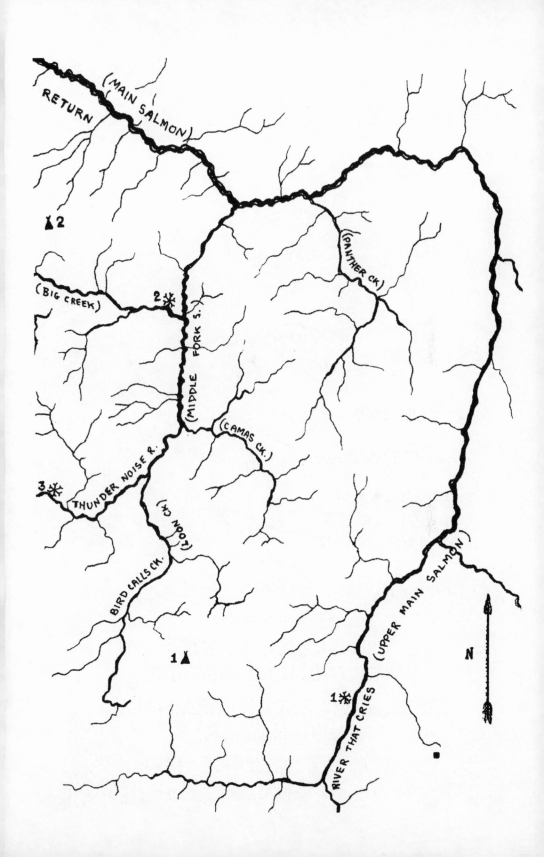

PART ONE
ERIK LARSON
ON THE FROZEN PRAIRIE

Chapter 1

Erik Larson stood within earshot of the two men, his sister standing beside him.

"Sorry, it's gotta be this way, Jon," Jack Slade said. "You've done your best. I got these other folks to worry about."

"*Ja*," Jon Larson replied quietly. "I understand. I expected what you'd say."

The men finished talking, and his father turned their way. His sister clung to him. Erik glanced into her worried face and squeezed her. He told her it would be okay. "*Det kommer att bli okej, Katrine.*" Erik spoke Swedish. His sister spoke English, but he hadn't learned much. He tried but felt uncomfortable around those who were not Swedish. He had not made friends the way Katrine had.

Slade approached them, but Erik's father waved him away.

Erik tapped on the wagon. "Papa's coming, Mama." His mother lie sick in the wagon bed.

She braced herself up; her light blond hair shone in the autumn sun, contrasting with her pale blue eyes and skin. She appeared drawn and thin.

Grim faced, his father addressed them. "They're going to move on. Afraid Mama Larson has the sickness. Afraid she'll make more sick and more folks will die."

Erik saw the pain and disappointment cross his mother's face. He felt his own hopes shatter. His mother nodded. She knew. Katrine clung to him harder, trembling.

His father glanced at him, the flash in his eyes telling him to be strong—that he depended on him. He pulled Katrine to him. "Katrine, you're going on with the Olafsons. They'll take good care of you until we catch up."

"But, Papa ..." Tears sprang to her eyes. "I want to be with you. I want us to be together."

"We will be ... soon ... when Mama Larson gets better. Then Erik and I will be right along. Now give your mother a hug and a kiss."

With tears in her eyes, the little girl climbed into the wagon bed and did so.

Erik helped her back down while his father gathered her things. "We'll see you soon, Katrine. Papa says maybe less than a week."

"But Erik, I want you to come with me."

That had been suggested, but Erik would have nothing to do with it. "I have to help Mama and Papa," he spoke quietly. "You know they need me."

"I need you too. I'll miss you."

"We'll be right behind you, Katrine," Erik replied.

"But what if you get lost?"

"We won't."

"But what if you *do*?" His sister began to panic.

"Then I'll come and find you."

"Promise, Erik?"

Erik hugged her. "Of course I promise, Katrine." He didn't want to follow along behind either, but he knew that if this were the sickness, it would be better for his sister to continue ahead with the others. "You have my sacred word, Katrine. No matter what happens, I'll come and find you."

With tears still in her eyes, she smiled. "Thank you, Erik." She threw her small arms around him and kissed his cheek.

The Olafsons' young daughter, Mia, came up, took his sister by the hand, and led her away. "Come on, Katie. You can ride with me. We'll play with my dolls." Mia seemed pleased that her best friend would now accompany her family.

Olafson clucked to his team and turned toward the trail. "See you soon, Jon." He reached down to shake hands. "I'll be saving some planting ground for you. Just you get Ruthie well."

"*Ja*, I will," Jon replied.

Bobbing and swaying, the wagon pulled into line behind the others as they headed northwest toward the barren, basalt-strewn hills.

In the back of the wagon, Katrine picked up one of the dolls and waved it at Erik. "We get to play." A smile showed on her face. "Good-bye, Erik. Good-bye, Mama. Good-bye, Papa. I love you."

"*Adjö*, Katrine. I love you too," Erik said softly and waved until he could no longer see his sister's bobbing, blond head. He bit his lip.

His father noticed. "Have faith, Erik. I'm thinking Mama Larson will be okay in a couple days. Then we'll catch up."

Jon turned to Slade. "Jack, I'll try to follow a couple days behind." Then, quietly, he added, "If this is the sickness like the others … well, Erik and I'll cut the wagon and catch up." Grimly, they shook hands.

"Sorry about all this, Jon. You've been a good hand. Got a good son and wife. Got a good daughter. I'll make sure to look after her." He pulled his horse back onto the trail. "We'll see you, one way or the other, Jon. Now I gotta get these folks through before more snow hits."

As they watched the train move out across the desolate land, Jon glanced at the gray autumn sky. "Weather's closing in, Erik," he said. "If we get hit by another early storm, no one's going to make it. They'll all be back here in one big, happy camp." He tried to laugh.

Erik studied the broken land. He remembered when they first entered the lava beds. When they turned north from the Snake River, they had entered the most desolate country he'd yet seen. Only sparse grasses, sagebrush, and prickly pear covered the jagged rocks. Black basalt jutted up in eerie, twisted sculptures, interrupted infrequently by stunted trees. Pronghorn and jackrabbits had been the only game. Sometimes a hawk or an eagle hung in the sky. The sun had been merciless. The wind drove dirt and grit into his eyes and ears. His eyes had stung. His lungs had ached. Slade said it was the alkali dust and to keep his mouth covered.

They had packed as much water as they could from the Snake River, but it quickly ran out. They had continued on, heading toward the butte that Slade said marked the point where the trail again headed west and where the next water source was. When at last they had reached it, they found only a trickle—hardly enough for the stock. They stayed several days, losing valuable time, nursing water from the seep until they had partially refilled their barrels.

That's when the Backstroms became ill, Erik remembered.

He turned to his father. "What if Mama *does* have the sickness?"

"Hush, Erik. She doesn't. She's just got a touch of mountain fever. It'll pass," he reassured him. "Come on now, lad. Let's fix a camp and get a fire going. Going to be cold again tonight."

Erik didn't know what to think. He wanted to believe this, but just a few weeks back, the sickness had taken its first life, the Backstroms' young daughter, then their son, and within days, the Backstroms themselves, an entire family.

What if Mama died? What if he got sick? … or Papa got sick? That was the real reason they sent Katrine ahead—the reason they wanted him to go as well. But he would have no part in it. His place was with his parents. The chill wind ruffled his hair.

He helped his father remove the harness from Smoky, the horse he had named, and Red, the ox Katrine had named. They had another ox, but it died early in the trip. From then on, Smoky pulled with Red. Smoky was a spotted gray—an old workhorse. It wasn't the best team for pulling a wagon, but it worked.

His father spoke. "We'll stay here tonight. Tomorrow or the next day, we'll get back on the trail, figuring on when Mama Larson can travel."

He helped his father hobble the animals. They couldn't afford to have them wander far.

"It's for the best, Erik. Mama Larson couldn't go on. The wagons couldn't stop anymore. When she gets some rest, we can continue."

"Sure, Papa," replied Erik. His heart wasn't in it, and he knew his mother wasn't strong—never was—not like the rest of them.

***

Morning came. They traveled but a few hours before deciding to camp. The jostling was too difficult on Mama Larson. His father took the rifle and hunted. It was a rifled musket, because he preferred its range. Erik cared for his mother.

"Well?" he asked when his father returned near evening.

"Saw some pronghorn but couldn't get into range. As usual, they see something move and just take off. Don't wait around like a mule deer to see what's up."

"Too bad they weren't mule deer. You'd have one for sure."

"Haven't seen any of them since we left the hills along the river. This basalt isn't mule deer country." He dismounted and began unsaddling Smoky.

They rested and hunted another day but killed only jackrabbits. The day after, they made a few more miles before stopping again. Another day was lost before Ruth began to feel better, but now the train was no longer within reach, and both Jon and Erik knew it. A storm blew in that evening.

***

Erik listened to the wind, growing distressed. Before, he believed they could catch up. Now, he feared that the snow would trap them and that his mother really would die. He envisioned himself and his father burying her along the trail and then continuing alone, trying to catch up.

Erik glanced at his mother. She looked pale and thin. He knew his mother's illness was different. She didn't worsen, but she didn't get stronger. The illness that took the Backstroms was fast. They had dug four graves inside a week. Afterward, Slade stopped the train for the men to hunt and for the people to rest, to regain some strength. That's when the snowstorm hit.

When they had started up again, Mark died. He was the Stiles' youngest boy. Erik saddened. He used to play with Mark. They had buried him in an unmarked grave for fear the Indians would dig it up. Then Mama Larson took fever. That's when the men met and decided that the risk was too great for more to catch the fever—they couldn't delay any longer. That was a few days ago. That's when the men had decided to move on ahead.

7

Erik felt an ache catch in his throat and a sting come to his eyes. He was thankful to be with his parents, but he longed for his sister, now many miles away. And now, he felt afraid.

***

Jon Larson stayed awake, thinking, listening to the blowing wind, hearing the sleet pelt the canvas, watching his wife and son as they slept. He could hardly bear the thoughts of what had happened. He had wanted so much to do well for his family.

He figured his wife didn't have the sickness—maybe a bit of mountain fever was all. He knew she wasn't as strong as the others. She seemed to be sick too often. Her slight build didn't help. Olafson had suggested he not go—not try to take her—but to stay in Minnesota and find land as they had originally planned.

Jon was done trying to find land. He left Chicago for land in Minnesota, but the land in Minnesota had been taken, some deal gone sour. It was not as Liljegren had promised. Then there was cholera and rumors of war. That's when Adolphson brought news of a valley out west, a good valley for farming, a valley of their own.

Adolphson had said, "Gold is being discovered. We can farm the land and sell the crops. The valleys are high and grow fine hay and barley, like in Sweden. There's good water. There are hot springs. We can make a good living."

Jon had seen it as an opportunity to raise his family, something he had prayed for for years, and he and Ruth were determined to try. Mostly he wanted to go somewhere to get away from the misery he had experienced in the city, away from the sickness, away from the friends he had lost. And he wanted to forget. He wanted to find the promises he had dreamed of when they left Sweden—the reason they had left the old country.

He didn't blame Slade. He thought Slade had done his job well, especially considering their run of bad luck after they turned north on Jeffrey's Cutoff. At first, it had seemed a good idea. Some Bannocks and Snakes had been attacking the emigrant trains along the Snake River, and the grass was gone along the old trail. Jeffrey's Cutoff still had good grass, and it swung them north, closer to where they wanted to settle.

Then the sickness hit, and they were caught in the blizzard. The train held up for several days while the snow melted and the trail cleared. That's when Slade told them to expect an early winter, and when they moved on, he pushed them hard. He had told them that the mountain passes might already be closed. If so, they'd need to abandon their wagons and belongings and continue on foot or turn south and try to find a safe place where Indians wouldn't discover them along the Snake River. No one wanted that.

When Ruth got sick, the men met and decided to push on. Slade agreed to get them to Fort Boise. There, some wagons would split off and continue toward Oregon Territory. Some might try to get to the goldfields that were opening up. Others, his group included, intended to head north, looking for land to settle.

Jon turned in his blankets. Now they were stranded, and his daughter was many miles away.

***

After the storm, the snow blanketed the prairie and the mountains now visible in the distance. Jon knew that, even by starting today, they wouldn't be able to cross them. If they did, it would be on foot. He hoped Erik hadn't realized what he now did. But he figured Erik knew. He was a smart lad.

Jon studied his sleeping son: slight build, blond hair—a handsome lad with vivid blue eyes and a bright, catching smile. He figured that when Erik reached his adult years, he would be much like himself—tough built and tall. At almost thirteen, Erik was just beginning to grow. But now Jon missed his son's smile and felt nearly defeated. The journey had been hard on them. His son now looked drawn and thin. *That's why we have to make it. My family needs to,* Jon fiercely told himself.

Gently, he woke him. "We're rolling out today, Erik."

"Great!" Erik replied, elated.

Jon softened his tone, sorry for what he had to say. "No. I'm leaving the trail. We're not following the train. I've decided we're going to find a spot to winter."

He saw the light leave his son's eyes.

"Okay, Papa," Erik whispered.

The boy made him proud. He never complained. He carried a man's load. He would do as he was asked. Now Jon prayed he wasn't letting him or his family down.

***

Jon swung north, away from the trail. All day they traveled across broken rock and barren prairie. The prairie offered no protection from the sun or the weather. The last storm had told him that. He angled toward the foothills to where there might be shelter. Their pace slowed as he tried to keep the wagon rolling across the steep flanks in the broken rock and sagebrush. He noticed none of the draws they crossed held water.

By late day, Jon began to doubt his decision. He should have turned west; he should have tried to follow the train; he should not have tried to reach the protection of the mountains. Now they seemed unreachable.

That night, they again camped on the open, windswept land. Twisted tufts of grass and sagebrush were fuel for the campfire, a fire that burned with quick heat and died just as quickly, a fire hardly able to boil water for soup.

Morning broke. The weather held. Snow-covered peaks now rose in the distance on three sides. They picked their way northwest, topping out along the rising plateau, now encountering a few aspen groves in the draws. Toward evening, thick timber appeared on the western horizon. Jon felt some relief. Surely there they would find water and perhaps a place to winter.

CHAPTER 2

FREE HAWK WATCHED HIS two sons, Otter and Badger, as they practiced shooting arrows at a rolling hoop. Whistling Elk's son, Raven, practiced with them. An early storm had left snow in the high county, and the elk would be moving, making them easy to track. Free Hawk had agreed with Whistling Elk to take Otter and Raven on a hunt. Each was watcher for the other's son, and both thought it time. This would be an important event for the boys. Not many boys successfully hunted elk before completing their vision journeys, and this would likely be the last hunt before the Twisted River Band struck its summer lodges and journeyed back to the protected canyons for winter.

Free Hawk rose, stretching his slender body to release the tension from sitting at length. Dressed in leggings and breechcloth, his bare torso shone a deep chestnut in the lengthening sunlight. His black hair swept back, loose except where he cropped it above his eyes. His wife, Shining Water, had braided a few hair strands above his right ear, which held a brightly colored red and yellow feather ornament.

When he reached his lodge, he found her outside, bent over the cooking fire with their baby daughter, Singing Bird, at her side. Her smooth skin, gleaming black hair, and sparkling brown eyes quickened his heart. She wore a simple sheepskin dress, softly tanned and held in the middle with a belt of fox. About her throat she wore a necklace of river mussel shell, silvery blue, catching the afternoon sun.

Without a word, he pulled her to him in a tight embrace.

"What's that for?" she immediately asked, pushing away, trying to return to her work.

He scooped up Singing Bird and swung her onto his shoulders, where she lit up with a giggling smile. "Ah, Singing Bird. The most beautiful woman of all the Tukudeka, and she asks, 'What's that for?'" He laughed.

Shining Water crossed her arms but now stood bemused.

"Ah, Shining Water. It is because I watch our two sons, and I remember my wife and daughter. I wish to show the Great Mystery thanks for my blessings, so I embrace you."

Shining Water shook her head, but her eyes had softened. "I think it is because my husband is hungry and wants something for an early meal." She began to ladle out some steaming stew, but Free Hawk touched her hand.

"No, it is for the reasons I say." Free Hawk spoke more softly, "I watch my sons at play, and I realize I have something important to ask of my friend Sees Far. Tonight we shall have a council fire. You shall see."

The light in Shining Water's eyes told Free Hawk that she already knew.

"See our sons." Free Hawk turned Shining Water so they could watch the boys.

They ran across the near hillside, chasing their arrows and the rolling hoop. Bare upper torsos bronzed by the sun, they were dressed in breechcloths and moccasins; their medicine pouches bounced about their necks.

Badger took a few running steps and rolled the target but rolled it in such a way that it bounced. Both Otter's and Raven's arrows went wide. Badger motioned at them, shaking his head as if in disgust, and then took off chasing the hoop.

Free Hawk laughed. "It has been eleven winters past, and still he is feisty like the badger."

Shining Water lowered her eyes. She remembered. "Yes, it has been eleven winters. He was the only male child born. The elk woman had a baby girl, but she was called to walk the sky trails." She did not say

Calling Cow's name for fear it would confuse her spirit, as she also walked the sky trails now.

Free Hawk drew Shining Water closer and looked into her deep brown eyes. "And when it came time for Badger to be born, we worried he would not survive. The time of year was wrong. It was during the cold seasons."

Shining Water watched Badger as he again rolled the hoop. "You worried you would never see him. The grandmothers looked at him and told me it would be proper to leave him in the snow. The cold season moons were severe. The people had little food. Some starved." She paused, remembering their words. "They said, 'If it is the will of the Great Mystery—the Maker—he will live to morning. Then you can take him to your lodge and care for him. But surely he will die, for he is winter born.'

"And after he came, as the grandmothers had said to do, I walked along the creek and set him down in the snow where the moon made shadows on his face. But when I stepped back, he stared at me—those deep, dark eyes of his—unblinking, unafraid ... and hungry." She laughed.

"I brought him to our lodge, and you tried not to show your surprise, because you knew I should have left him. But you knew, and I knew, the grandmothers had been wrong."

"Yes," Free Hawk agreed. "And you said, 'We shall call our son Badger, for he is strong like the badger.' And he *is* strong like the badger." Free Hawk glanced toward his son.

They watched a moment as Badger drew his own arrow and shot at the target, which Raven now rolled.

Shining Water smiled. "And it *was* difficult to keep him alive. And some of the people *did* mutter behind our backs that it was wrong to try to keep a little one alive, for surely if the people suffered, he would suffer, and it was wrong for him to suffer. But I had some camas that I had hidden that I crushed and mixed with my milk. And it was the elk woman's child that died, and it was Badger who lived."

Free Hawk shook his head, remembering. It had been a hungry winter, true, but a couple camp dogs escaped to spring, and Stands Alone had killed a fine ram a few days later.

An indignant cry arose from Badger. The younger boy held up the target, complaining to Otter. Two arrows were embedded near its edge. Free Hawk knew from his actions that one was his and the other belonged to Otter. He guessed that Badger claimed to be closer to the mark and that Otter disagreed. Raven, it seemed, wisely stayed out of it.

Ah, Badger, Free Hawk reflected. *You truly do possess the badger's spirit and are truly a gift from the Great Mystery.* He went out to the boys.

The boys looked up, expectant when he approached.

He took the target and examined it. "Two arrows in the same target. Both my sons shoot well." He nodded approvingly at them and studied their eager faces. Otter, approaching his fourteenth winter, clearly showed the beginnings of manhood: eyes bright, hair swept back like his father's and held with a piece of otter fur and hawk feathers, a sharp face, muscular upper torso. Badger was still boyish, slighter in build, rounder in face, but with keener, more spirited eyes.

Free Hawk sighed. "Badger, you should know this by now. Age, by even a year, gives you the second place."

Badger glowered then shrugged. He pulled his arrow and handed it to Otter.

"And, Otter, you should know this. As a successful hunter, you always give to those less fortunate."

Otter glanced away briefly. "Yes, father," he said. "Here, Badger, is your arrow."

Badger's eyes lit up.

Then he pulled his arrow free of the target. "And here is mine, little brother."

Badger didn't expect this and stared, confounded.

"You show me that, but for your age, you will be a fine hunter," Otter spoke kindly. "Father will agree that at your age, I couldn't hit a rolling hoop as well as you do."

Raven started to protest, "But, Otter, you need that arrow for—"

"No, Raven. Tomorrow we use real hunters' arrows, ones with the black-glass tips."

Raven could not comprehend. His father, Whistling Elk, was Otter's watcher, but he had said nothing about using the black-glass-tipped arrows.

Free Hawk laughed. "Do not worry, Raven. You shall have one as well. But tomorrow we shall see which man may use one. You know, as we all do, that to get a good mark on an elk, you should be lucky as well as skilled."

***

Evening approached, and with it a chill.

Young boys, Badger among them, ran through the camp, calling for the people to gather at the council fire.

Gray Owl stood quietly waiting. Smoke hung in the low areas, and on it the aroma of the evening meals. He listened to the happy talk as the people left their lodges and began to make their way toward the fire.

Wrapped in his elk-skin robe against the chill, his gray hair pulled back on the left and held with a white ermine skin, the dying sun etched his wizened face. He studied the summer camp, the camp they would soon leave. Five lodges stood highlighted in the long sunlight. He felt blessed. He was the one that the Twisted River Band of the Tukudeka—the *nimi*, or the people—turned to. During his years, he had seen their lodges grow in number from two to five. This was many for a band of the people. The Twisted River Band was respected among the Tukudeka, just as they were respected among those who knew the Tukudeka as the Sheepeaters.

He remembered this season at the star-grass meadows. The cold season had been difficult. He had worried that Little Fox would not live to see the new season. He worried that the greening-grass moon would be lean and that the people would go hungry. So before they left the winter camp, he went to a lonely place above the river and, for many nights, prayed to the Great Mystery, seeking an abundance of food at the star-grass meadows and successful hunts. And when they arrived during the star-grass moon, the meadows had rippled like a powder blue lake dancing in the sun. The *basigoo'nee'*—the camas—stretched from one side to the other. He remembered his joy. He knew too well that they did not appear in abundance every season. Some seasons, like the one just past, were sparse, and the camas cakes did not last through the long-nights moon. Those winters saw hungry bellies and starving children. In those winters, the old ones crept away to die, and the newborns perished so their brothers and sisters could live.

Now golden and russet grass, glowing in the faded light, filled the meadows. The shrubs had turned burnt orange, and the flutter-leaf trees were shedding their golden leaves. Beyond, the peaks stood cold and serene, blanketed by snow.

And the hunts, too, were good, he reflected. He looked at the five lodges standing silhouetted against the fading light. Where they were once built mostly of large piles of barren poles covered with brush and pine boughs, they were now heavily blanketed with hides. As the hunters brought in game, their wives and daughters tanned the new hides; their old bedding and robes were replaced with the new ones; and the old ones were added to their lodges.

He knew the Great Mystery had heard his prayers.

The people had now gathered. A young boy threw wood on the fire, sending sparks towering into the darkened sky, causing the fire to briefly flare.

Gray Owl turned to the people.

"Soon we will travel back to our winter homes in the river canyons. We are blessed. We will carry much meat and camas, for the season's gathering was good, and the hunters brought back many animals. The camp dogs will drag their bellies from their heavy loads."

The people laughed.

"Tomorrow, some of our hunters will once more go after the shaggy-neck elk to see if they might get one last robe for the coming winters. And if they do, perhaps we will have to eat a dog, because it could not carry this one more robe."

Again, the people laughed politely.

Gray Owl gestured toward Otter and Raven. "These two boys, who seek their visions next season, will accompany their watchers on a hunt tomorrow. But tonight is special, for Free Hawk wishes to name a watcher for his youngest son, Badger.

"We know a watcher can teach things a father cannot, for the young ones always listen to their watchers; they do not always listen to their fathers."

More polite laughter.

"This is the way of the people. How else will a young man know how to be? How else will he know how to act, unless he is taught?" He nodded to Free Hawk.

Free Hawk stood and raised his hand.

"My son, Badger, was winter born. The grandmothers did not think he would live. He will be young for a vision journey, even two seasons from now. But I know this day, he is not too young for a watcher. Indeed, today I watch him and see his good spirit—perhaps not always well directed, but always well intended."

Some of the people laughed.

"Nevertheless, it is clear that he is ready for a watcher, and so I have asked Sees Far to be watcher for my son, Badger."

The people murmured their agreement as a tall man, hair slightly graying, strong features, came forth.

"You know Sees Far as a father to many sons and a daughter and as a wise man and a good hunter."

The people nodded. They respected Sees Far. He had two wives. He painted the memories on the rocks, and many believed he would soon be the one to whom the people turned.

"I am now asking him to be father to yet another, a father and watcher to my son, Badger."

Sees Far turned and raised his hand to the people. "I should ask Free Hawk to be watcher for my sons Squirrel and Little Fox," he said with a slight smile. "But they are not of age."

The people, again, laughed politely. Sees Far had five children.

"Free Hawk," he clasped Free Hawk's wrists, "you honor me. I wish to honor you." He touched his hands to his chest. "With gladness, I will proudly be father and watcher to Badger."

Formally, Sees Far turned to the people. "It is an honor to be asked to be watcher to Badger. As my father before me, as his father before him, as is the way of the people, I will watch this young man. I will help him in the ways of the people. I will guide him to become a true man for the people. I give you my sacred word."

The people nodded and murmured their approval. They knew the seriousness of what Sees Far said.

Again Gray Owl rose and addressed the people. "I have discussed our winter camp with Porcupine Woman and Stands Alone; we have decided where we will travel."

The people listened keenly, for this was also why they waited at council.

"When our hunters return, I will ask you to pack well. The Great Mystery has blessed us greatly this season, so we have decided it will be a good season to return to River That Cries. River That Cries is a holy place. It is the place where our relatives of the Crying Mountain Band shall be. It is time for us to return to that place and give thanks for our blessings and see old family once more."

A murmur of joy spread among the people. Many seasons had passed since the people had traveled the far distance south and visited those relatives.

***

That evening, as the other hunters did in their own lodges, Free Hawk and Otter laid out their weapons. They knew tomorrow's success partially depended on good weapons.

Free Hawk reflected on his hunts of the past season. He had had good hunts, but still he hoped for an elk hide. They had seen very few elk and had taken none. Elk was the choicest of the meats; their hides were large and warm, making the best blankets and heaviest winter robes. Otter now grew tall and needed a new winter robe.

Free Hawk worked his hand along his sheep-horn bow, inspecting for weakness, and then along each of his prized arrows. He would craft more this winter. Though he needed but two well-placed arrows to bring down a fine elk—if he could get within range of the wary creatures—some arrows were always lost.

Tomorrow, he would give one of his arrows to Raven for whom he was watcher, but he hoped it would be Otter's arrow that found its mark.

He had fletched his arrows with owl feathers and tipped them with the black-glass rock. He was pleased with the tips. He had traded several fine sheepskin robes to Broken Blade, a Bannock trader who occasionally visited the Twisted River Band and who brought the obsidian from the burning-rock land far to the south. Some of the grandfathers still retold stories of how the earth heaved and tore itself open, leaving burning rock and jagged scars across the land.

Chapter 3

IN LATE AFTERNOON, JON brought the wagon to a stop at the top of a rise above a small valley. He turned to his son. "What do you think, Erik?"

Erik surveyed the tiny valley at which they had arrived—grassy and barren, except for a couple aspen groves and a dark spruce thicket spreading below. The pale grass contrasted starkly against the golden yellow of the aspens, many of their leaves already lying littered beneath their white trunks. A stream meandered through and pooled into a beaver pond. Beyond rose the snow-covered mountains.

The chill wind brushed Erik's face. "Might be a bit breezy."

"Up here, you'd be correct," Jon replied, "but near the creek against the bluff, I believe we'll be just fine." He lifted the wagon cover behind him. "We're here, Ruth," he said. "I think we can finally stop."

Ruth blinked and looked up, her face strained. "Thank the Lord."

"You doing okay?" Jon asked.

"I feel somewhat better but fear I won't be of much use."

"Don't worry, Ruthie," Jon whispered. "Erik and I will manage. Soon we'll have a nice, warm camp for you." He jumped down.

"Come on, lad. We best take care of the stock." He began to unbuckle the harnesses. "Not much time 'til sundown. I want to get a canvas up for the night."

Erik scrambled to join his father and helped pull the harness from Smoky and Red. He led the animals to the creek and let them water. He gazed back toward the wagon where his father continued unpacking. This would be home for a while, he realized, and a heaviness seeped in. He headed back toward the wagon for the tethers and hobbles. Until they built a corral, they couldn't risk letting the two animals wander, especially if Indians were near.

"Well, Erik, is the water good?" his father asked. "Do you think we can spend a winter here?"

"It looks good, Papa, but it's not home," Erik whispered.

"No, Son, it's not."

"And Katrine isn't with us." He felt the knot in his throat.

Erik returned to the creek and hobbled Smoky and Red where they could graze on the long meadow grasses. He stared at the pond. A few small trout broke the surface near the beaver dam. At least there would be some fish here. He wondered about game, however. They had seen very little on the high plains. Since his father had shot at some a few days past, they hadn't even seen pronghorn.

Back at the wagon, Erik found his mother busily gathering up items for their camp. "How do you feel, Mama?"

"I'm good, Son." She smiled. Some color had returned to her cheeks.

"You just rest, Mama," replied Erik. "I'll take those things on down. Going to get a cooking fire going and boil up some water. I'm planning a surprise."

"A surprise?"

"Just you wait." It troubled Erik how frail she looked. He knew she should have never tried to make this trip. But his father was set on it; Erik, too, had been anxious to go.

***

Erik noticed the blue and yellow glass vase in the bundle of goods. He remembered his mother's words: "… and my vase, Papa Larson," she had insisted. "That's just about all I've still got from my Mama Anderson, and it's about all I've got to remind me of the old country. For sure, we're taking my vase."

He remembered that his father had reluctantly said yes, but he had also told her not to get upset when the first bumps in the trail shook it to smithereens.

That had been months ago—back in the spring, back when they left Minnesota—a terribly, terribly long time ago.

Then every day it rained. The roads were sticky mud. They spent days prying loose one wagon and then the next just to go a few miles. It wasn't until after they crossed the Missouri River and headed west along the North Platte that the weather warmed. And all the way, his mother had carefully watched her blue and yellow vase. "It has the colors of the homeland," he remembered she often said.

Erik carefully put the vase away where it wouldn't be broken.

He helped his father with the cross spars of the lean-to. Although temporary, they wanted it strong. The wind from the prairie whistled cold through the valley. Already Erik wondered about this location, but this was the first good water and timber they had found.

Erik busied himself with pulling brush for their shelter from beneath the aspens and nearby timber. Brush was scarce. The meadow quickly changed from grass to sparse aspens to spindly spruce. Few plants grew under their dark black canopy. He took comfort in the numerous, bright reddish orange rosehips he found. They would make tea for his mother—"a good, hearty drink in the old country," she always said—his surprise for her. He also found bright red kinnikinnick berries. They looked like bearberries but grew low, hugging the ground, spreading themselves under the trees. The outer part was edible, and like the bearberry in Sweden, Erik suspected they would yield wax. He figured on making candles for Christmas.

Erik and his father finished their shelter as the stars began to appear in the velvet blue sky. The fire was welcome against the mountain cold. Erik seeped the rosehips and offered his mother the tea. She hugged him and sipped the tea; afterward, she lay down to sleep. Erik leaned against his father for warmth against the chill. His father pulled him near. His strength felt good. He studied his mother's quiet face.

"I think she'll be fine, Son." His father answered his unspoken question, trying to reassure him.

***

Erik stretched out under the canvas with his parents. Usually he and his sister had curled up in the bed of the wagon, helping to keep each other warm. He missed her. She was younger than him by four years. She was all he had. Now only God knew where she was.

Erik woke to blackness and a freezing chill. He wondered at the chirp of a bird, tentative but certain of a commencing dawn. Just a hint of light showed on the eastern horizon, but he needed to pee. He rolled out of his covers and stepped several yards away into the chilly wind, feeling exposed and vulnerable. "I hope nothing's out here, Lord, besides me," he half whispered. No matter how often he had walked out into the night, he feared the night and what it held—wolves, bears, or worse yet, a murderous Indian. He shuddered at the thought. All along the route, people told of their bloody deeds—how they snuck up to the camps, captured young children who strayed, and tortured and scalped them or made them into slaves. He shivered again.

He crawled back to his blankets, thankful again for his mother's warmth. However, as he drew near, he felt unmistakable shivering. A scared feeling flooded him. *Please, dear God, let her get better.* He drew close, trying to warm her.

***

Erik woke to the sun breaking upon him through a gap in the aspens. The sun came from the right of their shelter and would remain on the camp through much of the day before again becoming masked by aspens and pines. The hill rising to the west blocked the afternoon rays, but for the orientation of the valley, running north and south, it was the best they could do.

"Time to get moving, Son." His father was bent over, adding some tea to a pot of boiling water. He looked up. "I think we should build our cabin where the sun's shining." He pointed with the pot. "Over there by the creek."

Erik glanced upstream at the hillside. He noticed the spot of sunshine. He nodded. It wasn't where he had dreamed of building their cabin; this wasn't the high valley where they had intended to farm.

"We got our work cut out for us, Erik. Shelter for us. Shelter for the stock. Gathering hay for the stock. Hunting. Don't know when the winter will set in. Maybe a couple weeks, maybe a month. We'll be lucky to put up enough hay to see the animals through."

Erik heard his mother cough. He shot his father a worried glance and shook his head.

"We just got to do the best we can," Jon whispered, raising his eyes slightly.

"Cabin first, for Mama?" Erik asked.

Jon nodded and went to check on Ruth, taking with him some steaming tea.

***

They began to mark and clear a cabin site, but shortly after, Jon stopped.

"Erik, I know you want a cabin for Mama Larson, but I'm not sure that's the best thing right now."

Erik paused from his digging.

"We can manage with the wagon canvas for a while. But the stock have nothing. If bad weather sets in, they won't make it. You and I both know we won't go anywhere next spring without them."

Erik knew what his father was saying.

"If we get a corral built, we'll have a better chance of protecting them from predators, possibly Indians, if any pay us a visit."

Erik nodded. Reluctantly, he agreed with his father. "Good thing we made the lean-to strong last night." He realized there was little they could do if Indians did discover their camp and wanted their stock. They were on their own now—far from any help.

"Yes." Jon ruffled his son's hair.

***

Immediately they began work on the corral. They hunted for poles in the nearby aspen groves and the spruce thicket. Jon cut and felled them. Erik hitched up Red and dragged them in bundles up to a spot above the beaver pond. Here the stock would have access to water at one corner of the corral.

Ruth cooked a meal for the evening and made some coffee.

"Thank the good Lord and my Ruthie for fine Swedish coffee," Jon exclaimed as he held the steaming cup.

Erik also nodded his thanks. He raised his cup to acknowledge his mother but winced.

"Sore?" His father eyed him.

"Yes, but it's a good soreness, Papa. We got a lot done."

His mother rubbed his shoulders. "Better?"

He nodded. "Yes, Mama. Thanks."

"Got to take care of yourself, Son," his father continued. "We got a lot of work ahead of us."

***

The next day, they trimmed more poles for fencing. Again, the morning was cold, but like the past day, it heated quickly. Now, except for the snow-capped peaks in the distance as a reminder, the day seemed no different to Erik than mid August. They worked until noon when his mother called them to their shelter for lunch. She presented some flour cakes she had baked on the coals.

Erik hugged her. "Mama, I'm so happy to see you better." The flour cakes were the first she'd baked in some time.

"Not too tight, Erik," she whispered and smiled. "I feel stronger today, but I think I still have a long fight ahead. I'm going back to rest after you men get back to work."

Jon eyed her. "I don't know; I might take a short break as well."

"In that case, I'm going to check the beaver ponds for trout," Erik said. He stood and stretched. "Maybe I can go fishing later."

"Just stay near," Jon advised. "I want to get started again in about an hour."

Erik headed toward the stream. Besides finding a good fishing hole, Erik hoped he'd find a swimming hole. He hadn't had a good bath since they left the Snake River. They hadn't found enough water to even wash off the trail dust.

He followed the stream downward until it opened into another small pond. He skirted it, continued on to the next, which was larger, and then on to the next, which was the largest of the four. Heavy timber crowded the east side, but the west side was open and afforded easy walking. The last pond was partially dammed by boulders and a beaver dam near the outlet. Like the one nearer the cabin, the dam was old and in disrepair. Erik wondered why he hadn't seen any fresh beaver sign.

He chucked a pebble into the pond and watched as it sank. It settled, startling white against the black, muddy bottom. Erik decided the water was about five feet deep. Plenty deep for swimming. He laid aside his clothes and wadded in. Immediately the cold hit him. Although the day was warm, the water wasn't.

Gasping, he forced himself to wade farther, the mud squeezing up between his toes. Several small trout scooted away, startling him. Laughing, he kicked off the bottom. His breath left him as he sank into the frigid water, but it felt good. Quickly, he swam to the deepest section, turned, and swam back to the shallows where he climbed out, shivering. Once was enough. He brushed off the water and sat back on the bank, allowing the sun to dry him. Slowly, his warmth returned.

Erik felt some peace. His mother seemed better. Maybe they wouldn't have to build the cabin. Maybe she was well enough they could get back on the trail. Erik decided he'd ask his father that night if they should try.

Something suddenly hit the water in front of him, splashing his face. He sat up, looking around, heart racing wildly. Hearing his father's laughter, he relaxed.

"Ah, Papa, the water is great. You should try it. I'll even go again."

"Does look good," his father replied, squatting next to him. "Maybe later. Any trout?"

"Small ones," Erik replied. "I expect the bigger ones are hiding."

"Then you can try fishing later. Best we haul more timber while the light's still good."

***

The warm days ended; another cold rain moved through the basin, ending in snow, which soon blanketed the valley.

Jon and Erik began work on the cabin. Jon cut the first spruce, and they both limbed it. While his father began cutting another, Erik hooked up Red and dragged the first to the cabin site. By day's end, they had felled and dragged six logs to the site. They needed several dozen. The base logs, even for a small cabin, were taking much longer than anticipated.

Dragging the trees cut furrows through the snow and into the soil, creating black lines across the hill to the cabin.

"If we drag many more logs, we can plant a field right here, Papa."

His father eyed him. "The soil does look plenty rich."

***

That evening, they sat for dinner around a crude table. Ruth had gathered some kinnikinnick, heavy with red berries, and placed them in the blue and yellow vase. She brought out cornbread and venison, more food than usual.

"You know this day, Erik?" she asked.

Erik puzzled momentarily, then smiled. He knew. Although he didn't remember the exact dates, his mother remembered.

She hugged him. "Happy birthday, Son."

His father reached to shake his hand. "We do have a gift for you, lad." Erik was surprised. "I've been carting this all the way from Minnesota." He handed Erik a brown paper parcel.

Erik ripped it open. Inside was a skinning knife.

Erik shot back a huge grin. "Thanks, Papa. Thanks, Mama."

"Out here, you're going to need that," Jon continued. Then he laughed. "Son, you don't know how many times I thought about giving you that knife early. Sure could have used it by now."

"You can say that again, Papa." Erik carefully turned the knife in his hands and hefted it. He liked its weight. "Thank you so much." He hugged his parents. Then, quietly, he added, "I just wish Katrine were here."

"We do too," his mother replied.

"I still wonder if we couldn't have caught up," Erik said.

"Until last night when it snowed, I wondered the same," Jon admitted. "But, Son, you need to make the best decisions you can at the time with the information you've got and live by them. A man who always second-guesses himself doesn't get far in life."

"I know, Papa," answered Erik. "But it's hard."

"One thing I've come to realize these past days, we can do well right where we're at. Right here, Erik." He paused to make his point. "This valley isn't much different than where we were heading. We have what we need right here. You yourself noticed how rich the soil is. We need to finish the cabin and do some hunting, but then we should be okay."

That night, Erik thought about the past days. He thought about his new knife; the best gift, however, was that his mother seemed to be getting better.

CHAPTER 4

FREE HAWK AND WHISTLING Elk carried the young doe toward the meadow where the people would be camped for the evening. He and Whistling Elk had gone ahead of the people this day to hunt for them and to provide fresh meat. Already, Free Hawk could smell the smoke from the evening fires.

It was the sixth day they had been on the trail south toward River That Cries, and Free Hawk was thankful they didn't often journey this distance south.

He carried the doe to the center fire where the women gathered and soon began butchering the animal. Moccasin Woman rolled the hide and offered it to him. Free Hawk declined. "We already carry too much to the winter camps."

Shining Water shook her head. "It is true, but even so, we will find little from the previous seasons at River That Cries. We have camped there only once, and I don't have soapstone bowls or baskets. There, we don't own much."

"Perhaps, then, we shall keep the hide; you can use it to trade," said Free Hawk. He wondered how he would carry one more hide.

Shining Water nodded. "I will tan this hide when we reach our winter camp. We are close now. If we are lucky, the traders will come, and we will have enough hides for an iron pot."

Free Hawk nodded. He desired to trade for an iron pot for Shining Water and a steel knife for himself. He had hunted hard during the summer season and had extra hides and furs.

Shining Water soon had a stew simmering and, shortly, called her family to eat. As was customary, she gave Free Hawk his horn bowl first, then Otter his. She and Badger shared a third.

The boys quickly ate and returned to the meadow where other boys gathered for a game of kickball. Free Hawk shook his head. "You would think they would want some rest."

"Boys? Rest?" Shining Water laughed. "Our two will play until they fall down asleep. This you know.

"I will be glad when we reach our winter lodge," she sighed. "Each night that we are on the trail, I worry a night cat or bear will take Badger or Singing Bird."

"Ah, Shining Water," Free Hawk exclaimed. "You should not worry. The camp dogs will warn us."

"This is true, but I cannot help but worry they might wander off. It is easy to wander off when one is little and doesn't know where he is."

Free Hawk leaned over and stroked Shining Water's hair. "Our children will not do such a thing. You have taught them well. Even Singing Bird understands."

"Even so, I worry," she replied. "And I will be glad tomorrow night when we are in our own lodge and away from all the prying eyes." She glanced at Free Hawk, a smile tugging her mouth.

Free Hawk laughed. "On this, we can agree, Shining Water." He rubbed his nose against hers. "It is a long distance to River That Cries."

***

The morning light streamed through the conifers. Already, some of the people busily gathered their belongings. "It is time. Run and get the dogs," Free Hawk said, instructing his sons.

"Yes, Father." Otter replied. "Come on, Badger. They're probably with Weasel's dogs. That's where they usually go."

The two boys trotted off, looking for the dogs.

Free Hawk helped Shining Water roll the bedding and clothing into bundles. "If we continue having good hunts, maybe I should get more dogs."

Shortly, Otter came into camp leading two dogs. "Badger has the other two," he explained, breathing hard. "Our dogs get too smart, Father. They know we will load them down and that they will have to drag heavy bundles, so now they hide from us."

"Our dogs should be so lucky that their owners are good hunters." Free Hawk laughed. "At least they don't get eaten."

"It is like Gray Owl said, Father. They are dragging their bellies." Badger laughed as he brought the last two to their camp.

One at a time, Free Hawk helped Otter and Badger harness the dogs to their travois and then sent them on their way down the trail. Tails wagging, they padded off, following the people and the other dogs.

Free Hawk helped Shining Water lift her pack and adjust the head strap so her hands were free. He positioned the basket in which Singing Bird rode. "You get the best ride of all, Singing Bird," he said. The baby smiled, seeming to understand.

Shining Water picked up a staff and headed down the trail, Singing Bird bouncing on top. She met up with Moccasin Woman and her young daughter, Tiny Bird, and soon they were busily talking.

Free Hawk stepped to a lodgepole pine and took a sheep's horn from where it hung. He pulled some moss from it, checking its contents.

Badger watched, a concerned look.

"It is good," Free Hawk said, handing the small pack to Badger. He felt proud. The horn Badger carried held the coals from their last council fire. From it would be kindled the winter campfires. Badger positioned it on his back so he carried only his bow in his hands.

"I guess we get to carry the most, Otter," Free Hawk stated. "Even though a hunter should carry less so his weapons are free, in our case, we carry the most."

"I'm sorry, Father."

Free Hawk laughed. "In our family, it isn't the dog that will break his back, it is I that will break his back."

"We had good hunts, Father," explained Otter. "Even Badger was getting lucky with his bow."

Badger turned and glared. "I wasn't lucky, Otter," he protested.

"I joke, Badger," Otter laughed. "I told you the other day when we shot at the rolling hoop that you were good."

Badger seemed relieved. "But it is of you that they will sing a song tomorrow. You and Whistling Elk killed a shaggy-neck elk."

"I was lucky," explained Otter. "The elk turned in front of me. Besides, Whistling Elk shot it too. My arrow would not have killed it."

"But you had the first arrow, Otter. The kill goes to the hunter whose arrow first goes true."

"Badger is correct, Otter," agreed Free Hawk. "You shot true. Like a fine hunter."

They traveled in silence for a while.

"I am proud of both my sons," Free Hawk couldn't help but say. "I am proud of Otter for getting a good, shaggy-neck elk. But, Otter, you should agree with me that this is an important day for Badger. I am proud of Badger, for he is the fire carrier."

"Yes, Father," Otter agreed. He had once been a fire carrier. He *was* proud of Badger, for many reasons. Badger stood up for himself, even when the older boys teased him, which they often did.

Badger warmed in the praise and set his thoughts on returning to the river. A swim in the river would be good after this hot walk.

***

By late afternoon, the people could see the river below—a white ribbon weaving its way through the surrounding cliffs. Shortly, they reached the small grassy benches along River That Cries and paused to rest. Otter and Badger, along with other children, ran to its banks, glad to see the powerful, rolling waters sliding past.

The band turned upstream. Soon they came to where the Crying Mountain Band had chosen its winter camp. The people stopped briefly to visit. Already, four families had set up their lodges. Other families might come later. In this way, the people would be near their relatives during the long winter moons, and the young men could court women from other bands.

The Twisted River Band continued upriver to the next draw. There they found a bench near tall cottonwoods bordering a small creek flowing into River That Cries. Here the nearness of the canyon walls and the heavy trees would protect them from the coming winter winds. The bench was high enough above the river that most of the dense, cold winter air would flow from the camp and hug the river bottom.

In the timber, Free Hawk selected and felled trees. Most were dead—dry and stripped of their bark by the winter storms. He and his sons stacked them into a tall, conical shape about twice his height and covered it with brush and hides.

Inside, it was warm and dry with open space coming to just above his reach—good room to hang his bow and their belongings. He fixed a hide for the door—a small triangular opening facing the sacred direction, the direction from where the sun rose.

Shining Water brought in the prized elk hides and spread them opposite the doorway. She constructed a smaller pallet to the right for Otter's bed and another at its foot for Badger. Singing Bird would yet sleep with her. Although they were a family of five, a family of six to eight could sleep comfortably in such a lodge.

***

Again, the young boys ran among the people, calling to them to assemble. Shortly, they gathered near a cliff face to the side of the camp's center. One rock in particular was marked with numerous paintings of men and animals, depicting the past winters. It captured the spirits of the events of their lives.

Gray Owl addressed them.

"It has been many seasons since we have returned to River That Cries. Let us thank the Great Mystery that we are returned. We have truly been blessed with a good summer at the star-grass meadows."

He turned to Porcupine Woman and to Badger. "Let us light our winter fire."

Porcupine Woman, the woman who healed, shuffled forward. Bent over, graying hair, a wolf skin drawn about her, she beckoned Badger to come to her. Standing and feeling proud, Badger stepped up and removed his bundle. Carefully, he handed the sheep horn to Porcupine Woman.

"Have you carried this horn in a sacred manner, young Badger?" she asked.

Badger nodded.

"And have you kept the fire spirit alive?"

Again, Badger nodded.

"The people shall see." Gently, she pulled the moss from around the embers and scraped them into a nest of fine shavings. "If our winter fire does not catch, then the fire spirit has been broken." Softly, she blew on the coals as the people anxiously watched. However, almost immediately, a thin curl of smoke rose, and soon a bright flickering flame leaped into sight. "You have done well, young Badger. The fire spirit lives."

The people murmured their joy and sang the winter-fire song, softly chanting, then singing more quickly as the flames grew brighter and higher. Young boys threw new wood into the flames that now reflected from the people's faces.

Gray Owl's shadow danced across the painted rock.

"My people, it is time to recount the blessings we have received this season. We have had good hunts and prepared many cakes from the star-grass bulbs. We have a new child who will see her first winter, a daughter born to Black Legs and White Deer, whom they call Yellow Mink." He gestured for White Deer to come forward.

White Deer brought the child, cradled in her arms, into the firelight. Porcupine Woman took the infant and held her up to the people and their sounds of praise.

"Just as we count this new life given to us, let us remember those who now walk the sky trails," Gray Owl continued softly. "Let us remember the wise one, the one to whom we turned for many seasons. Sees Far shall paint his memory on the counting rock.

"I have also decided that Sees Far will paint the shaggy-neck elk that Otter killed. For one so young to bring down a mighty elk is a good thing to remember. Otter will surely be a great hunter and provider for our people."

Otter was pushed forward, and the people made approving sounds.

Otter's watcher, Whistling Elk, came into the firelight and began a slow dance to mimic the hunt. His muscled body rippled in the dancing light. Tapered forehead, eyes deeply set, his elk-tooth necklace vibrated across his chest with his medicine pouch as he danced. In a clever reenactment, Whistling Elk crept forward, looking, then gesturing, spotting the elk. He drew back his bow but did not release the arrow. He crept, looked, and again tested a shot. He lowered his bow. Then, in anxious actions, he moved rapidly to a different spot, drew his bow, and let the arrow race true.

He then became the elk, dancing, struggling, surprised at the arrow's bite, staggering, then dying.

During the dance, Otter stood tall and proud to the people's approving sounds.

Free Hawk warmed with pride. Both his sons were honored this day—Badger, the fire carrier, and now Otter, the hunter. He sought Shining Water's eyes, but knew it was not proper for her to show her joy. Instead, they would share their joy privately.

With the honoring complete, young girls took burning brands back to their lodges to kindle their own cooking fires. The smoky odor of burning cottonwood and mahogany soon flooded the river canyon. Families spent the remainder of the night visiting and celebrating their return to River That Cries.

***

Now was the moon of fattening animals. The salmon were returning to the river, and for the last weeks of autumn, the people fished and dried the meat in the yet warm days. Soon the mountain sheep and the mule deer would return to the canyon slopes to escape the snow now blanketing the high country. Each day grew shorter, and soon the sun would hardly show above the canyon walls. Then the river's edge would become stopped in ice, and the rains and snows would come.

In the lingering warmth, the people sought places to bathe or swim. Even in the winter, they chopped holes in the ice to bathe and gather water.

Eager to swim, Badger ran to the bathing place. Today he would swim with the older boys. Happy, he waded toward the rocks and the deep, quiet hole where they played.

Raven waited for him along with Coyote and Weasel. There were two older boys from the Crying Mountain Band, one he recognized as Quick Marten, son of Bold Bear. The other boy he did not know. Badger did not like Quick Marten.

The moment Quick Marten saw Badger enter the water, he challenged him. "Well, Badger, aren't you in the wrong bathing place? Shouldn't you still be with the old mothers and babies?"

The others laughed.

Badger was taken aback. The older boys often did this to him—unless Otter was around—perhaps because there were no others born during his first winter. But Quick Marten was no longer of the Twisted River Band. Surely Raven and the others would say something.

"No, Quick Marten. You know I am past my eleventh winter," he retorted.

"Well, you look like a skinny little girl. I think that you must still be a girl," Quick Marten mocked. "What do you think, Raven?"

"He does look like a skinny girl," Raven agreed. They laughed again.

The comment stung. "I am *not* a little girl," he shouted back. He stood up in the shallow water. "You can see I'm not a girl."

This only brought more laughter. "He sure looks like a girl to me," Quick Marten continued. "You should think so. Don't you?" He turned to the others, grinning.

They nodded. They couldn't resist tormenting Badger.

"You must go back to bathe with the women," continued Quick Marten. "Raven and I have decided. We won't let you swim here."

"You know I can't," protested Badger. "I *have* to swim here. I *will*." He continued to wade out to where they were on their rock, knowing he dare not back down. He knew Quick Marten could practically drown him if this turned into a fight, and even though Raven was Otter's friend, he knew Raven would be all too happy to help. However, he also knew there would be no end to their bullying if he didn't remain.

The others paused to watch the outcome.

Then, suddenly remembering what Otter had told him, Badger countered. "Quick Marten, if I'm a girl, then why didn't you go on your vision journey? You are a winter older than Raven and Otter, and they prepare to go when we return to the star grasses."

"It was because of my foot they didn't let me go," Quick Marten shot back, glaring.

"But I heard it was because they thought you were too weak," Badger pressed. "I think that makes *you* the girl."

Quick Marten sprang into the water, followed by Raven, and pushed toward Badger, intending to fight. Badger stood his ground.

"Hey, Raven! Hey, Quick Marten!" It was Otter. He waded toward them. When he was near, he addressed his brother. "Badger, it is not important that Quick Marten did not go. We'll all be going soon enough. Even you, Badger."

The boys stopped. They respected Otter. His words were true. The vision journey was too important to make light of it, and each considered it deeply from the moment he learned of its importance. A vision seeking marked the end of childhood and the becoming of a true man.

"Because Quick Marten was not able to go this summer, his family may join us at the star-grass meadows next season. He and Raven and I may seek our visions together," explained Otter. "That is what I heard Gray Owl talk about with Bold Bear."

Badger's heart fell. He didn't like Quick Marten. He had been happy when Bold Bear left to marry Running Doe and become one of the Crying Mountain Band.

Otter continued. "Little brother, you know you will go in two, maybe three, summers—maybe with Coyote and Weasel. We will all go. It will be good for the people."

"All right, Otter," Badger replied. "But I'm not a girl. And don't *anyone* say I am." He glowered at Quick Marten and Raven.

"He's not," Otter said. "He's my brother."

The others were silent. Quick Marten scowled.

The truth stung. Quick Marten knew that he should have completed his vision seeking. He approached his fifteenth winter. Badger *had* to remind them. He never did like Badger. If his family went with the Twisted River Band to the summer camps, Badger had better watch his back.

There was no longer fun in the swim for Badger, and he half wondered if he should return to bathe with the little children and their mothers. The younger boys looked up to him, especially because he had been fire carrier. He left the river, dressed, and headed to his lodge. He wondered where Chipmunk, Raven's younger brother, was. He wondered about going to hunt rabbits with him. Only a winter younger, Chipmunk often stuck around Badger.

CHAPTER 5

ERIK WOKE TO GEESE honking and the sound of their wings whistling as they passed above the cabin. He sat up, shivering, peering out through the gaps in the roof, straining to catch a glimpse of one in the gray morning sky. The sky was washed with heavy, low clouds. Snow clouds. Concern gripped him. He and his father had worked hard on the cabin, but the roof was only partially complete.

He stood up and tried to stretch. His shoulders and back hurt from sleeping on the hard ground. He pulled on his shirt, now becoming tattered, and his trousers, slipping the suspenders over his shoulders. He ran his hands through his lengthening hair. He thought back to his birthday. The weather had warmed for a few days, and they worked mostly on the cabin. Then the storms came. They started as cold rain mixed with snow, but the last ones were all snow.

He looked out across the small valley. Snow had gathered and piled under the aspens and in the shady areas. The pond had ice near the edges. The aspens now stretched spindly, naked fingers into the gray sky.

Erik glanced toward his parents' bedroll. His mother was all right, but she wasn't strong. Sometimes she coughed. She helped when she could, but Erik sensed unhappiness. Surely she missed Katrine. They all did. But she had him and Papa. *Shouldn't Mama be trying to do more to get strong?* he wondered, a little angry.

He moved to the hearth. It pleased him that they had constructed a crude chimney from sticks and mud scraped from the pond and that his mother now had a place to cook.

Actually, in the few weeks they had been there, he and his father had accomplished a great deal. They had built a corral and a stock shed. They had also cut hay for the stock and cut and stacked wood, and they had nearly finished the cabin.

Only, they should have been doing more hunting, he realized. No game passed near the cabin, and when his father did go, he frequently came back empty-handed.

Erik touched last night's coals. Finding them still warm, he raked them aside and exposed some glowing embers. Adding tiny twigs and wood shavings, he blew, watching in satisfaction as smoke tendrils rose. Blowing again, the shavings burst into flame. Carefully, he added more twigs until the fire had grown to a comfortable size.

"That feels good," said Jon as he leaned past his son, rubbing his hands. "How's the coffee coming?"

Erik turned to look up at his father. "I thought you didn't want me to fix anymore," Erik replied. "You wanted to save the last for something special."

"Could be that today will be special," he replied.

"How's that?" Erik filled the kettle and placed it on the fire.

"Maybe we'll finish the roof."

"I hope so," Erik responded. "I was really cold last night, and it looks like it's going to snow again. The canvas won't hold much weight."

His father dressed and then sat to pull on his boots, again rubbing his hands in the fire's warmth.

They sat silently waiting for the water to boil, allowing Mama Larson to sleep. She didn't sleep well when the cough hit her—usually at night—so they allowed her sleep whenever she could.

"What shall I fix for breakfast, Papa?"

"More trout if you got any, I 'spect."

Erik shook his head. "Sorry. I've pretty much fished out the ponds. I don't see trout anymore, except some tiny ones. I think the big ones have all gone south where it's warm." He grinned.

Jon eyed him.

"Well, at least they've all gone downstream to the river."

"That's a long ways from here, Erik."

"Yes, but I'll bet it's a lot warmer."

"I'm sure you're right, but we couldn't have made it with the wagon." Erik heard his mother stirring.

"Sorry, Ruthie," Jon apologized. "We didn't mean to disturb you."

"I'm fine," she replied. "Figured I'd get you two some breakfast today."

"How are you? You were coughing again last night."

"I feel good today, Papa Larson," she replied, "and that coffee is making me feel all the better. Wish we had some eggs and ham I could fix you."

"Don't *say* that, Mama," protested Erik. "That makes me really hungry."

"I have to agree," added his father. "Ham and eggs would beat fried trout any day."

"How about some pancakes with dried berries?" Ruth began gathering things to make breakfast.

The coffee was done, and Erik poured three cups. He savored his, sipping it, keeping his father company while his mother mixed the dough. Soon she had some cakes on the coals, and the odor filled the cabin, causing him a pang of hunger. She was too quiet, however. Erik watched as his father rose and went to her. She didn't say anything, but she showed him the flour bag. Erik could tell it was almost empty.

"It's about the same with the cornmeal," she whispered. But Erik heard.

"Now don't you worry, Ruthie," Jon said. "I'll think of something. Perhaps I can take Smoky and see if I can locate that mining camp Jack Slade said was somewhere in this country."

"I won't hear of it," she quietly protested.

"I can ride up there and back. You'd be okay for a week."

Erik went to them. "You can't leave, Papa. We need to finish the roof." Suddenly he felt scared. He didn't think he could make it alone with his mother.

"Erik, we're about out of flour as well as everything else," his father explained, shaking his head grimly. "We're stuck here for several more months. I've been avoiding going for supplies, but now I don't see any other option." He looked hard at him. "Think you and Mama Larson can tough it out for a week?"

Erik felt tears beginning to come to his eyes. He tried to nod. But he felt that if his father left, he'd never see him again. He sat down, head in his hands.

His mother came over and sat down, putting her hand on his shoulder. She realized how he felt.

"Maybe you should go hunting today while the weather holds," she suggested. "We can make it through to spring if we get enough meat put up."

Jon's mouth tightened. "I was planning on working on the roof …" He looked up, studying it. "The canvas seems to be holding … I guess except for the roof, we *are* pretty much fixed for winter."

But then he shook his head. "I don't know," he said quietly. "Lately, I've been hunting every chance I get, and Erik's always out trying to trap rabbits. It seems the game has disappeared. I'm not sure where to go anymore."

"Like I said, Papa," Erik lifted his head to look at his father. "I think the animals are all headed down the canyon to get food and stay warm."

"Okay, Erik." Jon got up and looked out at the sky. "Maybe we should try it. I'm thinking we're due another storm. If so, the game will sense it and likely be moving. We can take Smoky and head down the canyon a bit. We'd be gone a day, maybe two if we get an animal." He looked at Ruth. "You'd be okay?"

"I can certainly handle a day or two alone, and I sure don't see any game around here," she replied as she served them the pancakes. "If you don't go look for it, you won't find where it is." She ladled on some water-softened dried berries.

They sat down. Jon took their hands in his and said a prayer.

They ate in silence.

***

The next morning broke to a couple inches of snow, but it had ceased falling. The clouds drifted in patches, and the sky began to clear.

"Got the rifle?" his father asked as he opened and checked the cartridge case.

Erik saw him frown. He knew some of the caps and paper cartridges had been ruined, and he suspected they were now running low, but he didn't know how low. He was scared to ask.

Carefully, he pulled the rifle from its pegs and checked the load. "All set." He handed it to his father.

"Thanks, lad."

"Papa? How are we fixed for cartridges?" His voice cracked.

His father strode out into the snow and kicked it. "Look at this, Erik. Perfect tracking snow."

"Papa?" Erik followed. He couldn't let it go.

"Cartridges?" He tousled Erik's hair. "We're okay, Son. I just gotta make them all count. Now don't you worry."

Erik helped his father saddle Smoky. His mother brought out a package of food—leftover pancakes from yesterday—plus a small amount of dried venison.

Jon kissed Ruth and swung up onto Smoky. "We should be back before dark, Ruthie. But if not, don't fret. It means we'll be hauling out some meat," he explained. "Keep the fire going. Love you."

"Bye, Mama. Love you too," said Erik, hugging his mother. He swung up onto Smoky and positioned himself behind his father. "Come this evening, we'll bring you back a deer." He waved, smiling.

They rode Smoky double until they reached the breaks where the slope steepened and pitched downward. Frequently they crossed fresh deer tracks, all headed down canyon, but saw no deer. Jon had been correct. The new snow caused the animals to start moving.

By noon they had come to an abrupt ledge overlooking a vast, twisting canyon. A cottontail hopped out from under the rocks. Instinctively, Jon reached back to Erik for the rifle but paused. He wouldn't waste a round on a rabbit that would make but a single meal.

"Well, what do we do now, Erik?" Jon asked. "We haven't seen a blasted thing except tracks, and those make mighty thin soup."

"We aren't going down there, Papa," Erik replied. He looked to where thick pines marched down the rugged grassy slopes and disappeared over the edge. He could make out a ribbon of silvery water winking back between sheer cliffs and dense timber. He shuddered. "Smoky can't make it."

"Might have to, Son. All the tracks lead down," replied Jon. "We can hobble Smoky up here. As long as a mountain lion doesn't find him, he'll be fine."

"I was thinking about Mama. If we go down there, we won't get back until after dark."

"*Ja*, I know," Jon admitted. He glanced at the sky.

Erik glanced up as well and realized the clouds appeared to be closing in again.

"We can go down a ways and at least see if we can figure out what the animals are up to. Sometimes in weather like this, they bed down under the trees on the ridgelines. We might get lucky and spot one." Jon dismounted and helped Erik down. "If it doesn't look better, we'll head home. We can come back another day. Like Mama Larson said, at least we'll know where to look."

They tethered Smoky safely back from the rim where good grass showed through the thin snow and began to pick their way downward.

"Watch your step, Erik. This grass is slick. One bad slip and you'll wind up in the bottom."

"I'm watching." Gingerly, he followed his father. He suddenly had a bad feeling about the canyon. He sensed they weren't alone. Quickly he looked around, half expecting to see someone or something. A chill ran down his back, causing him to shiver. He tried to shake the thought.

Erik noticed the pines on the ridgeline had thinned. The south-facing slopes were barren of snow and, instead of timber, were carpeted with bleached grass except for areas of black, jagged rock. In places, the rock formed cliffs. The north-facing slopes were heavily timbered, and snow clung to them except nearer the river.

Suddenly, his father slipped and fell, sliding until he managed to jam his boot against a log.

Jon looked up. "Boy, much of that, and I'm going to be done for."

"I know, Papa," Erik replied. "This isn't good. This country is bad … very bad." The uneasy feeling had returned.

Jon checked the rifle and stood up. They paused a moment, studying the terrain below. It steepened.

Erik kicked his feet into the soil to improve his balance. "I don't think we can go down there, Papa."

He spotted an eagle below them, heading upriver, winging past effortlessly. He pointed. "Look, Papa."

"Well, now that's the way to travel this country." Jon grinned.

Erik followed the bird's flight as it first dipped toward a ridgeline then climbed back toward the gray sky and snow-covered peaks beyond.

"Good thing we're not hiking through that country." Erik nodded toward the peaks and shivered.

His father agreed. "*Ja*, I don't think anyone could make it through those."

Erik watched as the eagle dipped again toward a rocky, barren ridge. As it neared the crags, it suddenly shot upward, skimming the ridgeline, climbing free into the air, at the same time emitting a high-pitched *skr-e-e-e*.

"Look, Papa!" Erik cried. "There's some kind of animal."

"I see it too," Jon replied, voice quickening. "Can't tell what it is. Doesn't look like a deer."

"It looks like a ram, Papa. Only look at how huge the horns are!" exclaimed Erik. "Have you ever seen anything like that?" He felt a rush of excitement then saw more movement. "Wait, there's a whole bunch." Several more bighorns moved into view along the ridge crest.

"They do look a lot like sheep," Jon replied. "Well, I'll be. That old eagle must have been investigating, looking for a youngster or something."

"What should we do, Papa?" Erik asked. "Can we eat one?"

"I suppose we can. I don't really care for mutton, but it's sort of like meat." He kidded. "We've come too far and wasted too much time to not get one."

The band of mountain sheep now stared directly at them. Even though a good distance away, it seemed to Erik, they had heard them.

"We better try," whispered Erik. "I sure don't want to have to eat old Smoky or Red this winter."

Erik followed his father as he worked his way down, crossed the steep sidehill, and eased his way toward the rocky ridge where the sheep clustered, now blocked from their view by dense timber. Slowly, they crept upward, silent while on the grass, but crossing the rocky scree, loose rocks slid and clattered. They froze a moment then moved on. Before coming into view of the sheep, his father motioned for Erik to stop.

"You best stay and wait," he whispered. "If one of us should slip and make a racket, these animals will be gone. Alone, I might be able to sneak in and get a shot."

Erik nodded and sat down. He watched as his father crept upward into the timber and disappeared from sight. After long minutes, a shot rang out, echoing from the canyon walls. Erik scrambled toward his father. He knew Jon Larson rarely missed.

Another shot rang out. Erik's heart sank. There wouldn't be two shots if his father hadn't missed.

"Did you get one?" asked Erik, breathing hard, reaching his father. He stood on the rocky ridge, gazing toward the next.

Jon shook his head, mouth tight. "Nope." He pointed to the animals skimming over the top of the next ridge. "Looks like they're headed out of the country."

"You *missed?*" He stared at his father, frowning.

"*Ja*, I'm afraid so. I hardly got into view, and they were already heading up the next ridge. Probably heard us. Tried to get one. Then moved up here to get another shot. Missed them both."

Erik stood with his father watching the empty ridgeline until he realized that snow had begun falling. At first, the flakes fell softly. Then it turned into a thick flurry.

"Guess we're heading back," his father muttered, shaking his head.

"Guess so, Papa. Maybe we can come back in a day or two; now we know where they're at."

"That we'll do, lad. But we gotta figure out how to sneak up on them."

"I'll show you how," Erik offered, grinning. He knew his father was upset with missing. They needed the meat. He tried to make light of the situation. "You can wait on me next time. I'll shoot one."

"Guess so," Jon agreed.

It was late afternoon, and the gray shadows thickened.

CHAPTER 6

ERIK FOLLOWED HIS FATHER as they began to retrace their steps. The snow continued to fall and now covered the grass and rocks. He began shivering and found himself wishing they had killed a sheep.

He paused as his father came to some downed logs. Jon reached across, trying to balance himself on the slick snow. Suddenly, his foot went out from under him. The log caught his other foot and spun him around.

A sickening feeling flooded Erik as he watched helplessly. His father hit hard, sliding. The rifle flew from his hands, clattering as it hit the ground. He slid into a rock, hitting his head, spinning. He rolled and slid, now limp, into a ravine fifty yards downhill. Blood stained his trail in the snow.

"Papa!" Erik cried. He began sidestepping down toward his father. "Papa! I'm coming!" Erik slipped and went down, sliding, careening downhill. Desperately, he dug in his feet, catching himself. Gingerly he stood, heart racing, now skinned and bleeding, and continued edging his way downward to his father. "Papa!"

He saw his father begin to move. Relief flooded him. He was alive. His father turned slowly, moaning, trying to lift his head. "Blast it to blazes ..." He looked for Erik.

Erik reached him and saw him wince as pain flooded his face.

"Here, give me a hand."

"Take it easy, Papa!" Erik reached out and grabbed a hold. His father pulled himself up, trying to bring his feet underneath, but they gave way. Immediately he fell from Erik's grasp, grimacing in pain.

"Don't move, Papa. Let me look." Blood flowed from his father's head, trickled across his face.

Jon sat, breathing hard, blood soaking him. Erik removed his coat, pulled out his knife, and cut a long section from his shirt. He folded it into a pad. "Here, Papa, hold this." He pressed it onto his father's head and positioned his father's hand. Erik examined his ankle. He didn't see any protruding bones. "Maybe sprained?" Erik asked.

Jon didn't answer. Erik looked up and saw his father shudder and his eyes roll. He slumped backward, releasing the pad. He shuddered again. "Papa!" There was no response. Erik tried not to panic. He replaced the pad and held it tightly. "Please be okay, Papa." He discovered his hand shaking, trembling, and he tried to steady it. He felt nauseous as the blood seeped through the pad, warm, dripping from his fingers. Desperately, he held it tight. Finally, his father's bleeding paused, then ceased. Quickly, he tied the pad in place.

He straightened his father's crumpled legs and placed some dead branches under them to keep him from sliding. He covered him with his coat.

As the wet snow continued, Erik began shivering more intensely. He couldn't stop. Where he had cut away his shirt, he felt the cold wetness against his skin and began to feel chilled.

He watched his father's breathing, labored, sporadic.

Erik wondered if he should try to build a fire and wait for his father to come around. He realized that whatever he did, he had to get Smoky and get his father out of the ravine. He also had to get a blanket or something for himself. He surveyed the hill above. They were not far below the break.

"Papa, you take it easy. I'm going up to see if I can get Smoky over here." His father didn't respond.

Erik scrambled uphill, picking up the rifle, seeing it looked okay, and headed back toward the horse. As he climbed, the snow continued—soft, fat, wet flakes. Time pressed hard, and he felt panicked, nauseous.

Can't think about it, he told himself. He walked quickly, almost ran, toward the horse.

He tried to think how he would haul his father up. They didn't have much rope, only enough to secure some meat. They did have their blankets. They had prepared for the night if need be.

Smoky nickered as Erik came up to him. "Come on, Smoke. We got some work to do." He unrolled a blanket and wrapped himself in it, still shivering. He rolled the rifle into another, secured it, and swung up onto the horse.

He rode along the rim until he believed he was directly above his father. Dismounting, he led the horse downward, traversing the hill, and then switching back, dropping lower. Erik worried if the animal could handle the steep sidehill, but it seemed to have no trouble. The horse's weight enabled the animal to sink into the grass and dirt.

He spotted his father, a dark hump in the gathering snow. "Papa, we're here!" he hollered and waved. There was no response.

Carefully, he cut one more traverse until he was within a few yards of where the slope steepened. Now he didn't dare take the animal lower. The horse stamped nervously.

He patted the horse. "Stay, Smoke." He looped the rope he had around the saddle horn and stepped down to his father. The rope was well short. He'd have to drag his father upslope. He spread out the blanket and secured it to the rope. If he could get his father onto the blanket, Smoky could pull him up.

Sitting down above his father, one foot on each side of his body, pressing down into the rock and earth, grabbing his father's shoulders, Erik heaved himself and his father uphill a few inches. Slowly, breathing hard, fearing he would lose him, that he would tumble back down, Erik inched him upward onto the blanket.

The horse waited nervously, but didn't move. Exchanging his blanket for his coat, he bound his father into a blanket cocoon and scrambled back to the horse's head. "Good, Smoke," he said gently, steadying the animal. "Now come." He headed back across the hillside, his father's weight pulling downward. One step at a time, keeping his eyes on his father, he led the horse slowly upward. The ropes held. Several times he scrambled back to remove limbs in the way or to raise his father's shoulders so he could slide over the rocks. He knew he was being banged up even worse, but he knew of nothing else he could do. "Please be all right, Papa," he cried.

When at last they reached the break above the steep face, Erik felt some comfort. Smoky easily dragged his father across the snow.

Erik stopped and examined him. His eyes were closed, but Erik could see they were rolled up, only white appeared through his eyelids. "Wake up, Papa." He shook him. He wanted to get him up onto the horse. "Wake up." There was no response.

Erik felt the time slipping away. *I've got to get him back to the cabin. I have no choice. Even if it means walking all night, I have to do it. He can't survive out here.* He choked back the ache he felt.

He cut two long poles and, tying them at the apex, split them, laying one on each side of the horse. He cut more poles and tied on several cross pieces, using most of the remaining parts of his blanket and the rope. He led Smoky through the snow, testing the travois. The horse fought it briefly, but it would work if he could keep it out of the trees and gullies.

Erik dragged his father onto the travois and strapped him in. He used pine boughs to prop up his head and keep it stable.

He realized the snow had now turned into a steady, thick curtain. He brushed it from his eyes, squinting to see his way. Shapes were blurring together in the snow, and he realized the light was fading. Fear began to gnaw at him.

He headed uphill in the general direction of the cabin; his old tracks no longer visible. Even his coat was now soaked through, and he began shivering again. He wondered how much time he had left. He wondered how long he could survive. *I have not choice, Lord. I have to find the cabin.*

He struggled through the blinding snow for an hour, a deep gnawing fear growing inside. He began to fear he was lost. Reaching a divide in the valley, he couldn't decide what direction to head. Only a faint whiteness showed among the black timber.

Panicking, he began to sob. "Which way, God? Which way?" Surely they hadn't come this far to the north. He stood, swaying in the snow, knowing he would be unable to travel much farther.

A wavering sound, almost a whistle, came to him. He thought he could see a figure standing under the trees to his right. Mama! He couldn't believe his eyes. She had come to find them. He stumbled toward her. Then snow masked his vision.

He strained to see. Again he thought he saw the figure. "Mama!" he hollered and waved his arms. The figure appeared to be walking, heading upward, away from him. He felt a shiver race down his spine, and the hair on the back of his neck hackled as he suddenly became scared. *God, what is it?*

"Hello!" he yelled. "Help! I need help!" His voice was lost on the wind. The figure vanished. He strained to see. Nothing.

Struggling on, he reached the spot where the figure had been. No tracks. Nothing. Only swirling snow. But he still felt a presence. He tried to shake the feeling. Was something or someone watching him? He looked around, straining to see, but could make out nothing in the fading light and blowing snow. But he no longer felt fear. Strangely, he felt comforted.

He realized then that he was in the correct draw. The figure had brought him into the correct draw. "Thank you, God, for sending me help," whispered Erik. That was all he could reason it to be.

***

Ruth was worried sick, but she added another stick to the fire. If they were coming, they had to have a light. She brushed snow from the canvas twice, and already it refilled. Too much snow would tear it to shreds. The snow sifted in under its edges and between the logs, drifting into the cabin corners. She had already piled the remaining bedding together and pushed it closer to the fire. No matter what she tried, the snow continued to drift in, and the bedding was becoming soaking wet.

She ached for Jon and Erik to be home. She heard the rifle shots in the late afternoon. Certainly, they had gotten an animal, or by now, they would have been home. And now it was night. Given they had to dress out the meat, they should be coming in. She strained to hear something, anything. She nursed the fire, keeping the kettle hot.

"Dear, God," she whispered. "Bring them home safely tonight. Bring them home with meat."

She felt weak again and wanted badly to lie down. She struggled to remain awake. Finally, she heard what she thought was a shout. It sounded like Erik. Jumping up, she moved to the door and threw back the canvas. She heard the faint shout again. *It is Erik!* She tried shouting back. *They're coming!* She could barely make out their shapes through the swirling snow. Erik led Smoky, dragging something. *It must be a deer,* she hoped, *but where's Jon?* Then, heart catching, she realized it was Jon that the horse dragged.

Running into the snow, she ran up to Erik. "What happened? Is he okay?" She went to her husband.

"Mama, he fell," Erik managed. "He hit his head."

"Jon! Jon!" She reached down to him, brushing off the snow, pulling away the blankets.

Jon moaned.

"Oh, Jon!" Ruth began untying the ropes. Erik helped, and together they pulled him into the cabin and over to the fire.

Jon weakly moved his head. "Sorry … Ruthie," he managed. "Slipped … hit my head."

Ruth became frantic, sobbing as she began to examine him.

"D-don't know what happened," Jon struggled. "Fell … slid into a rock."

Ruth unbundled his bandages and examined the gash to his head—dark, bloody, swollen.

"N-now I'm here," he shuddered strangely. "Erik musta got me out of there." His eyes flicked around until they found Erik. "Th-thanks, Son. You've done good." Pain flooded his face, and he closed his eyes, shuddering.

Erik leaned heavily, shivering over the fire, soaking wet. "I only thank God we made it, Mama. God was with us for sure."

Ruth looked at Erik, half sobbing, half saying a prayer of thanks. She hugged her son. "God bless you, Erik.

"Heavens, you're soaked," she said, suddenly pushing him away. "Get out of those clothes and get dried off. You'll catch your death from cold." She started to pull off his shirt.

"I will, Mama." He pushed her hands away. "Got to take care of Smoky first. He's soaked wet as well. I'll dry off soon as I get back."

He grabbed a blanket to rub down the horse and headed back into the snow.

Ruth turned back to her husband, piled more wood on the fire, and began examining him. Only the cut on his head seemed severe. She saw him shudder.

"Let me get you something hot." She scooped out a mug of hot water and held it to his lips. He wasn't awake enough to take any. It ran across his face. She began to sponge his cuts, instead.

Erik stumbled back into the cabin, blowing snow following after. His mother helped get him out of his wet clothes and wrapped him in a blanket. She noticed his cuts as well and fussed over them.

"I'm okay," Erik mumbled. "Just some scratches. But I could sure use something hot." He shivered.

"Oh, my goodness. Of course!" She handed him a mug.

Erik held it to his face, hands shaking, and sipped. Looking at his father's silent face, he whispered, "Guess this is about as fine a track soup as I've ever had, Papa."

His mother looked puzzled.

"Papa said earlier that tracks make pretty thin soup, Mama. All we got today were tracks." He bit his lip, shaking, trying to keep from crying.

The wind whipped aside the canvas and blasted snow across them.

***

The night still black, Erik woke, shivering uncontrollably. The wind howled through the cabin. The canvas over his end had ripped loose and flapped madly. He could see the tattered shreds. It had quit snowing, and moonlight reflected from scudding clouds. Snow had piled in six-inch drifts across the floor and across his bedding.

He stood and tried to tie the canvas back in place. It was useless; the canvas was in ribbons. He'd have to get rope in the morning and tie it off.

"Erik?" His mother moved. "How is Papa?"

Erik realized she had dozed off while watching. "I don't know, Mama."

He noticed the fire had gone out.

He went to the hearth. In places, snow had drifted in strips across it. Only one or two coals winked red when he uncovered them. Despite the blanket about his shoulders, he shivered. He tried to relight the fire. Finally, it came to life. He piled on more wood, huddled in his blanket, and watched the fire and his parents as light slowly crept back into the eastern sky. An ache welled in his throat. He wondered if they would make it to spring. He wondered if he'd ever see his sister again.

Erik didn't realize the wet was his tears until one dropped onto his hand and glinted in the firelight.

CHAPTER 7

THE WARMTH AT LOWER elevation turned the snow into rain before it reached the canyon floor. Gray clouds masked the high mountains, but the people knew snow blanketed them. The frozen season was upon them.

Badger crouched on his favorite fishing rock, trying to snag another salmon. Although the salmon run was nearly finished, a few remained in the deep holes, and the people could always use more, especially during the days of the deep snow. The older boys had grown weary of fishing, and now Badger could do so without being tormented.

Today Badger wore his sheepskin shirt. Like his brother's, Shining Water had decorated it with a double row of dyed porcupine quills but in different colors. Badger was proud of the shirt and its handsome blue and green decoration. Few women were as skilled as his mother. He also carried his sheep robe, but while fishing, he had set it to one side.

"Hey, Badger."

He stood up and could see his brother splashing toward him, wading out toward his rock. The wind was cold, and he shivered. He had not worn leggings. Extra clothing would be dangerous if he slipped and fell in.

"You'll scare the fish, Otter."

"Yes, but you should hear this." He climbed onto the rock, dripping water from his leggings. He had carried his boots and sat to put them back on. "Father and some of the men have been talking. Some think the rifle shots were from Many Elks of the Big Sheep Band, because he has a rifle. But Father doesn't think so. He said the Big Sheep Band is too far; it's closer to the star-grass meadows where we hunted this past season." He straightened his shirt and crouched next to his brother.

They had all heard the rifle shots.

"Perhaps the shots were from the white trapper. I heard Stands Alone say that."

Otter shook his head. "Father doesn't think that either," he replied. "No one has seen the trapper for several seasons." Otter narrowed his eyes. "He thinks it's other white men."

Badger stared back, his heart racing. "White men?" He recalled some of the stories of these strange people.

"Yes. The elders have called a council to discuss this." Otter frowned. "But I wasn't invited."

"But, Otter, you haven't gone on your vision seeking."

"Yes, but I killed the shaggy-neck elk," he replied. "That is something important. I thought they would invite me."

Badger shrugged. The council did not concern him. He would find out soon enough what the men would decide. He wanted to snag a salmon.

"I think I will fish for a while."

"Ah, Badger," Otter replied, a hint of disappointment. He pulled off his boots and slipped back into the water to leave. "Men should worry about possible enemies, not catching a redfish, especially when we already have many." He shook his head and splashed toward shore.

Otter's words hurt, but Badger didn't budge. Sometimes he didn't wish to be bothered by things that concerned the men.

This was the best fishing hole for the salmon; it had been red with their fat bodies swarming into the gravel beds to lay their eggs. He laughed to himself, remembering. He and Otter had to chase them away in order to bathe; even then, sometimes the fish bumped against them. Some even skittered up the shallow creek that ran near the lodges, trying to reach deeper pools where they could spawn. Afterward, he and other boys picked up their spent carcasses and took them to the river to be washed downstream. Otherwise, they would stink or encourage a grizzly to visit.

Coyote and Weasel came toward him. "We are going to listen outside the council lodge," explained Coyote. "If you're not afraid, you can listen with us."

"I'm not afraid," Badger quickly replied. He wouldn't back down in front of them, although when not in Quick Marten's company, they usually treated him well. He had tired of fishing anyway.

He left his rock and snuck with the other boys to an area behind Gray Owl's lodge. Otter, Raven, and Quick Marten were already there. Otter gave him an approving look. He avoided Quick Marten.

Probably everyone knew the boys were behind the lodge, but no one ever said anything. It was somehow expected that young boys would try to listen in on council.

He couldn't make out the talking until he heard Fighting Bear's deeper voice.

"We should send men to find the man who fired the rifle, but there will not be enough light this day. We can wait."

"We should not wait long." He heard his father reply. It warmed Badger when he heard his father speak.

"But it is foolish to go now," Fighting Bear explained. "The snow is dangerous on the canyon walls."

"The snow will be frozen in the early day. Whoever has the rifle will not expect someone early."

He couldn't make out anything else until he recognized Gray Owl's voice. "Stone Hawk and I agree. We shall send four men. Whistling Elk and Cuts His Leg will pick two men. Before sunrise, they shall go."

Badger knew each band regarded these two men as their best hunters. More low talk ensued.

"So it shall be." He heard Gray Owl. "At first light, Whistling Elk and Cuts His Leg shall go with Free Hawk and Fighting Bear and observe."

Badger heard the men moving, shuffling toward the door. The council had ended.

Badger ran to the cover of trees with his two friends. Excitedly, they discussed what they had heard.

"What if it *is* white men?" asked Coyote. "Will we fight them?"

"Yes, we will fight them," replied Weasel. "My father says we must fight them, or they will kill us."

Badger was surprised. White men were very strange, but some of the people traded their animal skins with them and acquired wonderful things. He had never considered fighting them. "Why would the white men wish to kill us?" he implored. "We do not wish to kill them. The white men bring us good things like blankets and steel knives."

"True, Badger," Weasel replied. "Some white men are good. My father says some used to bring good things to us, but now they are changed. Most are bad—evil. They want our curved-horn and shaggy-neck robes but will not trade for them. They will take them."

Badger couldn't understand and resolved to ask his father about this thing. His father was wise. The Twisted River Band did not have enemies. They did not fight others.

CHAPTER 8

DAYLIGHT CREPT INTO A cloudless sky. At last, Erik could clearly see his father's face. He was unconscious, his breathing labored.

His mother sat beside Jon, trying to get him to take some water. He convulsed.

Erik was sick with fear. "How is he, Mama?"

His mother looked at him through tear-streaked eyes. "Not good, Erik. He hurt his head real bad. It's a concussion."

Desperation filled Erik. "What can we do?"

"I don't know. I'm doing all I know how. Keeping him warm and dry," she sobbed. "A head injury has ... has to heal itself."

"W-will he die?" Erik swallowed; he could hardly whisper the words.

"I-I don't know, Son," Ruth started to shake. "For sure, if you hadn't got him home last night, he would have died." She brushed away her tears.

"I had help, Mama," Erik admitted softly, almost afraid to say it.

"Help?" She stared at him.

"At first, I thought it was you. I thought you had come from the cabin to find us, but it was something else."

His mother sat silent.

"I saw a figure in the snow. It led me toward the right draw to take. I was going to take the other one," Erik almost choked on the hurt in

57

his chest. He realized that if he had, neither he nor his father would have made it back. "It helped me, Mama. I'm sure of it."

Ruth studied him, trying to understand. "Maybe it was an angel, Son. Sometimes God sends his angels when we are in trouble."

Erik wanted to believe her. "But if it was an angel, then Papa would be okay."

"I don't know, Erik." She covered her face with her hands and began shaking.

Erik felt everything slipping away, like sliding on ice. "Please don't, Mama." He touched her. "We'll pray."

She looked at him through her tears and nodded.

Erik piled more wood on the fire and then left the cabin to check on Smoky and Red. Both animals seemed to be doing fine. They had access to the creek for water and plenty of hay that he and his father had put up.

The animals also had shelter. Erik reflected that he and his father had spent more time building the stock shed than they had spent working on the cabin. Whenever he suggested they work on the cabin or go hunting, his father said that hay and shelter for the stock were more important. He repeatedly reminded him that, come spring, they couldn't go anywhere without the animals. They built a lean-to into the hillside, the sides mostly made of brush to dampen the wind, the roof made of variably spaced aspen logs and a few pines.

As he let the animals out of the corral, he studied the small shed. So far, it had worked well. Snow had piled on the roof and now insulated the inside. It seemed dry.

He headed back toward the cabin, remembering the work they'd done. His mother had helped where possible. She helped build the table near the hearth and took care of their belongings—the clothes chest, their clothes, the cooking utensils. She made hangers near the door for their tools—a couple axes, a saw, a spade—not many, but they were depending on communal use of other implements when they got to the valley.

Erik eyed the cabin. The unfinished roof sagged, and the canvas, laced with holes, flapped in the breeze. He and his father had managed to set a ridgepole and had laid in a few spars for rafters, but then the ridgepole cracked. They were going to replace it, but bad weather moved in, and his father decided it was better for his mother to be in the cabin than in the wagon. Instead of fixing the ridgepole, they had tacked up the canvas so she could move in and be dry. Now he realized the next snow would probably destroy what remained of the canvas.

Erik knew that somehow he had to finish the roof. Last night had been almost more than he could endure. Now his mother was trying to dry things out. "Wet clothes will kill a man faster than freezing to death," he remembered Slade saying during the first snowstorm.

He knew that with a proper roof, snow would pile up and insulate the cabin, keeping it warm and dry, like the stock shelter.

He took the ax, walked to the aspen grove, and began cutting poles, but he couldn't keep focused. He thought of how the figure in the snow had shown him the way. But he couldn't help but wonder about God. If God was really looking out for him, why had he let his father fall?

But maybe God had tried to warn him. Erik remembered the uneasy feeling he had before descending into the canyon. He wondered if it was the same angel trying to warn him, but he hadn't listened—he hadn't listened, and then his father was badly hurt.

He thought of his father, now back at the cabin, and could no longer cut poles. He returned to the cabin.

Entering, he glanced at his father. His mother looked up, eyes red, a scared look.

"I can't work with Papa in the shape he's in," Erik explained. He was glad he had come back. If nothing else, his mother needed him. "What can I do?" he asked.

"Nothing right now," she replied. "Just pray."

Erik stoked the fire and fetched more water. His mother looked haggard and exhausted. She sponged his father's head with water. He couldn't bear looking at him. His eyelids were partly open, fluttering, showing only white.

Erik sat next to him and tried to talk to him. "Papa, it's me, Erik. How are you?" His father didn't respond. Erik saw him quiver. He took the rags from his mother and dipped them into the snow-filled water. He patted his father's head. His eyes remained unfocused. "Papa, wake up. You're back at the cabin. You're going to be okay. You need to help me fix the roof. Snow is coming." He knew he rambled. He couldn't handle it anymore and gave the rags back to his mother. He sat, watching, praying.

Jon started mumbling something that sounded like cold.

"Come on, Papa. Wake up." Erik felt encouraged. He realized the cabin *had* grown cold. Despite the fire a few feet away, it was cold. Erik added more wood. There was no insulation. Large, open gaps remained between the logs.

Ruth piled on another blanket, giving Jon her own. Erik made hot packs of stones wrapped in rags and placed them at his father's feet. His mother lay beside him. Erik watched, stricken, unable to move, numb.

"Can I get you something, Mama? Something to eat?"

She shook her head and began shaking.

Erik again felt his world slipping away. He felt the same sickening feeling he had when he saw his father tumbling—when he realized he could do nothing. He bit his lip. *I've got to be strong. Help me, Lord. Help me be strong.* He went to his mother and patted her. "He'll make it, Mama. We'll make it." But his voice quavered.

He fixed his mother a cup of hot tea from some rosehips he had been nursing. They had almost no flavor, but the water was hot.

Evening gathered. He left the cabin and rounded up Smoky and Red to return them to the corral. He fed them and then chopped open the pond for water. The night had become bitter cold. His breath hung in clouds, and his face and hands stung. He carried wood up to the cabin. Its warmth was so welcome he almost cried.

He saw his father quiver. His mother sponged him and tried to give him water. He mumbled as if he were in Sweden. He talked to Katrine as if she were there.

Exhausted, Erik finally fell into a fitful sleep. He woke to a cry, then sobbing, then stifling quiet. Half asleep, he dreamed his father was falling again. Waking, he cried out. The sobbing was his mother's. First shock, then a great, empty grief flooded him. His father had died.

He got up to go to him. Stunned, he stood wavering until his legs gave, and he sank beside his mother. Tears came in great shudders. His chest heaved until it ached.

Somehow he found his father's still hand and took it in his own. "How can this be, Lord?" he cried. "How can this be?" He shook.

Then he realized. "Papa. Oh, Papa," he cried. "I didn't get to say good-bye."

CHAPTER 9

THE FOUR SHEEPEATERS FOUND the cabin by late afternoon. The climb from the canyon had been dangerous on the new-fallen snow.

The Sheepeaters generally avoided white men when they visited their canyon home in the past. So far, none had stayed. Some trapped but soon learned they could get more furs from the Sheepeaters by trading with them than by trapping their own.

The men were surprised by the cabin. They circled and came out in the timber on the hill above it, from where they could safely watch, crouching in the snow.

"This is strange for a white man to build his lodge in this place," observed Fighting Bear.

Cuts His Leg frowned, particularly troubled. "The Crying Mountain Band does not come here, but we hunt near here to the west. Why does the white man bring a rolling wagon here and build a white-man's lodge not far from us?"

"Perhaps he comes here to hunt," suggested Fighting Bear.

"No, that cannot be. You can see for yourselves that this is not good land." Cuts His Leg waved his arm toward the empty land to the south, turning his hand over. "We do not hunt here. This land is flat. Here the winds blow. There is no food. There is no water."

"At least this man has built his lodge near water and shelter," Whistling Elk observed, his mouth tight. "But there is still no food."

"I think he must be lost," suggested Free Hawk quietly. "He is many days from the wagon road to the south near the burning-rock land."

They spotted the horse and the ox making their way toward the fenced shelter. Fighting Bear debated on taking the horse. "It is walking free. I could own it. I think I shall."

"No," said Cuts His Leg. "We are here only to learn what is happening."

"We don't know how many guns they have," observed Whistling Elk. "The wagons have many white men and many guns. Maybe others are nearby."

"Fighting Bear and I shall look, but I think these white men are alone," replied Cuts His Leg. He motioned to Fighting Bear. The two rose and slipped away.

Whistling Elk and Free Hawk moved farther under the pines, wrapping themselves in their robes to ward off the gathering cold. They waited and watched.

A boy emerged from the canvas door and walked to the horse and ox.

Free Hawk whispered, "It is a white boy—maybe twelve or thirteen winters."

The boy opened the fenced area and led the animals into the shelter.

"A lodge for the animals," remarked Whistling Elk, surprised.

"It is a family of white men then," explained Free Hawk. "But I don't see the man. He should be out working."

"Maybe the man hunts."

"No. The horse is not gone."

"But he should hunt," observed Whistling Elk. "The roof hide is not strong. See it flap? And it has great holes."

They watched in silence as the light faded from the sky. Trees became black silhouettes. The boy came back out and went to the stream for water. He struggled, carrying the bucket back to the cabin.

"Ah, the little white boy does women's work," Whistling Elk scoffed.

When the boy raised the flap and went inside, they could hear a woman's voice. Afterward, there was silence.

Night had fallen when Cuts His Leg and Fighting Bear returned. The four crouched together.

"We found tracks in the creek—small man tracks with a horse. The horse dragged something," reported Fighting Bear. "We followed the tracks back toward the canyon rim. That is where the white man fired the rifle, but we did not see sign of any other white men."

"Where the horse came out of the trees, I found blood but no animal hair," explained Cuts His Leg. "I say the white man was injured, and the horse pulled him."

Whistling Elk nodded. "That is why we did not see a man. We did see a boy of perhaps thirteen winters. We also heard a woman's voice come from the lodge."

"Then this is a poor family of white men," concluded Free Hawk. "They will not bother the people."

The four rose and turned toward the canyon. Near the rim, they brushed snow from under the trees for a camp. They didn't strike a fire, but they ate some pemmican and then curled up in their robes. It would not be wise to walk down the canyon walls in the snow without light. It was a long distance to their winter lodges.

CHAPTER 10

DAYLIGHT FOUND ERIK AND Ruth still sitting beside Jon, drained. Silence filled the cabin. His mother sat without expression—almost without life, Erik thought.

Erik had forced himself to quit thinking. If he did start thinking, the hurt immediately flooded in. Then he found himself choking, struggling to understand, forming terrible thoughts.

Silently, he rose, pulled the spade from its pegs, and left the cabin. Smoky nickered and stamped impatiently when he came into sight of the corral. Erik realized that his father's death meant nothing to the animals, and he suddenly thought it strange. "Even death must wait while I care for you," he said without emotion. He pulled the poles from the gate so the animals could wander in search of graze.

He walked to the aspen grove on the knoll nearest the cabin—the one nearest the wagon—scraped away the snow and began digging. All morning he dug; his grief moving his empty body. While he dug, he prayed repeatedly that he and his mother would escape this high mountain prairie.

The grave was intentionally deep. Somewhere in his mind, Erik knew to make sure no animal would get his father. By noon he could dig no more. He slumped against the side of the grave and slid down, knees drawn up, head in his hands, the ache overwhelming. He found himself shaking, weeping. He couldn't stop. He wanted to remain in the grave. He no longer wanted to move.

At first he didn't hear her.

"Erik, honey," she called. "Come to the cabin. Have something to eat."

Erik looked up at her from where he sat in the cold earth. Slowly he stood and hauled himself out. He walked with her back to the cabin.

He tried not to look at his father's body, but he noticed the bandages had been removed; his mother had washed him, combed his hair, and dressed him in his good clothes. His father looked at peace—almost asleep.

His mother offered him some dried venison and a bit of pancake. "You need to eat, Son."

He shook his head. He drank only some water. He had no stomach for food.

They wrapped his father's body in a blanket and hitched it to Smoky. Erik dragged it toward the gravesite. Visions of dragging his father from the canyon flooded back. *But then he was alive,* he gasped to himself. Pulling his father out of the canyon was the hardest thing he had ever done. *And for what reason, God?* He nearly cried out at the thought. *I got him to the cabin, and you still let him die. Why?* The ache welled up, causing him to stumble. He couldn't move.

"Erik?" his mother called to him.

He pushed himself forward.

At the grave, they lowered him in and straightened his body. Ruth read a passage from their Bible. They tried to pray. She returned to the cabin.

Working silently, Erik filled the grave. There were a few rocks he had pulled from the hole that he placed on top. He fashioned a cross from aspens, and with the knife his father had given him for his birthday, he cut "Jon Larson" into it and placed it solidly at the grave head. The afternoon winter sun cast it into long shadows.

Chapter 11

Upon the scouting party's return, Gray Owl and Stone Hawk called a council. Again, Badger ran and hid behind the lodge with Coyote and Weasel and listened. When the men broke up, the people began to wonder what the news meant. The men reported a boy and his mother at a white-man lodge.

"My father thinks they were stranded or got lost from the others," said Badger.

"They must be lost, because no white-man roads are near," explained Coyote. "The wagon road is far away, near the burning-rock land, near where Black Legs' people are.

"Black Legs says there are many white men in his land, that they come in strange rolling wagons pulled by beasts that are like elk. They don't stay, but go on to Snake River. Black Legs thinks soon many white men will come and stay."

"Some people say there are white men near where the sun goes down," said Coyote. "They dig in the dirt like badgers."

"They are strange beings," Badger concluded. "I do not think they will come here. The canyon is too steep. They cannot bring their wagons here."

The boys sat in silence for a moment.

"My father said Gray Owl decided we should leave them alone," said Weasel. "He too thinks they're lost and will leave when the snow is gone. If they don't, our men will go and fight them."

"My father thinks they won't live long, and they'll die in the lodge they've built," said Badger quietly, making the sign for death.

The others looked at him, puzzled. No one had suggested this. How could anyone just die—unless the night cat or a hump-back grizzly got them?

"But they have a horse, so they can go far to hunt," countered Weasel. "They also have a white-man's elk that pulls the wagon. They won't die."

"They'll die because they're alone. They didn't see the man. My father thinks the man went away. Only the boy did work," said Badger.

CHAPTER 12

THE DAY AFTER BURYING his father, Erik found it difficult to do anything. He cared for the stock and brought in wood and water. He and his mother brushed the remaining snow from the cabin and tried to dry their blankets; otherwise, they sat unmoving, uncaring throughout much of the day. Evening came, and shadows filled the cabin. The sky remained clear. A faint star appeared through a gap in the roof.

"Tomorrow I'm going to close up the roof," Erik offered, noticing.

"Your papa said the ridgepole wouldn't hold."

"I know, Mama," Erik replied. "But I've got to do something. The canvas won't hold the snow anymore. It's ripped. Even if we repair it, it won't last. I've got to try."

"You try, Erik. We can't spend any more nights in the snow. Everything's wet," she choked. "We'll ... we'll both die of pneumonia."

Ruth was shaking, lips trembling, looking away. "Maybe it would be just as well," she whispered.

Erik felt stunned, hardly believing what he heard. "Don't *talk* like that, Mama!"

She lowered her face into her hands, pushing her thin fingers through her blond hair, shaking.

Erik rose to fix some hot tea. He added a small amount of the remaining sugar. "Here, Mama. This might help."

"Th-thanks." She took it, hands still shaking.

They sat, unspeaking, sharing the cup of tea. Ruth crawled to her bedding and curled up, drawing the covers about her.

Erik left the cabin to care for the stock. The night air was biting cold. His feet crunched the snow. Returning, he too crawled into his blankets, afraid to think.

***

Morning came. Quietly Erik dressed and pulled on his boots. "You rest, Mama," Erik whispered. "You deserve it. I'll take care of the animals, then I'll start on the roof." He slipped outside, scanning the sky. The weather remained clear.

He had done little work yesterday, and now he was behind. He worried. Work never ended. He spent every moment getting hay, hunting, bringing in wood, bringing in water. When they had first arrived, he went swimming—once—the only time he took a break. Now he hardly paused to splash himself to wash. And now, without his father to help, Erik knew he had to do more. If he wanted to fix the roof, he had to get ahead on other work.

Erik dipped water from the spot above the corral, a place where they had fashioned rocks into an icebox for storing their fresh meat, including the trout he caught. Now it was empty, and it scared him, reminding him of their desperate need for food. He filled the bucket and headed toward the cabin. He hauled water at least twice a day.

He cut more wood into lengths for the fire and stacked it near the door. The partial wall had dwindled, and he feared it wouldn't last the winter. The pine and aspen burned too quickly, and the sharp wind swiftly snatched away any heat.

Erik headed downstream to check the snares. Desperately he hoped to have a rabbit. He remembered he used to catch one every few days, but now he hadn't caught one since before his father's accident.

This day the third trap held a big snowshoe. *Thank you, Lord.* He trembled with thanks. He cleaned and skinned it, saving the heart and liver. He felt some joy. Instead of dried meat, tonight they would have fresh rabbit.

He returned to the cabin. "Here's a snowshoe, Mama. Was all I got. No sign of anything else, even though the snow makes the sign easy to see."

"This one is a blessing, Erik," she said. "Thanks."

Immediately she began preparing the animal. They had eaten little since Papa Larson's death and were hungry.

As dusk gathered, Erik went out to round up Smoky and Red. Red was back on the hill he liked, and Smoky was nosing for grass under the nearby aspens. Leading them back to the corral, Erik pulled down some hay and offered a handful to the horse. Smoky nickered as he pulled the tufts from Erik's hands. "Good Smoke." He patted the horse. "You gotta stay strong, boy, if you're gonna get me and Mama out of here next spring."

He turned and patted the ox for a moment. It shivered at his touch. "Good Red. You're hanging in there." He began to brush the animal. "I sure hope we don't have to eat you, Red. You better hope I get a deer soon."

He fetched more wood and water for the cabin. When done, he sat down, weary. His mother handed him a plate of boiled rabbit and a portion of the liver. With it they had a sprinkle of salt—nothing else.

"I was going to use some flour, Erik ... to make us some biscuits," his mother began, then broke down, shaking and sobbing. "I'm sorry, Son. It's been ruined. The last snow got it wet. I didn't know. I was too concerned about Papa Larson to ..." She covered her face, sobbing.

"Don't, Mama," whispered Erik. "It's okay. It's going to be all right." He patted her shoulder.

Ruth shook her head.

"Mama, I'll go hunting. I'll get a deer. We'll get the roof done."

Erik wondered if *any* food remained. He knew there wasn't much dried venison. He didn't know his mother had a bit of sugar and a small amount of coffee hidden away along with a couple of dry onions.

Night fell. Erik checked on the stock. A blanket of stars lit the frosty night sky. His breath hung before him. He knew he'd need to chop ice to get water in the morning.

Returning to the warmth of the cabin, he realized that he hadn't cut a single pole for the roof. He wondered if he were man enough to do so. He stoked the fire, crawled into his damp blankets, and fell asleep, exhausted. This was the second day after burying his father.

***

Erik rose at dawn and turned the stock loose to find grass. He scanned the sky and noted the high, hazy clouds, meaning a storm was likely coming—possibly in a day. He felt torn. He knew he had to finish the cabin roof as best as possible. He also knew he needed to go hunting.

He returned to the cabin for the ax. The dim light filtered across his mother's sleeping form—thin and pale. He choked back the panic and slipped out, heading toward the spruce trees below the cabin. Suddenly he spotted the tracks. His heart caught. *Man tracks!* A cold shiver raced down his spine. *Indians!* Frantically, he looked around, scanning the hill and trees. He saw where the tracks had wandered around and then headed uphill. They were old, partially filled by drifting snow. He returned to the cabin for the rifle and checked to make sure it was ready to fire.

His mother had risen and was stirring the cooking pot. "Are you going hunting?"

He started to explain the tracks, then caught himself. "No, but while I'm getting poles, if something jumps, I'll be ready," he said. "Maybe I'll get another snowshoe."

"I have some breakfast if you want." Ruth pulled the steaming pot from the fire.

Too hungry to refuse, he nodded and sat down. She ladled out some of the remaining rabbit.

Erik ate in silence, then headed back toward the woods. He scanned the hills carefully before setting the rifle against a tree. The clouds thickened.

He found two spruce about six inches in diameter and felled them. He yoked up Red and pulled the trees to the cabin. There he lopped off the branches and cut each to about ten feet long.

Erik dragged the two posts inside and dug two holes, each about three feet deep, toward the cabin's center. Lifting the first post into place, he slid it under the broken ridgepole and drove a number of stakes into the ground around its base. He set the second post in the same manner, believing the two posts would hold the weight of the bad ridgepole and the roofing material.

Saddling Smoky, he headed back out toward a large aspen grove. About half a mile out, he again crossed the tracks. He prayed the Indians wouldn't come back. At the grove, he quickly found and knocked over those aspens that were dead and dry. When he could find no more, he cut some of the live trees.

By nightfall, he and Red dragged the last bundle to the cabin. Exhausted from cutting and lifting, his hands blistered, his shoulders aching, Erik led Red back to the corral where Smoky waited to go inside as well. He threw down some hay and watched as they ate. "Poor fellas," he whispered. He realized both animals were growing thin and beginning to show the strain. "You need grain, not this worthless grass."

He went to the cabin for dinner. "How are we for water and wood?"

"We should be good until tomorrow."

"I'm glad. I can hardly lift my arms anymore," Erik murmured. He sat on the clothes chest and pulled off his boots. His feet were wet.

His mother took notice. "You got to keep your feet dry, Erik," she said. "I can't afford having you get sick."

"I'll be all right, Mama."

She fixed him a plate with some rabbit. "Thanks, Mama, but we should save the rest."

"This is the rest."

Erik considered this but was too drained and hungry not to eat.

His mother nodded. "You've done good today, Erik."

Erik warmed with the compliment. "Thank you, Mama."

"Try to dry your boots and get to bed. You're exhausted."

"Okay. Just let me check the stock. I want to make sure they get more hay." He worried now about their feed.

He pulled on his wet boots and coat and went back out. It had started snowing—scattered, light flakes.

He pulled down more hay and watched a moment while the animals fed. He knew, as any farm boy did, that the dried grass held little nutrition. When they arrived at the valley, there was very little green grass they could cut and properly cure. Most had already withered.

Leaving the stock, he checked that the poles were secure across the gate and headed back to the cabin. The firelight winked at him through the gaps in the cabin walls.

His mother had turned in. Too exhausted to talk, he slipped off his boots and trousers and crawled into his own bedding. Despite efforts to keep things dry, his blankets were still damp. The ground below was hard and cold. He mumbled good night.

***

Erik woke long before daybreak, shivering from the cold that waked him. Snow had sifted into the cabin, lightly covering things. Up, he pulled on his clothes, now frozen stiff from the night cold. His boots were also frozen. There was no grease to waterproof them. He lit the morning fire to bring some warmth to the cabin and put water on to heat. Satisfied that the fire was safe, he headed down to take care of the horse and ox and turned them loose, then shoveled out their manure.

Snow fell softly, and gray showed in the eastern sky. A light dusting had blown in during the night, perhaps an inch. A few straggling geese honked from the darkness, moving south. *Why don't you land here?* Erik questioned. *You'd sure be good in the stew pot.* He felt somewhat relieved. The clouds were light, or the geese wouldn't be flying.

His mother was up when he got back to the cabin.

"I figure I'll go hunting a bit, Mama. Maybe check around near the cabin. I wanted to finish the roof, but it's snowing. I don't want things to get any wetter."

His mother nodded. "If it lets up later, maybe you can start."

"I'm thinking that." Erik took the rifle down and checked the load.

"I'll have things ready in case."

"Thanks, Mama," he said.

Erik headed down past the ponds. The upper ones, except the one by the corral, were frozen. The lowest one, the largest, was partially open. Several times Erik had seen ducks on the open water but had never thought about shooting one. Now he did.

He saw nothing, but then noticed the cattails frozen in the ice at the pond's edge. He wondered why he hadn't thought of them before. They had dug and eaten cattail roots while on the trail last summer.

Fetching the spade, he began digging the roots from the mud and ice. He sank into the mud, and the icy water flooded into his boots, soaking his feet. The roots looked shriveled and mostly black, not white like those they had gathered during the summer. Possibly there would be something inside. He cut off the dead tops and carried the muddy clumps back to the cabin.

"These are cattails, Mama," he said, handing them to her. "They don't look like much, but maybe we can get a little food from them."

Ruth looked at the mostly black mud. She bit her lip. They were nearly out of food and beginning to starve. "Thank you, Erik. These are just fine. There might be a little good root left."

Erik turned and went to get more water for her to do the cleaning. The sky remained overcast; Erik reasoned more snow would soon follow. He had to fix the roof now or never. He pulled the canvas off and wrapped it over the wagon but only tied it lightly. Come nightfall, he hoped he and his mother wouldn't need to sleep in the wagon.

Erik climbed onto the ridgepole and began laying aspen poles across it. His mother handed them up as he worked.

He suddenly found himself nodding off and had to shake himself awake. He wondered how long he could keep this up. He was completely exhausted, and his body dragged. It felt as if he never completely woke up during the day. It was a long time until spring. The rabbit was all they had eaten during the past several days, and it didn't seem to give him any energy.

By the time he had laid half a side of poles, it began to snow. He ignored it. He had no choice but to continue.

He ran out of poles before finishing, and a gap remained at his end of the cabin. Instead of stopping to cut more, he laid the spruce boughs on the finished area, then the heavier spruce poles to weight them down. He noticed the roof sag as the weight increased. Even with the support posts, he worried it might collapse. He retied the canvas from the wagon over the remaining gap. It was near dark. The snow thickened. Already it piled on the new roof.

God, he prayed, *I've done all I can. Now I'm asking you to make this roof hold up.*

When he climbed down and stepped back inside the cabin, his mother greeted him. "It looks fine, Erik." She had already picked up the debris that covered their belongings and had given everything a good shake. She had also been boiling the cattails and now divided them into two mounds of gray mush. She handed Erik his plate.

Erik poked at them. "Not much good, are they, Mama?"

"Even so, Son, I think it's worth trying to dig more."

They chewed on the bland, stringy bits of fiber.

Erik said nothing. The cattails provided little—he knew that. He pushed the uneaten roots to the side. "Might have to slaughter Red," he said.

"No. We can't," Ruth protested. "Without that ox, we can't haul our wagon."

Erik didn't argue. He knew he'd do what he must when the time came.

"Maybe you can shoot some rabbits, Erik."

"Not worth the lead and powder, Mama," Erik replied. He knew there were only a few cartridges and even fewer caps remaining. "Don't worry. When I get this roof done, I'll take Smoky and see if I can't get us another deer. If I do, we'll be okay for a while."

Night had fallen. Erik went back out into the blowing snow to take care of the stock before turning in. He felt proud of the work he had done. Although his end of the cabin still needed some work, the cabin was already much warmer. Tomorrow he planned to finish the roof and chink the cabin walls with spruce boughs. While building the cabin, they hadn't been able to spend much time notching or smoothing the logs to get a tight fit. Now snow filtered through the gaps across his bedding.

Chapter 13

Erik woke to a sharp scream. He heard Smoky whinnying with fear and heavy thuds coming from the corral. He scrambled to get up.

His mother was awake, fumbling around. "Erik! Erik!"

"What is it?" he shouted, dragging on his trousers and boots. Something was after the stock, he realized.

The scream sounded again. A shiver raced down his spine. "Try to light the fire, Mama." He heard the animals thudding and wood splintering. He heard hoof beats and figured Smoky was out.

"Mountain lion!" he shouted. "It's after the stock!"

Erik grabbed the rifle and cartridge case and stepped out. The snow had quit, and the moon lit up the corral, reflecting from the snow. He could see shadows in the pen but not the horse.

Erik raised the rifle, cocked the hammer, and fired in the direction of the corral, hoping the noise would frighten the mountain lion away. A shadow darted up the hillside. Shaking with anger, he raced toward the corral.

He saw Red stumbling, struggling. A dark shape separated from the ox. Erik froze. *Another lion. A big one.* It stopped and faced him. Oblivious to the danger, Erik sprinted toward the cat.

"Get out of here!" he shouted, waving his arms. "Leave!"

The ox struggled up and thudded out of the pen, heading down the creek. The cat remained, crouched, facing Erik.

Erik sat down, tore open a cartridge, and loaded another round. Seating another cap, he cocked the hammer and pulled the heavy rifle back to his shoulder. Trying to see the lion through the sights in the moonlight, he squeezed the trigger. The explosion rocked him back. The cat leaped and bolted in the direction Red had gone. He heard the ox crashing through the brush and timber long after he lost sight.

Breathing heavily, Erik sat, a terrible hurt in his chest, unwilling to comprehend what had happened, the night now silent.

He heard his mother calling. Desperately he wanted to go after the animals, but he knew he couldn't do anything that night. He checked the snow and found bloodstains. With grief, he headed for the cabin.

He reloaded the rifle and placed it back on its pegs. His mother sat, shaking, looking questioningly at him.

"Smoky and Red have bolted down the creek," he explained. "I shot at one of the lions. I might have hit it, but there were at least two. I think one was a yearling cub still with its mother. I found blood in the snow, but I don't know if it was from Red or the lion."

"Oh, dear God," his mother said.

"It'll be okay, Mama. At first light, I'll go after them."

Erik saw the hurt come to her eyes as she shook her head. "If you go after them and ... Erik, you're all I have," she whispered, and began to shake.

***

Erik slept for a couple hours before waking and preparing to head out. He checked the rifle. He didn't want to carry it because of its weight, but he knew he might need it. He also packed a rope and a lunch of dried meat. "Good-bye, Mama," he said. "Hopefully I'll get the animals and be back soon. I should be back before dark."

"Be careful, Erik," his mother pleaded, coughing. "*Please* be careful."

Checking the corral in the gray light, he saw tufts of red hair amidst the blood. It was Red's. Erik realized that the lion must have gotten in some pretty good licks. Unfortunately, there were no blood marks where he'd shot at the mountain lion. He'd missed. Red's blood spattered the snow in the direction he headed. He followed the spots into the timber and downhill.

He heard brush crack and a whinny, and he looked up to see Smoky. "Oh, Smoke," he exclaimed. "Thank God. Come here, old boy." The horse limped toward him. Erik went up to him, but as he reached for his muzzle, the animal shied.

Grabbing the horse's mane, Erik steadied the animal. "Easy, Smoke," he whispered. "Easy, old boy."

Carefully, he examined the horse. A gash ran across one shoulder. One flank had puncture marks. Erik didn't know if it was from the lion or from running through the fence and timber. He examined his hoof. As far as he could tell, the hoof was okay. He led Smoky back to the corral, but the animal shied away. The horse still smelled the mountain lion as well as the blood. Erik ended up tethering him nearby. He would repair the corral when he got back with Red. He returned to the cabin.

"I've got Smoky," he stated. "He's been cut, but I think he'll be okay."

"Thank God," his mother breathed.

"I picketed him above the corral, because he still smells the lions. Can you take care of him while I go for Red? I don't want to ride him, because he's cut."

His mother nodded.

Erik returned to where he had found Smoky and continued following the tracks down the creek toward the canyon. The snow lay a foot and a half deep, but the ground under was mostly soft. The glare of the sun hurt his eyes, and he found he had to focus on the dark trees in order not to be blinded.

He thought about the deepening snow. Soon they would be snowbound, like the deep winters he remembered back in Sweden. He reflected on their journey from Sweden to America. He never understood why they didn't remain in Chicago; he didn't understand why they went to Minnesota; he didn't understand what happened to the farm his father was supposed to work. He realized his father hadn't told him everything.

It happened when Adolphson told them about the new territories, about the mining camps opening up, needing produce. Adolphson knew of a valley where some Swedes were settling. "You can grow cabbages as big as a person's head, onions bigger than a boxer's fist, and potatoes as big as feet," he had bragged. Erik liked those stories. "Oats and barley grow higher than your waist. Salmon run red in the streams. Deer and elk fill the valleys."

Often they had talked about that valley during the journey. "The sun shines long in the summer, like the northland. The snows are deep in the winter. Hot springs flow from the valley walls." How they had dreamed of having their own land—getting a new home. *Maybe Katrine is already there,* Erik remembered and shook his head. He had to find Red. They had to make it through to spring.

Erik followed Red's broken and stumbling tracks toward the canyon. Blood spots streaked the snow. He kept his eyes open for mountain lion tracks but saw none. He guessed if the cat had followed Red, it had followed from a different vantage point.

The sun warmed the forest, and clumps of snow slid from the boughs as he worked his way downward. Now grass showed through. Across the canyon, some slopes were barren. Erik marveled at how much warmer it was here than at the cabin. Somehow, the steep hills concentrated the warmth into the draw he descended.

He studied Red's tracks. They had become hard to follow, but then they climbed out of the creek. They went around the side of the hill into the open, then down again, into a second draw. From the tracks, he knew the animal was struggling and then running. With sickening realization, Erik knew the lions had followed.

He reached the top of the canyon where the walls steepened. Erik hoped the ox hadn't gone over the rimrock. At the edge, Erik peered down toward the thick scrub far below. Ravens hopped around the limbs of a snag; several on the ground flapped at each other. Erik's heart sank. It had to be Red. The ox was either dead or in serious trouble.

With a heavy heart, he edged his way downward, digging in his boots to keep from sliding. He spotted the river again, far below, silvery water peeking from the blue black trees along the barren canyon floor. No snow.

Red's body lay in a crumpled, torn mass at the base of the snag. Limbs and brush had been scraped up over it in spots, partly concealing it. Erik recognized it as a lion kill. Pad prints were visible in the soil. There were at least two sets, maybe more, a mother and her yearling cub or cubs. They had eaten their fill and left to sleep the day away. Erik knew they would return to eat more over the next several days. He was suddenly very glad he had the rifle.

"Poor Red," he whispered. "You were a good ox." He pulled his knife and cut off as much meat as he could carry. All the while, he worried the mountain lions would return. The thought of the lions watching him sent prickles along his back. He slung the meat and rifle over his back and headed back up toward the rim.

He suddenly slipped, barely catching himself. His father's accident flashed vividly back, and he shivered. He couldn't let that happen to him. Angry, breathing heavily, he climbed upward, making certain of each step.

Tears of frustration and helplessness hit him as he topped the canyon. Oblivious to the world around, he sat, exhausted. *Why, dear Lord, is this happening to us? What have we done so wrong?* He couldn't stop his thoughts although he knew they were wrong.

***

Ruth anxiously waited for Erik, keeping the fire going. She tried to get Smoky back into the corral but saw that the fence was ruined. She took a few armloads of hay to him. He pawed at it and ate. She brought more wood into the cabin but felt very tired—the stress was telling. Her cough was back. Now she began to fear the worst. She feared Erik wasn't going to make it back. Night came, and he still hadn't returned. She kept the broth and remaining boiled meat hot, and she prayed.

She dozed for a while, then slept. The night turned to morning. She woke, hearing his faint calls. The tone said he was all right. She began to shake, and tears streamed down her face. "Praise the Lord," she said. "My son is coming home." *For thirteen, he's a strong boy, but he's still a boy.*

She pushed aside the canvas on the doorway and looked toward her son's voice. "Erik," she found herself saying, voice cracking. She spotted him, waving from across the snow. She waved back, trying to shout, but realizing Red wasn't with him, her heart sank.

When he reached the door, she could see the turmoil in his eyes. He slung down his pack and hugged her, shaking. She knew he was upset and wanted to ask why but didn't.

Silently, he pushed away. She watched as he brought Smoky up and picketed him near the cabin. He made two more trips to the shed and brought up some hay. She realized it was in case the lions returned, and she felt a shiver of fear.

Erik came inside, sat down, and pulled off his wet boots.

Ruth noticed one of the soles was coming off and that his feet were blistered, red, and raw. She bent down to examine them. "Erik, dear," she said softly. "Your feet look terrible." She got a blanket and began to dry them.

He sat with his head in his hands as she patted his feet and put on some salve.

"Maybe you can stay here tomorrow and take care of your feet."

Erik didn't reply.

Ruth saw the blood on his hands and now feared the worst. Finally she asked, "So you didn't find Red?"

Erik bit his lip. "Yes, Mama, I found him. But the mountain lions found him first. He was dead and half eaten." Erik started to shake. "I'm sorry, Mama."

Chapter 14

"See, Father," exclaimed Otter, smiling triumphantly. "They *are* curved-horns." He pointed across to the cliffs that came to the river's edge upstream above the camp.

"They will be difficult to hunt," replied Free Hawk, studying the animals, pleased but doubtful they could reach them.

"We should try. Raven and Whistling Elk can come."

"It would be good to get one. I should like to begin making a new curved-horn bow."

"But, Father, you have *two*," protested Otter. "What would you do with another ... trade? I need to build a horn bow, not you."

"True. But let's see which hunter gets this curved-horn; he can decide what to do with the horns." He laughed at his son. "And if Whistling Elk and Raven come with us, perhaps they will get the curved-horn, and they can decide."

"There will be more than one, you wait."

They watched the ridge for a moment. Despite the far distance, Free Hawk could make out several animals. His son fidgeted nervously, clearly anxious for the hunt.

"All right. Go tell Raven and Whistling Elk. I'll have Shining Water prepare our food."

Otter sprinted off toward Whistling Elk's lodge through the light snow that covered the ground. Deeper snow lay in drifts from earlier storms and filled the ravines and shady areas.

Whistling Elk and Raven quickly arrived. As the boys prepared, the men moved aside to briefly discuss the hunt.

"This may be a good day for one of our sons to get a curved-horn," said Free Hawk. "If so, you or I should make it into a good horn bow."

"I shall hope it is Otter, and you can make the bow. He killed the shaggy-neck elk," replied Whistling Elk.

Free Hawk laughed. "Perhaps both our sons will be lucky—for they are both becoming fine hunters—then we can both work on bows. It would be good to work on a bow during the long winter moons."

"We shall hope for two good curved-horns, then."

They journeyed a short distance up River That Cries until they found downed trees partially across it. Removing their leggings and winter boots, they walked across on the logs to the shallow side, leaped into the water, and waded the remaining distance. They paused to dry themselves and then dressed.

With Free Hawk leading, they began their slow climb toward the rocks above. Ridges peeled away from the higher mountains above and steeply plummeted into the river. Sometimes a ridge extended out over the river and ended in a series of cliffs. Other times the ridges ended in barren, grassy slopes—slopes so steep they were nearly impossible to climb. In that case, the hunters made a series of traverses. Always they were careful not to dislodge rocks. One the size of a fist could easily knock a man from his feet or worse—it could kill him if it should strike his head.

Grass blanketed most of the south- and east-facing slopes, but either brush or heavy timber blanketed the north- and west-facing slopes. Following a contour around a ridge often meant moving from grass into brush and trees and then back out into open grass. A predominant shrub, ceanothus, grew thickly on the north and west slopes, its large branches growing downhill, curving up off the ground. Neither man nor animal could move uphill against its springy limbs. Similarly, nothing could travel uphill in the heavily timbered areas where trees, living and dead, crisscrossed in crazy jumbles.

Game adapted to the steep slopes by bedding down on the ridgetops where they could observe danger approaching from below. They chose ridges where one side dropped into heavy timber, and the other opened onto brushy or grassy slopes. In this manner, the animals could graze in the open and retreat to the heavy timber if threatened. Over the years, they had created the trails that now crisscrossed the ridges.

The Sheepeaters followed what game trails there were, even if it took them farther away from where they wished to go. Game found the easiest routes, which eventually emerged onto the ridgelines where walking was easier.

The sun came out, and the new snow began melting.

"Remember," Free Hawk said, addressing the boys, "when the grass is wet, it cannot be climbed against. Walk a long way across it and then walk a long way back, being satisfied with moving only a man's height upward.

"Also, when the wood is without bark and is wet, it's like water on ice. One step on wood hidden beneath snow will always take the legs of a hunter." He gestured at the snowy caps already seeping water, blanketing the broken limbs that littered the hillside. "Today is such a day to watch."

He knew the boys would remember. As watcher for Raven, he had often instructed him, and he knew Whistling Elk similarly instructed Otter. But as the grandfathers advised, boys constantly needed reminding.

Free Hawk intended to approach the sheep from downwind and above them if possible. Wind currents moved down the canyons in the evenings and up them in the mornings during the hot summer days. They moved similarly during the winter but on a lesser scale. No animal was ever surprised if hunted from below or from upwind.

Free Hawk paused and studied the ridge they followed. In a short distance, it would end in a series of sheer cliffs that dropped into the river. These were the cliffs visible from camp.

He turned and moved rapidly on a traverse upstream, then cut back, gradually gaining elevation so they would be on a safe bench above the cliffs. The river dropped as they climbed, now heading back downstream toward the sheep. They were a couple hundred feet above it when he led them out onto the bench. Scanning the ridge where the sheep had bedded down, he realized they were still too low. He called softly to Whistling Elk, pointing uphill, indicating a route that would take them higher and above the sheep, motioning for him to lead.

Whistling Elk began edging around the knoll, moving upward with the others following. The river lay directly below, churning white against the cliffs.

A branch kicked up when Otter stepped on it, catching his leg, throwing him off balance. He stumbled and then stepped quickly with his other foot, but his leg buckled as he tried to catch himself, and he pitched forward, crying out in surprise. Frantically, he grabbed, but there was nothing to catch.

Free Hawk watched, stricken as his son slid over the edge. He saw him trying to push himself from the rock face, trying to get himself out into the water, but he bounced and fell, hitting the water sideways. When he came up, one arm moved; the other was limp. His head bobbed as he tried to turn himself and swim out of the rapids, but then the water dropped into seething white over the ledges created by the cliffs.

"Otter!" Free Hawk cried, stunned, a desperate feeling flooding him. He dropped his bow and frantically climbed down toward the river. He watched the water swing his son into the rocks then suck him into the rapids beyond. "Otter!" he called again, voice choking.

Both Raven and Whistling Elk scrambled downward as well. It was a mistake; their paths ended on the cliff above the river.

Free Hawk wanted to throw himself into the water ... wanted to go after his son. He watched helplessly as Otter, no longer struggling, was swept from his sight by the pounding whitewater.

Racing back up and around the rocks and recrossing the river, the hunters ran along its banks calling and looking for Otter. Raven ran the distance back to camp to summon help then continued downstream to inform the Crying Mountain Band. Soon many people walked the banks looking for Otter—all clinging to hope that he had climbed out.

Free Hawk saw Badger among those frantically looking. He heard his younger son repeatedly crying out for his brother. Heartsick, an ache almost overwhelming, he let out a cry. "How can this be, Great Mystery? How can this be?" He ran to Badger; together they searched the river until exhausted. He found Shining Water, also beside the pounding river, softly wailing. He held her. Badger continued to wander aimlessly, calling his brother's name.

Sees Far found Otter's body not far downstream where it had become wedged under a rock outcrop. He pulled him from the water and carried him back to the camp. The wailing began as he came into sight. The others turned from the river and followed, joining in the wailing.

The people mourned throughout the night and into the next day. Shining Water cut her hair and blackened her face and arms. Free Hawk and Badger blackened their faces and shoulders.

The people bundled Otter in the elk hide from the elk he had killed at the summer hunting place. Free Hawk and Whistling Elk carried Otter's body and, with the people following, climbed far above the camp into deepening snow, to where the canyon broke into rimrocks. They placed his body, dressed in his finest clothes—the shirt similar to Badger's with its double row of porcupine quills—and wrapped in the elk skin, on a large, isolated rock that had separated from the rim. Beside him, they placed his bow and arrows, and about his neck, his medicine pouch.

Other Sheepeaters' bodies, wrapped in their robes, had also been left along the same rim. Their bleached bones, shredded robes, and remnants of personal items could be seen among the rocks. The breeze still found bits of feathers and hides to worry.

River That Cries lay far below. Beyond it, the canyons unfolded in broken grandeur as far as the eye could see. And beyond the canyon rim, snow-covered peaks touched the blue winter sky.

This was the place where the eagles—the messengers to the Great Mystery—came to hunt and soar. Here was where the spirits lived. Here was where Otter's spirit—the one who hunts the elk's spirit—could now find its way to the sky trails.

A deep sadness descended on the Twisted River Band. It was a great loss to lose one so young, one in his fourteenth winter, one not yet a true man. Already the one who hunts the elk had shown he was kind to others, and others turned to him; already he had shown he had a good heart and spirit; and already he had shown he was a skilled hunter and a good provider. Now he walked the sky trails.

Free Hawk kept company with Shining Water and Badger while they mourned. Where his son should have grown to be a strong hunter and an important member of the Twisted River Band—where he should have married and had sons and daughters—now there was emptiness. A burning ache welled within his chest. He deeply missed his son. He glanced at Badger's face and saw the hurt there as well. He knew Badger missed him. He gave thanks he still had Badger and little Singing Bird.

CHAPTER 15

ERIK STARED AT THE swirling snow through the gaps in the cabin. He and his mother were snowbound and now in desperate trouble. They had eaten the ox meat. Their only remaining food was a small portion of dried meat. Erik hunted near the cabin almost every day. The snares were no longer effective. Rabbit tracks showed where they scampered through the snow past the snares. He dug more cattails, gathered even the shriveled rosehips, and tried to find pine nuts remaining in the opened cones. Always he carried the rifle and kept his eyes open for the mountain lions in case they should return for Smoky.

When he didn't hunt, he tended to the cabin. He carried water, collected and hauled wood, and cared for Smoky—fed him, chopped ice to open up his water, and walked him. The horse now had trouble finding grass except in a few sheltered areas under the trees where a little remained. What looked to be more than enough hay to last the winter was rapidly dwindling.

More and more he thought about leaving the cabin and going down into the canyon for protection and food. He was certain there were deer and mountain sheep in the canyon bottoms.

"Mama," Erik began, sitting down to a bowl of broth, "I think we ought to move to the canyon to get out of the snow." He tasted the weak broth.

"I will hear none of that," she replied, sitting down with him. "I could never make it that far, and you and Papa Larson both said the horse couldn't make it."

He looked at her directly, hoping he could make her understand. "I think I can find a way for Smoky to get down. He can carry you most of the way."

"Even so, I'm not strong enough," she protested. "I'm not well." She spooned some of the broth but took none.

"You are, Mama," Erik persisted. "You can do it. I will give you the remaining meat. When we get to the river, I can catch trout. There we will have food. Here we don't have any." He let the broth drip from his spoon, clearly showing it had no substance.

His mother shook her head. "Maybe you can go hunting here and get a deer." She didn't return his gaze.

"Mama," Erik pleaded. "That's what I've been trying to say. There are no deer here. They have gone to the canyon to get out of the snow, where they can get food. Here they would be dead. They *aren't* here!"

His mother didn't reply but let her spoon drop.

Erik softened. "Mama, before Papa died, when we went hunting in the canyon, we saw sheep. He agreed with me that's where the animals went in winter. The canyon is protected. That's where they can get food."

His mother just sat shaking her head. He could see her tears.

"Erik, if we go down there, if I even make it … I-I don't think I'd ever make it back. I-I cannot leave your father," she sobbed. "We'll die in the canyon. I don't want to die there."

"Mama, I promise you if we go there, we *will* come back. Next spring, we'll come back. *I'll* get us back. Then we can leave and go to find Katrine."

She sat shaking her head.

But Erik now realized her true reason—she didn't want to leave Papa Larson. Erik gave in. He whispered, "Don't worry, Mama. If you don't want to try, then we won't go. We'll be fine. I'll go hunting. I'll get some food. Next spring we'll go back to the trail." He patted his mother's hand, but he didn't believe a word he had spoken.

***

Morning came. He made certain his mother had wood and water. "Mama," Erik said, "I was thinking about what you said last night— that I should go hunting. Please don't try to stop me. I've decided to take Smoky and go back to where Papa and I saw the sheep so I can get one."

Ruth knew she couldn't argue, but she felt the world crumbling about her. They needed food. She bit her lip. If Erik ran into trouble, they'd both die. She couldn't survive without him.

"I'm going to be safe, Mama," Erik continued. "I'll try to be back by dark, but I don't think I'll make it unless I get lucky. Expect me tomorrow."

Ruth didn't reply. She knew Erik must go. She finally understood that there was nothing but snow on this empty prairie. Even here in the shelter of the bluffs and the trees, the animals were gone.

"If I don't get back by dark, I'll fire a shot to let you know I'm okay."

"And if you're not okay?"

"I *will* be, Mama," Erik said. "I feel God is telling me I'll be okay."

Ruth helped him pack his gear, including a bedroll and a canvas for shelter.

***

Erik saddled Smoky but couldn't ride him at first. The snow was too deep. He led him through the snow, intentionally angling west to see if he could find a better way into the canyon, one the horse could traverse.

It took better than half the day to reach the canyon wall. To the west, he could see a valley. If he could drop into the valley, he could follow it all the way to the canyon floor. On another day, he would search for a way.

Erik continued for a while, now riding Smoky, doubling back. He kept above the canyon rim. He wanted to come out on the ridge where he and his father had seen the sheep. Already he had jumped some rabbits and grouse. But he would not waste any rounds on them, not just yet. He had thrown a stone at a grouse but missed. It disappeared below him, sailing off into empty space. The rabbits scampered out of throwing range. If necessary, he would shoot a rabbit and come back another day for a sheep.

Erik came out of the timber onto a series of open brush- and grass-covered hillsides that plummeted toward the river. *Good game country.* He studied the hills descending toward the river, a jagged ridge leading downward between them. He thought again about his father's accident and hesitated.

But this time there was no uneasy feeling. Instead, he felt a comforting presence. He looked around, straining, trying to see something under the trees, but he saw nothing.

He dismounted, picketed Smoky, and checked the rifle. He began working his way downward along the narrow ridge, keeping his eyes sharp for game. He hoped the ridge wouldn't end in a cliff, but more or less, it did. Rocky bluffs fell away on three sides.

He moved out to the point and paused, scanning the countryside. A grassy knoll and brushy draw with patches of snow spread below him. He saw no game. He decided to sit for a moment.

Suddenly, he heard crashing below to his left. Two massive bull elk, with dark, shaggy necks and shoulders and large branching antlers, broke from the timber, trotted across the open slope, and dropped into the next draw. Heart beating rapidly, Erik pulled up the rifle and tried to sight in on the rear bull, figuring it was a hundred yards away. When they reappeared, they were already over the next ridge and moving upward out of the steep canyon, far out of range. Erik wondered what had spooked them and began to panic. *What if that's all? What if I don't see more?* The thought flashed that he had already seen rabbits, grouse, and elk. This was good game country. There had to be more.

He heard softer thudding and turned to see a string of cow elk moving rapidly out of the timber into the open below him. One paused and looked in his direction. Erik tried to sight in behind her shoulder. It bounded away. In desperation, he swung the rifle toward the rear cow, which seemed to stumble, but then she trotted after the others. Erik squeezed off a round. The explosion shattered the silence and rocked him back onto his rump. Quickly he scrambled up and fumbled out another cartridge. But the cow was down. "Thank you, dear God!" Erik exclaimed. And for the first time in months, he let out a whoop of joy. "Thank you, God! Thank you!"

He jumped to his feet, heart pounding, and headed toward the cow. He froze. A man emerged from the timber and walked quickly toward the elk. *An Indian!* In desperation and anger, and without thought, he ran the remaining distance to the elk, shouting and waving, "Go away! Go away! It's mine!"

Three other Indians came into view. All had bows and moved toward him rapidly, gesturing and talking excitedly. They advanced to within a few yards; one raised his hand, palm out. Erik knew it meant peace, but he leveled the rifle at him. He was protecting his elk. *Stupid,* he realized instantly. A couple of the Indians paused and notched arrows to their bows, partially raising them. Erik realized that if they wanted, they could fill him with arrows even if he did manage to shoot one of them. The thought mystified him. *How can I think that? How could I kill anyone—even an Indian?*

The other two gestured at him and then toward the elk, grinning. They pointed at his rifle and back to the elk. It seemed they were trying to congratulate him. One pointed to the other and mimicked drawing a bow and releasing an arrow. He pointed to the elk. Erik nodded. He lowered the rifle but kept it ready. He slowly raised his hand, palm out. The Indians lowered their bows and returned the sign. Relief immediately flooded him. He decided they wouldn't hurt him. If they had intended to do so, they already would have.

The men were about his father's age, although one was younger, probably only a few years older than he, Erik realized. They wore breechcloths, leggings, and furry boots. Their hair flowed free, except for those who wore a small braid with an ornament. They wore small pouches about their necks and quivers across their shoulders; otherwise, their shoulders were bare, even in this cold. Maybe because they were hunting, Erik reasoned.

Erik stood by as they advanced to the elk and wrestled it over onto its other side. Immediately, Erik spotted the two arrow shafts imbedded in the ribcage. His stomach turned. His legs gave way, and he sat down heavily in disbelief. He had hit the elk, true, but this wasn't his elk—it was theirs.

He felt tears stinging his eyes. Unable to move, he sat while the men skinned and began butchering the animal. One pulled a portion of liver free and, making a sign, offered it to Erik. Numbly, he took and held it, unsure of what to do.

Scowling, the Indian that offered it took it back, cut a bit off, and made a sign as if to eat. He offered it back to Erik. The others watched.

Now knowing what they expected, Erik gingerly put the warm piece of meat into his mouth and, without chewing, swallowed. He tried not to grimace.

Laughing, the Indians made agreeable sounds and took bites. They resumed their work, working rapidly in the lengthening shadows.

Erik no longer felt fear toward them. He knew they didn't fear him. How could they? He was just a boy.

Erik stood awkwardly by, wondering how he could make them understand that he and his mother needed this elk. Twice he thought about gesturing to them but didn't. Maybe they would leave some scraps. Maybe he should go after the other elk.

The Indian who had first approached him seemed most wanting to communicate and occasionally addressed him. A sharp face, friendly eyes, he looked strong, a red and yellow feather ornament hung from his braid. This Indian, Erik decided, he would call Talker. As Erik watched Talker, he spread the elk hide and placed chunks of meat on it, gesturing and talking to Erik.

Shortly, they had quartered and divided the elk. Only a few bones and some entrails remained.

Talker addressed Erik, gesturing toward the canyon. His gestures were clear: he wanted Erik to follow.

Erik shook his head. "No, I cannot," he said. "My home is on the canyon rim." He pointed.

Evening crept into the canyon. Heavy shadows cloaked its depths. The air held a deep chill, and the sun slipped from the highest parts of the hills. Erik suddenly wanted to follow. He wanted to go with them to the canyon floor, to where there was no snow, to where it was warmer.

Talker again gestured toward the river and beckoned to him. Erik shook his head. Talker frowned and shrugged. He and the other three men hoisted their loads and headed back in the direction they came. Erik choked back a sob as he realized they had left a large portion of meat for him.

He placed the meat in his makeshift pack and carefully retraced his steps back to Smoky. Night had fallen. He could see his breath, and frost coated the brush and grass. The snow had crusted. The stars were strung brightly from horizon to horizon.

Erik thought about returning to the cabin. He feared his mother would be worrying. He did not want to spend the night away, but he knew it was too risky to head back from this far away. He rolled out his blankets, wrapped up in the canvas, his back against some overhanging rocks, and tried to sleep. The night air froze in his nostrils. Coyotes yapped and argued with each other, almost singing. They no longer frightened Erik as they had when he first came to this country. He knew they were probably cleaning up the elk remains. *Please, dear God, let Mama be okay,* he prayed. *Keep me and Smoky safe tonight. Thank you for the elk.* Finally, he slept.

***

Long before daylight, Erik woke from the cold. His boots were stiff. The one with the broken sole had ice lodged in it. He picked it free before wedging his foot back inside. He knocked the frost from his bedroll and canvas and rebundled them. The elk meat had frozen through as well. Erik thought about having some for breakfast but knew his mother would be worried sick. He packed Smoky and led him toward home.

Erik began to encounter much deeper snow and became uncertain of his direction. He angled toward the creek that ran past his cabin and, at last, cut across it. Nearing the cabin, he thought about firing a round but knew it would make no difference. He would be home soon enough. Every round was precious.

***

His mother wouldn't let him hear the end of it. "How could you not fire the rifle? How come you didn't let me know you were okay?" she asked him, coughing. "I worried myself half to death."

Erik tolerated the drumming and was beside himself with hunger as the odor of cooking elk filled the cabin. Never had anything smelled so wonderful. When at last he tasted it, he trembled with gratitude, closing his eyes, savoring the rich flavor. Never had he tasted such wonderful meat. His mother quit hammering on him the moment she tasted her elk as well. Erik thought he saw tears come to her eyes, and he smiled to himself.

"Erik, this is wonderful," she said. "You can go hunting any time you want." She reached over and hugged him. "You need to go back right away and get the rest of it before some mountain lion does."

"Mama, this is all I got," he said quietly.

"I don't understand, Erik. An elk is much bigger than a deer." She coughed. "You hardly got anything."

"I met some Indians, Mama," Erik began softly—he had to tell her the truth—and he told how the he and Indians had shared the kill.

Afterward, Ruth would have nothing to do with Erik returning to the canyon. "The only reason they didn't kill you was because you shot the elk," she said. "The next time they catch you, they'll butcher and eat *you*. You're not going."

Erik listened long enough to let his mother wear herself down. He realized she had been coughing a lot since he returned home. Maybe she had been crying all night. Maybe the cabin got too cold last night. Gently, he addressed her. "Mama, this elk meat is the only food we have. In a few days, I'll have to go back to the canyon and go hunting again." He got up to complete his chores. He would not argue with his mother any longer. He knew it was worrying her and wearing her out.

CHAPTER 16

THE SEASONS WERE CHANGING; the sun was no longer as low on the southern horizon. Erik presumed it was late February, but he no longer cared what date it was.

A snowstorm blew in. It snowed without letting up for several days. Snow lay four feet deep on the level. Drifts reached eight to ten feet deep. The horse was largely confined to the corral, and Erik could no longer travel far to hunt. Footpaths through the deep snow connected the cabin to the creek and to the corral. Erik and his mother were again desperate for food.

Erik tried again. "I think we should go down to the canyon for sure now, Mama."

His mother went white. She sat for a long moment. "Erik, we've talked about this. Even if we find a place where there aren't Indians, they'll soon find us. And when they do, even if they don't hurt you, they'll hurt me."

"Why, Mama? What makes you so sure?" Erik demanded.

"Don't you remember the stories?"

Erik remembered. "Yes, I know that Indians attacked the wagon trains. I know that they tortured and murdered people. But these Indians are different. They helped me. They're friendly."

"Indians are heathens," his mother whispered harshly. "They do vile and evil things to women."

Her tone frightened him. "What evil things?"

"They force themselves onto women, and afterward, they torture and kill them in horrible ways."

Erik didn't understand. His mother was adamant, so he gave up arguing. It took a lot out of them both. Her coughing worried him.

"Okay, Mama," he said. "You rest. I'm going hunting around the ponds for a bit."

Erik took the rifle, knowing he wouldn't see anything—not near the cabin—and he couldn't travel very far in the snow, especially without Smoky. He felt it was hopeless, useless, but he knew nothing else to try.

The longer days and sunlight had caused the snow to crust, but it wasn't strong enough to support his weight. He broke through and floundered. Struggling to lift his legs, he waded his way toward the spruce thicket, breaking and pushing the crust before him.

Keeping to the tree wells where the snow was shallower made traveling easier. He hoped a squirrel or even a bird would show itself. He was ready to shoot anything that moved.

He was surprised when a snowshoe suddenly bounded from a tree well in front of him and scampered to another a few feet away. His heart quickened and he trembled, realizing how desperately he needed this animal.

The rabbit froze, blending into the white snow. Erik could make out only its unblinking eye and black nose. Slowly, he raised the rifle and fired. Snow around the hare exploded, but it bounded away. *I missed!* Angry, heart pounding, Erik crashed forward into the next tree well and after careful searching, again spotted the rabbit. It had gone a few yards and stopped. Shaking, he reloaded and fired, then again, and then a fourth time. The hare bounded out of sight into the willows where Erik couldn't follow. In frustration, an ache in his chest, Erik turned back toward the cabin, angry with himself for having stupidly wasted the rounds. Very few remained.

***

The firewood was now gone. Erik had long ago used the dead wood from the nearby timber. Now he cut and dragged green trees to the cabin. The wet wood burned stubbornly, with little heat, and its smoke filled the cabin, nearly choking them.

Keeping the fire going consumed him. It was the only life in the cabin, or so it seemed. The fire kept them warm, gave them light, heated their water, *made* them alive. Erik woke now two, sometimes three times during the night and got up to stoke the fire. He worried, irrationally, that if it went out, he wouldn't be able to start it again. Somehow he felt if it were to go out, they would both die.

They went three, then four days without food. His mother continued to cough. Her eyes were becoming shadows, and she shook. He saw how her bones pushed out under her thin, pale skin. She no longer got out of bed. His mother was dying. He fought the realization. He didn't want to concede. Desperately he wanted to fight.

Without food, he wondered if he had the energy himself to survive. When they had first had no food, he ached to eat. He daydreamed of the wonderful meals his mother used to make—of cornbread and beans, of venison steaks, onions, and potatoes. He dreamed of salt pork and dumplings and, most of all, baked apples. He dreamed of having one of those meals, of eating all he wanted, of not being hungry. Now he was numb to hunger. Now he found himself tired, wanting to sleep, and more and more, he found himself thinking about slaughtering and eating Smoky. Then he would shake the thought. Smoky was his only way out. *Our only hope of escape.*

One morning, Erik discovered the snow had crusted to where it held his weight. He decided on one last desperate gamble.

Carefully, he constructed a travois, set it aside, and then took the rifle to go hunting. He walked effortlessly across the crusted snow to the timber where he had last seen the snowshoe. *Probably the last rabbit in the country if an owl hasn't already got it,* he thought. He searched a long while until finally he spotted it. Carefully he raised the rifle, cocked the hammer and checked the cap, took aim, breathed out, and squeezed the trigger. *Please, dear God, let me get it.* The explosion shook the woods, and white smoke drifted before him.

He lowered the rifle and saw the rabbit sprawled in the snow, red. "Thank you, Lord." Shaking, he retrieved the snowshoe. The rifle ball ruined a third of it, but they had food.

He chopped open the pond again for Smoky to drink and pulled down some of the remaining hay. He went out later and pulled down more. He saw that very little remained, but he knew Smoky would need every bit he could get. After tomorrow, if any remained, it might not matter.

He boiled the rabbit to save all the nutrients. He got his mother to drink the broth; she couldn't get any meat down. "Come on, Mama," he pleaded. "You have to eat some of this. It will help you." She wouldn't.

Erik ate a good portion. He was so hungry he shook. Nothing—not even the elk—had ever tasted so good.

It took a long while for him to sleep. His mother's breathing was raspy, and he listened, scared. Whenever her breathing paused, he shot awake, frightened. He feared each time would be her last. He remained awake, uneasy about what tomorrow would bring, but he knew his decision was correct.

***

Erik left the cabin at first light. He was satisfied—the crusted snow held his weight. He readied Smoky.

Returning to the cabin, he heated the remaining rabbit and gently woke his mother. "Mama, I have some breakfast." He knew she wouldn't get up unless he forced her to do so.

Rolling over, she struggled to push herself up and then shook her head.

"Come on, Mama, have some breakfast with me." Erik held up the steaming pot.

Shaking, she slowly stumbled to their makeshift table where Erik ladled some into a bowl.

Erik watched as she tasted only a little before she set the spoon down. She was gaunt, pale, and shaking. Her eyes had sunken into even deeper shadows. It scared him to realize he'd been avoiding looking at her. Desperately, he prayed he would say the right words—would convince her. He dared not think what he'd do if she didn't agree.

"Mama, today I will take you out of the snow." He didn't allow her a chance to protest and spoke rapidly, trying to sound convincing, strong, like he remembered his father talking. "You have to trust me; I can do it. I don't know when another storm will come, but we need to go now. You must agree with me."

She shook her head. A tear squeezed from her eyes. "Son, you go if you must. L-leave me here with Papa Larson."

Erik felt stunned, like being drenched with ice water. "*Never*, Mama! Never." He didn't expect this. "We will both go … or we will both die here." He could hardly say it.

She started to sob quietly, shaking her head. "No, Erik, no," she said. "Even if I wanted to go now, I can't make it."

"But you *can*!" He pushed the bowl toward her. "Eat. The rabbit will give you enough strength." Erik protested angrily, "Mama, you want to live? You want to see Katrine again?"

She shook harder, her breath wheezing.

"Mama, *I* want to live. *I* want to see Katrine. I've tried, Mama, but I can't do it here. *We* can't. There's too much snow. We don't have food." Erik cried. "I want to live, Mama." He rose and went to her, burying his head against her shoulder, shaking, holding her. "I want to live."

His mother stroked his hair and whispered. "I'll try." She pushed away. "Promise me one thing."

He nodded.

"If I should not make it … if I should die … you will bring me back here … to be with Papa."

Erik was shaken. "Don't think such a thing, Mama. You will make it. We'll both make it."

"Promise me, Son."

Tears in his eyes, barely able to nod, he whispered, "Okay, Mama. I promise."

***

Erik led her out to the travois where Smoky stamped impatiently, already loaded down with some of their things: a kettle, the ax. He bundled his mother in the blankets and tied the canvas around her to keep out the snow.

In the early morning, the travois slid effortlessly across the crusted snow. Erik led the way. Although the crust supported his weight, Smoky broke through and floundered. Erik calmed him and coaxed him into bounding a few more steps before he stopped again. Smoky labored hard, but valiantly the horse followed. Erik worried they wouldn't make it to the timber before he gave out. He headed west toward the valley he had spotted while hunting.

He encouraged his mother. "Mama, we're doing good. Smoky will be all right when we get to the timber. You'll see. Hold on." She didn't respond.

When at last they reached the timber, the snow thinned and softened. Erik undid the travois and rested Smoky. Immediately the horse began pawing the snow for grass under the trees. He found none. Erik was heartsick. He didn't rest long.

When they finally hit the creek along the valley floor, Erik paused for Smoky to get water and gave some to his mother. Along the creek, tufts of grass poked out from the snow and reached over the water. The horse tore up mouthfuls whenever it could.

Travel through the timber was treacherous. Fallen trees blocked the way. Often Erik had to scout out a path and then come back to get Smoky and his mother. Frequently he had to climb the valley flanks to get around the downed timber.

Evening approached, and Erik found himself exhausted and beginning to panic. They were still a long distance from the canyon and were still in deep snow. Desperately, he continued onward until the light grew flat, and it became difficult to see.

Sweeping out an area under the trees, Erik pulled his mother under the boughs. He unsaddled and picketed Smoky where he could get water and grass along the creek.

Erik tried but couldn't light a fire. He used most of his charred cloth before giving up. He could no longer see, so he saved the remaining tinder for morning.

The night air grew cold, and clouds scudded in. Stars winked in and out.

He offered his mother some of the cold rabbit, trying to get her to eat. "You need to eat, Mama. You need your strength. I might not be able to get any food for a while." She only turned away. He wondered if she was refusing the food for his sake. He fought the thought. Was she willing to die so that he might live? Erik wouldn't allow himself to believe it.

"H-have some water," he encouraged, choking on his thoughts. This she took.

He was too exhausted to argue, to try again to force her to eat. He took his own blankets and lay next to her so they could share their warmth. His mother wheezed and coughed weakly.

He patted her back. "We'll get out of the snow tomorrow, Mama. You'll see. It will be warmer in the canyon." He gazed at the night sky through blurred eyes. *Maybe when we get down … maybe when we find food, and Mama sees I have enough for myself, maybe then she'll eat. Then she'll be all right.*

***

The next day, the clouds thickened. The air felt cold and damp, like snow.

Again, his mother wouldn't eat. Erik ate most of the remaining rabbit. He couldn't stop himself. He was too hungry. He was drained from fighting the snow and downed timber.

Rain mixed with snow began falling shortly after they headed out. The going was even more difficult. The valley became narrow and steep. Erik repeatedly climbed its flanks to get around the downed timber. He struggled to keep the travois from sliding down the slope; he struggled to keep Smoky headed in the right direction. Dense trees faced him. He stumbled and slipped from exhaustion. The canyon bottom remained a terrible distance away. He rose, struggled on, but slipped again. "Why, Lord?" he cried out. Too exhausted to rise, he rested a moment. His body wouldn't move. He wanted to sleep. *Maybe it's okay. Maybe it's okay to die now. I tried, Lord, didn't I?*

He lay a long while in the snow until a soft whistling crept into his foggy thoughts. He struggled up, heart quickening. *The angel!* He strained to see in the timber but saw nothing. But he thought it had to be his angel. "Thank you, Lord," he whispered. "Thank you for telling me I'm right to do this." He trudged on, heading in the direction from where he heard the sound.

Unexpectedly, he encountered a game trail that entered the draw. Fresh tracks angled downhill toward the creek. *This is what the angel was trying to tell me!* Tears sprang to his eyes. *Thank you, God.* "We're on a trail, Mama," he said choking, elated. "It looks like it goes toward the canyon."

Smoky's hooves now kicked up dirt through the thin snow. At any time, Erik expected to see a deer or an elk, and he kept the rifle ready. He saw nothing larger than some snowshoe hares.

The valley broadened, and the river came into view. The ground leveled, and Erik found the feeling surreal. No longer did he fight his footing to stand up. He gazed in awe at the cottonwoods and pines towering on both sides.

Reaching the river, he paused in disbelief. The river that looked like a thin ribbon was fifty yards wide and roiled angrily over the boulders littering its bed. In places, it pooled beneath rock outcrops before dropping as whitewater into the pools below.

"Mama! We're down! We're here!" He went back and sat beside her, breathing heavily. "We're in the canyon."

His mother's shadowed eyes flickered; she rolled her head, trying to nod.

Erik realized he had no time to pause. Evening approached. The falling snow thickened.

He laid a long pole into a spruce for a shelter frame and piled brush over it before pulling the canvas over the top. He brushed away the snow down to barren earth, cut fir boughs, and piled them inside. He had hoped there would be no snow. He remembered seeing a barren canyon floor from when he had been hunting. Since then, of course, it had snowed. He wondered if there would be none farther downstream.

"Here, Mama." He helped her inside. He patted the blankets and made sure she was as comfortable as possible.

He picketed Smoky where he could get water and grass, where the grass poked through in clumps. He was glad, because Smoky could graze all night if he wanted.

Painstakingly, he gathered kindling and fuel for a fire. Carefully he built a nest for his charred cloth—painfully aware that if he failed in starting this fire, he had no more. Fumbling out his flint and steel, he paused, then struck a spark, then another. It caught. Quickly he blew it into a small flame. Soon a warm fire snapped brightly. He put water on to heat and piled more brush on the shelter. The snow now piled thickly on their shelter.

He wanted to go to find the Indians, but it was now dark. Once he thought he smelled faint smoke when down by the river. He guessed their camp was close.

Again, he tried to get his mother to eat—all that remained was a broth made from the rabbit bones and scraps—but she refused. Erik thought again that she was giving up. She was letting Erik have the food so he might live. She was allowing herself to die. *Why, Lord? Why?* He cried silently. *I got her here. We are safe. Please let her get well.*

Erik didn't sleep. His mother's breathing scared him as it had before, and he thought about the coming morning.

CHAPTER 17

AT DAYBREAK, ERIK BROKE and reboiled the rabbit bones. He drank some of the broth and then woke his mother.

"Here's some broth, Mama." He got her to sit up. "Mama, I'm going to see about getting us some food." He did not want to say exactly what he intended. "Here, have some broth. Please, Mama." She took some. "I'll be back in a few hours. If you want more, it will be here." He set the pot in the corner of the shelter where she could reach it. "There's also wood next to the fire. ... Are you going to be okay?"

She nodded weakly, lay back down, and curled up into a ball. Erik felt frantic. He knew he had to find help. He covered her with the blankets and then pulled brush in front of the door.

He swung up onto Smoky, hoping the horse had the strength to carry him. He headed downstream, figuring there was less snow and thus, more likely, a campsite.

Within an hour, he spotted the camp across the river. He found a place where the river ran shallow and coaxed Smoky into the water. Smoky shied at first but then splashed across. There Erik discovered a well-traveled trail.

He rode into the Indian camp. Dogs came yapping, and people spilled from their brush lodges to meet him. He stopped Smoky and gave the sign for peace. "*Hej.* Hello," he greeted.

Several men stood with their bows. Women and children gathered around. Clearly they wondered who this person was, riding a horse into their camp in the middle of winter.

Children came up to Smoky, trying to touch him. Erik motioned for them to stand back. He feared the horse might shy and step on one of them, but the children didn't understand.

Badger was among the children surrounding Erik. He stood in awe. Here was a white boy, perhaps a little older than he, riding a horse. He knew this must be the boy who shot the elk that his father had spoken of. He must have come down from the white-man lodge on the canyon's rim, but why?

An elderly Indian came forth, greeted Erik, and returned his sign of peace.

Erik believed he must be a chief of some sort. He wore a shirt with porcupine quill designs and hair fringes. He also wore fringed leggings with more porcupine quills decorating the outside of each. His hair was gray, nearly white, and pulled back and held on the left side with white ermine skins and owl feathers.

Erik dismounted. Another Indian, whom Erik recognized as Talker, took Smoky. A boy about his own age, slightly built with shoulder-length hair, followed Talker. Erik wanted to protest but knew it was foolish. He forced himself to trust them with his horse. He was completely at their mercy.

He gestured to the Indians for them to follow and pointed back upstream toward his camp.

They ignored him but made him sit and brought a bowl of hot meat. The chief made a gesture for eating. Erik pushed the bowl away and motioned again for them to come with him. "I need help," he said, trying to gesture his meaning.

He realized they would do nothing until he ate. Besides, he was starved. He wondered just a moment where the spoons were before he reached in with his fingers and began picking out hot pieces of meat. Immediately he recognized the flavor as elk. Smiling, he bowed his head. "Thank you. This is good." The Indians smiled in return, pleased with his response. He ate more, quickly finishing the bowl. He wiped his mouth across his sleeve, smiled, and nodded again. "Thank you." They tried to bring more, but he waved his hand. "No, thank you."

He tried to think how he could get them to follow—to know he needed help for his mother. He found a woman and pointed at her. He pointed to the woman, then to himself. He pretended to cradle a baby.

The Indians looked puzzled. *Was this white boy saying he was a mother?*

Erik continued. He doubled over as if sick, pointed back to the woman and then back up the trail. "My mother," he pointed upstream, "is sick." He bent over. "She is back at my camp." He pointed. "She needs help."

The chief seemed to understand. He nodded and pointed at Erik, mimicking the same signs.

Erik gestured for the Indians to follow and started back along the trail. They remained seated. Erik stepped up and took the chief's hand. The old Indian immediately pulled away, shaking his head, but then he rose. He spoke briefly with a group of men. Three moved forward, including Talker. Talker addressed the boy who turned and left but soon brought up Smoky. Erik led the horse. It would be impolite for him to ride while they walked.

Erik felt hopeful. They would find his mother. They would know what to do.

He reached the place where he had crossed the river and waded into the water, still leading Smoky. The cold from the water took his breath. As it deepened, he prayed it wouldn't be over his waist. The current tugged at him, almost causing him to slip on the slick, cobbled bottom.

The Sheepeaters paused, not eager to wade through freezing water, but with Erik leading, they did.

Erik was numb from cold when he reached the shelter. He ran to it and pulled away the branches. His mother woke somewhat when he shook her. "I have brought help," he said. "The Indians who helped me get the elk are with me."

When his mother saw the Sheepeaters, she cringed and grew frantic. Barely speaking, she hissed, "Send them away. They are heathens." Her chest heaved.

Erik was shocked. "How can you say that, Mama? They are here to help. I brought them."

"Please, Erik. Send them back," she rasped.

The Sheepeaters made motions for his mother to follow and moved to pick her up. She drew away and screamed weakly, "Get them away! Get them away!" She shuddered.

Erik waved the Sheepeaters back and sat next to her. "Mama, they want to help. I think they want to take you to their camp."

In a wheezing, halting voice she replied, "I-I told you I didn't want to come here … I wanted you to leave me … at the cabin … with Papa Larson." She struggled to talk. "We cannot go with them. We will be lost to God."

"No, Mama," Erik replied. "We will not be lost to God. I will not change. I will still believe, and if you believe, they will not change you.

"These people aren't like the Indians in the stories. These Indians will help us. I know."

She didn't respond. She squeezed her eyes tightly and clenched her hands to her face. Her breathing came fast and shallow.

Erik gave up. A huge hurt filled his chest. *How can she do this? Doesn't life mean anything to her? Doesn't Katrine mean anything? Don't I mean anything?* He stood up and went to Talker. Pointing at his mother, he made a sign for sleep and pushed his hands away and apart.

The Sheepeaters talked briefly among themselves, gesturing. They understood.

Talker entered the shelter and carried Ruth out. She pounded him weakly with her fists. Erik heard a strange cry, a voice he didn't recognize. She quit hitting after a few moments. Holding her tightly, Talker waded into the river, heading for their camp. The other two Sheepeaters followed.

Frantically, Erik bundled their things and ripped the canvas from the shelter. Clumsily, he lashed the bundle onto Smoky and splashed into the river, trying to catch up to his mother and the Sheepeaters.

Talker carried her to a spot near some of the lodges and gently laid her down. Erik ran over to console her. Her face was screwed up tightly. Talking gently, he patted her. Her eyes flickered open, then closed, but her face relaxed.

Several of the men began building a shelter similar to the ones scattered throughout the village. A woman brought a bowl of hot meat and then began building a fire pit.

"See, Mama, they want to help. They are building us a shelter. They have brought us food." He tried to give her some, but she didn't respond.

Two women brought some hides and piled them inside the shelter. The men helped Erik carry his mother inside. The chief came over and studied her. He pointed at the meat and gestured for Erik to feed her. "I'm trying," he replied. He tried to wake his mother. "Mama, you need some food."

Erik got some water and sponged his mother's face. Her breathing was raspy; she slept fitfully. Erik sat watching. He didn't know what else to do. The chief sat outside, watching as well. One of the women kept the chief company and added fuel to the fire. A younger woman brought two bowls of simmered meat and set them beside the fire.

An ache welled within Erik. These people, to whom he was a complete stranger, were trying to help in the only way they knew how.

Erik sat next to his mother, trying to sooth her. She felt hot. Her breathing was raspy. Her eyes flickered, but they didn't open. "Mama, it's going to be okay. They know what to do." He sponged water onto her and put water to her mouth. The water dribbled off.

Erik began reliving his father's death—only this was his mother. He felt his chest tighten and his breathing catch. He was back on the ice, slipping, unable to stop. Desperately Erik wanted things to stop— for things to be okay again.

Rain mixed with snow began falling. One by one, the Sheepeaters rose and returned to their own lodges to keep dry.

Erik's fire began to sputter in the rain, dying down into tendrils of white smoke. He threw on more sticks. The smoke increased until a twig finally dried and ignited. He heaped on more wood but knew it wouldn't last the night.

Feeling emotionally numb, he pulled his blankets around himself and drew up against his mother, again listening to her shallow breathing. Her struggle against the Indians and arguing with him seemed to have sapped her remaining strength.

***

Morning came. Erik wondered about Smoky, but the horse was not in sight. He had to trust the horse wouldn't wander far and was capable of getting food. He found the Sheepeaters outside watching.

He talked to them as if they could understand. "My mother and I are thankful you have given us food and shelter." He said trying to gesture the meaning.

"My name is Erik Larson," he said pointing to himself. "Erik Larson." He pointed to his mother. "My mother is Mama Larson. Mama Larson."

"Who are you?" he pointed to the chief, then back to himself, "Erik," and to his mother, "Mama Larson."

He patted his chest. "I am Erik. Erik." He pointed back to the chief, opening his hands, shrugging.

"Aishi-mompittseh. Gray Owl." The chief patted his own chest and repeated. "Gray Owl."

Erik felt immense relief. "Aishi-mompittseh," he said and smiled.

Gray Owl pointed at him. "You are Er-ik. Er-ik."

"Yes!" exclaimed Erik. "I am Erik." He patted his chest. He pointed to his mother. "Mama Larson."

Gray Owl mimicked. "Ma-ma Lar-son."

Erik nodded. This man understood. As they talked, the others gathered around, watching, listening.

Erik pointed to the other Sheepeaters and asked their names. He learned that the man he called Talker was known as Free Hawk. The two other men were called Whistling Elk and Sees Far. Of course, he did not yet know what their names meant. He only knew the sounds to make.

He returned to care for his mother. The Sheepeaters left him alone while he did. Soon one of the women brought more food. His mother didn't waken. Erik grew more desperate. "Mama … Mama Larson." He gently shook her. "Wake up." It slowly dawned on Erik that she wouldn't waken. Things were terribly wrong. Erik bowed his head into his hands and began to shake. *What do I do, God? What do I do?* He sat there a long while before he realized Gray Owl stood near, watching. He looked at Gray Owl, tears in his eyes. "What do I do, Gray Owl?"

Gray Owl didn't understand his words, but he leaned over and examined Ruth.

"See, she has a fever. She no longer opens her eyes when I call her," Erik tried to explain. "Mama, Mama. Wake up." Again, he gently shook her.

Gray Owl left. Shortly he returned with the older woman. "This is Porcupine Woman," Gray Owl said. "She has strong medicine. Now she says she will help."

Erik didn't understand the words, but he realized the woman must be a healer. His mother had said the Indian healers prayed to evil spirits. He felt a tightening in his throat. *I can't allow this. Mama would never approve.* He wrestled with stopping the medicine woman but knew he was the one who had asked for help.

The old woman pulled out some plants and sprinkled them in the fire chanting. Erik felt a weight pressing his chest. *Dear God, if you don't approve of this, somehow let me know.*

He knew the Indians used plants that could heal. *Please let the plants be okay, God. Don't let her pray to an evil demon.*

Free Hawk and Whistling Elk carried Ruth out of the shelter and placed her on an elk-skin hide near the fire where Porcupine Woman prepared her things. Other Sheepeaters gathered to watch.

Erik moved to where he could hold his mother's hand, but Porcupine Woman gently removed it. She looked into Erik's eyes and muttered, "You must not interfere with my medicine, white boy." She gestured for him to leave.

Erik sat back, praying.

Deliberately, Porcupine Woman opened the fur bundle and laid out some rattles, some plants, and some bones. She poured water into a shallow horn bowl and crushed dried plants in her hands, allowing them to sprinkle into the water. All the while, she stirred the tisane, she softly chanted and sang.

Please, God, Erik prayed, *let this be acceptable. Help my mother.*

Porcupine Woman's tone sounded as if she talked to his mother as well as to unseen persons. It was a begging tone.

She took a bundle of grass, started one end burning, blew it out, and fanned the smoke. She cupped her hand through the smoke, spreading it, and again began chanting. Her voice started low and calm, but soon it became more agitated. She took bones and placed them on Ruth. She touched her face and lips with the tisane. She repeated the process—more smoke, more touching, more tisane. She placed a bone near Ruth's throat, sucked on it, and spit. She did this twice before resuming her chanting. Now her voice became demanding.

Porcupine Woman sat back, chanting, eyes closed, voice rising and falling. Erik didn't move. She chanted more vigorously and then suddenly stopped. She looked at Erik and spoke rapidly at length in a comforting tone. Picking up her items, she straightened and rebundled them. Rising, she pulled her robe about herself and left. Free Hawk carried Ruth back into the shelter.

Erik saw no miracle, no change in his mother. Her breathing remained raspy and shallow. Erik looked to the faces of the other Sheepeaters. They appeared confident, expectant. No one doubted Porcupine Woman.

Erik was unsure what to do. At last, the younger woman brought more food and hot water. He thanked her. "I am Erik. What is your name?" he asked. The woman smiled, seeming not to understand. She and the other Sheepeaters now departed, going back to their own lodges. Erik realized that they felt they had done all they could. He sat alone with his mother.

Erik took the food and water to his mother. He sponged her forehead. She slept, but strangely. He talked to her. "Mama, it's me, Erik," he whispered. "The medicine woman tried to help you. I've been praying." He bit his lip. He was losing hope.

"Mama, please get better." He lay next to her, exhausted, finally sleeping.

He woke to his mother's labored breathing. A sickening fear flooded him. *Please, no! Dear God, no!* He felt his mother shudder and heard her last breath sigh out.

Erik knew. The ache overwhelmed him. He could not understand. *Why, Lord? Why?* The tears began and wouldn't quit. He tried hard to stop, to not cry, but he couldn't.

The women heard him. Soon the younger voice began a quiet wailing. Other voices in the camp took it up until there came a soft wailing—rising and falling throughout the village. Erik felt a strange, brief comfort and cried without shame.

CHAPTER 18

BY MORNING LIGHT, ERIK knew what must be done. Feeling numb, he found Smoky. He bundled his mother's body in the canvas and a blanket and lifted it onto the horse. He led Smoky back across the river, constructed another travois, placed his mother's body on it, and headed upstream. Three Sheepeaters followed.

If it killed him, he would return to the cabin where he would bury her next to his father. That is what she had asked. That is what he had promised. At the time, he didn't accept the possibility. Now he knew and was angry. *I was wrong to try to bring her here.*

Erik again camped at the spot where he had when he first started down into the canyon. He built a small fire for warmth and pulled his blankets about himself. Free Hawk came over and offered him some dried meat. He took some and nodded his thanks. Free Hawk talked quietly in a comforting voice, gesturing toward his mother's body. Erik understood, but he waved him away and turned his head. He wanted to be alone with his thoughts; nevertheless, he was glad the Sheepeaters had followed him.

Free Hawk moved to the side where the other men rolled out their own robes under the trees. "The white boy mourns," he explained, "only he does not paint his body black or cut his hair."

Sees Far shrugged. "Maybe now he will leave and go to where there are other white men."

"But that is far to the south near the burning-rocks land. He is too weak to travel that far in the snow," explained Free Hawk.

"Yes, he is too skinny." Whistling Elk glanced over to where Erik huddled under the trees. "But as Gray Owl asked, we shall watch over him. He sees something about this boy in a dream."

The Sheepeaters pulled their robes about themselves and lay back among the trees.

***

By midday, Erik reached the cabin. The Sheepeaters had walked ahead, helping pack the trail, making it easier. Still, Smoky labored hard.

Erik studied the cabin. It brought no joy, although it had been home for several months. He noticed that some of the roof had collapsed, and snow filled the end where he had slept.

Erik found the spade and immediately began digging his mother's grave, working first through the deep snow, then into the earth below. He dug the grave in the aspens next to his father's. The Sheepeaters sat quietly watching.

When evening overtook his work, Erik cleared out the debris from the good end of the cabin and started a fire. He put water on to heat and gestured to the Sheepeaters to come inside. Politely, they shook their heads but left him some dry meat, and departed, heading back toward the canyon. Erik realized he was now alone—completely and utterly alone.

***

The Sheepeaters camped near the canyon rim where they found barren earth under some trees. They didn't start a fire. There was no need.

Whistling Elk spoke. "The white boy is foolish for digging the hole in the earth for his mother. Her spirit will not be able to find the sky trails." He gestured toward the evening sky.

Sees Far and Free Hawk glanced to where he pointed, nodding. Stars now appeared above the canyon rim.

"And why does the white boy stay in the broken-down lodge? Why doesn't he build a good shelter?" asked Whistling Elk. "Are all white men as strange?"

"I think Gray Owl was wrong to have us follow this boy," suggested Sees Far. "Maybe he is old now and sees things, even in his dreams."

They laughed softly.

"No, the white boy is foolish," said Whistling Elk. "There is no food near his lodge. It is two moons until the grass is green. The horse will soon die. He will soon die."

Free Hawk shook his head, thinking. He didn't understand the white boy, but he saw his courage, his bravery. He saw how he brought his mother to the people. Maybe that is what Gray Owl had seen— why he asked them to follow and look after him.

"We will return and tell Gray Owl that the white boy will die," said Sees Far.

***

Erik spent a restless night. He could see stars peeking through some of the gaps. In early morning, he finished the grave and dragged his mother's body into it. He found the Bible in the clothes chest and found a good passage. In the empty stillness, he read aloud until he choked on the words and tears stung his eyes. He filled the grave, fashioned a second cross, and engraved it "Ruth Larson."

He stood a moment and surveyed the small valley and cabin. Unbroken snow stretched in all directions. The dark conifers marked where the canyon began. He felt immensely alone and very small.

Erik returned to the empty, silent cabin. He carefully wrapped and stowed the Bible back inside the clothes chest. He sat for a while, then discovered himself trembling. "God, I don't understand," he began, talking to the empty stillness. "I prayed for help. You sent your angel to show me the way. Twice you brought me to safety. But you let my parents die. Why?" He felt his hot tears hit his hands. "I'm sorry, Lord. I don't know what to think anymore. It doesn't make sense." His soft sobs broke the silence. "I-I don't think I'm going to talk to you anymore—bother you anymore."

After he said it, a great sadness and hurt flooded his body. He found the ache back in his chest; it hurt to breathe. He shook. He found himself thinking terrible thoughts. *Maybe I should walk out into the snow until I die. Who would care?* He felt shamed by his thoughts, but he couldn't help himself.

He saw the blue and yellow vase on the table and picked it up. He pushed his hand across his eyes, wiping away the blur. He turned the vase, studying it. His mother had said it was his grandmother's. It was special. *Maybe to Katrine it would be special.* He felt a little better remembering his sister. *We still have each other. I'll find Katrine. She will care. She deserves to know what happened to Mama and Papa.*

***

Erik spent the remainder of the day searching for hay for Smoky. Smoky had to make it to spring if he ever hoped to survive and go for Katrine.

At last, he found a draw where the wind had exposed the grass. With his knife, he cut all he could and hauled it to the stock shed. Now he noticed other grass clumps showing in the trails where the sun had melted the thin snow. More showed where the wind swept the hillsides bare. He felt a ray of hope.

He tried to repair the cabin roof. In the early day, he walked easily on the crusted snow. He pulled more poles up to the cabin for the roof and for firewood. By midday, the crust softened, and he began breaking through, so he stopped.

He thought about taking Smoky to the canyon to try hunting another elk, but he knew the horse was weak. It would probably kill him. Instead, he returned to the woods and hunted snowshoes until late evening. He spotted one and wasted two rounds before he was able to kill it. He knew the meat would only last a couple days. Already he wondered where the next meal would come from. He had a single remaining cartridge.

He found himself talking aloud just for the sound of something besides the whistling wind. Other than his single-sided conversation, there was no life—nothing moved, nothing broke the silence.

Erik felt deeply alone. He talked to Smoky. He found himself staring at the two crosses on the hill. He felt he had been alone for many days—not just a few.

He looked at the white landscape. Spring did not appear to be anywhere near. Instead, gray, heavy clouds began rapidly pushing in, not from the north, but from the southeast. Suddenly frightened, Erik realized it was the direction for a spring storm. By the afternoon, the sky was full of thick, blowing snow.

Driven by wind, it was a dangerously wet snow, the kind that could kill stock. He feared for Smoky and headed out into the storm. The flakes melted on contact with his flesh, soaking him, trickling down his back under his coat. At the shed, the snow poured in. The door faced the wrong direction for southeasterly weather. Smoky huddled against the far side; water ran across the floor. "Poor Smoky. Hang in there, boy." He patted the horse, already wet and trembling, and rubbed him down with a blanket. "As soon as it lets up, I'll come dry you better."

He tried to secure a blanket across the opening, but the wind whipped it away. He tried again, managing to secure one part. By then, he was shivering; his teeth chattered. Much longer, and he'd be in trouble. He returned to the cabin. Tried to dry off. Stoked the fire.

All night and the next day, the storm raged. Now evening again, Erik huddled in his wet clothes and blankets beside the sputtering fire. The snow continued to blow in through the gaps between the logs almost unrestrained. Snow filled the cabin and piled on his blankets, soaking through.

Erik stayed awake trying to keep the fire going, trying to coax out some warmth. He took wood from the far end of the cabin, worsening the amount of snow coming in. Never had he seen the snow pile so fast. He found himself shivering uncontrollably.

Finally, he slept, only to waken soon after. He thought his mother was beside him. "Mama," he murmured. "We'll make it."

Coming fully awake, he realized she wasn't there; he felt the deep hurt and ache for his parents all over again.

Then he fell back to sleep. This time his mother came into the cabin. "Wake up, Erik. You need to dry your clothes." She built the fire higher, and Erik got up, taking off his wet clothes and spreading them before the fire. The warmth flooded him.

"Erik," she said. "I'm not upset about the Indians anymore. We can live in the canyon, if you want. We can live with the Indians. You were right. The prairie here is too harsh. Papa Larson agrees. Tomorrow, I will go with you to the canyon."

Erik felt a warm comfort.

"I'll see Papa Larson and tell him you're okay. When I get back, we can leave."

"Mama!" Erik woke with a pounding headache, shivering uncontrollably. It had been a dream, but it had been all too real. Erik tried to shake it. He stumbled about the cabin in the darkness trying to find dry wood for the fire. It had died.

He couldn't relight the fire in the dark. He pulled wood over the coals to protect what remained from the wet snow until morning. He sat and watched the sky to the east, shivering under his wet blankets, worrying about Smoky. His headache was relentless, and he continued to shiver uncontrollably. He fumbled to get more clothes from the chest, not caring what they were, knowing they would get wet as well, but at least he might survive to morning.

Gray finally streaked the sky. Snow lightly fell. Nearly two feet had fallen. He found dry tinder and relit the fire. Gently, he added wood until he had a fire large enough to dry the wet fuel as it burned. Anxious, he left the cabin to check on Smoky.

Erik found him soaking wet and trembling. He knew the horse was in danger of getting sick. He spent a good hour trying to rub him dry. His blankets became soaked. He tried to dry the blankets over the fire, then returned and tried to dry Smoky some more. The storm weakened. For hours he worked between tending the fire and drying the horse. Finally, the sky cleared, but then the temperature dropped. He brought the last of the grass he had cut into the stock shelter and rubbed down the horse a final time. He left the blanket over the animal and tried to tie it beneath its belly.

Erik spent another cold, damp night in the cabin. He slept only a little. By morning light, he had made his decision. The horse was in poor condition. Erik knew he couldn't afford to lose it. He could never walk out of here by himself. Deliberately, he rolled some more utensils and his father's knife into his remaining blankets. He wrapped his rifle with the single remaining round and placed it under the rocks and logs near the hearth. He would not need the rifle where he was heading.

When the sun rose full on the snowbound landscape, Erik was already breaking a fresh trail, leading Smoky, heading him back toward the canyon. If they would have him, he would live with the Sheepeaters until he was capable on his own. Then he'd take Smoky and leave this terrible country. He'd go to find Katrine. She deserved to know what happened. Maybe the dream was a sign.

"I'm sorry, Mama. I'm sorry, Papa. I have no choice." Erik talked just to hear something human. He started to say something to God but stopped himself. The prairie was dead silent. Only an occasional gust whistled its song as it kicked up the new-fallen snow.

CHAPTER 19

ERIK REACHED THE SHEEPEATERS' camp late afternoon the next day. They came out to greet him, seemingly happy to see him again. He greeted them and returned to his old lodge where he threw in his blankets and the few items he had brought. Everything was as he had left it, as if they had expected his return. He did not try to picket Smoky but let him wander. He shook with hunger, but already the Sheepeaters brought him food. He sat and ate in their company, repeatedly signing and saying, "Thank you."

Late in the night, snow mixed with rain began to fall. The shelter leaked in a few places, and Erik had to move to keep away from the drips. His blankets were still wet. He realized it would be snowing at the cabin. Here it mostly melted on contact.

Erik spent the night thinking. He no longer allowed himself to think of his parents. It only brought ache. Instead he resolved to survive. He would not beg from the Sheepeaters. It wasn't right. He would show them he could provide his own food. He longed for his rifle, but with a single round, it was not much better than a club. It was better he had brought other things, like the ax and his father's good knife.

When morning at last came, he noticed a couple Sheepeater boys, maybe a year or two younger than him, sitting near, watching. They were dressed in skin shirts, leggings, and breechcloths and wore a type of furry boot. He guessed it was because of the winter snow.

"*Hej*, I'm Erik," he offered. "Who are you?" He pointed questioningly. The two shook their heads, laughed, pointed back, mimicking, then took off for their lodges.

He rebuilt his fire and gathered wood. He added brush to his shelter, hoping it would stop the leaks. He hung up his blankets to dry, but it still rained softly. He gave up and waited for the rain to stop.

Some other Sheepeaters came up the trail and stopped by his shelter. He greeted them. They nodded and watched until the three men he had come to know came over and greeted them. They pointed at Erik, talking and gesturing, and then turned and went into one of the lodges. Erik soon heard happy talking.

He wondered why he wasn't invited to their lodges. He was back with the Sheepeaters, but it was as if he didn't exist. He felt silly.

Erik decided to go fishing. He wandered down to the rocks where earlier he had seen one of the boys fishing with a snagging pole. A couple poles lay on the bank. He took one and, wading through the icy water, climbed up onto the rock. He peered into the deep pool beyond to where he could see several trout suspended in the blue green water. He crouched, waiting until one drifted near, then swooped with the pole. The moment he moved his hand, the trout scooted out of reach. Patiently, he waited. The same trout slid back into the pool. He tried again. The trout slipped away.

Laughter came at him, and he looked up to see the same two boys pointing and laughing. They mimicked his awkward jabs, making fun. Erik's ears burned. He climbed from the rock and waded back to the bank, ignoring the boys. He returned to his shelter and crawled inside. *I'm going to have to beg to live,* he thought. *If I had my rifle, they wouldn't laugh.* He decided he had to get a bow.

No one brought food. Maybe because of the wet weather, the Sheepeaters mostly stayed in their lodges. If people came near his shelter, they stood at a distance and watched, but then returned to their own lodges. He worried even more what to do. At last, Gray Owl came and sat outside his shelter.

"*Hej*," Erik greeted and waved. Gray Owl made a sign back.

Erik found it hard to do, but he rubbed his stomach and made an eating sign. "I'm hungry." He pointed to the rocks in the river and made a sign of thrusting the snagging pole. "I tried to get a trout but couldn't." He shook his head and rubbed his stomach again. He felt embarrassed and miserable in doing so. He couldn't look Gray Owl in the eyes.

Gray Owl understood. He called to a nearby child and spoke to him, making an eating motion. The child ran into a nearby lodge, and the woman who had helped Erik, whom he now recognized as Moccasin Woman, promptly returned with a bowl of meat.

Trying not to tremble, Erik choked his gratitude, "Thank you." He gestured.

Gray Owl spoke and gestured to Moccasin Woman. Erik found it strange, but just as much as they spoke, they also signed with their hands. Most signs he understood.

Erik ate. When done, he turned the bowl upside down. Otherwise, Moccasin Woman would have immediately taken it to get more. He had learned that mannerism.

"I need a bow." Erik gestured, pulling back on an imaginary bow. "I need arrows." Again, he gestured. He repeated his message.

Gray Owl spoke abruptly, mimicked shooting a bow, and turned his hand over like the bowl. The meaning was clear.

"Why not?" Erik shrugged.

Gray Owl simply repeated his gestures. Erik didn't know what else to try.

The rain renewed, not heavy, but a steady drizzle that quickly soaked things anew. Gray Owl and Moccasin Woman returned to their lodges.

Erik was again alone with his thoughts. Already he worried about needing to ask for food again.

He went out to check on Smoky. There was no shelter where he could bring the horse in out of the rain. He would have to build one. The horse nickered when he walked up. "Good Smoke." Erik said. "I'm glad you made it. Now you need to get strong. Come spring, we will go to find Katrine." He caressed his muzzle, and Smoky bobbed his head. Erik pulled some grass and fed it to the horse, just to feel the animal pull it from his hands.

Erik returned to his shelter, his clothing wet. He had been so long in wet clothes that he was forgetting what it was like to be dry. Still the rain came. It steadily sifted down through the pines and cottonwoods. Erik built a small fire inside his hut to try to dry his blankets and clothes. He heated a pot of water and went back out into the rain, looking for rosehips, the only thing he knew he could find in the winter to eat. The rosehips were badly shriveled and mostly no good, but he found enough to make tea. He had decided he would not beg for another meal this night.

Exhausted, he lay back in his blankets. Drops of rain shattered into cold spray on his face.

He slept until the dripping rain and his shivering woke him. His blankets were soaked. The fire had died, and the coals were soggy. He would need to wait until morning to start another.

Sleep didn't come, and he began thinking about his parents. He couldn't help the tears. He was shivering and crying, and he was unable to stop. "Please, dear God. Stop this infernal rain," he began, but he didn't know if he should pray anymore. He didn't know where God had gone, or—he could hardly believe his thoughts—if he existed.

Morning brought more of the same. Erik didn't see any of the Sheepeaters. He decided they were staying out of the rain. He left his shelter to check on Smoky.

He couldn't find the horse. Frantic, he ran through the camp looking and whistling. Nothing. He climbed up past the lodges along the creek where he could see the grassy hillsides. No Smoky. Some of the Sheepeaters came out and watched.

Shaking, Erik ran up to Gray Owl. "Have you seen my horse?" He asked, gesturing.

Gray Owl understood and pointed to an empty lodge. "Fighting Bear found your horse and has taken him away. He took his wife and daughter and is now gone to live with the Lemhis."

Erik was stunned. He didn't understand the words, but he understood the gestures.

Feeling numb, Erik stumbled to his shelter and collapsed. He now knew he would never leave this place. His mother's words flooded back: "If we go to the canyon, we will die there." He wondered about his angel. He could no longer sort out his thoughts. Nothing made sense.

Rain filtered in. He couldn't stop it, so he tunneled back to where it was somewhat dry and sat shivering most of the day. He heard Sheepeaters talking, occasionally singing.

More visitors came up the trail, and he went to his door to watch. They stared briefly at him before entering one of the lodges. He could again hear the happy voices. He watched as they moved from lodge to lodge. *If only someone would come to my shelter. But I belong to no one. No one cares for me. And they let Fighting Bear take my horse.* The tears came back.

Near midday, the rain turned to a misty shower and gently stopped. Fog floated along the river and hung in the cottonwoods. Erik walked among them, looking for more rosehips. He knew of nothing else to eat.

He did not wish to ask for food. No one really wanted him here, it seemed. He ripped his trousers on the brush while returning to his shelter and felt the wet cold on his skin. He realized how badly his clothes were tattered. They had been wet for too long without proper care. He had already pulled the broken sole from his boot. He longed for a warm elk skin or sheepskin like those the Sheepeaters had. He longed for a dry lodge—something, anything that was dry.

Returning to his shelter, he bundled his belongings into his blankets and dragged them to the fire near the camp center where sometimes the women cooked meals. He piled some wood on the coals and called out to the Sheepeaters.

"I am Erik Larson," he proclaimed. "I came to you for help. You tried to help my mother. You have given me food. I am thankful to you for your food. But I cannot take your food. I have nothing to offer in return. Even my horse is now gone. I do not have weapons, so I cannot hunt. I cannot fish. I cannot talk to you. I do not know your ways."

The Sheepeaters began gathering around to watch the strange white boy's antics.

When they did, Erik opened his blankets. "This is all I have remaining. I want to give it to whoever wants it." He took out the kettle and offered it to Moccasin Woman. He gave the ax to Stands Alone and his flint and steel to Gray Owl. He handed his knife—his father's birthday gift to him—to Sees Far. He didn't remember who took his father's knife. It was too difficult to bear. Other items, including the blankets, he gave to whomever stretched out a hand. "Now, I have nothing." The Sheepeaters stared back in silence.

Impulsively, Erik leaned down, pulled off his boots, and threw them into the fire. Likewise, without thought, he stripped off his torn trousers and shirt and threw them in as well. He watched as his white world smoldered, then burst into flame. He clasped his arms about himself and, crying, said, "Now I am nothing. I cannot live by myself. I cannot be Erik any longer." Great shudders overcame him.

One by one, the Sheepeaters shook their heads—*this is truly a strange white boy.* Turning, they walked back to their lodges.

Erik could not understand. He began to shake and, without knowing what was happening, sank to his knees. He felt the chill from the mist surround his body. He knelt shivering for a long while. He realized that the Sheepeaters would leave him to die. How stupid he had been to come here.

***

A heavy robe fell about his shoulders as a voice came to him, startling him. "Get up, little white boy." The voice belonged to Free Hawk.

Erik first thought Free Hawk would send him back to his own shelter, but he directed him toward his own. "Shining Water says we have room in our lodge."

Erik entered the lodge, trying to meet Shining Water's eyes as he did. She didn't glance at him, only indicated a place near the door for him to sit. The baby girl watched with big eyes. The boy, whom Erik recognized as Badger, one of the boys who often laughed at him, glared.

Erik nodded politely to Badger. "*Hej.*"

Badger spat back, "You aren't my brother." He rose and left the lodge.

Erik understood the younger boy didn't like him and didn't want to share his lodge.

Shining Water made a motion as if to go after Badger, but Free Hawk stopped her. He indicated instead for her to give Erik some food.

Erik ate hungrily, and although he wanted more, he left his sheep-horn bowl turned down. He signed and said, "Thank you."

All the months of his ordeal on the prairie flooded in. For the first time in many weeks, he felt warm. He was dry. He was safe. He pulled the elk hide around himself and again signed, thank you. He felt the world about him beginning to spin. He could no longer keep his eyes open. He slumped back, curled up in the animal skins, and slept.

PART TWO
SKY EYES

TO BE CALLED A TRUE MAN

CHAPTER 20

ANGRILY, BADGER WALKED TOWARD the river. What he had done was completely unacceptable. It was his mother's lodge. He had no right. He had heard his mother tell his father that if he were to decide to allow the white boy into their lodge, she wouldn't object.

Badger didn't know his father's thoughts. His father had simply risen and gone to get the white boy. He wouldn't have done so, however, if he didn't agree with his mother. Badger had no right to question his father's decision. But he didn't like the white boy. He acted silly. He did stupid things. All he did was take the people's food.

True, the white boy had owned a horse and had shot an elk, but Whistling Elk and his father had also shot the same elk. Now he had let the horse wander and Fighting Bear claimed him. No one was surprised when Fighting Bear took Singing Wind and left. Now his son, Runs Fast, was angry. But Runs Fast was sixteen winters and didn't live in his mother's lodge any longer. Runs Fast could decide for himself what to do.

Badger knew that a horse was the most wonderful of all possessions. A horse made a man wealthy. It made him a mighty hunter and warrior to whom the people looked and admired. But none of the Twisted River Band owned horses. Horses didn't live long in the canyons. They couldn't be ridden on the steep hillsides. They stumbled and fell and broke their legs.

Badger had come to the river's edge. He looked out at the gliding green water that formed pools around the swimming place and the rock from where he fished. Chipmunk stood there with a snagging pole, fishing.

Badger watched the river glide past, thinking, until Chipmunk came over and sat beside him.

"Is it true the white boy will be your brother and live with you?"

"No!" Badger snapped. "He's not my brother!"

Chipmunk recoiled. "But he will live with you?"

"Yes. My mother asked my father, so it is."

"But, Badger, that is not so bad. You saw the white boy's giving away. They say it's good for a man to have a giving away, especially when bad things have happened. Surely the Great Mystery will now give him good things."

"Yes, Chipmunk, he did a good thing."

"Now he will receive acceptance from the spirits," Chipmunk continued. "Maybe now, nothing bad will happen to him."

"But maybe he doesn't know about the giving ceremony, Chipmunk."

"I think he does, Badger," Chipmunk insisted. "Some people got good things from him—pots, knives—those are good things. It begins the giving circle. Now those people will give to others. Soon some of the people will give good things back to him."

Badger shook his head, but he wondered who would give things to the white boy.

"Yes, Chipmunk," agreed Badger. "But I don't like him, and I don't want to live with him." He sighed. "But I'm too young to leave my mother's lodge. I have not yet completed my vision seeking. I'm not yet a true man."

"Maybe the white boy has gone on his vision seeking, Badger," replied Chipmunk quietly. "He shows many qualities of a true man. The people think so."

"But he's stupid, Chipmunk," Badger protested. "You saw him fishing. He tried to catch a river trout with a snagging pole. He knows nothing. The snagging poles are for redfish or the big spring trout."

"That is true," Chipmunk agreed. "The river trout are too fast to snag. They are for practice with our spears. Everyone knows this."

Badger gazed beyond to the main current of the river, its whitewater pounding unceasingly, ever moving down the canyon. This was near the place where his brother died. Suddenly he felt lonely. The one who hunts the elk had been his companion. He was more a true man than this white boy was. Yet the one who hunts the elk had left him. It had been the Maker's will.

No one knew the days of his life, but Badger wondered why the Maker numbered some with so few. He did not understand. A heaviness entered his heart, but he wouldn't allow himself to dwell on his brother. His brother was happy now. He walked the sky trails. Now the one who hunts the elk would watch over him.

And now the white boy was brought to live with him. *Is this also the will of the Maker?* he wondered.

Badger stood up. "Ah, Chipmunk, if we were but older, we would understand things."

Chipmunk looked up, puzzled.

Badger smiled. "You should go back to fishing while the older boys stay away."

He watched Chipmunk return to his rock. He decided there were many things he did not understand. Perhaps in time he would talk to his watcher about these things.

***

Badger returned to his lodge and entered. He looked at neither his mother nor his father. He knew he had been wrong. He saw that the white boy slept. *Maybe he is but a winter older than me, but he looks skinny and weak. Perhaps, if I'm lucky, he won't live long.* He sat on his robes, studying him. *I hope the others don't make more fun of me because of him. He'll do stupid things and make me look stupid as well. Now that he doesn't have his rifle, he can't hunt. He doesn't know about animals. He doesn't know how to live.* Badger lay back, watching the breeze rustle a feather near the lodge opening. *Well, I won't help him. If my father wants him, then he can worry about such things.*

CHAPTER 21

ERIK WOKE LATE IN the morning, wondering at first where he was, feeling the strangeness of the animal hair robes against his skin. He saw the sun was fully up. Only Shining Water and Singing Bird were in the lodge. Shining Water was bent over, busy with some sheepskins.

Without looking up, she spoke. "Little Dugumbaa'naa Buih-nee` sleeps long. That is good." She went outside to the cooking fire and brought back a bowl of meat. Erik signed thank you and ate.

He sat, wondering what to do, knowing he had to pee. He stood with the elk robe and walked to the bushes. He guessed he would wear the robe. Maybe Shining Water would find him some clothes.

He felt strange. Now he had a family to care for him. For the first time in many months, he didn't have to haul water, cut firewood, stoke a fire, feed a horse—he felt sad remembering Smoky.

He couldn't help it. He picked up some of the downed cottonwood branches and hauled them back to the lodge. He noticed that some of the boys stared at him. One snickered and pointed. Erik ignored them and dropped the load of wood next to the cooking fire. Shining Water looked at him quizzically but said nothing. She beckoned him into the lodge where she handed him a pair of moccasins and a sheepskin top. The top was made from two sheepskins sewn together with openings for his head and arms.

Erik tried on the moccasins. They were somewhat large, but they would do. He could feel the twigs and rocks under his feet.

He slipped on the sheepskin top. It felt strange on his bare skin. It reminded him somewhat of a dress, and he felt a little foolish wearing it. He realized he had to be careful not to bend over too far. Maybe it was up to him to make the coyote leggings that the men wore. Maybe his family needed more skins or was poor. He realized he was doing nothing yet to help them.

Repeatedly, he signed and said, "Thank you." Shining Water nodded, smiling.

Free Hawk returned with Badger. Each was given a bowl of food. After he had eaten, Free Hawk addressed Erik. "Ah, Dugumbaa'naa Buih-nee`," he signed and said, "I see Shining Water has given you some proper clothes and moccasins."

Twice now, he had heard the strange address. He believed it was the name they now called him. He also understood Shining Water's name and that Free Hawk talked about the clothes, so he replied, "Thank you for the clothes."

Free Hawk stood and pulled a wrapped bundle from the poles of his lodge. Unwrapping it, he pulled forth a bow and several arrows. "Now you must learn to become a hunter. This is a bow for a boy. It will be good to bring down rabbits. When you are a man, as when Badger becomes a man, we will make curved-horn bows to hunt the sheep and elk. There will be plenty of time for that."

Erik was dumbfounded. Although he didn't understand what Free Hawk had said, he understood he was being given a bow. Repeatedly he signed thank you.

Free Hawk spoke to Badger and beckoned Erik to follow. They walked to the painted rock where Gray Owl sat on his robe. Free Hawk spoke to him. Badger began piling wood onto the fire.

Young boys ran through the camp crying for the people to gather.

After the people had arrived, Gray Owl stood, the morning sun gleaming from his graying hair and weathered face. "My people, we have had some sad times this long winter season. The one who hunts the elk now walks the sky trails." He gestured toward the sky, the sun shining from the bundles of hair edging his shirt. "The boy who helped the men get the elk and his mother came to us, but his mother now walks the sky trails." He looked toward Erik. "The boy left us, but he has returned. When he did, Fighting Bear and his family left the people and took the boy's horse. It is sad that some have left us."

The people murmured. They knew all too well the consequences of losing a hunter.

"But the white boy showed us that he wants to be a true man," Gray Owl continued and signed. "He has given us all that he had. Now Free Hawk has agreed to take the white boy as his own. We agree that this is good.

"He shall be known as Dugumbaa'naa Buih-nee`." Gray Owl looked up and pointed to the blue sky and then to his eyes. He turned Erik toward the people. Erik now knew his new name meant Sky Eyes. "We will teach him to be one of us. He shall be one of the people."

The people murmured their agreement, but Badger scowled.

Free Hawk stood and addressed the people. "I am pleased to call Sky Eyes my son. He will learn the ways of the people. Just as the one who hunts the elk made me proud, and just as Badger, the fire carrier, makes me proud, one day Sky Eyes will make me proud."

He turned to Whistling Elk and spoke softly. The man was silent for a moment, but then nodded. Free Hawk continued and signed, "I ask Whistling Elk to be watcher to Sky Eyes."

Whistling Elk stood and clasped Free Hawk's arms. "It is an honor, brother friend, to be called watcher for your new son Sky Eyes."

He placed his hands on Erik's shoulders. Looking hard into the boy's eyes, he firmly spoke. "I will do this for my brother friend, for I owe him everything. Although I failed the one who hunts the elk, I will not fail you, Sky Eyes. You will be a son to me. This is how I will honor my brother friend."

He addressed the people. "I shall be watcher to this young white boy. I will teach him the ways of the people. I will guide him to become a true man. To you, I give my sacred word."

The people murmured their approval.

Erik grasped only some of the meaning of what was said. His heart raced. He knew Whistling Elk would now play an important part in his life.

Erik didn't know what to do or say, so he simply signed and said, "*Aishenda'qa nimi.* Thank you the people."

His comment brought murmurs and smiles. The white boy was learning their language. But Runs Fast scowled. Because of this white boy, his father had left the Twisted River Band and taken with him his new wife and baby daughter. He would have gone with his father, but he hoped to marry Sweet Grass or Quickly Smiles—whoever favored him. But now he questioned his decision. His father was gone. They would no longer share the hunts. It was a far distance to the Lemhis to visit. He didn't believe the little white boy was a fair trade. He felt his anger rising.

***

As the people returned to their lodges, Gray Owl called out to Sky Eyes. He had pondered the boy from when the hunters told of how he had killed the elk and sat unafraid while they prepared the meat. He had been amazed when the boy gave away all that he owned and then burned even his clothes. Surely he knew then that if someone did not take him, he would soon walk the sky trails. Instead he trusted his life to the people, and Free Hawk accepted him. The boy had shown great courage.

Sky Eyes came toward him. Gray Owl shook his head. *Surely the Great Mystery has brought him to the people. Surely he has already been blessed with a spirit helper.*

Erik stood quietly, curious as to what Gray Owl wanted.

"I too am pleased you have come to the people, Sky Eyes. You have shown much courage to do so," he signed and said. "You must learn to become a skilled hunter. Your watcher and your father will help you become one, but a good hunter must also be able to start a fire. You must have back your flint and steel." He opened a parcel and handed him his flint and steel.

Erik was baffled but took and clutched his flint and steel.

"I also want you to know you have made my heart glad." Gray Owl touched his chest.

"*Aishenda'qa,* Aishi-mompittseh. Thank you," Erik said, bowing, humbled.

Gray Owl nodded, rose, and shuffled toward his lodge.

CHAPTER 22

THE WEATHER WARMED, AND the days grew longer. The river began to rise from the melting snow. Snow had long ago left the canyon floor but still blanketed the highest peaks. Trees and shrubs turned green with new leaves. It was the greening-grass moon.

When Whistling Elk took Erik on his first rabbit hunt, Erik could barely notch an arrow and hold it against the string. Badger and Sees Far joined them. They waited patiently for Erik to take the first shot. His arrow flew but a few feet, skidding into the dirt in front of the animal. The rabbit bounded away, and Badger laughed. After that, Erik noticed that Badger wasn't around when Whistling Elk took him hunting. He figured Badger didn't wish to be seen with him.

Erik took his bow and practiced alone. He didn't want even Whistling Elk to see how miserable he was. After trying again to hit rabbits for a while, he decided he had better luck by throwing stones at them. He was no good. His arrows wouldn't fly straight.

The other boys had no trouble killing rabbits. Often Coyote and Weasel waved them in front of him as they carried them to their lodges. Badger always showed Erik his before presenting them to Shining Water. Erik overheard her say how proud she was of her "young hunter."

Erik found himself left behind when the other boys hunted or played. He figured they avoided him. He grew frustrated with sitting in camp by himself and resolved to help in some manner. He began carrying water for the animal skins in which Shining Water cooked, and regularly, he gathered firewood for the cooking fire.

"You do women's work," Coyote signed and said to him one day while Erik gathered wood. "Why do you do women's work? Is it because you are no good with a bow?"

Erik didn't answer although he partly understood the message.

"Maybe he wishes to be a woman," chided Weasel, signing. The boys, including Badger, laughed.

Erik's ears burned. He saw nothing wrong with helping Shining Water. "I do not wish to be a woman," he tried to sign and say.

The boys burst out laughing, doubling over, pointing. Erik realized he had said something terribly wrong.

"You *are* a woman," replied Weasel, making the unmistakable signs.

Erik grew angry. He tried to ask why they thought helping their mothers was being a woman. He didn't know the words and, in frustration, gave up.

The three left, glancing over their shoulders, still laughing.

He picked up the bundle of wood, dropped it in front of the lodge, and went inside.

"Sky Eyes," Shining Water addressed him, "you are troubled?"

Erik sensed she was concerned for him, but he couldn't explain.

***

Sometimes Erik helped Shining Water and Moccasin Woman gather plants. The canyon was now lush and many blossomed. Moccasin Woman explained this was a good time to find the healing plants.

Together the two women dug rosebush and snowberry roots from which they made a tisane for healing. They gathered kinnikinnick—the red-berry plant—which they dried and made into a type of tobacco for the men to smoke at council. Erik wondered if they made rosehip tea or ate the kinnikinnick berries as he had done.

When alone one day, Erik recognized the unmistakable fragrance of mint. He quickly found the young plants, pulled some, and took them to Shining Water. She smelled them and gestured for him to hang them to dry. Instead, he seeped them in hot water. Erik savored the almost forgotten taste and, feeling proud, offered some to Shining Water. She tasted it, then pushed it away. Gently, she tried to explain, "This is a medicine plant for healing. It is not to be used as a drink."

Erik didn't understand.

Shining Water asked him, signing, "How do you know about the mint and rosebush?"

Erik couldn't explain. He came to learn them while coming west; they often collected useful plants.

She laughed gently at his silence. "Perhaps someday you will become a medicine healer or a holy man."

Erik shrugged. He understood "holy man." *I just want to be able to hunt,* he thought.

"Thank you for being Sky Eyes," Shining Water said and signed.

Erik was confused but felt the appreciation.

***

One day, Free Hawk killed a badger. Both Erik and Badger were standing by, near the lodge, when he brought it in. Immediately, Shining Water brought out her stone knives to skin it. She placed Singing Bird nearby to play on some robes.

Erik watched as she slit up the badger's stomach and then down each leg. She pulled the skin back and cut the underlying tissues away, rapidly peeling the hide back. Several times the animal slipped, and she struggled to get it back into position.

Without asking, Erik squatted next to her and held the badger.

Shining Water looked up, a puzzled look, but when Erik held the animal firmly, she continued her work.

Badger stood apart, watching, arms folded, mild scorn on his face.

Coyote and Weasel approached. Seeing Erik helping Shining Water, they pointed, laughing. Badger quickly turned and joined them, walking away.

Erik ignored them.

The hide free, Shining Water retrieved a number of sharpened pegs she had piled near the lodge. With a heavy, rounded stone, she drove in a couple through the edge of the hide, pinning it to the ground.

Erik helped by stretching the hide and holding the pegs, until the pelt was tightly stretched and pinned.

Taking a sharpened piece of quartzite that fit her hand, she began scraping the hide, peeling up bits of flesh and tissue. She tossed the bits to the camp dogs that had come around.

Erik took a similar stone and tried doing the same along the other edge but was ineffective. He wished he had his knife.

Shining Water gripped his hand that held the stone. "Hold the stone like this." She pushed it against the hide. Erik was surprised at her strength. She removed her hand, and Erik tried by himself. This time he pushed a small bead of flesh off the hide.

Shining Water nodded and smiled, then continued rapidly scraping the hide.

Finished, she took the round stone and dashed open the badger's skull, picking out small pieces of bone and then scooping out the brains with her stone knife. These she began mashing into a paste along with an equal amount of deer brains from a previous kill.

Erik felt queasy watching her mix them.

Shining Water must have noticed. She smiled and began to explain. "Long ago, when the people first came to this land from the burning-rock land, they didn't know how to make good clothes, but they were the best hunters. The Great Mystery—the Maker—saw that only the Tukudeka could catch all the animals he had put on the earth, and he was pleased with the people because they used all the animals." She paused and signed the words she had spoken so Erik would understand.

"The Snakes and the Bannocks were good at catching some of the animals, but not all of them. And they used some of the animals, like the fleet-foot deer and the big-ear deer, but not all of them.

"But the people used all the animals—the rabbit, fox, coyote, wolf, and badger, the big-ear deer, shaggy-neck elk, and night cat, even the weasel, mink, otter, and fisher, and of course, the curved-horns." Rapidly and excitedly, she made signs for each animal.

The parade of gestures was comical, and Erik smiled. "But what animal is this?" He mimicked her when she curled her two index fingers downward, one on each side of her mouth.

"The night cat." She made signs that mimicked a cat crouching and stalking.

Erik laughed. Of course, it was the mountain lion.

"Well, the Maker saw that the people used all the animals, so one day, he decided the people, and only the people, would know the secret of making the best hides. So the Maker sent Otter Woman. She showed the people how to use two brains for each hide, not one. But each animal has only one brain." Shining Water shook her head and laughed. "That is why only the best hunters can catch enough animals to make the best hides. That is why the Tukudeka make the best hides."

She sat back, smiling, patting the mixture into a ball.

"I will need some ashes and a bowl of water." Shining Water gestured as she set aside the brain mixture and rose to take care of Singing Bird. Erik ran to get the ashes and water.

Shortly, Shining Water returned and began kneading the brains into the hide. Erik joined her, the mixture oozing and sticky between his fingers and knuckles.

Now Shining Water took the ashes and mixed them into the water. She soaked the hide for a while and then, sprinkling more ashes on the inside surface, rolled it up into a ball.

"We shall bury this. In a few days, we will dig it up and scrape off the hair. Then I will make you men some hunting moccasins. I will make yours first, Sky Eyes, for you helped make the hide." She signed the words, so Erik mostly understood.

***

One day, Erik practiced with his bow a short distance from camp. He smelled onions and noticed where many blossomed. He located a sharp stick and began digging some. In a stew, they made all the difference. He looked forward to taking some to Shining Water. He had a pile when Coyote and Weasel appeared. They watched a moment, then snickered.

"Only women dig onions," Weasel mocked, signing.

Erik paused from digging and stood up.

"Look, he holds a digging stick, like a woman," added Coyote. "And he wears a woman's dress," he said scornfully, also carefully signing the words so Erik understood.

"Onions are good," Erik tried to say and sign back. "Why not dig for them?"

"Women and girls dig onions," Weasel said again, signing. "You must be a woman if you dig onions."

"I am glad I am not Badger and have to sleep with you in my lodge," Coyote continued. "Maybe some man will marry you and make you his wife."

Both boys laughed loudly, mockingly.

Erik's ears burned. He dropped his stick. He understood sufficiently what they said. He left the onions and picked up his bow and arrows. He walked away, the boys' laughter ringing in his ears.

This is not working. I have not learned how to hunt. They see me as a woman, doing a woman's work.

At a rock near the river, he sat watching it glide by. *I must learn to hunt. I must be able to do a man's work.* He chucked a rock into the water and watched the current swallow it.

CHAPTER 23

ONE MORNING ERIK WANDERED alone to the river, wondering if he should try again to fish. He eyed the frothy river, full from the spring runoff. Although he was a good swimmer, the river frightened him. It was rising and now pounded loudly and violently through the canyon.

He noticed several boys fishing with the snagging poles. Badger stood on a rock farther out in the river. The steelhead, large like the salmon, were moving upstream. The people said it was too hard to get a steelhead. They swam too fast and didn't stop in the shallows to spawn like the salmon. Erik half wondered if Badger was trying to snag a steelhead to further show him up.

Erik had tried to be friends with Badger. He tried to help whenever there was something he could do. Together they cut young syringa shoots for new arrows. But whenever Badger seemed to warm to him, Erik did something stupid. Invariably, Badger's friends would see and laugh. Then Badger joined in the laughter and ignored him.

Today Erik watched him standing near the churning water, trying to snag a fish. The other boys were nearer the shore. Erik remembered Runs Fast. He had been the young elk hunter present when Erik got the elk. Now it appeared he was helping Quick Marten and Raven, but Quick Marten was pestering Badger.

Erik knew something about fishing, even if he wasn't good at using the snagging poles. He knew the trout liked the hole near the large rock where the three older boys stood. He doubted Badger would have any luck where he was—the water ran too fast.

As Erik watched, Badger turned angrily toward the other boys. He turned back and watched the water. Suddenly Badger sliced his pole through the water and jerked it upward. He had nothing. Quick Marten mimicked his antics, laughing. Raven and Runs Fast joined in. Erik knew what Badger felt.

Badger waved his snagging pole at Quick Marten. Quick Marten poked back, parrying away Badger's pole. In desperation, Badger lunged. Quick Marten knocked the pole aside and, in doing so, knocked Badger off balance. Badger's pole flew, and he fell hard into the churning river.

Without thought, Erik pulled off his sheepskin and ran toward Badger. He saw him come up and turn toward the shore, paddling madly. In moments, Badger would be pulled into the main current where the water swept upward into huge piles. Erik sprang onto the rock next to the other boys and leaped into the water after Badger. The cold took his breath; he gasped for air but focused on Badger. Strongly swimming toward him, he grabbed the floating pole.

Badger was swept into the pounding water; his head went under. Erik lost sight of him until he bobbed back up, eyes panicky. Badger paddled madly, desperately trying to break out of the current. Erik swam into it. The heavy, turbulent water pushed him under. Shaken, he came up, eyes searching for Badger. He spotted his bobbing head and pushed the pole toward him. "*Ta tag i pålen!* Grab the pole!" he yelled.

Badger's eyes widened as he saw Erik in the water with him. Madly, he grabbed for the pole but missed. Both were caught in the main current, being swept toward the pounding waves.

Erik angled for Badger, swimming hard, trying to keep from being pushed under again. He pushed the pole toward Badger. "Grab it!" Water filled his mouth, and he choked.

Badger grabbed and held on. The frothing water dunked him at the same moment.

Immediately, Erik turned and swam toward shore. He knew to ride the current and not fight it. He struggled to keep his head out of the water and to hold on to the pole.

The water swept them downward past the camp. Desperately, Erik kept swimming, hoping the current wouldn't sweep them farther out but push them toward shore.

He felt his body going numb from the cold, and he struggled to hang on. Finally, his feet bumped the bottom. Breathing hard, lungs aching, he grabbed a root on the bank and swung Badger in next to him. Dragging themselves out, they collapsed from the numbing cold.

People had gathered on the bank and watched, stricken. Now they shouted. Quickly they wrapped robes about them and helped them to the nearest fire.

Erik's teeth chattered; he shivered uncontrollably. He felt Shining Water's hands as they dried him with a soft fur. Another person brought a hide warmed by the fire and wrapped him in it. He was offered hot water, most of which he splashed on himself while trying to get it down. Slowly, his warmth came back. His shivering calmed. He regained focus. He sat dazed, thinking about what had happened.

***

The Sheepeaters gathered near the council rock, amazed by what they had seen.

"The Great Mystery watches over both Sky Eyes and Badger this day. For certain, if Sky Eyes had not gone into the water. Badger would have been lost. Like his brother, Badger would now walk the sky trails. Sky Eyes pulled him back from the water spirits."

"None of the people swim through the water like Sky Eyes. His arms came out of the water and made him go quickly. He reached Badger at the edge of the fast water."

"And Sky Eyes was clever. He took the snagging pole and reached it out to Badger. And when Badger missed, Sky Eyes swam into the fast water and reached the pole out again."

"Sky Eyes was brave; he didn't fear the water spirits."

"Surely, he is like the otter. Maybe the water spirits are his friend."

Later, Stands Alone, the one who enforced the people's will, met with the young men.

He addressed Quick Marten. "Although you are of the Crying Mountain Band, when you're with us, you know you're responsible to us. You have not completed your vision seeking, yet only those who have not reached three winters do not know to play around a river high from spring melt. The water spirits are lonely. They don't care that you intend to play, that you swim, or that you fish. They will be happy to take a person's spirit so his spirit may never walk the sky trails. You are the cause of Badger falling into the river," he told him. "You shall not visit here again until you show more understanding of how a true man should act."

Without even a glance back, Quick Marten headed down the trail toward his own people. It would be a long time before his heart would be glad to see the Twisted River Band.

"Raven, you approach the season of your vision seeking. You also should understand your responsibilities to others more. Free Hawk has already lost a son. You should think twice before you would allow his second son to be lost."

Raven stood quietly, head down. He looked up. "Yes, Uncle. I would not want the people to remember me as the one who caused the people to lose a hunter. I am in Badger's debt." He stood, waiting.

"And the people shall expect you to fulfill that debt," Stands Alone said. "That is all, Raven."

Raven turned and went to seek Badger. The one who hunts the elk had been his best friend. He suddenly felt miserable. He owed it to the one who hunts to care for his younger brother, not torment him.

"Runs Fast, you have completed your vision seeking. You are a true man of the people. You should have stopped Quick Marten and shown the right example."

Runs Fast stood, a scowl on his face.

"Your father would be disgraced to know you stood and watched Badger fall. You did not reach out to him. Now others say that Runs Fast did not have the courage to go after Badger before he was swept into the fast water.

"Your father would be sad to know that Sky Eyes, who is new to the people, showed more courage for a stranger than you did for one of your own."

Runs Fast's ears burned. He swallowed hard and stared steadily at Stands Alone. He knew he should accept this, but the hurt overwhelmed him.

"I would have reached for Badger ... but the stupid white boy got in my way and jumped into the river. It is lucky that both he and Badger do not now walk the sky trails. Talk to the white boy. He—"

Stands Alone held up his hand. "Do not disgrace yourself further, Runs Fast. I am the one whom the people ask to say these things so that you may understand the proper manner of being a true man. I won't say these things to the people but only to you, for in your heart, you know the truth."

Runs Fast stood defiantly. For certain now, he did not like the little white boy.

***

"It was a brave thing you did for me, Sky Eyes," admitted Badger, signing.

"Thank you," Erik signed and said. "It was not right what Quick Marten did."

Badger nodded. "I don't like him, but it was my anger that made me stupid," he signed as he spoke. "I hope my brother is never lost because of anger toward me." His eyes were steady as he signed and said the words.

Erik didn't completely understand, but he understood "brother." He smiled and nodded.

Free Hawk had been watching and listening. He addressed them. "Today, both of my sons have made me proud." He rose and pulled down a bundle from the back of the lodge. Unwrapping it, he pulled forth Larson's knife. "I have this for you, Sky Eyes. You gave it to me when you first became a Tukudeka. I have kept it to see how my son would be. I now return it to you, for you have given me back my son, Badger."

Shaking, Erik took the knife, humbled. He couldn't believe the gift. He knew Free Hawk didn't own a steel knife; yet Free Hawk returned his father's knife to him. His eyes misted.

Shortly after that day, Shining Water also brought Erik a gift—a breechcloth, leggings, and a shirt. He no longer wore the sheepskin robe like a dress. Erik felt proud in his new clothes. They were comfortable; they gave him freedom to move, to run, to hunt. Only to bathe or sleep did he ever take them off.

CHAPTER 24

"GOOD," SIGNED AND SAID Badger. "Sky Eyes has shot another rabbit, and again it is a clean kill. His arrows go true."

Erik smiled and picked up the rabbit pierced by his arrow. The boys headed back at a trot to take the rabbit to Shining Water to add to the stew.

***

Now the snowy white, yellow-centered syringa blossoms cascaded down the draws. Their fragrance, mixed with the new pine and fir, filled the air.

Once, a black bear wandered near the camp with new cubs. Badger pointed her out to Erik. "The men will not hunt this bear; her cubs are too new," he said and signed.

"We call this the new-sheep moon," he said. "You can see the lambs with their mothers." He pointed to a ridge where Erik could just make out a band of sheep. "Soon the big-ear deer will have fawns. During the new-sheep moon, there are many animals, but soon they will leave because in the canyons it grows hot. Already the mountain big-ear deer have left. Only those deer that live in the canyons remain."

Badger suddenly slapped his back, examined what he held pinched between his fingers, and laughed. "We also leave, because the mosquitoes and biting flies come."

"And the winter camp grows old and smelly," said Erik, holding his nose.

Badger laughed again. "Yes, that is true as well."

***

It was good when the weather warmed. The people could bathe—not just splash themselves with cold water.

Erik and Badger went to the river in the early morning. Erik swam out into the current, rode it downriver for a distance and then swam back to Badger.

Badger shook his head. "Why do you do that, Sky Eyes? Surely the water spirits will take you."

Erik paused and stood in the shallow water where Badger waded and bathed. "No." He shook his head. "If you swim like me," he mimicked swimming and pointed to himself, "the water spirits will not take you."

Demonstrating, he swam across the river and back. "See," he said, returning.

"Maybe your name should have been Otter Swims," Badger said, laughing.

"I can show you how."

Badger shook his head. "Perhaps some day."

They left the river and lay on their stomachs in the sun near the bathing place. This was the first spot where the sunlight touched the canyon floor, and they timed their morning bath so they could lie in the sun's first warm rays.

After a while, Erik sat up and watched River That Cries as it ran past them, cool and dark. Insects, wakened by the sun, buzzed over the sullen waters. Occasionally one hit the water's surface, dancing, skittering across. Trout had now quit feeding, so they were safe.

Erik felt good. He had not felt good for many months. He wondered about his sister Katrine, now nine years old, somewhere west, hopefully at the high valley. He missed his parents, and an ache welled within him.

He looked around at Badger lying on the warm rock, appearing content. He looked past to the people, happy, busy, moving about the lodges, working on hides, cooking. *This is my family, now,* he told himself. *This is my life for a while. The time will come when I am able to leave. Then I will. Then I will go and find Katrine. For now, I am a Tukudeka. I am one of the people.*

Badger sat up. "What are you thinking?" he asked, touching his head.

"About being here with my brother and being happy." Erik signed "brother" and "happy."

"I am happy you're here as well," Badger replied, signing.

Sees Far found the two boys. "Ah, here are the lazy boys," he chided. "Come with me. Whistling Elk waits."

They rose, dressed, and fell into a jog behind as he took them past the lodges to a thick stand of mountain maple. Whistling Elk was seated near a small fire, pieces of arrows laid out in front of him.

"Ah, Sky Eyes and Badger," he greeted the boys. "In short time, we will go to the mountain meadows to hunt. It is time to finish some hunting arrows—perhaps an arrow that will bring down a shaggy-neck elk."

Both Erik and Badger felt a quick excitement. Sheepeater boys did not get a chance to hunt the elk. For this to even be discussed was a proud moment.

Whistling Elk took a section of arrow and pulled it through a hole in a rib bone. "For an arrow to fly true, it must be as straight as possible." Small slivers of wood curled from it as he pulled. He put it to his eye and sighted down it, then handed it to Badger. Badger examined it and handed it to Erik. "See, it is straight, Sky Eyes."

Whistling Elk compared the piece to two others of similar size. Carefully, he notched each end of the short shafts and checked that they fit tightly together. He dabbed the ends into a small stone bowl that held a bubbling liquid that smelled to Erik like pinesap.

Now Whistling Elk pulled a length of sinew from some boiling water, hammered it on a stone, and shredded it into threads. With the sinew, he quickly bound the three pieces together at the glued joints, creating a single shaft about fourteen inches long.

Whistling Elk picked up an owl wing, pulled some pinion feathers, and split and cut them into six-inch lengths. He glued them into grooves along the butt of the arrow—three opposite each other—and secured them, front and back, using sinew. He explained, "Feathers from the night bird don't absorb blood and soften. They keep stiff and fly the arrow true." He cut a notch in the end of the arrow for seating the bowstring.

Whistling Elk opened a small leather parcel. Inside were six beautiful obsidian points. Badger caught his breath.

"Yes, Badger, these are hunters' points. When last Broken Blade was here, I traded for them. That was when his son, Black Legs, remained behind and married White Deer." Whistling Elk touched one, examined it. "Now before we hunt the shaggy-neck elk, I will make them into fine hunting arrows."

Badger picked one up and handed it to Erik. "These come from the land far to the east where Broken Blade's people are. They say the ground shakes and boiling water shoots high into the air."

Erik nodded. He wondered about the land. He ran his finger along the obsidian point's edge and quickly noticed its sharpness.

"You may lose an arrow. It may break when the animal falls. But you must try to never lose a point," Whistling Elk explained. "If your arrow should miss its mark, you should seek the lost point and hope it didn't break." He placed the point in a notch he had cut and bound it in place with glue and sinew.

"That is why you practice on rabbits with white-rock points, Sky Eyes," Sees Far added. "Only when you are a true hunter will you use the black-glass points."

Whistling Elk sighted down the finished arrow, now about sixteen inches in length. He handed it to the boys for them to inspect.

CHAPTER 25

As THE SHEEPEATERS PREPARED to strike winter camp and head for the star-grass meadows, Whistling Elk and Sees Far spotted some mountain sheep coming down to the river.

"We won't see the curved-horns in the mountain meadows. Perhaps one of these has good horns," suggested Whistling Elk. "If so, it would be a good time to take Sky Eyes and Badger hunting."

"Yes, though they hunt with boys' bows, they can bring down a curved-horn if they send their arrows true."

"Come quickly," Whistling Elk called to Erik and Badger, seeing them near the river. "Today we will hunt the curved-horns."

Giving a quick cry, the boys raced to their lodge to prepare. Pushing their way inside, Badger reached up to pull down their personal bundles. "We shall need something to eat, Mother."

The boys sat and pulled on their hunting moccasins and selected two of their best hunting arrows.

Free Hawk entered the lodge, observing the activity.

Badger explained. "Today, Father, we are asked to go on a hunt with our watchers. We will hunt the curved-horns."

Shining Water busily packed dried meat into the pouches, which the boys wore looped through their waistbands. She paused and turned away. The memory of the one who hunts the elk was too new.

"Hunt well, then," Free Hawk replied. "And we shall see about making a horn bow." He thought about his own charge, Raven, but decided it was not proper to join them on this hunt. He should not interfere with his sons' watchers. His sons would learn better from them than from him.

Whistling Elk and Sees Far took off on an easy jog, followed closely by Erik and Badger. After jogging a distance, they stopped and rested and drank from the river. The sun beat warm in the canyon bottom.

Erik and Badger noticed Whistling Elk and Sees Far move to the side. "I think they shall try to lose us, Sky Eyes," whispered Badger.

Erik shrugged. "Perhaps. But if so, I think Whistling Elk will not lose me." Erik now knew this was how their watchers helped prepare them to be strong hunters. He remembered the first few times. Whistling Elk would quickly lose him, then hide and ambush him. The others laughed at him. He hated it. He remembered that Sees Far never lost Badger. And if he did, Badger always seemed to figure out where he would be. But now, he realized it was all part of the game. And now, he could usually keep up.

Whistling Elk turned up a steep, grassy slope, moving fast. Sees Far continued downstream.

Erik and Badger exchanged knowing looks and followed their watchers.

Whistling Elk trotted into a draw, jumped across the narrow cleft, and disappeared, weaving under the buck brush until he came out on top of some jagged rocks.

Erik, right behind, trotted into the draw, almost hesitated about jumping, but then frantically launched himself over the gap. He scrambled up, dodging the wicked spikes on the brush, and emerged on top of the rocks where Whistling Elk had been. He remembered times before when he had misjudged the brush and jabbed himself. It wasn't infrequent to return to his lodge with several long, bloody scratches.

Erik caught up to Whistling Elk moving quickly across the rocks, jumping from one to the next. Carefully, he watched Whistling Elk's steps and matched them. If his left foot came down on top of a rock, his landed in the same place—stride for stride.

Whistling Elk finally paused. Lungs nearly bursting, breathing heavily, Erik reached him. He bent over, gasping for air, but was pleased. He had stayed with Whistling Elk.

Whistling Elk, chest heaving, smiled. "You run well, Sky Eyes."

He pointed toward the sheep. They were still a good distance away. Then he pointed down toward a separate ridge. Erik saw Badger and Sees Far below, moving rapidly upward.

Whistling Elk turned and continued following the ridge. Erik followed closely behind, dodging the trees, jumping the brush. They raced, one trying to shake the other, the other determined to best the master.

Erik wondered about all this dodging and leaping until one day he nearly came down on a rattlesnake awakened by Whistling Elk's passing foot. Somehow, in mid air, Erik twisted and came down on the opposite side of the snake. Neither Whistling Elk nor Badger needed to tell him that was why they played this game.

Whistling Elk aimed to where the ridges joined. Erik pushed himself hard, trying to keep up, his lungs aching and heart pounding. Whistling Elk slipped down the ridge, taking cover, motioning Erik to do the same. Excited, Erik realized they were setting an ambush for Sees Far and Badger, and he was part of it. His breathing came hard; he could hardly endure the ache; he prayed for it to slow.

Sees Far and Badger came to a stop in front of them. "We have beaten Whistling Elk and Sky Eyes," said Sees Far, breathing heavily.

Whistling Elk reached out and struck Sees Far. The man spun in surprise. Erik tried to tag Badger, but Badger had seen Whistling Elk and already turned. Instead, Erik tackled him to the ground, rolling with him, his bare skin against the pine needles and gravel. They came apart, laughing, gasping for breath.

Whistling Elk resumed the lead, walking now, angling upward for the rocky cliffs and the ridge farther upstream where the sheep were bedded.

At the rocky cliffs, he slowed and cautioned his followers, pointing. "Curved-horns." At first, Erik didn't see the animals, then one of the mountain sheep stood and began moving slowly down the ridge.

With signs, Whistling Elk sent Sees Far and Badger down and around. He and Erik headed up and above the animals. Quickly,

Whistling Elk moved upward, slipping into the rock clefts, scrambling up one face, crossing a rock chute to another, and then climbing up another rock face.

Erik assumed Whistling Elk would cautiously sneak up on the animals. He didn't. Instead, he picked a route that hid them from sight until they came out above the sheep.

He froze and motioned for Erik to come forward. Carefully he notched an arrow. Erik did the same. Easing out above the animals, they studied them. There were no rams, only ewes and newborn lambs. Whistling Elk stood up and waved to Sees Far.

Turning to Erik, he shrugged. "There are no good curved-horns— just mothers and their young, Sky Eyes. There is no need to kill a female with its young when we prepare to go to the summer hunting camps so soon. Already we have too much to carry."

The mountain sheep, seeing the hunters, scrambled to their feet, bounded away down the other side of the ridge, and then crossed to the other.

Sees Far and Badger soon joined them. They rested, taking a moment to eat. The day's lesson was finished. Erik called it a lesson, but the Sheepeaters never did. They simply did what they needed to do. Often they repeated the same games, but Erik never tired of them; neither, seemingly, did the other boys.

The wind whipped down from the canyon rim. The air had cooled. Erik shivered with the chill as his perspiration evaporated. He wished suddenly that he still wore his winter shirt. Looking across the river canyon, Erik studied the ridges piled one upon the other. The uppermost were jagged and rocky, still surprisingly white with snow. The ridges falling away from their flanks were carpeted with dense black timber.

Whistling Elk suddenly jumped up, saying something to Sees Far. Quickly, they headed back down the route they had come. Erik was soon on Whistling Elk's heels and Badger on Sees Far's. The four of them leaped and jumped their way back down the ridge at a dangerous, but exhilarating, pace. One trip, one stumble, and a person could break a leg or worse. But this was not something Erik thought about.

Chapter 26

THE PEOPLE VISITED ONE last time with their friends and relatives from the Crying Mountain Band. Early the next morning, they left the winter camp, heading upstream. Everything they needed for the summer hunts, they carried on their backs or in their arms. The camp dogs dragged travois bundled high.

Erik recognized the place across the river where he and his mother had stayed when he brought her to the Sheepeaters. He could make out the remains of the broken shelter, now just brush in the shadows. Memories flooded back, and he felt the hurt well up within. The water was deep and fast. He remembered wading across the frigid water, leading Smoky. He remembered Free Hawk, now his adoptive father, carrying his mother back across. Tearing his eyes and thoughts away, he hitched up his pack and stepped back on the trail. *That was another time,* he told himself, *to which I can never return.*

They camped the first night, several miles upstream.

Continuing upstream the next morning, River That Cries turned west and quickly became constrained by high columns and walls of brightly colored volcanic tuff—yellows, tans and browns, reds and oranges, and whites. Smelly hot springs seeped from the draws, forming brightly colored clays. This place they called the paint pots.

"Come, Sky Eyes," Badger signed and said. "We will gather some paints for marking the rocks and our arrows."

Badger scrambled up a cobbled watercourse toward a rocky shelf. A seam of bright red cut across the moist ravine. Taking a stick, he pried out gobs of the bright red orange clay. "Here, this is one color I use."

Erik also peeled out a gob. It looked like blood and stained his hands. The boys wrapped the gobs in a small skin.

Badger searched higher. "Here is some of the white." He pried out several gobs. "This is the sacred color. When Raven goes on his vision journey, he will paint himself with white."

After collecting the clays, Erik half expected the Twisted River Band to head back downstream. He was somewhat surprised when they continued upstream. Volcanic tuff now outcropped along both sides of the river, forming grotesque formations in some places. The golden yellows and subtle reds mixed with the stark white spires reminded him of the aspens in autumn.

They turned north up the next creek, quickly climbing out of River That Cries canyon until they reached the canyon rim where the steep slopes began to taper and the timber grew thick. Again, the people stopped, prepared their meals, and rolled out their robes to sleep.

Morning came. The Twisted River Band continued toward the west, climbing higher. Now small, marshy meadows dotted with bright blue blossoms appeared. Frogs leaped from under Erik's feet as he followed Badger through the many wet places. Their croaking music filled the meadows.

By late afternoon, they reached a large, rolling meadow, blue flowers thickly carpeting it. Snow-capped peaks rose in the blue sky beyond. A doe bounded away, her fawns hidden somewhere in the bright green brush. The people moved to the edge, to the timber, and spread out to set up their lodges.

Erik helped Badger and Free Hawk drag and set up poles. Shining Water gathered brush. Singing Bird followed her mother, dragging smaller pieces. By evening, the new lodge was complete.

Gray Owl called for the people to gather. He gave thanks for their safe journey back to the star-grass meadows. The people paused to remember the one who hunts the elk. They gave thanks for Yellow Mink who had seen her first winter. Then the remainder of the evening, the people gathered around smoky cooking fires, talking happily, sharing their meals with each other, celebrating their return to the star-grass meadows.

***

The people settled into the routine of hunting and gathering. The days drifted by. Most were warm, the skies bright blue, becoming punctuated with white, billowing afternoon thunderheads that brought occasional violent storms.

Erik and Badger immediately began hunting the smaller game that boys hunted—birds, squirrels, rabbits—just as they had in the canyon. Always, they would bring the animals back for Shining Water to add to whatever stew simmered in her cooking pouch.

The men brought in the larger game. The women skinned the animals and tanned the hides. The meat was roasted or put into stews; any extra was dried.

Erik saw how hard Shining Water always worked.

"Why does Free Hawk bring you so many hides to tan?" he asked one day. "We don't eat all the meat, and you feed some of the hides to the camp dogs."

Shining Water leaned back from the fox hide she was scraping. "Your father is a fine hunter; he is able to get many animals." She pushed her scraper across the hide. "You should know for two hides, only one is tanned."

"Yes, I remember."

"You should know too that the Great Mystery has given us many different animals. I use each for what it is best. I use coyote for your leggings. I use sheep or big-ear deer for your breechcloths and shirts. I use badger for hunting moccasins. And marten and fox I sew onto big-ear hides to make winter boots. Every animal has its own use, and there are many different uses, so your father brings in many animals."

"But won't you have more than enough for the clothes we need?"

"Yes. And Free Hawk will try to get even more. Maybe he will get a night cat or wolf. He hopes to trade for fine things from Broken Blade. He wishes to get me an iron pot and himself a steel knife." She continued her work. She looked up at him and smiled. "You ask many questions, Sky Eyes."

Erik wished he hadn't asked the last question. It hurt to realize Free Hawk desired a steel knife and yet had returned his father's knife to him. He touched it where it hung on his belt.

Now more than ever, Erik helped Shining Water. He brought firewood in each time he returned to camp, and he checked and kept the water skin filled. He noticed that the other boys no longer made fun when he did. Maybe they had decided that white boys did women's work and that was just the way it was. Sometimes Badger helped him, but only when it was clear no one could see him.

***

That day, they passed where the women had dug a large pit and lined it with rocks for baking the camas.

Shining Water was bent over nearby with a digging stick, prying the small bulbs from the black earth. Singing Bird was at her side, her own small stick in her hands, jabbering at her mother, sticking it into the damp soil.

"I see my sons go hunting again," she addressed them.

"Yes, Mother," Badger replied. "We go after rabbits before they all disappear."

Shining Water leaned back, picked several bulbs from a clump of damp soil, and tossed them onto a stack, their blossoms forming a large, sky blue pile. "Hunt well," she replied. "I still need many rabbits if I should make new robes."

"We will," replied Erik. He was determined to bring in many. Shining Water was making a summer robe. She left the tails attached and sewed one rabbit opposite another so their white, fluffy tails made a beautiful line down the robe's back. Sometimes she decorated them with bird feathers so its owner knew his robe. Erik knew she worked on one for him, and he looked forward to having it during the cool summer evenings.

Some women were building a fire in the oven, preparing to heat the rocks that would bake the bulbs. "I hope Mother makes many

159

star-grass cakes," observed Badger. "Some winters, that is all we have remaining before the greening-grass moon returns."

***

Some days the boys would have a game of kickball. Someone would construct a ball out of hide stuffed with other scraps of hide or bits of wood. Two teams faced off, and an elder tossed the ball into the center. Shoving and kicking each other, both teams kicked at the ball as they struggled to kick it successfully to a small peg at the opposite end of a field. Mostly, one person kept kicking at the ball until he lost it. Erik and Badger sometimes won, because Erik would roll the ball to Badger.

Today they watched as the men played. It appeared a complete ruckus. Yelling, grabbing, and tripping, the men knocked each other down to get to the ball.

"We should join them," observed Badger. "You can roll me the ball. Perhaps we'll win."

Erik thought about it. The boys' games were rough enough. Many times he ended up with a bloody nose or bruised shin. The men would run right over him.

"Come on." Badger stood up.

Reluctantly, he rose. He couldn't back down. Soon they were running madly about, trying to get to the ball. But anytime they did, an elbow or leg flew in their direction, and they'd back off.

Free Hawk collided with Sees Far, and the ball came loose, landing near Erik's feet. He took it and rapidly advanced outside the group of men, now thundering toward him, yelling. At the last second, he rolled the ball to the far side toward Badger. The men switched directions, thundering, yelling, heading toward Badger.

Suddenly, he felt a sharp pain in the back of his leg. He somersaulted forward, rolling, hitting his shoulder hard. He came up, head spinning, dizzy. He felt another kick to his back and gasped, crying out in pain, his eyes filling with tears. He rolled out of the way as another blow landed in the dirt next to him. Somehow he scrambled to his feet. Runs Fast stood, staring him in the eyes, an ugly look on his face.

"Ha. The little white boy cries," he spat. "You want to play with the men? You are weak. You should go and play with the old women and little children." He shoved hard and Erik went down.

Struggling up, he glared at Runs Fast, shaking.

"You don't belong here, little white boy. You don't belong with the people," he hissed. "You have brought bad medicine."

Erik was stunned, scared by what Runs Fast said.

"You shall never become—"

Cheering men interrupted Runs Fast. Sees Far reached over and thumped Erik.

"We won, Sky Eyes," Badger shouted. "No one was near me. I kicked it to the peg."

Runs Fast turned away. Erik looked at Badger. "That's good." He tried to smile.

"Shall we play again?"

"No. I don't think so." Erik turned and hobbled toward the lodge.

Badger ran to catch up. "What happened?"

"I got my knickers wrung," he said in Swedish, trying to smile, and gestured by hitting his hand with his fist.

Badger looked puzzled.

***

Almost daily, Erik and Badger hunted together or practiced with their bows and arrows. Often they hiked to a small, shallow lake full of frogs and small trout. They had an ongoing competition to see who could spear a swiftly darting trout. There were no overhanging rocks or logs on which to stand and from which to get a good angle for spearing. Instead they waded out and stood on the muddy bottom, spears poised, until a trout drifted near.

"Stand still, Sky Eyes. You scare the fish."

"I am still."

"No, you shiver like the trembling-leaf tree," chided Badger, signing.

"I'm trying." It was difficult to stand perfectly still in cold water.

Suddenly Badger's arm shot down. He pulled forth a flapping trout. "Ha, got him."

Erik sighed. "Looks like you win, Badger. I'm tired of trying to spear these tiny fish. I hope we can go on a real hunt soon."

"Yes," Badger replied. "Sees Far says perhaps when he hunts for the shaggy-neck elk, I will go at least to help carry meat. I'm sure Whistling Elk will say the same for you."

"I'm hoping so."

They headed back to their lodge for their hunting bows and arrows. Maybe they would find a grouse. The grouse roosted high up in the spruce trees, hiding behind the needles, making difficult targets. However, the meat was tasty, different than venison, and they sometimes used the feathers for fletching rabbit arrows or for decoration.

On returning, Erik came over the knoll above the place where the women bathed. Quickly Smiles and Sweet Grass, older sisters to Coyote and Weasel, stood in the shallow water scooping water onto each other. Erik saw them and immediately squatted down in the tall grass. There was nowhere else to go. He would be seen. It was not right for him to look upon the women while they bathed, even if they were not much older than he was.

He hissed at Badger who was just coming over the hill and motioned for him to sit. Badger sat, but slowly, his eyes following the girls.

Erik couldn't help but gaze as well. He felt drawn to what he saw, but he also felt frightened. He waved at Badger and tried to say, "We must leave."

He felt a funny fluttery feeling in his belly and was strangely drawn to Quickly Smiles. She was but two seasons older than he was, but he could see that she was fully a woman, as was Sweet Grass.

Badger didn't move. He just watched.

Erik signed again and said, "Leave. Don't look."

He jumped up and scrambled down the way he had come, soon out of sight. Badger followed after, smiling.

Erik couldn't shake the picture of Quickly Smiles, her beautiful smile, her breasts. He couldn't help what it did to him.

Badger joined him under the trees, laughing. "Oh, come on, Sky Eyes. You see the women naked all the time," he said, signing.

It was true, Erik recalled. He tried to explain, "It's just … Quickly Smiles looks beautiful to me now."

Badger raised his eyes and smiled.

***

That night, Erik lay in his robes remembering and seeing Quickly Smiles again. Maybe this was a good thing. Until now, he had no time to consider someday marrying, becoming a father. Until now, he had struggled with every ounce of his being just to survive—to stay alive. He resolved he would have to learn the proper way for meeting and courting a girl.

CHAPTER 27

SEVERAL EVENINGS LATER, GRAY Owl invited Erik and Badger and the three boys, Raven, Coyote, and Weasel, who were near the time of their vision seeking, to his lodge. They crept inside and seated themselves around the small fire, adding the small bundles of wood each had brought to the pile.

"You see five young men here tonight. All of you are within a season or two of your vision seeking," Gray Owl began. "I think it is a good time to tell you of my first vision seeking."

The boys grinned, looking knowingly from one another to Sky Eyes. Perhaps only he had not heard the story.

"My journey was in my fourteenth summer. My father friend and watcher was the one who remembered for the people. He was the son of the first grandfather who brought the Twisted River Band from the fiery, black land. The first grandfather taught the one who remembered well. He was one of the first people who decided we should not live in a place where there was war between the people."

Gray Owl snapped some twigs and added them to the fire.

"In the first days, there were only two families to come to Twisted River. Today we have four families and other bands. We also have four grandmothers and grandfathers and twelve children. Most important, we have five boys who approach the time they will become men."

Gray Owl knew his listeners would be patient with him as he told his story. He knew as well that almost all had heard his story. Yet he knew, as his father had told him—and as his father's father had done— that a young boy would not learn unless he was taught. He would not know how to act unless shown, and a young boy needed constant teaching.

He turned toward Erik. "We are blessed by the Great Mystery that Sky Eyes has come to us. We will not forget that he gives to us all he has. We will not forget that Sky Eyes has already shown us how a true brother should be."

Erik felt his cheeks flush, and he cast his eyes down. For Gray Owl to praise him before the others was an honor. He looked quietly at the small fire.

"We seek a vision to seek our helpers for life and to continue to seek the Great Mystery's help and blessings for all the people. This is what I was taught as a boy, and this is what I will teach you." Gray Owl looked in turn into the eyes of each boy. Each slightly bowed in return, acknowledging Gray Owl.

"My journey was in the star-grass moon after the snow spirits returned to the north and after the people returned to the summer hunting places," he spoke softly, waving his weathered hands toward the north and then back. "The one who remembered took me to a sacred place, the place to which he had been before my time. He took my clothes and painted my body white. He gave me sweet sages to burn. He made me pure for the Great Mystery. Then he told me to seek a high place, stand before the Great Mystery, and pray.

"And so I did—farther and higher than I thought possible," he said, spreading his hands upward and gazing upward. "There I sat alone, praying continuously that I might have a vision.

"I did, but not on my first night." He shook his head. "And not on my second ... It was late on the third day. I had all but given up hope—that the Great Mystery did not find me worthy.

"But then an owl came to me from out of the setting sun." He cupped his hand, the sign for the sun, and turned it over. "He flapped to the ground and came up to me.

"He told me, 'Chipmunk,' for that was my boyhood name, 'I have come to you. You will see many things. Some you can help. Some you cannot help,'" Gray Owl said, opening his hands outward, pushing them away, and then cupping them toward his chest.

He stirred the fire, causing it to flare up brightly, casting his shadow against the lodge.

"The owl did a dance on the rock. He went three times in the direction of the sun. Then he went three times backward," he said, mimicking the dance with his fingers. "All the time he said my name, 'Chipmunk, Chipmunk, Chipmunk.'

"Suddenly a great snake fell from the sky and hissed at my feet." He replicated the writhing form of a snake with his fingers. "It looked at me and then made a great circle in the direction of the sun and then a great circle against the sun." He waved his arms to mimic the circle. "It rose up and bit my foot then turned to bite the owl. But the owl was too fast for the snake, and it flew up into the sun," he said, waving his fingers, like a flying bird, up and up. "Then coming back, the owl grabbed the snake in its great feet, and it flew away back to the sun."

Gray Owl picked up some sage, broke pieces, and dropped them into the coals. As the smoke rose, he grasped each boy, in turn, by his shoulders and gently pulled him near the smoke. With his other hand, he fanned the smoke, spreading it about the boy's head and shoulders.

"When I returned to the Twisted River Band, the one who remembered brought me to the one who healed. He took the sting from the bite on my foot and then told me about my vision. Some of that I can say to you. Some of it, I cannot. Part of the vision meant I would lead the Twisted River Band to the canyon and the meadows for three seasons. Part meant that my helper would be the owl, the most sacred of all birds. And so I received my name, Gray Owl.

"'The snake was danger,' the one who remembered told me. 'As I took the Twisted River Band to the canyon and to the meadows, it would follow. Sometimes it would strike at the people, but sometimes it would not. In the end, the owl would overcome the snake. That is what I see this day,' the one who remembered said." Gray Owl tossed the stick with which he was tending the fire into the flames.

"I learned other things as well about myself and the Maker." He sat back, closing his eyes as if remembering. Suddenly, he snapped back, alert.

He turned to Raven. "Raven, in a few days you will seek your vision." He turned to the others, spreading his hands. "Soon you shall all go ... Some of you may not succeed. Each of you should pray to the Great Mystery now and each day for success. Listen to your watchers each day. Your watcher will help prepare you.

"Now that is all for this night."

Quietly, Erik and the others rose and, one by one, left the lodge.

CHAPTER 28

IT WAS DECIDED THAT only Raven would make his vision journey. Some argued that Coyote and Weasel should also attempt theirs. Others argued that they should not. They had observed Raven during the summer hunting camp. He had grown taller and stronger; he had grown apart from the other boys. Coyote and Weasel, closest to Raven's age, didn't demonstrate the same strength or skill. Raven often hunted with Runs Fast. Together, they had brought back a fine black bear.

Young boys ran through the camp, calling everyone to gather near the center fire.

Free Hawk prayed for the Great Mystery to protect Raven and find him worthy.

His father, Whistling Elk, also said a prayer for his son.

The people thrummed and cheered as the men led him away to take his sweat bath and to prepare. From there, they would take him far into the mountains to begin his quest.

***

Late the next day, Raven's escorts returned. Later, the last men, the chasers, also returned. They had not caught nor even seen Raven. The people were in good spirits. Another boy would soon return to them a young man.

The day was warm and sultry. Erik and Badger decided to hunt the high meadows to see if they could find a badger den. They headed in the direction Raven had gone.

"The white-star flowers bloom, Sky Eyes," observed Badger. He gestured to the clumps of bear grass sporting tall spikes of flowers scattered among the alpine fir.

Erik thought the clumps slightly resembled the yucca he had seen coming across the desert, but the grass blades were more slender and fell in large, stiff mounds. In the center rose one or two tall spikes, reaching to two feet, supporting tight clusters of creamy white flowers. He examined one—each flower was a tiny trumpet. Thousands of tiny trumpets composed the large globe that ended in a central protruding tip of unopened buds.

"They look like a woman's breasts," Erik replied, mimicking, cupping his breasts.

"Maybe a white woman's breasts," Badger laughed.

"Are they useful?"

"The people use the grass to make small baskets," replied Badger. "Elk eat the blossoms."

"Then we should go to where they bloom to find elk."

"But they grow everywhere. You'll see." Then Badger signed and added, "You should know this. The grass is dangerous to step on when you're on a hill. Like a wet log, it will take your legs out from under you."

Erik remembered slipping on the clumps of bear grass scattered in the canyon when he and his father had been hunting. Without blossoms, he had mistaken it for common grass.

Now breathtaking, the white globes—bobbing, white ghosts—peeked out from among the dark trees.

They entered a dry basin with short, bright green grass clumps growing around its dusty edges—a good place for badgers. Beyond were the rugged peaks toward which Raven journeyed.

"Raven should have success," Erik signed and said. "The weather is good. The chasers did not find him."

"The chasers only catch lazy boys," Badger replied. "All boys know this is a test, but if you show you can hide and be strong, they will let you succeed, even if they could catch you."

Erik wondered about this. He had heard the stories—how the chasers were to test each boy. If the boy wasn't ready, the chasers would catch him and not allow him to seek a vision. Gray Owl stressed it was important to be strong before a boy was allowed to try for a vision.

"I hope Raven has a vision," Erik added. "Gray Owl says sometimes a boy doesn't have one."

"This is true. I remember one. The one who saw the falling star, he didn't have a vision. He was son to Stands Alone, older brother to Quickly Smiles. The chasers found him. Before he tried again, the night cat took him.

"Three seasons ago, Runs Fast went on his journey," Badger continued. "Before that, I don't remember any who sought visions."

"There should have been two vision seekers this season," Erik said quietly. "The one who hunts the elk should have gone. He surely would have come back a true man."

Badger looked away. He couldn't think of Otter. He wondered about the ways of the Great Mystery. Now Sky Eyes had come to live with him. He was a good brother, but he wasn't the one who hunts the elk. "We all know the one who hunts the elk would have gone," Badger signed and said. "But the Great Mystery did not think so. Now he watches from the sky trails. Perhaps his spirit will go with Raven."

Erik thought about what Badger said. Everything the Sheepeaters said, every moment of their lives centered on their beliefs in the Great Mystery and the spirits. Erik hadn't talked to God much since his parents died. "Do you really believe the spirit of the one who hunts the elk is with Raven?" Erik tried to sign and say—there was no Sheepeater word for the concept. Spirits existed. There was no word that suggested they could or could not.

Badger nodded. "His spirit is where it wishes to be."

Erik wanted to ask about the angel, perhaps a spirit, he had seen in the woods. "Have you ever seen spirits?"

"No, but I see the work they do, always," Badger signed and said, somewhat confused. He wondered why Sky Eyes would ask such questions. The spirits revealed themselves only when they wanted.

Often they simply left signs. "Only a few times do the people *see* the spirits. But always the spirits tell you when they are near."

Erik thought about telling Badger about the angel, but the memories were too personal. Erik had told Badger his father had died, but he never explained how. Always he felt responsible—he didn't listen to the angel's warning.

***

The boys searched the basin but found no sign of badgers. They found several marmot mounds and dens but decided not to hunt them.

The sun now beat down, and the air was dead, interrupted only by brief gusts. The clouds built rapidly above. Already they could see lightning over the peaks to the north and hear the muted thunder.

"Raven must be in the rain," observed Erik, signing.

"I am sure he has found a safe place," replied Badger.

The clouds soon drifted overhead, blocking the sun.

"The clouds come, Sky Eyes," said Badger. "We should also seek a safe place. We are too near the cloud spirits."

Erik eyed the advancing thunderheads. Lightning flashed across the sky.

"They can see us in this open area," continued Badger. "Perhaps one is angry with us or our parents and will send his anger at us."

They broke into a jog. A brilliant flash and explosion jolted them. Instinctively, they ducked as the crackling reverberated from the surrounding rocks. Large, heavy raindrops began to spatter. They continued to trot toward camp until the clouds opened and the rain, mixed with hail, hammered down, soaking them to their skin. They found shelter under dense trees and sat shivering, waiting for the storm to pass.

When it eased, they continued toward camp. The people had taken the hides and food that had been out to dry into their lodges and had secured them. Rain now hammered down on the lodges, breaking into spray on the poles and brush, running in rivulets across the matted ground.

Erik and Badger squeezed through the flap into their lodge, shaking off the rain. Shining Water was sewing and Singing Bird played with a rattle. Shining Water looked up and acknowledged their return.

Free Hawk was seated, working on an arrow. "Ah, so a little summer rain brings the brave hunters home?"

Badger shrugged. "We were near home, Father. We did not find a badger den, and being it was the heat of day, we were done hunting."

Free Hawk nodded. "Then you shall work on arrows?"

"That would be good, Father." Badger pulled their personal bundles down and handed Erik's to him. Carefully Badger unwrapped his and began work where he had left off—smoothing and fitting the short shafts together as Whistling Elk had demonstrated. He found himself wishing his lost brother had been with Raven on this journey. Outside, the rain thundered down. Occasionally a flash of lightning and a crack of thunder caused him to flinch.

***

In the early morning, faint smoke drifted into camp through a washed, blue sky. The younger boys watched for Raven's return, each anxious to be first to spot him. Instead they spotted two smoke columns to the north. By midmorning, the smoke thickened to a pungent odor. Some of the people worried that a fire could threaten their lodges. Several hunters left camp to check on the fires' locations.

Erik and Badger chose to climb the peak to the north so they could also see the fires. As they climbed, the smoke columns grew. The largest column tripled in size, and the second doubled. They could also now make out two other thin streamers farther west.

It took until midday to reach the highest point. The top was flat, about ten feet by ten feet, composed of loose and broken granite fragments. It afforded an unrestricted view in all directions. The wind kicked at them.

The view took Erik's breath. In all directions lay mountain peaks, and beyond them, more peaks, and more, separated by dark-shadowed canyons. Most peaks cradled snow banks and small lakes. He looked to the southeast, trying to pick out where the cabin was. Peaks blocked his view. The prairie was also far beyond his sight. He felt some sadness. The cabin was a terribly far distance away.

White, puffy clouds spotted the horizon to the west and east. Heavier clouds, billowing tops of yellow and orange, appeared to the north. From time to time, flashes of lightning split their heavy black bottoms. The low rumble of thunder followed long moments afterward.

"There, Sky Eyes, you can see the fires." Badger pointed to the northeast. Two large columns of billowing, gray white smoke rose into the sky. The largest was clearly west of the river. The second largest was in the canyon below their sight, blocked by the rim. Two smaller columns were visible to the west and were on their side of the river.

Erik pointed toward the smaller fires. "If those grow, Badger, they might reach our lodges."

"Perhaps, Sky Eyes," Badger agreed. "We shall tell Gray Owl about them. They will probably not get large, however. Most fires don't."

Mesmerized, they sat and watched. The largest fire ate its way rapidly up the mountains across the canyon. A thin line of flickering orange snaked from the canyon bottom across the flanks of three ridges, making a sweeping arc toward the tree-covered rim. They watched as the flickering line advanced uphill. In minutes, the flames reached the rim, sending towering, bright orange tongues into the sky.

The fire cloud was a writhing, living thing. The brown-stained white and yellow mushrooming tops roiled and churned. White smoke erupted from near the base and leapfrogged its way up the column edge. Nearing the top, it turned from bright white to yellow, then to orange brown.

"Green timber must create the white smoke," suggested Erik.

Badger nodded. "Yes. The green timber has water."

The wind shifted toward them, bringing the acrid taste and smell of smoke. Bits of ash rained down. Erik became nervous. Hot ash could ignite other fires. He touched the ash and was relieved to find it was cold.

"I don't think the fires will reach the star-grass meadows," said Badger. "Even the two near ones will burn out when they reach the rim. They won't burn across the meadows."

"Probably there is too much water."

"Fires eat their way up hills very fast," observed Badger. "Even animals cannot outrun them. But they crawl their way down. All animals can outrun them."

Erik watched as the largest fire slowed, and its flames quieted. He figured it might burn slowly across the broken meadows, but when it reached the snowy peaks, it would die.

"I hope Raven remembers," Erik said, signing.

"All Tukudeka know this," Badger replied.

***

The fourth day came. Eagerly the young boys watched for Raven. The fires to the north continued to grow, casting their summer hunting camp into orange shadows. Smoke filled the air, stinging the eyes. Ash rained down. The elders decided to move the camp to get out of the smoke. They headed farther east. They didn't worry that Raven wouldn't find them. Anyone could follow a camp trail. The people became concerned, however. Raven hadn't returned.

***

By noon the fifth day, Raven had still not returned. Now some of the women began the soft wailing for a person lost. Four hunters departed camp. They would attempt to find him. Erik and Badger feared for Raven.

***

On the seventh day, the men returned. They had been to where the fires burned. There had been no birds to show where a body might be. There was no sign of Raven. The women wailed. Surely the boy who killed the bear now walked the sky trails.

Erik was cutting alder shoots for rabbit arrows with Badger when he heard the news. He found it difficult to comprehend what had happened. What should have been a proud and happy moment was now sadness. He glanced at Badger, wanting to speak of this, but

174

this was not something of which the people spoke. Badger had lost his brother, and now Chipmunk had lost his. Erik felt sadness for Chipmunk.

Feeling empty, Erik half-heartedly finished stripping the shoots of their leaves. He wondered if he had the strength to succeed on his own vision journey next season. It was expected he would go. Coyote and Weasel would also surely go. He decided it best to put it out of his mind.

He motioned to Badger to take the shoots and, then alone, wandered to a small meadow were he sat looking out at the mountain peaks in the direction of his cabin. He thought of his parents. He wondered if it would have been better for him to die and for them to live. He tried to imagine how Whistling Elk and Moccasin Woman felt. He wondered how Chipmunk felt. Raven was gone.

He wondered again about God. Why did he allow his mother and father to die? *I did my best. My prayers—nothing—kept Papa from dying. And there was nothing Porcupine Woman or I could do to heal Mama once she gave up. How could you allow this, God? And yet, you sent your angel to lead me, and I lived. Why?*

He wondered about Katrine. Maybe she made it with the Olafsons to the mountain valley they wanted to farm. Maybe he would learn a way to leave the Sheepeaters and go to find her.

He suddenly felt terribly alone. They had traveled a long distance from their winter camp on River That Cries. He had looked for the way back to the cabin from the mountain peak. Even if he had the chance, he did not know for sure in which direction to go. An ache welled within him.

Chapter 29

The nights now had a nip. Sometimes frost covered the auburn and tan meadow grasses. Steam rose from the ponds in the mornings. Throughout the mountains, the aspens turned gold and leaves fluttered down. Soon the people would return to the canyons for winter.

Erik recognized this as the time he and his parents had arrived the valley where they had built their cabin. He tried not to think of those times, but he couldn't help it. He turned fourteen. He thought of the knife his father had given him for his last birthday. Now it was Sees Far's. He touched his father's knife. He was pleased to have it.

The men prepared to hunt elk. The people prized their meat and thick hides, which made the best winter robes and blankets. However, the people took but a few. They were uncommon and spooked easily—running great distances, far faster and farther than man. Erik recalled the Sheepeaters' joy when he shared killing the one last winter. Thus far, the hunters had only seen a cow and her calf.

Sees Far decided now was the proper time to teach Badger and Sky Eyes about making arrow points. A man needed strength and control in his hands before attempting this craft. Sees Far had collected several pieces of jasper from near the paint pots and had saved a large piece of jasper for this day. Now he retrieved it and called to the boys.

He took them to the area under the pines where he often worked. Chips of red and brown jasper lay scattered about.

"See," explained Sees Far, "the best shards are found in the heart of the stone. Large, sharp pieces come from its heart." He held the chunk of jasper on his lap and, taking a rounded cobble, struck the core near its edge. The blow sent a tapered sliver of bright red jasper splintering off. Quickly he struck off another and then another. Each shard, about two inches long, already resembled a sharp-edged arrow point.

He offered the core to Badger. At first, Badger had no success. Either he hit the core too close to the edge, pulverizing it into tiny bits, or he hit too much toward the center, bouncing the cobble off. Finally, he succeeded in striking off a good shard.

Sees Far handed the stone to Erik. Erik also troubled with the stone but was pleased when he finally stuck off a shard.

"Good. You now have shards from which to work."

Sees Far laid a thick piece of leather across his thigh and picked up the tip of a deer antler. He held the shard against the leather. "Push the horn tip against the edge to flake away small pieces from the underneath." Sees Far pressed the antler into the stone, making a clicking noise as it chipped the stone. Small slivers sheared off the underside and spilled to the ground. Clicking rapidly, he pressed off flakes. He slightly turned the jasper to expose fresh surface, and pressed off more flakes. "See, the slivers come from the bottom."

He turned the shard over. "After going around and shaping, do the other side."

The boys mimicked Sees Far.

After several tries, Erik was amazed when he successfully struck off his first sliver of jasper. Almost like magic, a small piece broke away. He pressed and clicked again; another sliver split away. They were not long like those Sees Far produced, but they were slivers nevertheless.

Sees Far watched the boys' progress. He knew only through practice could they find the point buried inside the stone and make it reveal itself. He resumed work, rapidly flaking and shaping his arrow point. Occasionally he took another stone and knocked it across the point, further refining its shape. "Every Tukudeka must know how to make arrow points," he said. "If he were ever lost, a knife or arrow point could save his life." He told about the Sheepeater who fashioned a bow

177

and arrows while on his vision seeking and brought meat back to feed the people. Badger, of course, knew he spoke of Free Hawk.

Sees Far finished several points before either Badger or Erik had fashioned a single one.

Indeed Erik broke the notch from his just as he neared finishing it.

Sees Far laughed gently. "It is not completely lost, Sky Eyes. Shining Water may be able to use it as a rabbit scraper."

Erik turned the piece in his hand. Even with the broken end, he was proud of what he had accomplished. He looked forward to using obsidian.

***

Wisps of steam lifted from the pond the following morning while Erik and Badger bathed. The water was frigid. They stood for a moment, shivering in the sun, and said a prayer. Neither Sees Far nor Whistling Elk had indicated they wanted the two boys that day.

"We should go to the high places and try to find a shaggy-neck elk," suggested Badger.

"That is far to go," signed and replied Erik. "I don't think Free Hawk will allow us."

"It would be two days," continued Badger. "But that's where the shaggy-neck elk are. If we could find a shaggy-neck, the people would be pleased and would make a song for us."

"That would be good," agreed Erik.

They ran back to the lodge to ask.

At length, Free Hawk spoke. "A night away is good training, but it's unlikely you can travel far enough to find a place the hunters have not already searched.

"Yes, you should go. But take a robe, each of you. The night will be cold. You are not yet on your vision journeys."

"We will have fire," Erik said, knowing he could always start a fire with his flint and steel.

"That would be good," agreed Free Hawk who then added, "Be watchful for the night cat. He is always where the deer and elk are. Take good arrows and watch your trail behind."

They decided to head northeast toward an area the hunters hadn't tried much. And instead of directly climbing upward, they angled across the ridges so they could check out the draws between and see more country.

All day they crossed the gentle ridges of aspen and fir. As they topped each ridge and entered each valley below, they searched for sign. They encountered fresh bear sign—scraped trees and scat—and saw some mule deer, but they saw no elk sign.

By evening, they came out onto a small lake nestled in the arms of a mountain peak. A few scraggly trees grew above and around the flanks of the lake, but the peak itself was rocky and barren. They had reached timberline. The elk wouldn't be above timberline.

The late afternoon sun lit the peak as if it were on fire. Its stark beauty reflected perfectly from the crystal waters. Erik whistled softly and signed, "Look, Badger, it looks like gold." Only he didn't know the word for gold, so he used the Swedish word, *guld*.

They paused to rest and sat a moment on the white granite boulders overlooking the water. The scrubbed lake bottom was sharply visible. A small stream ran from the end and disappeared below them into a deepening valley, thick with black spruce and golden aspens. Near the trees, they could see the torn up mud where the elk had wallowed, and now they caught their musky odor on the evening breeze.

Badger whispered, "Sky Eyes, we have found the elk."

"Yes, I see too," Erik replied. "We should stay here tonight and search for them in the morning."

Quickly, they moved to the sheltered side of the lake where the elk wouldn't hear or smell them, where the sun would first touch in the morning, and where the rock cliffs would ward off the cold wind.

Clumps of bear grass grew thickly. The flower stalks had died and now rustled with small seedpods. Figuring they would burn easily, Erik gathered some along with dry twigs and weathered grass. Building a nest, he took the flint and steel and struck a spark into it. Quickly he blew the spark into a tiny flame. Adding the twigs, the fire grew into a warm, comforting blaze.

After some pemmican, Erik and Badger rolled out their robes next to the rocks. They sat watching the fire. It reflected warm against them.

Erik watched the flames lick across the aspens. He felt a comforting peace, almost as if his angel had returned. He glanced around, half expecting to see it. He felt his eyes mist as he realized his angel's significance. *I'm alive because of my angel.* An ache rose in his throat and he choked back a quick sob. *I'm sorry, Lord. I was wrong to doubt you. There are many things I don't understand, but as sure as I'm sitting here, you sent me the angel. You protected me.* He glanced at Badger. He also seemed lost in thought. Erik knew the Sheepeaters didn't understand many things either, but they accepted them as truth. They didn't have a word for belief. They accepted the Great Mystery without question. There was no doubt as to his existence or that of the spirits. In some ways, Erik envied Badger's faith.

Impulsively, he stood. "You and I pray to the Great Mystery in the morning after we bathe," Erik signed and said. "I am accustomed to praying to the Great Mystery each night as well. I do it quietly to myself. My people call the Great Mystery, God."

Looking puzzled, Badger frowned slightly.

"I am thankful for this day, and so I would like to offer a prayer this night to the Great Mystery," Erik explained. He stood and faced the fading light to the west.

"Here we are, Great Mystery, as you created us. We have good thoughts to you. We thank you for this day, for our lives ... for being brothers. Let us use our lives for the people.

"We also thank you for this lake and the mountains. In the morning, we ask you to help us find the elk. Amen."

Badger questioned, "Amen?"

Erik laughed. "That's how we end a prayer."

"I think your prayer is a good prayer, Sky Eyes," Badger signed and replied. "I think the Great Mystery will listen to you."

They curled in their robes to sleep; their clothing was their pillows. It was not good to wear clothes to sleep. They would grow smelly and wear out too fast.

***

Erik woke instantly to the scream. Cold fear crawled down his back; he felt his scalp prickle. The scream was a distance away, but Erik knew it was a mountain lion.

Badger scrambled for his bow. "Night cat," he whispered harshly.

Erik sensed the fear in Badger's voice. He knew the Sheepeaters feared the mountain lion, as did he.

Their fire had died. "*Snälla, gode Gud.* Please, dear God," Erik said, scrambling from his robe. "Let there be live coals." He patted around with his hands, fumbling, until he found the dry twigs he had stacked. He tossed them onto the warm ashes.

The scream pierced the night again, this time seemingly from above them.

"He knows we're here," Erik said again in Swedish, feeling the chill wash over him, as he remembered the attack at the cabin. Thoughts of Red flashed through his memories.

Badger crouched, peering into the darkness, bow held ready, notched with an arrow.

On hands and knees, feeling that any second the mountain lion would be on his back, Erik puffed on the coals. Smoke rose. Shaking, he pulled dry tufts of grass and tossed them on. Stars brilliantly studded the sky, but there was no moonlight. *Perfect cover for a mountain lion*, Erik realized.

He blew again. The grass caught and blazed into a brilliant yellow light. "*Aishenda'qa, Pia-mukua*," he whispered. He realized that he had used the Sheepeater words for Great Mystery.

Soon the light danced off them, sitting huddled, backs against the rock. Erik threw on more wood and tried to laugh. "They don't like fire," he said. "Too bad. I bet we looked like an easy meal to him."

"I would have had him," Badger finally spoke. He still firmly held his bow, notched with an arrow.

"I know you would have, Badger."

"Sees Far says the night cat does not scream when it hunts," Badger signed and said. "He speaks truth, but it is hard to think the night cat does not hunt you when you hear his scream."

"Why does the night cat scream?"

"Like all animals that seek a mate, sometimes they become angry at one another and wish to fight. There are probably two night cats."

Erik felt his skin crawl again. He remembered the two at the cabin but one, he was certain, was a yearling. "Then I am glad we have a fire."

Neither Erik nor Badger slept. Neither wanted to admit his fear of the mountain lion, but it was an animal to fear. At last, as the gray light crept into the sky, they fell asleep.

***

Erik found himself back at the star-grass meadows. The sun was warm, and he and Badger were at the bathing place. Quickly Smiles bathed alone. She saw Erik, but instead of turning away and casting down her eyes, she smiled at him. Slowly she stood, water streaming from her beautiful body. Erik realized this was a sign that he was allowed to court her. He approached, feeling an excitement storming through him. She reached to touch him. The feeling that gathered within his middle, sharpened.

"Sky Eyes." Badger shook him. "The sun is up and warm."

Erik woke, the feeling and dream interrupted. Suddenly embarrassed, he checked to see that his robe covered him.

"Come on, I have to make water." Badger moved to the side.

Erik couldn't move. He couldn't let Badger see. He knew what caused the feeling. He tried to dress before Badger returned.

Badger stopped up short. "You are silly, Sky Eyes," he said, "to worry about that."

Erik understood partially. He wanted to talk, but didn't know how.

Badger dressed. "Come on, let us look for elk."

***

Beyond the first line of trees, below the lake, they reached the wallow: a small meadow of scattered clumps of bear grass. Several areas were trampled into shallow muddy bowls where the elk rolled to cool off or to relieve themselves of insects. A herd of five cows was bedded down around the edge, near the timber.

As they watched, a bull bugled, startling them. Moments later, it wandered out of the timber on the far side, bugled again, and crossed the wallow toward the cows.

Erik turned to Badger, signing, making a motion to notch an arrow.

Badger shook his head and signed, *Our bows are not strong.* He began to back away slowly.

Erik followed, careful not to catch a twig.

Safely away, they burst out into excited whispers.

"Did you see the shaggy-neck elk?" exclaimed Erik. "It was huge!"

"Maybe if a hunter gets it, he will make a horn bow."

"We must come back with the men when they hunt the elk," insisted Erik, excitedly.

"If only we had curved-horn bows, Sky Eyes, we could have taken that shaggy-neck elk." Badger frowned and waved his chokecherry bow. "I will be glad when I get one.

"Come. We must hurry to tell the hunters," he said and broke into a jog.

"Perhaps you're right, Badger," said Erik, laughing as he suddenly remembered what Badger had said yesterday. "Perhaps the people *will* make a song about us."

CHAPTER 30

THE SNOW RETURNED TO the high country, and the Twisted River Band began its journey back to the canyons. They headed north, crossing the peaks where Raven had gone and where the lightning had started the fires. They dropped down onto Bird Calls Creek and followed it to Thunder Noise River, which they followed for two more days until they reached the mouth of Twisted River.

There the people paused briefly to celebrate and give thanks. This was the river from which they took their name and by which other Sheepeaters knew them.

Crossing, they headed west upstream for a day, now along familiar trails, trails bordered by sheer cliffs, until they came to a place where the canyon broadened and a small stream entered. They had reached the winter camp, the camp of their grandfathers. They gathered at the painted rocks while the winter fire was kindled.

Gray Owl rose and gestured to the sky. "It is time to give thanks to the Great Mystery. The hunts have been good. The hunters killed two shaggy-neck elk from the herd that Sky Eyes and Badger found. They brought back much sinew, bones, and fine hides.

"The gathering was also good. The women and dogs could almost not carry all the star-grass bulbs and pemmican.

"Most importantly, we should be thankful for our five good hunters and four young men who will soon become true men." He paused as the people murmured their approval.

"But there is sadness as well. The one who hunts the elk walks the sky trails, and the boy who would be a man and killed a bear also walks the sky trails. A strange white boy has come to live with us, the one we call Sky Eyes. He swam in the river like the otter and pulled Badger from it. But Fighting Bear took the white boy's horse and went to live with the Lemhis."

The people murmured and some softly wailed.

"Stands Alone and I have decided. Sees Far shall mark the season by remembering the boy with eyes of sky and those who have gone to walk the sky trails."

Sees Far began painting. He painted Sky Eyes on the memory rock. Then he began painting the spirits of the one who hunts the elk and the one who killed a bear.

Runs Fast was not pleased. As Sees Far painted he turned and complained to Black Legs.

"Why do they count a memory for the little white boy? I killed the bear along with the boy who was lost. The elders should have considered that worthy."

Black Legs shrugged.

"And Gray Owl should have said *six* hunters to be thankful for." Runs Fast scowled. "I have completed my vision seeking, and I bring meat to the camp."

Black Legs adjusted his robe. "Perhaps it's because you were at the river when Badger fell in."

"Yes. The little white boy foolishly jumped in after him," Runs Fast admitted. "Stands Alone told me it was my fault. I didn't stop Quick Marten, and I didn't reach out my pole to Badger."

Black Legs nodded. He knew what the people had seen.

"That is not truth. I am not watcher for Quick Marten, and I would have pulled Badger out, but the little white boy got in my way." Runs Fast glowered, then spoke icily. "I do not think the little white boy is good. I think he brings bad medicine."

Black Legs raised his eyes.

"It is because of him my father leaves the Twisted River Band and the boy who killed a bear walks the sky trails." Runs Fast lowered his voice. "I think he brings a bad spirit." He spat as if he had a bad taste. "I say, Black Legs. We should watch out for the little white boy."

"I think you think too much, Runs Fast," replied Black Legs, trying to laugh. "If you think a bad spirit is with him, you should tell this to Gray Owl."

Runs Fast didn't laugh. "Perhaps you are correct. I should speak to Gray Owl."

"Come, I shall have White Deer prepare you something to eat. We will go hunting later. The people will see you're a good hunter."

***

It was always good to return to the winter camps, especially to the camp of the grandfathers on Twisted River. This was the best of all their winter camps.

This winter, the Big Sheep Band wintered downstream from the Twisted River Band. Sees Far was pleased, for he could visit with his son, Gray Knife, and his young family.

Upstream, hot springs bubbled, scalding from the riverbank. Here the people soaked animal horns to soften them. They then shaped and straightened the horns, fashioning them into bows, bowls, or even snowshoes.

Sometimes elk came near this camp when the snow pushed them out of the high country. One grassy hill above the camp was a place the people called the hill where the bulls come. There the bulls shed their antlers. The people gathered them and made them into ladles or bows or used them to chip points.

Many mountain sheep came to the cliffs above this winter camp and to the areas east, near to where Twisted River entered Thunder Noise River. The sheep seemed to prefer the rockier exposed slopes that were mostly free of snow.

On the south side, the mule deer also came. They didn't live among the elk, for the elk could reach high for the food where they could not. On the south side, the deer had thick browse and cover.

Although this was their favored winter camp, the Sheepeaters knew it couldn't be used every season, for if it were, it would be hard on the land. Soon the animals would not come, and the people would starve. There would be no wood for the lodges or for the fires. Even the lodge areas would become dirty and smelly from the people. It was good to go to other winter camps, but their hearts were especially glad to see the familiar canyon of Twisted River.

***

The days were yet warm in the canyon bottom. Broken by afternoon storms, some cold, the weather warmed soon afterward. Erik enjoyed the warm days, because once more, he could swim the river. The water had not yet cooled. He was having some luck teaching Badger to use his arms in more than just a dogpaddle. The two boys had gained some respect from the other boys as well. They showed they did not fear the water spirits. They swam and played in the moving water where the water spirits lived.

***

That day Erik and Badger decided to visit the cave where the grandfathers had marked the winter counts and left messages for other Sheepeaters. They decided they would make their own marks on the rocks.

Climbing to the cliff face, they walked along its bottom until they reached a small shelter cave into which they could hardly squeeze. They had brought tallow, charcoal, and some of the red clay from the paint pots.

Badger mixed the clay into the tallow, then painted the red onto his hand. Carefully, he positioned his hand on the wall and pressed hard. He left a clear print of his palm, fingers, and thumb. "There. I have placed some of my spirit on this wall so all will know that Badger has been here and is part of this place."

Erik followed in a like manner, placing his print to the left on the open wall. "There is my spirit as well," he said.

Badger mixed the black paint. Impulsively, Erik dipped his fingers into it and below his handprint, carefully wrote, "Himmel Öga."

"What is that?" asked Badger.

"These are picture words for my name, 'Sky Eyes.'"

"That doesn't look like 'Sky Eyes.'"

He reached over and wrote below Badger's print, "Grävling." "And that says 'Badger,'" Erik said.

"No," Badger insisted. "Your picture words don't say 'Sky Eyes' or 'Badger.'" Emphatically he signed as he spoke.

Erik studied Badger's serious expression and couldn't hold back his laughter.

Badger grew indignant. "But they don't." He said and signed even more strongly in case Sky Eyes didn't understand.

Erik replied, still laughing, "In my picture words, that's what they mean."

"Quit it, Sky Eyes." Badger pushed him backward down the slope, then tackled and wrestled him in the sandy soil until he sat astride, pinning his arms.

Erik gazed up. "They are different word pictures," he tried to explain but couldn't without also signing.

He pushed himself up and carefully signed and explained. "Different pictures mean the same thing. A white boy who can read my picture words would know they say 'Sky Eyes' and 'Badger.'"

To clarify, he climbed back to the shelter cave. Carefully he painted a black badger below Badger's name. Only Erik didn't paint a stick figure. He painted a close likeness of a badger with bandit eyes, large claws, rounded bearlike ears, and narrow eyes—those he painted red.

"There, Badger, for you, a real one," he said.

Astonished, Badger stared. No one painted the real animal. Sky Eyes had done magic. Quietly he said, "Sky Eyes, this badger ... Truly, you have captured its spirit."

Badger drew an arrow from Erik's quiver and one from his. These he bound with a strip of leather. "Two brothers," he signed and said, "share one life." He placed them well back, directly below the prints.

They sat for a moment in the lazy warmth of the cliffs. Below them the river ran sparkling in the long shadows, cool, green, and deep. Sparks of light, created by the sun catching the buzzing insects, darted in and out of the shadows, sometimes dropping down to touch the dark waters. Erik wanted the moment to last. He felt peace.

CHAPTER 31

Now in great numbers, the salmon returned to Twisted River. More came each day—well into the fattening-animal moon—until their rosy sides turned the river crimson. Erik and Badger had to chase the salmon out of the way to go swimming.

Twisted River was a smaller stream than River That Cries, and the men constructed willow and rock weirs around a few places, forcing the salmon to swim through narrow gaps. Many fish crowding against the narrow areas didn't wait. Impatient to move upstream, they hurled themselves over.

The Sheepeaters lined the narrow gaps with their snagging poles and snared the salmon crowding through. They hauled the flopping fish to the bank where the women and girls waited to kill and prepare them for drying. Just as soon as one man brought a fish to shore and returned to the gaps, the next man carried another to shore.

Erik and Badger took their own positions on a rock near a swift chute of water and tried to snag salmon coming through. Whenever one caught a fish, the other helped him haul it to the bank. Many weighed thirty pounds; some weighed more.

Erik's arms ached from hauling the struggling fish to the bank. But he was happy. At least in this way, he helped his family.

The men erected willow frames for drying and smoking the salmon. The women cleaned and split the salmon lengthwise to their tails and then hung them over the thin willows, head end down, to cure. Since Erik was fishing, he loaned his knife to Shining Water who was most pleased and proud. The other women used stone blades. The children kept watch over the drying fish and swatted the flies to keep them from laying eggs that would hatch into maggots. They also built smudgy fires under many of the racks. This helped keep the flies away as well as helped impart a nice flavor to the salmon.

The people kept at a feverish pace for several days until drying salmon hung everywhere. The camp took on an eerie orange appearance from the hanging carcasses. Erik thought the racks looked like clotheslines draped with bright orange-colored clothing. At first he liked the salmon smell, but as the camp filled with the odor of smoke and drying fish, he grew to dislike it. Outside his own lodge, Free Hawk and Shining Water had two racks of drying salmon.

The run continued long after the people had harvested all the fish they wanted.

In the quiet, Erik and Badger returned to the river to watch the spawning salmon. Erik was mystified by their single-minded intent to spawn.

They watched a female in the shallows vibrating her tail and stirring up the gravel. The fish flicked up small bits, which the current carried away downstream, eventually forming a depression.

A male hovered nearby. Another male encroached on the redd, and the male dashed at it, sending a wake of water off behind him.

"The males fight to drive off the others until the female is ready," explained Erik.

When the redd was complete, the female vibrated vigorously, releasing hundreds of bright reddish orange eggs above the shallow gravel nest. The eggs sank and bumped along the bottom, settling among the pebbles. The current picked up a few and carried them off.

"Now the male will spill its seed," observed Badger as the male quivered beside the female, releasing his milt in a white cloud over the eggs.

As the cloud cleared, Erik knew only some of the eggs would be fertilized. The fry that hatched in late winter would then drift downstream and grow into adult salmon. Those salmon that survived would return from the ocean in a few years to this same spot and spawn.

The female returned upstream and stirred up more gravel to be carried onto the eggs to cover and protect them. The eggs that weren't covered floated away where other salmon or trout destroyed or ate them.

"Now they will die," observed Badger, bluntly.

The two spawners grew listless and turned on their sides. No longer fighting to stay upright, the current carried them downstream. Other dead and dying salmon bumped past, floating downstream. Eagles lined the riverbanks below to feed on them.

"I'm glad that humans don't die after they try to make a child," Erik said softly. He couldn't imagine having one child and then dying, never being able to see his own child.

"I'm glad too, for I'd be dead," Badger replied, laughing.

Erik shook his head. He didn't understand.

"You are silly, Sky Eyes," Badger said, still laughing.

They watched a moment longer as the current swung a dying salmon into a quiet section of water and washed it up against the shore. Its gills slowly worked their last—its life's purpose complete.

As before, the young boys walked the banks and dragged the dead salmon back into the current so they wouldn't rot and stink up the river—at least not anymore than they already did.

CHAPTER 32

ERIK WOKE AND GAZED through the small gap in the ceiling at the thick, falling snow. Now that the heavy snows had come to the canyon, the people rarely left their lodges; they slept well into the mornings. Sometimes the people from the Big Sheep Band came to visit. Other times, people from the Twisted River Band went downstream to visit with them. But the days were quiet, signaled now by a hush, a silence.

Shining Water whispered to Singing Bird and rustled quietly about. Erik noted she had already started a small fire and that Free Hawk had left the lodge. Badger still slept, his furs a mound against the side of the lodge.

"Good morning, Mother," Erik greeted, sitting up. "Good morning, Singing Bird."

"Good morning, Sky Eyes," Shining Water replied. "We are all like mice in our winter nests. Not wanting to get up." She laughed softly.

Erik knew she would turn away while he stood and dressed. "Come on, Badger." He nudged him with his foot. "We should take a bath this morning."

Badger sat up. "No, Sky Eyes, it's too cold," he muttered, still partially asleep. "Look outside. It's snowing."

"All the better to go to the hot springs."

"But they smell."

"Then we shall bathe in the river." Erik laughed. "Which do you choose?"

"The river."

Waiting for Badger, Erik tossed a dry branch on the fire. He followed the smoke wisp to the top of the lodge where it collected momentarily, meandering around the bundles of drying arrow shafts before sifting through to the outside. Free Hawk, like Whistling Elk, was a well-respected craftsman. He had made many of the finest bows the men of the Twisted River Band owned, as well as many of the arrows.

"Where's Father?" asked Badger, pulling on his winter boots.

Shining Water pulled a parcel down from the ceiling. "Probably with Whistling Elk where you and Sky Eyes will go." She opened the hide and pulled out some dried camas cakes. "Why do you ask?"

"He works on the curved-horn bow. I want to watch."

"I think you watch too much." Shining Water built up the fire and set up the tripod holding the water bag. She rolled the round cooking stones into the fire and tossed the camas into the bag.

Erik knew Shining Water would serve them a meal about midmorning and then a second one in the evening. But like all the women, she always had a meal ready for visitors, no matter when they arrived.

She unwrapped some dried meat and began breaking it apart. "Perhaps some boys would go hunting and get their mother a fresh rabbit or squirrel for their meal?"

Erik realized she wouldn't ask them directly, but it was clear she was tired of dried meat, as was he. He figured the comment was more of a suggestion to him and Badger to go somewhere because no hunters would venture out when it was snowing.

Singing Bird crawled toward the fire. Erik picked her up and returned her to the far side of the lodge. "Little Singing Bird knows the fire is hot," he said. "Here." He found the doll he had made for her. "Show Sky Eyes what you can do with your doll."

Singing Bird's eyes lit up and she smiled. "Sleep." She made a rocking motion. "Feed." She drew the doll toward her breast.

Erik laughed. "Yes, Singing Bird. You will be a good mother." He patted her. Erik found he played with her a good deal and kept her from underfoot of Shining Water. He wondered if it was because he was inside the lodge more, but he also found himself thinking of Katrine.

"Come, Sky Eyes," interrupted Badger. "Let us bathe." He pushed aside the lodge cover and stepped out into the falling snow, his robe pulled about himself.

***

Later, Erik and Badger went to Sees Far's lodge to visit Weasel. Coyote was already there.

"When it snows all day, we have nothing to do," explained Badger. That was the polite way to ask to visit.

"We shall play a game of bones then," offered Weasel. "I will be the first shaker. You can bet against me."

Erik was pleased he remembered to leave his knife at home. Always when they played this game, Weasel tried to get him to bet his knife. Instead, he had brought some rabbit arrows and a few of the jasper points he had recently made.

Badger laid out his stone points with a worn stone knife and several rabbit arrows. Coyote was bolder. Along with several stone points, he produced a hunting arrow with an obsidian tip. Erik thought him foolish and remembered how the wives of the men who bet hides and weapons got angry when their husbands lost them.

"What is the bet?" asked Weasel, his eyes bright as he shook the bones.

Each of the boys threw a stone point into a pile on a piece of leather.

"Just a little point? You are frightened I will win? Where is your bravery?"

They shook their heads, refusing to be goaded into losing too much too soon.

Weasel threw the bones. Erik felt a quickening excitement. Two came up marked.

"Ah, you are lucky. No one wins." Weasel laughed. He gathered up the bones and began rattling them again. "Now you shall bet more?"

Nodding, Badger threw in another point.

Erik knew Weasel wouldn't likely throw the same hand twice, but he held back. He knew the game could last for hours, well into the night, and he had a better chance of winning when he was the shaker. He waved his hand.

"Ah, Sky Eyes is not brave?"

"No, I'm not," Erik replied, laughing.

"I am," Coyote said loudly, and he threw in a second point.

The bones came up with three marked.

"Ah, I win my pick!" exclaimed Weasel. Deftly, he picked up three points.

***

After the snow ended, the sun warmed the camp. Erik and Badger took to the trails to check for game. They passed Weasel and Coyote who were busily tramping out a long path in the snow.

Weasel greeted them. "After this night, we shall have a snow-snake track," he exclaimed. "Maybe Sky Eyes will be brave and bet his knife on his snow snake. He wouldn't bet on the bones."

Erik had no idea what he was talking about and turned toward Badger, frowning.

"Come on, Sky Eyes," he said. "I'll show you. We'll make a snow snake. But like when Weasel shakes the bones, I wouldn't bet against him."

Erik remembered their game. By late evening, Weasel had finally won Coyote's hunting arrow. Then, strangely, they had to leave the lodge. Sees Far's wives, Swift Swallow and Magpie, were tired of visitors, he had said.

Badger took him to a stand of alders where he finally selected a thick sapling and began cutting it, hacking it with his stone blade. Erik offered him his knife.

Badger grinned. "You're lucky to have a steel knife." Quickly he cut the sapling.

He cut another. "This one is for you."

They carried the alders back to the lodge, and Badger showed him how to make a "snake" and "thrower." The snake, about eighteen inches long, reminded Erik of a small ski with a turned tip at one end and a pointed butt at the other. The thrower, also about eighteen inches long, had a cup carved into one end.

"See, it fits the snake." Badger demonstrated by fitting the snake into the cup of the thrower. "Now we will go and practice."

By morning, the snow-snake track was icy slick. By the time Erik and Badger arrived, Weasel and Coyote, along with Chipmunk, were already sending their snakes down the track. Taking turns, running up to a starting point, each boy flipped his snake down the track. If it landed correctly, it slid beautifully, straight and fast.

Weasel's snake slid almost to the opposite end. He turned to Badger. "Shall we bet now?"

"No," exclaimed Badger as he came up. "But you will see how to throw a snake." He ran to the line and expertly sent the snake down the track. It slid far past the others. He raised his eyes to Weasel and motioned to Erik. "Your turn, Sky Eyes."

Erik felt a rush of jitters. He didn't want to be embarrassed. Although he and Badger had practiced, it wasn't on a track, and his snake frequently stuck in the snow.

Anxious, he ran up to the line and flipped the snake. It landed and slid for a nice distance but caught something and skipped up crazily.

The others laughed, but it was more because of the comic path the snake took.

Running to get their snakes, they turned to send them the opposite direction.

"You still want to bet, Weasel?" Badger eyed him.

Weasel shrugged. "Perhaps later," he said. "Now we should see who can hit the target."

Runs Fast showed up and watched for a while, purposefully laughing whenever Erik flipped his snake.

Erik remembered the game of kickball and felt a knot tighten in his stomach and a bad taste form in his mouth.

"Here, I will show you all how to do this game." Runs Fast stepped forward. "Let me use your snake, Badger." He took the snake. "I challenge the white boy. We will throw three times."

Erik stood disbelieving, wondering how Runs Fast could do this. He didn't agree to a challenge.

"I challenge him for his knife."

Impulsively, Erik's hand went to his knife. His heart raced, and the bitter taste grew. Nothing meant more to him than his father's knife. He knew he couldn't out throw Runs Fast. But he also knew that if he was fairly challenged, he would show weakness by backing down. Anger welled within him. "I'll take—"

Badger interrupted. "And what do you have to offer if you lose, Runs Fast?"

"Ha! I won't lose, so I don't offer anything."

The boys gathered around anxious for the competition, but they knew the challenge wasn't fair. Runs Fast had to offer something equal.

Badger quickly grabbed back his snake and stepped back, glaring at Runs Fast. "Sky Eyes will not take your challenge. All of us know you cannot match his knife."

Runs Fast tried to retake the snake, but Badger turned away.

"Come, Sky Eyes," he said. "We shall wait until Runs Fast can match your knife, if ever he can." He spat the words.

"Let the little white boy speak for himself!" shouted Runs Fast after them, his face reddening. Badger made him look foolish. He turned to the other boys and tried to laugh. "Of course I can match the white boy's knife. They are just afraid I will win, because I will."

"His name is Sky Eyes," protested Chipmunk. "You should call him Sky Eyes."

"Bah!" exclaimed Runs Fast, and he stomped off.

***

During these shortened days, the sun only lit the canyon floor for a few hours before the canyon rim again blocked it. There were no hours of dawn or sunset, just a time of gray light before the sun peeked over the rim and again after it sank below.

After a storm, when the snow clouds cleared and the sun shone, Erik watched the sunlight on the highest peaks to the west. He could see a few upriver through a gap in the canyon walls. The peaks were rugged and treeless, blanketed in thick snow. When the dying sun lit them, they took on an eerie, pink or orange glow. Their blue and gray contrasting shadows etched them sharply against the steel blue winter sky. Erik treasured the moment. *The alpenglow,* he remembered. Badger told him it was the cold spirits dancing before they went to sleep.

Clear days and nights were broken by regular storms that pushed through the canyon three to four days apart. During them, winds blasted through the canyon, breaking trees, rattling the lodges. Snow piled deep on the leeward sides and drifted to depths nearly covering the lodges. Inside, the people stayed warm and dry.

The people began to talk that it was a strange winter, a deep winter. They feared many animals would die, that hunting would be poor during the coming season.

It was after one of the heavy snows that Erik woke, and the night was still black. He could see the brilliant stars through a small gap in the ceiling. He had to pee, but he realized that something else woke him. He heard happy whispering coming from where Free Hawk slept. Erik found himself embarrassed. During the summer months, he and Badger knew to be away from the lodge for these times when brush was pulled over the door. Perhaps they only whispered to each other, Erik decided, but he found himself thinking of Quickly Smiles. He did not know yet the proper way of getting to know this girl. Once he had smiled at her, but she looked away. He knew he must talk to Stands Alone, but he also knew he was not yet considered a man. Until then, how could he block the feelings he had? He didn't understand.

Silence returned to the lodge. He lay awake a while longer before making obvious rustling noises. Then he stretched and dared to sit up. He slipped on his winter boots. He was glad the night was black, but he wrapped his robe around him when he left the lodge.

He walked toward the edge of camp, wondering. He stood for a moment and watched his breath—frozen clouds hanging in the still air—and the patterns he made in the snow. He thought he could discern soft lights—pink and green—flowing across the snow. An eerie light enveloped the camp. Above him, there was no moon, only the blazing, cold stars. Turning, he looked toward the mountain peaks and felt a rush of sudden joy.

Billowing curtains of soft green and pink lights, flowing from one side to the other above the pale peaks, lit the sky. *The northern lights!* He remembered them from Sweden but had never seen them in America. Shimmering, wavering, he watched the reels of color, light blues and greens tipped with pink, wavering back and forth, reaching and streaming in high feathery veils across the northern sky.

He raced to the lodge. Crawling to Badger's robes, he shook him. Whispering, he tried to get him to understand, to come outdoors. He pointed to the moving lights, which now penetrated the lodge in places. Seeing them, Badger immediately let out a thrilled cry and scrambled to stand up and dress.

"*Daka'bi mukua!* The cold spirits have come!" he exclaimed. Everyone woke.

Free Hawk and Shining Water joined them, carrying Singing Bird outside. They called to the others. Soon the whole camp was up, talking excitedly, walking out into the open. With their robes about them, their breaths caught in the frozen air, they gathered in the snow where they could gaze up to the heavens.

The lights shimmered, now mostly green veils. Already Erik realized they were less intense than what he had seen. Still, the people watched, eyes wide, whispering, pointing.

Gray Owl addressed the people softly. "This is a sign from the cold spirits, where the snows sleep. The winter will be long. But it is also a reminder that we are blessed. More children will be born this spring. The lights shine on us with gladness and favor."

Porcupine Woman came over, gazed intently at Erik, and muttered something to Gray Owl.

Gray Owl continued, "Porcupine Woman says the lights have chosen to show themselves to Sky Eyes. He is blessed, because the spirits show themselves to him. The lights have shown favorably to the people, because he has come to us."

The people's eyes shifted to Erik. He understood the kind looks, but he wished Gray Owl hadn't said what he did. He wasn't special. He didn't want that responsibility. He felt awkward and embarrassed and cast his eyes down. It was polite to do so when praised.

CHAPTER 33

CHIPMUNK AND SQUIRREL RAN through the camp. "Come. This night Gray Owl tells us a story."

Erik looked questioningly at Badger. "Are we not too old for a story?" he asked.

"No, Sky Eyes. Gray Owl's stories are for everyone. Sometimes even the grandmothers come and bring pine nuts and dried meat.

"Besides, what else is there to do tonight?" He kicked at the snow, sending a spray toward Erik.

Erik quickly kicked a spray back, laughing as it hit Badger's face.

Crowding inside Gray Owl's lodge, Erik noticed Coyote and Weasel were present. He also noticed their sisters, Sweet Grass and Quickly Smiles. When his eyes fell on Quickly Smiles, his heart quickened. She glanced briefly at him and smiled before casting her eyes away.

"Ah, Sky Eyes, she likes you." Badger shoved him in the ribs.

"Quit it." He shoved back, face reddening.

Gray Owl began, "You should all take a lesson from your little brother, Red Squirrel."

The youngest listeners' eyes grew larger, and they turned to each other, giggling.

Badger whispered, "This is a little child's story, but now it is not polite for us to leave."

Erik whispered back, "That's okay. I like all the stories." But Erik was thinking about being near Quickly Smiles.

Gray Owl continued. "Today you see the little red squirrel scamper about, chattering and scolding. But that was not always the way it was.

"In the beginning of days, when the Maker created each of the animals, he had a helper create some of them for him, and the helper didn't always do a smart job," Gray Owl said, sweeping his arms in an arc and cocking his eye at the youngest boy.

The youngsters laughed. They knew Gray Owl meant Coyote. Coyote was the trickster. He didn't always do what the Maker wanted him to do.

"You mean Coyote," the small boy spoke, eyes big.

"Sh-h-h-h," the others quickly responded. "It's not polite to interrupt."

Gray Owl eyed the boy. "Yes, of course I mean Coyote." He smiled, shaking a finger. "Coyote is a very funny being.

"Well, Coyote was to create an animal much like the red squirrel is today, for that is what the Maker had in mind, but Coyote decided the squirrel should not talk and would just lie around eating nuts whenever he was hungry." Gray Owl paused. "I think Coyote didn't want to listen to the squirrel chatter, and it was he, Coyote, who wanted to just lie around eating all day."

Some of the children giggled.

"So the first squirrels were fat and sat around just eating nuts wherever they found them on the ground." Gray Owl made chomping noises, eyes sparkling.

"But Coyote forgot that there were owls, martens, fishers, and weasels. Soon these animals began gobbling up all the red squirrels, especially the marten." Gray Owl pretended to be catching small animals, stuffing them into his mouth, and gobbling them. The small boy shied away.

"Well, it wasn't long before most of the red squirrels had disappeared," Gray Owl said, shaking his head sadly. "Red Squirrel had lots of nuts to eat, but not saying much, he became accustomed to seeing his friends getting eaten up by the other animals. But this didn't bother him as long as he wasn't getting eaten.

"Coyote also forgot about the cold spirits and the snowy moons. When the cold spirits brought snow, it covered all the nuts, and then Red Squirrel got hungry and skinny because he couldn't dig through the snow and find the nuts," continued Gray Owl, shaking his head sadly.

The children joined by making sad eyes and shaking their heads as well.

"Coyote told the Maker he didn't think he was wise to make all the animals that ate Red Squirrel, and he wasn't wise to make the cold spirits that brought the snow.

"'Ah, but it is you who are not wise, Coyote,' said the Maker." Gray Owl deepened his voice to mimic the Maker. "'You seem to forget it was you who knew best what Red Squirrel needed. You didn't think that other animals would eat Red Squirrel. You didn't think that something would hide the nuts. Soon there won't be any red squirrels.'" Gray Owl made an even sadder face.

"Coyote felt sad. He had messed up," Gray Owl said and eyed the children. "As usual," he added brightly, and they laughed.

"So the Maker told Coyote, 'Coyote,' he said, 'I will give you a chance to make things to help Red Squirrel.'

"So Coyote went to his favorite rock to think about how he'd help Red Squirrel." Gray Owl put his chin in his hand and pretended to be thinking.

"Coyote couldn't ask the Maker to take away the cold spirits. He couldn't ask the Maker to take away Owl, Marten, Fisher, or Weasel. Every animal had its purpose. *No*, thought Coyote. *It wouldn't be good to undo any of what the Maker has done.*

"Coyote needed to think of a way to fix the cold spirits to not bring snow and cover the nuts. So Coyote sat on his thinking rock, thinking. Soon his mate came out and said loudly, 'Coyote, all you do is think.'" Gray Owl spoke in a louder, squeaky voice. "'Come quickly and help me gather up these berries for supper before the wind blows them away, and we can't find them.'

"So Coyote went with his mate and gathered up a huge pile of berries for dinner. And suddenly," Gray Owl narrowed his eyes, "Coyote realized that if Red Squirrel would just gather up the nuts before the cold spirits came, then perhaps he would have a pile he could find in the snow."

Gray Owl used his coyote voice. "'Ah, that is it! I will make it so Red Squirrel can pile up nuts,' said Coyote. 'Red Squirrel can then find them when the cold spirits bring the snow.'

"And so Coyote made Red Squirrel with tiny hands to gather up nuts and with big cheeks to carry the nuts so he could gather and carry lots of nuts to a place where the snow wouldn't be too deep." Gray Owl cupped his hands, puffed out his cheeks, and bobbed like a squirrel.

The children laughed, and Erik glanced toward Quickly Smiles. He couldn't help but notice how her eyes sparkled and how she laughed right along with the youngest child. *What a beautiful woman,* he thought. *Somehow, I must get to know her.* He couldn't tear his eyes away.

"And now in the deep snow, Red Squirrel can find piles of nuts under the trees where there is not much snow. And if he finds one, since there is a big pile, he can find enough to last him through the deep-snow moon.

"But then Coyote had to figure out what to do with Owl, Marten, Fisher, and Weasel to keep them from eating Red Squirrel. So he climbed back up on his thinking rock, and he thought and thought until his mate came out again and said to him loudly, 'Coyote, all you do is think. Come quickly and help me catch fish for dinner before they swim away,'" Gray Owl said again in his louder squeaky voice.

"So Coyote went with his mate and caught some fish. It was easy to catch fish, just like catching Red Squirrel, Coyote realized. *If fish could talk, they could warn each other when danger was coming,* Coyote thought.

"'Ah, that is it! I will make the squirrel so that it talks,' said Coyote. 'Red Squirrel can then tell all the other squirrels to watch out when Owl, Marten, Fisher, or Weasel come around.'

"And so Coyote made it so Red Squirrel could talk. But like Coyote often does," whispered Gray Owl, looking to the listening faces before him, "he did it too well!"

The children laughed. They knew about chattering red squirrels.

Again, Erik stole a glance toward Quickly Smiles. This time, he thought she smiled toward him, and he smiled back. She giggled and turned away, whispering to Sweet Grass who glanced his way. Embarrassed, Erik looked down.

"Now the red squirrel talks all the time, chattering and scolding, chattering and scolding. Even when he doesn't need to warn others of danger, he just talks." Gray Owl eyed the youngster who had spoken out of turn. The little boy turned his eyes away.

But suddenly, the boy turned back. "That is a good story, Grandfather," he said. "But you said it was a lesson Red Squirrel taught to the people."

"Ah, you *are* a good listener, Little One." Gray Owl was pleased.

"The people, like the red squirrel, should always keep watch for danger and warn others of danger. Do not just watch them get eaten up. The other lesson is that the people, like the red squirrel, must make baskets and store food for the deep-snow moons. If we don't do these things, we won't know when hungry animals are coming to eat us, and we won't have food for when the starving moon comes."

Eyes wider than ever, the children nodded, agreeing.

Erik laughed to himself. It was a silly story, but it made sense for the people to teach in this manner. It was certainly more fun than sitting in one of the classrooms he remembered.

"That is enough for one night," Gray Owl said, eyes bright. "We are blessed by the Great Mystery to have so many children; especially so many young children." He drew his robe about himself, signaling to his visitors that it was the polite time to leave. "Remember to thank your parents and the Great Mystery."

The children rose obediently and left the lodge, whispering among themselves about Red Squirrel and silly Coyote.

When they were out in the snow, Badger nudged Erik. "I saw you looking at Quickly Smiles," he whispered. "You should be careful." He laughed.

"I can't help it, Badger," replied Erik. He felt warmth within even though the snow crunched underneath and his breath hung in the frosty air.

CHAPTER 34

THE SNOW-EATER MOON CAME, and the deep snows quickly left the canyon. Spring returned. The people began to look forward to the summer hunting camps.

"Come, Sky Eyes," said Badger. "Father works on his curved-horn bow."

Erik put down the wood he was carrying and joined Badger.

"I hope you or I can soon get a good curved-horn so we can work on our own bow."

"Yes," replied Erik. "But soon we go to the star-grass meadows where there are no curved-horns."

Badger sighed. "I know. I wish we had gotten a curved-horn when we hunted with our watchers."

"Perhaps Father will give you a bow," suggested Erik. "He has two."

"That would be good, but he makes them to trade. Everyone knows he makes the best bows. Everyone has his bows—well not Whistling Elk and maybe Black Legs, but they have horn bows, anyway."

"Then he doesn't need to make one for anyone."

"But he wants to trade with Broken Blade for a steel knife and things for Mother."

Erik realized again what it must have meant to Free Hawk to give him back his father's knife. He felt humbled. He didn't know how, but he resolved to get him a steel knife.

They found Free Hawk sitting next to a small fire, adding a few hoof shavings to the glue he boiled.

"Ah, here are my sons," he greeted them. "Soon you will build bows like this one," he said, gently lifting the bow.

Erik could see how his work had progressed since early winter. He had since added a midsection, joining the two horn wings. The midsection was about five inches wide and tied with rawhide.

Free Hawk laid a strip of sinew along the outer curve of the bow and glued it into place.

"I will talk to Whistling Elk and Sees Far. They should take you to get a curved-horn with good horns." He laid and glued on a second piece.

"They try," Badger replied. "The other hunters get curved-horns, but they take their horns to a certain bow-maker who makes them bows." He glanced at his father. "But he does not make his sons bows."

"Ah, but do you forget that a certain bow maker has given each of his sons a boy's bow? Bows that he also made ... from the chokecherry tree?" He eyed Badger while he added more sinew, continuing to laminate the strips to the bow.

Badger replied, "Yes, and they are fine bows. Sky Eyes and I get many rabbits, and we get fur animals, but they are too weak for us to get curved-horns or shaggy-neck elk."

"Perhaps you forget that one should be expert with a wood bow before he gets a curved-horn bow?" Free Hawk dusted the bow with fine clay and set it aside to cure. He turned toward Badger, arms resting on his knees.

"Badger *is* an expert, Father," said Erik in Badger's defense. He knew Badger's frustration. "Even I am becoming a good shot."

Free Hawk took the sinew, beat it on a rock, and began stripping it into long, hairlike strands. "And I agree," he said smiling. "But the grandfathers teach that a father should not do something for his son that he can do for himself, or the boy will not grow to be a true man." He took two strands and laid a third and fourth, overlapping them about midway. He began rolling them together with his palm on his leg. He added two more strands to the mid area of the single strands and continued rolling them. In this fashion, the strand continued to grow in length, four strands thick.

The boys were silent.

"Do not be disappointed. You will be glad when you make your own bow. It will be something of which you can be proud," continued Free Hawk. He added and rolled in new sinew until the strand was over twenty feet. Then, very subtly, he smiled. "And perhaps if someone should give you a curved-horn bow, you will be able to make more to trade and get your wives good things."

Erik's heart caught. He nudged Badger and gave him a cautious smile. Badger nodded. Both recognized Free Hawk's hint.

Free Hawk folded the strand into thirds and inserted a small stick into each end. "Now take this, Badger, and hold tight." He handed one of the small sticks to Badger.

Rapidly, he twisted the other stick until the length shortened to a fine, three-ply cord. He tested it by pulling against it, pulling Badger off his seat. "Good. It can pull a boy." He laughed. "It should send an arrow." He rubbed it with bear fat. "That is enough for this day. I will hang these back in the lodge where they will cure from the fire's heat."

Free Hawk rose, his sons following. The day was nearly gone, and Shining Water should have something ready to eat.

CHAPTER 35

THE STAR-GRASS MOON RETURNED. The people from the Big Sheep Band struck their lodges and visited for one last time with the Twisted River Band. Afterward, they turned downstream toward River of No Return. Their favored summer hunting camps were far to the north and east across the big river, in the mountains above Cold River.

The Twisted River Band traveled upstream and northwest from their winter camp. It took three days to reach their summer hunting spot, some high meadows and small lakes scattered beneath white, rocky peaks.

After the lodges were finished, Gray Owl led the people in giving thanks to the Great Mystery for their safe journey. He also gave thanks for the birth of a boy. Named Little Elk, he was the second child born to Black Legs and White Deer. He thanked the Great Mystery that Black Legs had come to the Twisted River Band. A new hunter and family greatly strengthened the people.

Some of the grandmothers whispered that they hoped Runs Fast would marry Sweet Grass or Quickly Smiles and begin his own family. He was of age, and since he was of the Lemhis, Runs Fast could marry into the Twisted River Band.

Badger told Erik of this when he heard.

Erik felt as if stabbed. He couldn't breathe. He wanted Quickly Smiles. From the day he had seen her in the meadows, he knew he wanted her. When she was near, his breath caught, and he became clumsy. And whenever he caught her smile, he warmed inside. But he knew he wasn't of proper age to court her—he hadn't completed his vision seeking. His heart caught at the thought of his vision journey. In a few days, he would go. *Please, dear Lord. Don't let Runs Fast court Quickly Smiles. Let him seek out Sweet Grass instead.* The image of Runs Fast with Quickly Smiles turned his stomach.

***

The flashing-sky moon arrived. It was decided that four boys were of age and ready for their vision journeys. Four had never before gone to seek their visions during the same season.

On the night preceding, Erik could not sleep; neither could Badger. When Erik observed Badger rise and carry his robe outside the lodge, he rose and followed.

Outside, Erik found him seated on a smooth rock beside the creek. The night sky was alive with stars.

"Why are you here?" Erik breathed, whispering.

"I am thinking and cannot sleep."

"What if one of us should fail? Is that what you're thinking?"

"You will not fail, Sky Eyes," replied Badger. "Although you are with us but one summer, you are strong."

"You are worried, then, that you will fail?" exclaimed Erik.

Badger didn't reply.

"Brother," came Erik's words softly, "you will not fail."

"I am young. It is only because of you, Sky Eyes, that I go."

Erik knew this was true. Some thought Badger was too young. *He is but thirteen winters—one more winter—let him still be a boy.* Runs Fast especially said so. He argued Badger was not strong yet.

But others argued that Badger and Sky Eyes were like one. For one to remain a boy while the other completed his vision journey would not be right. They also knew Badger was winter born and but a few moons younger—not a full winter.

The moon had cast her white light across the waters. It sparkled from the numerous hidden marshy areas. Except for the croak of frogs and whirr of bats, the night lay silent.

"We are both ready, Badger," Erik comforted. "We will both succeed. But now we must sleep. Soon enough we will go without sleep."

"Yes," agreed Badger, rising silently and returning with Erik to the lodge where they both soon slept.

***

Whistling Elk and Sees Far crept into the lodge in the early gray light and gently shook their charges. In silence, the two boys rose and, escorted by their watchers, crept out into the stillness of the new day. Already some of the men were gathered, and Coyote and Weasel stood nearby with Free Hawk and Stands Alone.

Erik walked quietly with the others away from the village to the lake. The path was well worn, but long blades of dew-soaked grass reached out and brushed his legs, causing a chilly wetness.

At the lake, he waded out into the calm, silvery water, feeling the coldness and the crispness of the water against his skin. Steam wisped from its surface. That morning, he bathed in earnest, carefully preening the dirt from his fingernails, his ears, even twice washing his hair. Whistling Elk had taught that it was important to be as clean as possible for acceptance to the Great Mystery.

Sees Far began a soft singing prayer as they washed. He prayed to the Great Mystery to grant them success during their vision seeking.

Shortly, Erik emerged and stood beside Badger on the bank, water streaming from him to the muddy shore and in tiny rivulets back to the meadow lake. He turned to where the sun rose, its rays just now beginning to touch the uppermost boughs of the lodgepole pines.

Sees Far spoke the new day prayer for them. "Great Mystery, today four boys stand before you to greet the new sun and to begin their journeys to become men. Fill them with courage. Give them pure hearts. Let them be acceptable in your sight."

The sun's rays now touched Erik, sparkling as they lit the still-clinging beads of water on his shoulders and chest. Momentarily, he stood, bathed fully in the golden glow. Erik felt the warmth strike him. *I am here, Great Mystery—Sky Eyes. Be with me. Accept me.*

He and the others dressed and returned to Whistling Elk's lodge, where the grandmothers had prepared the journey meal. Erik wasn't particularly hungry, but he knew he would need to eat for the journey ahead. Even so, he didn't eat more than usual—to do so would have been impolite and shown weakness.

Erik savored each bite, remembering. Never, since he had come to the Twisted River Band, had he known hunger—unlike his days on the prairie. Soon, however, he would again know hunger. He didn't fear this part of his journey, rather he respected it.

Now the village was awake, and the people excitedly gathered at the council fire. Gray Owl addressed them. "This day, the Great Mystery smiles on us. One summer ago, we saw a boy off on his journey, a journey from which he did not return. We were all saddened that the Great Mystery should take this young man from us. Now this day we have before us four boys who will attempt their own seeking.

"We have prayed for these young men. I, in particular, have prayed. Even before the one we lost, I prayed. And I can share with you this: I have a vision that this summer will be good. Today we send four boys out to make themselves known to the Great Mystery. We will pray to the Great Mystery that he sends them back to us as men."

Whistling Elk led the boys away as the women made trilling sounds of encouragement and praise. They traveled to a sheltered place above the camp along the creek. Here were two sweat lodges. This was a private place away from the camp—a place where a man could be at peace and pray.

The men started two fires and began heating smooth rocks. They filled and placed water bags inside the lodges. Gray Owl instructed the boys to set aside their clothes and to sit, to be silent, to pray.

To Erik, the lodge resembled an upside down bowl. Hides had been stretched tightly over a willow frame and were anchored around the base with earth and rocks. A small opening was positioned to face east and was covered with a hide flap from which a path led to a fire pit.

Gray Owl spoke. "I asked the Great Mystery to place a special blessing upon these lodges. They hold a special purpose. Now you shall enter, take your first sweat, and prepare in earnest for your journey to become true men."

Erik followed Badger as he crept into the darkened, tiny, domed room. They seated themselves facing the door. The flap fell, plunging them into total darkness except for tiny shafts of light streaming through small holes. Erik sat, squatting on his haunches—something he had never grown comfortable doing—his eyes adjusting to the darkness. He could make out the small earthen pit used to hold the rocks. Between them was the water-filled hide and sheep-horn bowls for dipping. The roof was within a forearm of his head, and if he stretched out his foot, he could touch the opposite side.

He was silent. This was a time for prayers and cleansing. Whistling Elk had taught him what to expect, but he felt anxious. He grasped hands with Badger for good wishes.

All too soon, the lodge flap was raised, and one by one, some large rocks were rolled in. Using a short length of aspen, Erik helped Badger worry them into the pit. He felt the heat beginning to immediately radiate onto his body and fill the cramped space.

With Badger, he scooped water onto the dull, glowing rocks. The water exploded, sizzling and popping, into billowing clouds of intensely hot steam, enveloping them in stifling heat. They ladled on more, and again the steam hissed and boiled, now pressing its weight outward against them. Both gasped. Sweat and water dripped from their bodies.

The heat was overwhelming. Erik gasped for air, choking on the heat. Instead of purity, he prayed for survival. He prayed for the door to open. The steam and heat pressed in—suffocating him—stopping his breath. Water streamed from his hair, stung his eyes, poured from him. He fought to concentrate, to relax, to draw a breath.

He saw Badger, how he sat head down, legs crossed, hands limp on his knees. Badger took quick, short breaths.

Erik adjusted his position to mimic Badger's. His panicked feeling eased. Soon he mentally escaped to the river, to the canyon, to where he swam in the cool current and felt its tug against him; the blue sky stretched above. He prayed.

As the steam subsided, he and Badger again dipped water onto the rocks, and again great torrents of steam erupted, enveloped him, pressed against him. Erik again fought for control, and soon, he again floated on the river. Now the rocks cooled, and the steam lessened.

The flap opened, and cool air washed in. Sees Far rolled in more stones; the flap fell; they poured water; the steam exploded. Erik remained cloistered in the lodge with Badger, sweat and water running freely from them, carrying away the dirt and grime.

Erik prayed. He remained as quiet as possible and breathed carefully, slowly, his eyes closed. He no longer floated in the river. He now saw the Great Mystery to whom he prayed. *Please, God, let me succeed. Let me receive your message.*

Then he welcomed the heat. It felt as if a heavy blanket were wrapped about him, pressing into him. The waves of liquid warmth bathed and hugged him tightly. He no longer felt naked but felt enveloped inside a warm cocoon.

From the sounds, he knew Coyote and Weasel had finished, but he was content to linger in the warm, enveloping steam. He prayed for acceptance and felt the hurt, worry, and pain ebb away.

Whistling Elk and Sees Far threw back the flap. "It is time."

The cold rushed in, shocking Erik. He emerged with Badger, squinting in the brilliant sunlight. A tingling sensation washed across him; thousands of tiny invigorating needles pricked his skin. He felt clean and fresh and more alive than he ever remembered.

While he and Badger stood, their watchers took sage and vigorously rubbed them dry. They tossed the sage into the fire. Erik watched as it smoked and burst into flame. Whistling Elk had explained that the white smoke would carry away the last impurities.

Whistling Elk and Sees Far gave them their breechcloths and moccasins and told them to dress. All else—leggings, shirts, robes, and weapons—would remain behind.

Stands Alone motioned for them to follow and led off, heading toward the jagged, white rock peaks. He followed a brook, climbing over downed trees and large, white, fractured boulders. The creek tumbled through a narrow cleft and around torn logs and brush. Then, abruptly, the brush and timber ended. Erik could see they had reached timberline. Before them spread a broad meadow matted with short-stemmed grasses and alpine flowers. White-star flowers, supporting their creamy white globes, grew in scattered clumps above the basin.

Stands Alone stopped near a seep where the water had pooled. "You shall begin your journeys here and return here."

Erik glanced around. Before them rose the jagged peaks. Perhaps the very peaks he had studied from their winter camp on Twisted River—the peaks that had been touched last winter by the northern lights. But turning, Erik could not glimpse the river he knew lay far below. A thick, blue green forest carpeted the canyon walls and descended downward into the shadows.

Gray Owl now spread a small hide and formed a depression in its middle. Here he placed the powdered white clay he had carried from the canyon and mixed it with water. He prayed to the Great Mystery. The four watchers bent and scooped out handfuls and began painting the bodies of their charges. Gray Owl explained. "This is the sacred white clay that is pleasing to the Great Mystery and that invites him to send you a vision."

Erik stood, feeling the brush of Whistling Elk's fingers and the coolness of the clay. His heart quickened. In only moments, his journey would begin. Soon after, the chasers would follow. He dared not think of failure. He took comfort in knowing there were only two chasers. There was some safety in numbers. Nevertheless, he felt that he and Badger would be the two pursued—Badger, because they considered him too young, and himself, because Runs Fast blamed him for bad medicine, which brought Raven's death.

Shortly, he stood next to Badger, fully painted with the gray, sticky clay. Pure white when dry, it wouldn't easily come off, nor was he allowed to remove it. Only through exposure during the journey was it permissible for it to come off. In the meantime, the white would stand out like a light to those pursuing.

Gray Owl motioned for them to sit near a small fire he had built. The fire's heat helped dry the clay. He pulled out bundles of sage and, igniting them, fanned the sweet smelling smoke toward Erik and the others, muttering prayers. Ceremoniously, he immersed each of them in the smoke, circling the smoking sage three times around their bodies. "This sacred smoke now carries away all bad thoughts, all things impure that still linger and might displease the Great Mystery."

Erik shook his thoughts about Runs Fast.

Now came the moment of parting. Whistling Elk took Erik aside, giving him his blessing and prayers. Erik nodded his thanks, and choosing his direction, headed away at a trot. It was the time of the long summer light. Erik knew it would be several hours before darkness fell. Only then would he and the others be safe from their pursuers. Until then, they had to prove their skill.

Erik realized that Badger headed roughly in the same direction as he, toward the tallest peak.

***

The watchers observed until their charges had disappeared, then turned and headed solemnly back toward their lodges. Gray Owl remained behind.

During their return, the watchers prayed. Free Hawk knew the personal loss of a son and prayed for his second son, Badger. He also prayed for his adopted son, Sky Eyes. Last season, he had prayed for his own charge, the boy who killed the bear, but his prayers were unanswered. What caused the Great Mystery not to hear his prayers last season? Would he not hear his prayers this season as well? Free Hawk shook his head. A longing for Otter welled within him. He did not understand the ways of the Great Mystery.

Runs Fast and Black Legs now approached Gray Owl. Both had quietly followed at a distance, hidden. Their task was to test the boys—if possible, to catch one or more before the first night fell. If they succeeded, it would be seen as a sign that the boy was not ready and should wait another season.

Gray Owl seated them, their backs to the boys. For a long while, they waited as Gray Owl ensured the boys each had a good start. Gray Owl strongly wanted each to succeed. If so, this season the Twisted River Band would be greatly strengthened.

Finally, Gray Owl addressed them. "You are our newest young men and have recently completed your test. Just as you were pursued, you are asked to pursue these boys. It will do the people no good to call a boy a man if he is not worthy. It will be an insult and a great danger to the people. But remember also to judge well. A boy who shows courage and wisdom can be overlooked. But only you can make that decision."

Runs Fast told himself that neither Badger nor the white boy were ready to be called men. They wouldn't be overlooked. Today he would prove his name and catch them both, and if not both, then at least the white boy.

Dismissed, he and Black Legs trotted together, also toward the highest peak.

Gray Owl watched, wondering at how quickly the men moved. Already he worried he had allowed them to leave too early.

Gray Owl knew the animosity Runs Fast harbored toward Sky Eyes. He always felt Sky Eyes had a spirit helper, sent by the Great Mystery. He guessed it was Sohobinehwe Tso'ape, a spirit of the trees, for this spirit would live near the white-man lodge. He worried. Besides bringing Sky Eyes, it could have brought bad things as well. Perhaps Runs Fast was right. Perhaps the white boy had brought bad medicine to the Twisted River Band. If so, it was now in the hands of the Great Mystery. The chasers would complete their task.

Chapter 36

Erik ran fast and hard, trying to keep the thought of the pursuers from his mind. He wished the sun were not as high. He wondered how he would stay hidden until nightfall. He desperately wished he were less visible.

It seemed to Erik, although he tried, he couldn't keep out of sight of Badger. It occurred to him that he and Badger must have picked the same destination. Erik adjusted his direction and headed more westerly, toward where the sun now hung in the sky.

Already his breath came hard, and it made him realize he was moving too fast, too hard all at once, like a nervous rabbit that ran recklessly until caught by the coyote. Erik tried to calm his feelings and run smart, but he couldn't keep the pursuers from his mind.

He reached a rocky knoll, then a steep sidehill strewn with rocks and clumps of bear grass. Above him rose steep cliffs, snow banks clinging to their bases.

Sweat streamed from his matted hair and stung his eyes. Trying to wipe it away made it worse. The clay, now sticky mud, also stung. Sweat tracks ran down his arms and hands. Deliberately he angled toward the notch in the rocks above. Nearing the saddle, he slid down between white granite boulders and studied his back trail. He caught movement below. *Black Legs!*

To his right, he saw a white flash. *Badger!* Like a white ghost, he stood out against the dark gray crags. He watched Badger scurry quickly from one boulder to another, trying to keep hidden.

Erik's heart caught. Below Badger, but headed directly toward him, was Runs Fast. Erik felt dread seep in. Badger was trapped—he couldn't move without being spotted. Unable to tear his eyes away, Erik watched as Runs Fast closed the gap. Certainly Runs Fast had spotted him or he wouldn't move so deftly. Erik's thoughts raced furiously. Badger would fail. He—Erik—would become a man; his brother would remain a boy.

Erik felt alone and vulnerable. He knew Black Legs would soon be on him. Impulsively, he stood, showing himself. *Catch me, Black Legs. Badger and I can be boys for another year.* Erik fought the feelings of failure already flooding in and choked back the hurt. *How can this be happening? How can Black Legs and Runs Fast come so far, so fast, and catch us?* A bad taste filled Erik's mouth as his anger grew.

He stood in full view, looking for Black Legs. He saw no one. He thought of waving to attract attention, but that would be wrong. The pursuers would know something was amiss. No one gave himself away.

Erik turned to climb a rock outcrop, unsure of what to do. Runs Fast had nearly reached the spot where he last saw Badger. Erik could no longer watch. He scrambled upward. A rock turned under his foot, tore loose, and clattered down the face. He caught sight of Runs Fast turning in his direction.

Instinctively, he pressed into a rocky crevice. He knew Runs Fast could not see him. *But why does Runs Fast head this way if he sees Badger?* It no longer mattered. Erik was the one trapped, and soon Runs Fast would catch him and Badger would escape. Suddenly Erik realized the tables were turned. *I will remain the boy. Badger will become the man.*

Still Erik held his place. He wanted to give Badger as much time as possible. Surely Badger had checked his back trail by now and had seen Runs Fast. Surely he knew to remain hidden. But Erik realized that if he could see Badger, Badger could see him. He wrestled with himself. *Badger will do exactly what I would have done for him. He'll show himself and try to pull Runs Fast toward himself!*

Stay down Badger, Erik prayed. *Please, God, have him stay down.*

He saw the movement of white. *No, Badger. Don't. Not for me!*

Erik leaped up, scrambling upward toward some brush. He avoided looking back. He didn't want Runs Fast to know he'd seen him. Runs Fast wouldn't rush him until he got closer unless he knew Erik had seen him.

Reaching the brush, Erik turned slowly, surveying behind himself. If he made it to the top, he could sprint down the other side, giving himself a better chance of escaping.

***

Runs Fast heard the rock clatter and immediately caught the flash of white. Although he couldn't make out which boy it was, something told him it was the white boy. Runs Fast was both elated and disappointed. He had spotted Badger and would soon catch him, but he wanted the white boy most.

"I will catch you, little white boy," he breathed. He headed toward the movement. Sky Eyes would be his. The little white boy would never become a man. Abruptly Runs Fast saw more movement in the timber even farther to his left. *A third boy!* Runs Fast was elated. Certainly he would catch the white boy, possibly another. He would show the people that the boys were not ready—that indeed the white boy had brought disfavor to the people.

***

Erik reached the saddle, lungs aching, gasping for breath, frustrated and angry. How could he have been so badly mistaken? Runs Fast should have turned back by now.

Gaining the other side beyond the saddle, he stopped cold. No sheer drop fell away into protective timber as he had expected. Instead, before him stretched a barren, rocky basin with a snow-rimmed lake. Beyond, he could see another. To the east rose a ragged mountain peak. Farther beyond, he could see where the canyon must lie, marked by a line of dark conifers. He had crossed into the River of No Return drainage. There was nowhere to hide. Runs Fast would easily see him.

He decided that his only chance lay in racing down and across the basins. Maybe he could make it to the black timber in the canyon beyond. Runs Fast would know he had spotted him, but he could not pretend to seek cover when there was none. If he were caught, at least he would lead Runs Fast far away from Badger.

Erik scrambled downward from the saddle toward the first basin, jumping, careening off broken boulders, leaping smaller ones, scrambling over the larger ones. He had no pretence of hiding—only of escaping to the trees—*far, ah, so terribly far.*

Sounds of clattering rock reached his ears. Runs Fast must be behind him.

Erik concentrated on the obstacles before him. His wind returned a little as he hit the spongy surface of the alpine meadow edging the lake. He reached the cover of a few scraggly spruce at its outlet. Recklessly, he raced for the line of trees.

He entered the trees. The slope steepened. He leaped downward between clefts of rock, dropping over his height and more, to rocky benches below. Following a twisting brook, Erik reasoned it would soon plummet steeply toward the canyon below. He figured he could lose Runs Fast in the brook's narrow cleft that opened below him. *Surely he won't follow me. It's too steep and dangerous. If he does, maybe he'll fall. I'll get away.*

***

Runs Fast was surprised when he reached the notch and saw the white figure already far below, racing fast, crazily across the barren rocks and snow. He felt angry. The white boy had known he was behind him, and now he had a head start toward safety.

He laughed. The foolish white boy headed toward the canyon. He couldn't do his vision seeking in the canyon. Even if he didn't catch him, the white boy wouldn't succeed. *But perhaps he will become lost. Maybe he will fall to his death or be caught and eaten by the night cat.*

Runs Fast slowed his pace. There was no need to run as hard. He would trap him on the canyon's edge.

He was surprised at how hard his own breath came. The white boy was stronger than he suspected. Perhaps the Great Mystery *was* with him. But Runs Fast shook the thought. He paused, memorizing the edge where Sky Eyes disappeared into the trees.

"Go on, little white boy," he whispered. "Soon the night will be upon us, and I will be forced to return. By then I will have driven you far away; it will not matter. You will fail or you will perish." The foolish white boy would do his work for him.

***

Erik continued to crash viciously through the increasingly thick underbrush, now leaping fallen snags, landing many feet downhill, jarring each time he hit. He felt like the bounding deer—leaping crazily, dangerously.

Branches gashed and tore his thighs and legs. Sharp sticks and rock fragments punctured his moccasins, cutting his feet. His arms and upper torso were scratched and raw; he bled. Still he ran.

Suddenly he burst from the brush to empty space before him. He clawed frantically to stop his tumble. Then, as the nearness of death struck him, Erik began to shake uncontrollably. He collapsed, panting in a heap at the edge of a jagged black cliff. Strangely, the river that he knew must lie below remained hidden.

Erik hid in the brush, heart pounding, noisily gasping for air. He tried listening for his pursuer and tried to figure his next move. He heard twigs snapping, and his heart froze. This hadn't been a game, he realized. This wasn't how it was supposed to be. The people had said that if a chaser grew near and you had showed good effort to avoid capture, the chaser would let you go. Runs Fast had not given up. Even now as evening approached, Runs Fast was coming. Erik realized that Runs Fast was determined to catch him, and now he was trapped, cowering like a rabbit, on a cliff face.

***

Runs Fast paused. He knew the little white boy was somewhere below him. He knew he had stopped running. He was hiding. Perhaps he was cornered. Runs Fast grinned. Judging now from the terrain ahead, the little white boy was trapped. It was simply a matter of time. The white boy was his!

***

Cautiously, Erik approached the sheer drop. The rock was an ugly, black, sharp-edged, crumbling material. It had already cut his moccasins, and his feet bled.

Erik thought briefly of turning back and trying to sneak upward past Runs Fast. He quickly dismissed this. He had no choice but to descend.

Erik quickly scouted the edge, checking and rechecking for a route down. He began to panic, because he knew Runs Fast would soon be upon him. Returning to his original spot, he began to scramble downward. Perhaps it would lead nowhere; he had no choice but to try.

He reached a dizzy drop. Above him was sheer crumbling rock and below was a small ledge. To try to go up and around would mean being caught. He wasted no time and dropped down. Hitting the ledge, he fell backward, catching himself. The drop put him out of sight of the cliff's rim.

He angled across the ledge toward the brush. Evening, at long last, was upon him. Shadows grew long. The canyon below was deep in dark purples and blues.

In the shadows now, Erik reached the safety of the steep, brush-covered slope. He walked northward toward a ridgeline that would take him back to the alpine peaks. He felt weary. He had run all day. Now his legs shook and trembled and no longer wanted to work. He collapsed at the first trickle of water and drank. The sky had gone to a violet, now deep indigo blue. Faint stars appeared. The approaching darkness closed in. Erik lay until the welcome coolness of the spongy moss turned cold. Feeling at last that he was safe, Erik rose and began climbing back toward the peaks.

***

Runs Fast reached the jagged cliff. Broken bits of basalt showed where Erik had been. *He's trapped*, thought Runs Fast. *He can't find his way past.* Runs Fast felt certain he'd shortly find the little white boy. All he had to do was listen and search carefully. With his speed, he'd quickly catch him or send him over the cliff to his death.

Runs Fast headed south, expecting to quickly find his prey. He reached a knoll that offered a good view of an open ridge leading back toward the peaks. Expectantly, Runs Fast searched the ridge. Surely the little white boy would be there.

He searched patiently, studying every detail of the hillside. He listened for a twig breaking, a sliding rock, a bird flying up, anything that would tell him with certainty where the little white boy was. Strangely, only silence reached him. He saw no movement.

Evening shadows gathered. Runs Fast grew uncertain. He wondered if the boy had headed north instead. But that direction was impossible because of the cliffs. Runs Fast jogged north until he reached another point from which he could survey the north ridge—wicked black, jagged rocks. The light faded. Still he saw no sign of the boy. The only route north would be below the black cliffs. The little white boy was incapable of that.

Runs Fast returned to where Erik first came out onto the cliff and reexamined the marks. A feeling of desperation seeped in. How could a stupid little white boy sneak around him? Only a fool, a smart fool, would have attempted to drop down below the cliffs. But there, staring back, were the signs from someone having gone down the cliff. Now difficult to see in the twilight, Runs Fast studied the broken bits of basalt, streaked with blood. The little white boy had climbed down the face, but how? Then he smiled. Perhaps Sky Eyes was far, far below. Perhaps he fell. Maybe tonight the coyotes would find a new meal.

Feeling satisfied, Runs Fast turned for the ridge leading toward the notch. He would need to travel long into the night to return to the star-grass meadows. He wondered how he would explain his absence to the elders.

Chapter 37

WHEN ERIK REACHED A small alpine lake, the moon was rising. Nearly full, its white light lit the rocks as it crept slowly across them toward the still, glassy water.

Erik found an overhanging rock protected on two sides and crawled underneath. The alpine grass was scrubby, and the rock was gravely against him, but he was too exhausted to care. He knew he could not really keep awake this night—perhaps tomorrow. Today, like an animal, he had been hunted. He was certain. He knew Runs Fast blamed him for bringing misfortune, but it was more than just that. A dreadful feeling told him that if Runs Fast had caught him on the cliff, he would have pushed him over. Of that he was certain. Erik shuddered. He couldn't shake the feeling. He knew that when he returned to the people, he would have to watch his back.

His shivering increased, and he cupped his knees to himself tightly, burrowing farther into the rocks, still slightly warm. He stared across the pond, now fully reflecting the glowing moon, cold and silent. He need not worry about sleep—his shivering would keep him awake.

He watched the stars turn in the sky about the North Star, slowly, imperceptibly. The moon seemed to hang over his shoulder, but finally, it disappeared.

***

The first bird twittered. Another soon answered, and as the morning's gray light bled into the sky, more joined until the basin filled with their twittering and calling. Morning had arrived. Erik had dozed only a few times. The cold and his shivering kept him awake, not his prayers. Erik felt hungry, but he was no longer allowed to eat.

He continued past the small lake and climbed toward the sculpted peaks. Today no one would pursue. Today he would reach his special place and stop to seek his vision. Even though the others may have already spent their first night at their seeking places, it didn't matter. This quest was between himself and God.

Erik came out onto a broad basin marked by scrubby trees. Sculpted glacial granite cliffs rose on all sides. A large lake, separated by a thin ridge of scoured rock where two more lakes lay, filled the basin. He reached the shore and skirted it, heading toward the cliffs beyond. To the east, a sheer, black cliff rose into the sky. Before him, trout lazily swam away from the shore, heading out toward the deeper shadows. That was good; not many of the high lakes held fish. On the far side, a rugged mountain peak, now bathed in the rosy morning light, beckoned to him.

The beauty transfixed him. Perhaps no other man had ever seen this place. Perhaps God was now revealing it to him for his vision quest. Erik realized that if Runs Fast hadn't chased him so hard, he would have never found it.

Erik climbed to a rocky ledge. Overhanging rocks rose above. Below, they dropped away into empty space, spilling downward into the lake. He watched the gray and white robber birds cross the expanse below. Only this ledge kept him tethered to the earth. He gazed, spellbound.

He thought he heard a faint whistle. A chill crawled up his spine as he felt the presence. It had been a long time since his angel had visited—but then he was no longer certain it was an angel. He strained to see something, to hear something, but he decided his ears played tricks.

Carefully, he studied the basin looking for his unseen companion. He saw nothing, but the feeling of its presence was strong. He felt comfort, not fear. He was no longer alone.

He removed his breechcloth and moccasins. Like the giving ceremony, he now had nothing. Now it was him and his Maker. Now he could cry for his vision.

"I want to talk to you, God. I pray you hear me this day. Listen to Sky Eyes. Listen to me, to whom you have given life and a spirit. Listen to me this day and every day. Send me a vision. Show me what you have in mind for my life as you have done for the Sheepeater boys for years before me.

"Find me acceptable, please, God. I know my body is now streaked with dirt and blood. The white, sacred clay has almost rubbed away. Don't hold this against me. I tried. I know I've not always done what is right in your eyes. But this is me, Sky Eyes, whom you created. Accept me as I am. Let me receive your vision, Great Mystery."

He sat a moment, surveying the beauty before him, thinking. Surely there was no finer place to talk with God. *I know I'm not supposed to believe in spirits like the Tukudeka believe. Mama and Papa taught me this. But you do send your angels, and for certain, there are demons in the world. But I think you also left part of your spirit in this world you created. I think that is what the Tukudeka feel—what I'm now able to feel.*

He stood and again spoke. "I see this great beauty before me, as I have each day I've been in this land, even when things have been hard, and I know you are here in every living animal, in every living plant, in every stone—you are here.

"Perhaps the only place you aren't is in a man's heart who has rejected you. Therefore, you are everywhere else. It's your spirit that is within all else."

Erik gazed deep into the blue sky above the peaks. "Now show me, Great Mystery, what you intend for me."

The sun was fully overhead, and Erik was thankful for the remaining clay protecting his body. He sat back in the shade of the overhanging rocks. No breeze yet stirred this place. The warmth radiating from the rocks, which had felt good at first, now felt uncomfortably warm.

He looked out to the vast distances north to the horizon beyond the great, unseen river. Small, snowcapped peaks blended into the white clouds.

He studied each peak from its summit down along each ridge, exploring each nook, each open spot, each rock outcrop, each clump of trees, until the ridge flowed into the gray blue depths of the canyon below.

The peak to his right gently ascended from the south—tree covered, gnarled, and broken—but on the north, it suddenly dropped hundreds of feet, stark and sheer, as if some giant hand had gouged away half its bulk. It was dark, almost black. At its feet were two small alpine lakes, deep green and intense blue.

Dark ribbons of rock and fractured ledges crisscrossed its broken black face—barren, naked rock, dark and brooding, almost sad. Erik decided the dark gashes were indeed down-turned, sorrowful eyes. The mountain reminded him of a boy, dark eyes, gazing sadly to the north. Sad Boy Mountain, he decided to name it.

He wondered what had been seen over the ages that had saddened the boy. Perhaps a Sheepeater boy had come here to seek his vision. But his vision was sad, and he hadn't been able to return and tell his people. Instead he became the stone mountain, forever sorrowful. Erik tried to shake the thought, but he couldn't.

Erik returned his gaze to the hidden canyon below. He thought again of his old cabin. He thought of Katrine. *Someday I will go to find her. Perhaps next spring when I'm older.* Then Erik realized his thoughts had taken him from the purpose of his quest. Firmly he told himself, *The old life is gone. For now, I am a Tukudeka seeking his vision. Please, Great Mystery, take from me all the thoughts of old. Give to me thoughts of this life—the people's life. Help me receive my vision.*

The sun grew warmer and with it, Erik's thirst. He wanted not to drink. He knew his chances for a vision were increased if, in the eyes of the Great Mystery, he had suffered and presented himself humbly, denying himself food, clothing, water, and sleep—things needed by an earthly body but not by a spiritual body. Only by denying himself these things and concentrating on his spirit would he be found acceptable to the Great Mystery.

Erik's thirst grew. He knew he needed to remain strong. He needed water. Carefully, he climbed down to the lake. Kneeling in the spongy grass at the edge, he drank deeply. How good it was, icy cold in the summer heat. A smooth boulder rested half above the water. He jumped out onto it and stared down at the watery world beneath. The bottom was visible far out toward the middle.

The lake was oval except where it squashed up against the cliff and rocky rubble. Several small springs bubbled from under the rocks to feed it.

He watched a pair of large trout swim lazily past, suspended, casting their shadows onto the yellow brown bottom. The shadows moved across the lakebed, bobbing up and down in the varying depths, following the trout. Unafraid, the trout drifted into the darker, deep water and disappeared.

Something red on the opposite shore caught Erik's eye. He jumped off the rock and skirted the shore to investigate. A narrow band of rust-colored rocks emerged from the ground and ran in a jagged line to Sad Boy Mountain where it merged with the black cliff. Erik dug up some of the red. He realized it was much like the red clay he and Badger had gathered at the paint pots. He collected more and then ripped up several spreading dogbane shrubs. Shining Water had called them striped cupflowers and had once used their milky sap for medicine. Erik thought he'd try mixing the sap with the clay to make paint.

He continued around the lake and paused at the outlet. It was clogged with broken logs, some floating, some submerged. Torn from the cliffs by avalanches, they had floated across the lake and collected here. The creek funneled down into a small pool below the outlet then spilled quickly into a narrow ravine where, twisting and turning, it cascaded down toward the river far below. Several large trout swam leisurely in the small pool. Erik guessed they were spawning.

Drinking again, he left the lake and climbed back to his perch. Cloud shadows came and went now, cooling him briefly from the summer heat and bright sun. To the north, he watched large thunderheads forming. As they grew, their tops reached ever higher into the blue. Their dark bottoms drifted slowly toward the east. Erik hoped it would rain. He was not allowed to bathe until his journey was finished. Now he longed for a bath to rid himself of the heat, grime, and sticky clay. Erik prayed as he watched the clouds build.

Movement below broke his concentration. Rock rabbits—pikas—scurried from rock to rock. He thought they looked like large mice, except they had stubs for tails and bigger ears, giving them a rabbitlike appearance. Shortly, one paused and emitted a high-pitched *e-e-e-e-k*. Another answered from across the talus. Back and forth their tiny calls sounded.

Erik found a stone and crushed the dogbane stems, collecting the sap in a depression in the rock. Adding the red earth, he mixed it into a paste. Carefully, he painted his hand, and as he and Badger had done, he placed his hand on the rock under the protective overhang, leaving his handprint. Part of his spirit was now captured for all time at this spot. Satisfied, he sat back.

The shadows stayed longer now as the thunderheads steadily built. Now and again, a breeze, stirred up by their churning and billowing motion, buffeted his ledge.

Erik caught himself nodding. He was exhausted. The night had been cold. It appeared that soon rain would be upon him. The clouds to the north were black, marked by flashes of light, followed at length by the dull rumble of thunder.

"Please, dear God," Erik prayed. "I want to receive a vision, but please protect me and the others. Perhaps I was foolish to pick this spot, but its beauty captured me and held me here. Forgive me. Find me acceptable in your eyes." He shivered as the cool wind from the thunderheads buffeted him.

Erik wanted to sleep but dared not. He studied where the sun stood—now lower on the horizon. His head felt fuzzy.

***

Erik watched as the sinking sun began to lengthen the shadows. The rain hadn't come except for a welcome spatter across his rock ledge. It created pockmarks on his body, so it looked as if he had a strange disease.

He longed for his vision journey to be complete. Still he remained— the watcher of his lands below—lands now turned golden in the fading light. Nightfall approached.

The trout busily fed as the shadows lengthened. Smaller fish leaped from their liquid world like tiny darts of silver, then plinked back into the silvery, blue green waters. The larger trout seemed less anxious.

They simply broke the surface, gobbled in heavy slurps, and rolled back down, roiling the water upward behind them.

The lake, now gone silver in the fading light, was a mass of circles and blips—circles that caught silver on one side and pink on the other, expanding, moving uniformly outward until interrupted or joined by other rings—a lake of silvery rings.

Now the first stars of evening appeared. Faintly, one by one, they came into view in the indigo sky.

To the south rumbled the thunderheads. Their billowing tops lit up frequently, luminous yellow white, from the imbedded lightning. Softly, the rumbling followed.

The world swam before Erik's fatigued eyes. Stubbornly he prayed. He dozed and abruptly woke from a vivid dream. He wondered if it was his vision, but then he found himself still on the ledge.

The moon rose, bathing the world in an eerie light. The world was more than black and silvery white. Erik discerned subtle colors: snow glowed with a slight pink cast; granite showed a soft blue tinge; the transparent lake, through which the moonlight filtered, shone a pale blue green.

Erik studied the moonlight reflecting brightly from the snow, creating sharp contrasts with the blue purple banks in shadows. It had a mystical appearance. Resembling lights scattered throughout the basin, each mound of snow glowed like a slice of moon come to earth. The granite also glowed but with less light and was crisscrossed by long, blue black shadows cast by the alpine firs.

He returned his gaze to the lake. Never had he seen such light. It reflected from the surface—soft, blue green, radiant, and soothing. More striking, it penetrated the lake to its rocky bottom and, reflecting, created a glow, a living glow, a light like none he had ever seen—soft, wavering, almost beckoning him to join.

Slowly the moon climbed to its zenith, changing the reflected light from the lake. It picked out a spot within the lake that glowed eerily, a brighter green than elsewhere.

Erik moved farther back against the rocks but felt no warmth. He began shivering again and curled tightly into a ball, clasping his knees against himself. Hunger nagged him, but the ache was not as terrible anymore. His thirst had returned, and his head throbbed with fuzzy, unfocused thoughts and prayers. God was his partner on the ledge with him. He had talked so long and constantly with him that he just accepted he was there beside him, still talking. Half dreams came and went.

The cold increased, and Erik worried. *What if I'm not strong enough? What if I freeze to death?* Surely he wouldn't freeze, but still his warmth, and perhaps his life, could be stolen by the night cold.

He got up, stood shakily, and walked in circles on the ledge, studying his shadow as it moved with him around and around in a slow, shuffling circle. As he came into the moonlight, he felt odd, since surely he must stand out like a ghost. Then he crossed into the shadows, turning his back on the moonlight. He watched his shadow lead him, shrink smaller, and then turn and walk behind him as he came back into the light. Shivering, he walked into the light, but it was light without warmth. He imagined the moon to be the sun. He tried to feel warmer as he entered its light. He imagined he did.

Again, Erik felt his head swimming. He sat and watched the eastern sky—watching, watching for the first sign of light, praying for mercy, praying his vision would come.

CHAPTER 38

ERIK WOKE AS THE sun rose and warmed him. Quickly stumbling up, standing, swaying, he grew immediately angry. He had fallen asleep. If he slept, a vision would never come.

Thirst burning within, Erik forced himself to go without drinking until the sunlight walked down the mountain to the lakeshore. The twitter of birds again filled the basin and was soon joined by the high-pitched *e-e-e-k* of pikas.

A buck, antlers in velvet, paused at the lake's outlet to drink. He had appeared so quietly, stealthily, Erik hadn't noticed until he saw movement on the water. He wondered if this was his vision. Everything about him seemed much a blur now. Sometimes he didn't seem part of the world. He found himself caught up in his thoughts, and the thoughts were becoming reality, not separate from his being as they should be. For times the fuzziness cleared, and he focused back on the world around him. Then, without consciousness, he found himself coming back awake as if asleep, as if in a dream.

The young buck was real. He drank and watched around himself; tugged at some of the young brush near the stream's edge; and when Erik looked again, he was gone.

The day quickly warmed. The sun beat down hot. Erik didn't curse the heat, his hunger, or his thirst. This was part of his test—the sacrifice he had to make to become worthy of a vision.

Head swimming, eyes blurring, he stumbled back to the lake for a drink. It helped. His head cleared; the throbbing eased. The world returned to reality for a moment.

Thunderheads now towered above Sad Boy Mountain, high into the vivid blue above. Over his shoulder loomed other thunderheads, white, luminous mushroom tops anchored by heavy blue black bottoms. Steadily, the clouds built in the afternoon heat. Now and then fitful puffs of wind caught his ledge, pushing his hair around, spilling it before his eyes, stirring the waters below, bending the trees.

Erik envied the flight of the birds that rode the drafts of the clouds, as it seemed to him, for fun. Certainly they weren't hunting. They swirled on their wings, rising higher and higher until they slipped away to descend in spirals and again come into the swirling, unseen drafts of rising air.

He stood at the edge, empty space falling away below him. He raised his hands and arms into the breezes now steadily pushed by the churning clouds. He felt enveloped in the wind, almost as if he too could leap out and fly with the birds. He laughed at the feeling from the wind buffeting his skin, as he stood exposed to the approaching storm.

Erik startled to a flash of lighting and booming thunder. The sun was gone, masked by heavy clouds; the wind hissed across his ledge. Thunderheads with deep, black bellies filled the sky. Another flash lit the black cliff face before him, closely chased by crackling, booming thunder. The echoes reverberated from the mountain behind him, booming.

He suddenly felt as if his unseen watcher was gone. He suddenly grew afraid. He felt alone. The lightning was close. The wind buffeted him, picking up bits of stone, flinging them across the ledge, bouncing them stinging off his skin and the rocks behind him.

He retreated to the overhang and watched an angry sheet of rain approach. It had broken away from Sad Boy Mountain. It was as if the lightening had ripped apart the thunderheads, and they now poured out rain in a rage. The rain turned the lake into a churning, gray black mass along its advancing line. Erik watched in awe but also in fear. He had nowhere to go.

A flash lit up the basin as lighting struck trees near Sad Boy Mountain. It flickered momentarily, a brilliant ribbon from cloud to rock, then abruptly disintegrated into a dozen balls of liquid fire that raced downward, bouncing and skittering across the ground, some to the lakeshore. The explosion of thunder came instantaneously, vibrating the ledge and reverberating from wall to wall. The trees burned brightly but died out shortly to a small blaze. Erik felt terror. He had no protection except the rocks at his back.

He felt pricking on his arms and legs and looked down. Each tiny hair stood erect. Now a slight singing—a buzzing—low pitched at first, then higher, came from numerous places around him, like a thousand bees. He felt his hair standing on end. He shoved himself back under the rocks, watching and afraid.

The singing buzz increased. The rocks began glowing with ribbons of green fire. Like a myriad of snakes weaving in and out, the glowing light flowed from rock to rock, up and across, standing, wavering in long luminous fingers toward the angry sky. The singing increased to a buzzing whine.

The world exploded as the lightning struck, splitting into fierce white light and heat as it met the rocks above in a tremendous blast. Erik felt the force and found himself deafened, blinded. He grabbed at his ears and writhed in pain, fear, and blindness. A strong acrid odor hung in the air. He knew only that he still lived, and painfully, he opened his eyes. He saw the rain advancing, spattering below him. The ringing in his head subsided; his ears hurt.

Huge drops of rain spattered with the wind across his ledge. They disintegrated into a stinging spray that came under the protecting rocks.

Now wave after wave of pelting rain washed over the ledge, slamming against him. Erik gasped and shuddered as the cold hit. He tried to move under the rocks to avoid the storm's full strength. It was no use. The rain slammed into him in frozen torrents, driven by the wind into every nook and cranny.

He found himself shivering uncontrollably. Water ran in sheets from the rocks. It became a curtain above his back, cascading off the rocks into a torrent about his head and shoulders. The thundering noise all but drowned the reverberating explosions of thunder.

The sting increased; the rain had turned to hail. He pulled his breechcloth over his head and shoulders. Hailstones rocketed at him, hitting with stinging force, bouncing away crazily off the rocks in all directions. He cowered in a ball, keeping the breechcloth over him, allowing the hail to slam into his back and shoulders. Torrents of icy hailstones and water ran in sheets over his head and shoulders. "Dear God, please stop it! Please," he cried. "I cannot take it! I cannot take it!" He could hardly take a breath without breathing in the icy spray. His shivering became convulsive. The noise, deafening.

The hail piled in small, white drifts about his feet, some snaking away in torrents over the rock's edge. Erik gasped in shuddering breaths, trying to breathe during the storm's rage. He could feel his body being pounded and numbed by the stinging hail and now feared for his life. "Please, dear God," he sobbed, "Stop the hail. I cannot take it."

Lightning lit up his ledge repeatedly and thunder reverberated in booming echoes. Erik went numb with cold. He felt his strength weakening. He couldn't fight back. His body was shutting down. He struggled back. He envisioned his naked body lying on the ledge, white in the pounding rain.

Abruptly the hail paused. He looked up to see light beyond the clouds. Another sheet of rain mixed with hail hit. Erik cowered again, protecting his face with his battered and stinging hands. It paused, ending in a spatter and sprinkle. Light glowed from the wet rocks. Sheets of rain still filling the basin moved slowly away.

Erik turned, chilled, shivering uncontrollably. He brushed the water from his body. The storm moved south. "Thank you, God," he whispered. "Thank you."

The light behind Sad Boy Mountain increased until the glow reached under the clouds. Erik danced vigorously to warm himself and prayed for the sun. He rubbed his arms and legs. The breeze chilled him as the water began to evaporate.

Everywhere lay heaps of hailstones. The lakeshores were white as if blanketed in a heavy snow. The entire lake basin had turned into an incredible winter wonderland—a frozen landscape. Green leaves that had been stripped from the trees and shrubs lay scattered on the white.

The dull roar Erik now heard was the myriad of streams of new fallen rain running from every rocky ledge, every crevice, racing downward in gurgling streams carrying the frozen, icy hail off the mountains, down to the lakes below.

Erik shivered uncontrollably. His body was pounded and bruised, and his head ached. He continued to dance and pray for the sun. The clouds moved slowly. He gazed earnestly toward where the sun lay hidden. Slowly, slowly they lifted; at last, the beams broke through.

The warmth flooded his body, and Erik cried out in joy. Never had he endured such freezing, numbing cold. Never had he withstood such a brutal force.

He stood clasping his shoulders facing the sun, tears in his eyes. "Thank you, God." The warmth began to return. The numbness began to fade, but he could hardly stand he was shaking so badly. He sank to his knees.

He looked himself over. All traces of the white clay were gone. His scratches were washed clean, now marked pink and red by scabbed lines of dried blood and healing skin. His body felt numb, pounded. He ached. Shakily, he sat back.

The sun felt good. He sat, unable to move, soaking in its warmth. The pain eased. The heat returned. Below him, the hail melted rapidly.

The birds resumed their nervous twittering. The pikas returned. All seemed glad to have survived the storm.

Erik felt the unseen presence return. Somehow, this time, it felt nearer. Erik scanned the basin carefully. It seemed to be from his right. Was this his spirit helper? Did it bring his vision? If so, why did it wait?

Then he shivered. He wondered if it could be evil. The Sheepeaters had never talked about a person's helper being evil. Was it possible? *Please, dear God, if this is a spirit from you, let it be good. I don't think I can handle any demons.* Erik found himself wondering about his prayers. Things were all mixed up. He didn't know what to believe anymore.

Then his uncertainty passed. Surely the spirit was benevolent. Already it had helped him twice. He tried to relax. For some reason, the spirit seemed content just to keep him company, to watch.

Erik felt his own joy returning as his strength came back. But now he wondered if he could survive another cold night. Slowly, dreadfully, he realized if he had no vision this night, he would need to eat and sleep. He wouldn't succeed. The Great Mystery wouldn't accept him. He wondered if God really did test him. "Please, Great Mystery, find me worthy of a vision."

Things began to grow fuzzy again. He sat blinking, watching the sun sink, his head swimming, fading in and out. The heat had returned, and he almost found himself wishing for a light, cooling rain. The sky faded to gray. The thunderheads were far to the north. Their white mushroom tops occasionally lit up brightly. *I now know what it's like to be consumed by the wrath and fury of a thunderstorm,* he thought. *Never again.* He watched as the sun slipped below the peaks and felt the coolness of evening come.

He sat quietly gazing back out across the alpine lakes. The shadows grew long, and the light dimmed. Another night approached. He studied Sad Boy Mountain. *Maybe it was sad because all along it had known I would be coming here some day, and it knew I would fail.* Erik felt a knot welling up within.

The setting sun caused Sad Boy Mountain to glow. Erik stared, struck by the beauty. Hours ago, he had been in the bowels of hell. The world had been an angry, wild maelstrom; now, once more, it was at peace. The orange-lit mountain reflected from the silent lakes at its foot.

To the north, other peaks picked up the pink and orange glow. The forested canyons grew darker, more somber—grew lavender, then purple blue.

Erik felt at peace, as peaceful as the basin before him. "At least, Great Mystery, you have revealed to me things I've never seen or felt before. If I don't have a vision—if this is the way it is to be—then I shall accept this."

Night gathered; the moon rose. Erik fought to stay awake. He caught himself fading in and out of consciousness. He walked in his circle as he had done the night before.

He sat, his back against the yet-warm rocks. He studied the moon's soft glowing face. He reached out to try to touch it. It had climbed above his basin and glowed, shimmering, reflected in the quiet blue green pool below. Soft shadows crept across the waters and land, bringing the landscape into vivid detail. The world before him spun into fuzziness, and Erik's head fell. He shook it and gazed back across the velvet darkness at the shimmering moonlight. Again it grew fuzzy.

***

Suddenly Erik looked up into the eyes of a mountain lion. *I should be afraid,* he told himself, but he wasn't. Coldly, he studied the cat as it began to pace back and forth on his ledge. In turn, the cat starred back as if it had not expected to find the ledge occupied. Erik told himself he should run, but there was no place to go.

The cat continued to eye him as if daring him to move. Erik knew to move would invite an attack. He sat stone still, eyes on the mountain lion, still surprised by his lack of fear. "Well, God," he whispered. "If I can survive being pounded by rain, lightening, and hail, I expect I can survive this guy."

The lion turned and approached him and sat a few feet away. All the while, its green eyes studied him. "Sky Eyes," she said. "You know you were foolish to come on this vision journey."

"Yes," replied Erik, admitting to himself he had probably made a mistake in seeking a vision. He was not the least bit surprised that the mountain lion had spoken to him.

"The vision journey is for Tukudeka boys who would become men—not for little white boys who are lost in this country, who cry when they are hurt or when it rains hard on them."

"I'm sorry," replied Erik, lowering his head. "I think anyone would have cried in that storm. And I still want to have a vision. Is it so wrong for me to have a vision, even if I'm not a Tukudeka?"

"A helper has to bring you a vision," explained the lion.

"Hey, how about you?" He lit up with the thought and opened his hands to the lion. "Can't you bring me a vision? I'm not afraid of you. Haven't I shown this? All Tukudeka are very afraid of you, you know."

"Yes, they are," the lion replied. "But that's because they don't understand me. You seem to. But let's not talk about your vision." The lion sounded somewhat perturbed. "You seem to have forgotten what you did to me, haven't you, Sky Eyes?"

"What do you mean?" Erik sat back, troubled, watching the lion as she paced, her tail twitching.

"You drove me away from your cabin, remember?"

"Yes, I remember," replied Erik, and he suddenly grew fearful. This cat would not be his helper.

"I was hungry, Sky Eyes." The cat stopped and sat, staring at him. "And you drove me away. Me and my children."

"I'm sorry," replied Erik. "But I didn't want you to eat our ox. We were hungry too. Maybe that's why Mama Larson died, you know. Because of you, our ox ran away." Erik shook his head. He could feel the ache build as memories of blowing snow and that winter night crept back.

To his surprise, the mountain lion hung her head. "I didn't know that, Sky Eyes. I didn't know you ate the ox too. I'm sorry."

"Well, actually, we didn't want to eat Red. Red and Smoky pulled our wagon. We were going to a valley where we were going to farm," Erik replied softly.

The mountain lion looked back at him. "But Mama Larson's happy now. You know she watches over you," the lion said. "And she's not mad at you for becoming a Tukudeka. She understands."

Erik couldn't believe what he heard. The mountain lion knew about his mother. Now he wondered if he was asleep and dreaming all this. He pinched himself and stood up. No, he was awake. The lion watched as he stood.

"Tell me about Mama," Erik blurted. "What about Papa too? Is he okay?"

The lion looked away. "Sh-h-h, Sky Eyes. It's not for me to tell you those things. Just know things are okay.

"Look," the lion said, "I came to talk to you tonight because although you seek a vision, what about Katrine? When will you seek her, Sky Eyes?"

Erik was surprised and suddenly ashamed. "Soon," he replied. "I haven't forgotten. That is one reason I seek a vision, to become a man, to leave the Tukudeka."

Erik caught movement in the moonlight below along the lakeshore. Two bull elk had come to the shore to drink. Erik walked to the edge and watched them. He could tell by the large branching antlers and the frosted white look of the shaggy coat that one was very old.

After the elk had watered, they faced each other. Erik wondered why their antlers were not encased in velvet. It was still early summer; they should be. The two bulls backed away and then launched themselves at each other. The crash of their colliding antlers rang across the basin. Erik watched, amazed at their power. After recoiling, they backed away and again, lowering their heads, came back, crashing, locking their antlers again. The older bull seemed to have no trouble pushing the younger one around.

Erik had always wondered about elk battles, and he watched amazed. Suddenly he shouted down to them. "Why are you fighting? It's not autumn yet."

They paused. The larger bull looked Erik's way.

"All elk fight," he replied. "We fight for our mates. We always have."

"Why don't you share?" questioned Erik. He always wondered why one bull had to have so many cows.

"Why don't *you* share?" retorted the elk.

"I'm not married," replied Erik.

"Ah, but you have Quickly Smiles for whom you will fight," replied the bull.

Erik felt stunned. He hardly knew Quickly Smiles. Why would the elk talk about her? Why would he want to fight for her? "How do you know that?" Erik called down.

"We know those things, Sky Eyes."

Erik shook his head and started to tell them he would soon leave the Sheepeaters and Quickly Smiles when behind him he heard another smaller voice calling his name. Erik turned. He noticed the mountain lion was gone. In her place was a tiny pika. He couldn't help himself but to call out upon seeing the tiny creature. "Well, hello, little fellow. Welcome to my home."

"Your home?" the pika squinted at him as he squeaked in his high-pitched voice. "This is *my* home, Sky Eyes." The pika squatted back on his hind legs. "You are here but for a short while on your vision journey. When you leave, my family and I will move back."

"I'm sorry, little pika," murmured Erik. "I didn't mean to chase you from your home."

"Oh, no bother, Sky Eyes. We have plenty of homes," he replied, coming closer. "We always have one we can go to. Besides, my family and I have rather enjoyed watching you. You know you're funny, Sky Eyes. You talk a lot, but no one answers you."

"Oh, that is my praying, little pika," Erik replied. "I pray to the Great Mystery and seek my vision. I do not think it's funny."

"Well, no, that's not what I meant either," said the pika. "Now sit down Sky Eyes, before you fall asleep." He sat back on his haunches, studying him with his big eyes. "I want you to listen to a story I have to sing for you."

Erik returned to the rock overhang and sat. He rested against the rock, wanting to sleep. He watched the pika beginning to circle in the moonlight. Each time it completed a circle, it climbed onto the stone and faced him. Then it climbed down and began again. Now it stood on the rock and faced him.

Erik grew fearful. "But if you sing me a story, I might fall asleep, and I won't have my vision."

"Do not worry about that, Sky Eyes. Do not worry. My song is a good story. Besides, you must listen to my song before you can have your vision. That is what the night cat would have told you."

"In that case, I will listen to your song story, little pika," murmured Erik, and he settled back, eyes heavy.

The pika climbed into the moonlight on the rock and began singing his song story. It was a high, sweet melody—soft and beautiful. Erik couldn't believe his ears. How he longed to share this music with Badger. He concentrated on memorizing the words, the music, but now he was fighting to stay awake. How he longed to sleep. And the melody continued and brought to him memories of his mother. How he longed to share the song with his mother. She would have enjoyed this song. He could see her now, back at the cabin. The roof was fixed. Papa was there. The sun shone brightly; the cabin was warm. Erik felt a comfort he had missed for many months and gave in at last to sleep.

CHAPTER 39

THE PEOPLE WAITED ANXIOUSLY the third day with hopes a vision seeker would return. It had happened before. None wanted to reveal their feelings, yet it was important to the Twisted River Band that these boys would return as men. Weasel had not succeeded. He had returned the second night. He had been caught in a hailstorm. The people accepted it though there was an unspoken disappointment. Weasel would go another time. This was their way. No one would say anything against him—at least not openly.

Stands Alone questioned himself. *Why did Weasel fail? Weasel was stronger than this. No boy should give in because of a storm.*

Already Gray Owl and the others had expressed their displeasure in Runs Fast. When Runs Fast returned in the early morning of the second day, far beyond any prudent time, Gray Owl and the others questioned him. Runs Fast explained he had spotted the little white boy and in doing his duty, followed him north to the canyon of River of No Return. He said he didn't know what the white boy was thinking, for no boy ever traveled that far. Perhaps he didn't know what was expected of him. He followed the boy to the canyon's edge and looked for him, thinking he might have fallen. When it grew dark, he decided to turn back. However, the look in Gray Owl's eyes told Runs Fast a deep hurt.

Free Hawk was also concerned by Runs Fast's actions. Sky Eyes knew what was expected. Although he was not surprised Sky Eyes would travel far, he knew he had to have reason to travel to the canyon. Runs Fast had pursued—pursued long after he should have. A fear nagged him. Perhaps there was more. But Free Hawk shook this feeling.

None returned on the third day.

***

The noon sun of the fourth day woke Erik. He had slept a long time. He sat up, remembering his strange dream, and suddenly knew. There was the rock the pika had sat on to sing his story. Erik longed now to recall the melody, and his heart ached when he couldn't. Yet it also filled with joy. His quest was finished. He shook his head.

He stood and faced the morning sun, arms outstretched. "Great Mystery, my heart soars with joy. You have answered my prayers. You have accepted me as worthy." He had succeeded. He would now eat and head back to the star-grass camp.

Gingerly, Erik made his way down toward the lake's shore. He found himself stiff and sore. His body ached from being hammered by the hail.

Hunger and thirst had been his companions for so long, he almost felt he didn't need to eat. He went to the small pool below the outlet. The trout hugged the bank, seeking safety. Carefully, Erik reached his hand into the water, deep below the drifting trout. Suddenly he brought it up, like a bear fishing, and scooped one onto the bank. It flopped helplessly in the grass. He continued fishing until he scooped out a second. There were more, but two would be enough.

He took the trout and headed across the basin toward the stand of timber he had seen struck by lightning last evening. If any smoldering wood remained, Erik knew he could light a fire. If not, he would eat them raw.

He climbed to the trees; smoke still curled from the burn. Scorched black shrubs radiated outward from the trunk. Erik kicked into the orange duff and turned over some winking red coals. Gathering some wood, he soon coaxed the coals into a blaze.

Erik roasted the two trout and ate, licking his fingers, savoring the rich taste. He wondered about catching more but was anxious to head home. This was the fourth day. He lay back in the grass, feeling relaxed and full. He realized he had slept a long time, but it had been good. His body needed it.

Looking again at the ledge, he decided on one last thing before beginning his journey home. He collected more of the red earth and mashed more stems of spreading dogbane. Carefully, he added some paintings below his red handprint—some paintings that captured his vision.

It was now late afternoon. Erik headed toward the saddle between Sad Boy Mountain and the peak that had been at his back. He figured the saddle would lead to the shortest route.

He began climbing, but the cirque headwall steepened. Huge rock slabs blocked the route. He slipped trying to scale one and decided against trying again. He tried a second route. Again, he found the wall too slick, crumbly. He scanned the wall, looking for a safe way up, but he couldn't see one. Disappointed, he turned back. He realized he wouldn't have enough light to make it back before nightfall. He realized he needed to backtrack.

He headed back the way he had come and began working his way around the edge to the south. Before he moved beyond sight, he took one last look at what had become so familiar—his lake, his ledge, Sad Boy Mountain. He knew he would never again see this place. Before he turned, he thought he heard the quiet wavering whistle once more. For some reason he felt that whatever it was, it would no longer follow.

Soon he encountered the basalt flows and the chute where he had climbed up out of the canyon. He studied the way above him to see if he could continue upward and climb back out on top in this direction. He shuddered to think he might have to climb down and then around to the ledges he had traversed. It occurred to him he would be unable to climb from the last ledge. He looked at the route above him and began scrambling upward. *Maybe I won't have to.*

Carefully, he worked his way out onto the crumbling, black face. Erik avoided looking down. If he slipped, there was nothing to stop his fall. A queasy feeling filled his stomach. The black rock crumbled into pebbles and bounced from the face. Frantically, he struggled to keep his grip. Slowly, he edged his way upward, hanging tightly to a few scrubby alpine firs that protruded from the face.

At last, he gained the top and pulled himself upright. Now he looked down. The sight made him dizzy.

He turned and headed up through the alpine basin toward a ridge of smaller peaks. He considered climbing the ridge but realized night would catch him. It would be better to remain here for the night. He searched for food but found only a few pink-blossomed onions. He dug and ate the bulbs, enjoying their sweetish taste. He crawled under some overhanging rocks and behind some brush where he could sleep. This was his fourth night away. *Perhaps Badger is already back and sleeping in a warm lodge,* he thought. He slept in fits because of the night chill.

***

The morning of the fourth day, the people went about their work and play as usual but with frequent gazes to the mountains. That day the remaining vision seekers should return, whether or not they had been successful. To stay out longer would risk their lives.

Young boys walked up the slopes to where they could keep watch. Late morning, one shouted and waved back to the camp. The women took up a joyful trill, and the people turned out to watch for the returning seeker. Someone called out that the youth was Coyote.

From the manner in which he held himself, all knew he had been successful in his vision journey. Free Hawk proudly greeted Coyote and then solemnly led him to Gray Owl's lodge. There he would eat and rest and share his vision.

Mid afternoon, more shouts echoed through the camp. Badger returned. He too, from his carry, had been successful. Sees Far quickly ran to meet his charge and as quickly, to the accompanying trill, led him to Gray Owl's lodge. The grandmothers took food and drink to the newest one who had returned.

The sun slipped below the horizon. Free Hawk wandered to the edge of camp, concerned, eyes scanning for any sign of his adopted son. Whistling Elk joined him. Both sat silently as the dusk gathered.

Whistling Elk spoke, "Perhaps he encountered some trouble, and it will take another day. Sky Eyes will not travel at night."

Free Hawk shook his head, knowing Whistling Elk was trying to lessen his concern.

"I share this with you, Whistling Elk, for you are my brother friend, and you have honored me by being watcher to my son, Sky Eyes.

"During the days both my sons seek their vision, my heart has ached. Though my heart feels strongly for my son, Badger, it also feels strongly for my son, Sky Eyes."

Free Hawk turned to Whistling Elk, hoping he would understand. His feelings for the boy surprised even him.

"When he stood naked in the rain at the council rock, after he had given away all that he owned, I thought he was foolish. No one would have him. Surely he would die, which was as it should be.

"Then Shining Water told me she would not object if I found room in our lodge for the white boy. And I remembered my son who hunts the elk. The one who hunts the elk would agree that I take him as my own.

"I looked at the white boy in the rain." Free Hawk suddenly found it hard to talk, to explain. "Something told me to take this boy, and my heart went out to him."

Whistling Elk listened. His heart also ached for Sky Eyes. Where the boy had come to the people stupid and awkward, he had come to learn their ways. That was two winters ago. Now he attempted a vision seeking. He shook his head.

Brilliant stars now appeared above the rocky peaks. Free Hawk searched in hopes of spotting a campfire. Sky Eyes was good at starting a fire. But there was none, only the empty night sky and the soft murmur of the wind.

"If he has a helping spirit as Gray Owl says, then the spirit will see him home," said Whistling Elk. He rose and turned for his lodge.

When Free Hawk crawled into his robes, he said nothing to Shining Water. Singing Bird was softly asleep in her place. Free Hawk gazed upon her small form. *Is she our last child? If Sky Eyes is lost, it would not be good to have but two children.* He felt comfort knowing Badger was safe in Gray Owl's lodge, but he felt a tremendous emptiness for his other son.

"My heart aches for him as well, my husband," whispered Shining Water.

Free Hawk was surprised that she expressed her thoughts. She must be learning this from Sky Eyes. He never hesitated to share his thoughts. Free Hawk wondered if it might not be the right thing to do after all.

"Tomorrow I will seek him," Free Hawk replied.

Shining Water appeared shaken. "But you must not. That is not our way. He must complete his quest on his own. If the Great Mystery has taken his spirit home, it—"

Free Hawk made the quieting noise, and Shining Water looked down.

"He is our son, and his ways are different. I will go to see where he is. I will not assist him," he explained. "That is all."

***

At first light the fifth day, Erik woke. Remembering his vision, he felt giddy. He had succeeded. That day he would return to the people. He would be named a true man.

He drank from a small seep and began working his way up toward the ridgeline. Carefully he picked his way among the boulders and climbed up the near vertical side. He worried it would again be like the cliff near Sad Boy Mountain. If it turned out to be so, he would need to backtrack even more. But then, he could see his route to the ridge. It would only take time. Cresting the top, he paused in disbelief.

He stood on the ridge confused; the mountain breeze buffeted him. The star-grass meadows didn't lie below. Instead another scoured alpine valley and another naked ridgeline lay in between. How had he traveled so far from the camp? Where had all this country come from? How could Badger's mountain still be so far to the south?

Erik sat down to think. Behind him was familiar country. To the north was the black cliff he had dropped below. The alpine basin where he ran from Runs Fast had to be beyond it. He had to be correct. Instead of a single ridgeline between him and the summer camps, there were at least two, maybe three.

Disappointed, he knew it would be near evening at best before he made it back. When he had dropped into the canyon to escape Runs Fast, he had moved farther away from the star-grass meadows. He had not made a loop.

Topping a large boulder, Erik jumped to cross a gap, something he had done hundreds of times, but his foot slipped on loose pebbles, twisting. Desperately trying to regain his balance, he plunged off the rock's face. In a sudden burst of pain, he was swallowed into blackness.

***

Toward noon on the fifth day, sadness filled the camp. No vision seeker had remained away for five days. They remembered the boy who had killed the bear and how they went to find him but did not. Some had already begun the mourning noises.

Gray Owl wondered why Sky Eyes had not returned. He wondered if Sky Eyes's spirit helper had abandoned him. He could not understand why the Great Mystery would do this, however, if he had truly brought him to the people.

With a heavy heart, he called for a council of the men, including the vision seekers who had returned. Reluctantly, he spoke. "I have thought about this and though Sky Eyes has not returned, we shall have the naming ceremony tonight. Tomorrow we shall go to look for him."

The men nodded their approval until the pipe came to Free Hawk. "No," he said. "I will not hear Badger's new name until I seek my second son." He looked at Badger. "I will go today. I shall have Runs Fast lead me to the place where he last saw Sky Eyes. There I will see if I can find what has become of him."

When the pipe came to Runs Fast, he declined to speak. Not many seasons ago, he had returned to hear his new name. He wondered now what had caused him to think this white boy wouldn't be missed.

"I cannot disagree with what Free Hawk wishes … to seek his lost son," replied Gray Owl. "The boy of light hair has meant much to us." He spoke of Sky Eyes as if he walked the sky trails, an address that was not lost on the Sheepeaters. "However, I fear it is not good for us to delay this important time for our new men. This day they have earned.

We shall have the naming ceremony tonight and seek the boy with eyes of sky tomorrow."

It appeared the matter was closed until Badger took the pipe and spoke.

"Grandfather, I have not spoken as a man at council until this day. It is not good that I must speak in this manner for the first time I address the council, but I would also wait to hear my new name until after I find my brother. I would not be here tonight, awaiting a naming ceremony, if it had not been for my brother, Sky Eyes." Badger deliberately avoided addressing him as if he were lost. "I am certain Sky Eyes lives."

"How is this so?" asked Gray Owl.

"Yes," the others wondered.

"This I can feel in my heart as a true brother does. I do not wish to take a man's name until I see my brother well."

Gray Owl listened. "You speak with your heart for your brother with eyes of sky, and this is good. But we do not name you just for yourself. We name you for the people as well."

The men began to rise to leave when a scratching came at the lodge flap.

Weasel entered—eyes downcast. He walked between the men and sat before Gray Owl. He glanced briefly at Badger before looking to Gray Owl, a request to speak.

"Weasel, you wish to address us?" Gray Owl questioned.

Weasel didn't look up but nodded.

"This is unusual, Weasel, but you have earned this opportunity to be heard this day," Gray Owl replied.

"I confess I have heard your council and your decision about my brother friend. I could not keep away when I learned you were to discuss this." Weasel spoke quietly but directly to Gray Owl.

The others grew angry. How could Gray Owl allow a boy who failed his vision seeking to speak at the council? Runs Fast in particular protested angrily, but Gray Owl quieted him. "Runs Fast has had his opportunity to speak, and though Weasel did not succeed, I have allowed him to speak, and so he shall."

Runs Fast stood as if to leave but thought better of it and sat back down.

Weasel continued. "Four boys of the Twisted River Band began their vision journeys a few days ago. Two have returned as men. I returned as still a boy. I said it was because of the hailstorm, and this is true. But there is more. Perhaps I could have succeeded, but I did not try. It would not have been right for me to do so. I should have returned a boy, no matter. I failed." With this, Weasel paused, quickly looked at Runs Fast, and drew a breath. In that moment, Runs Fast's eyes flashed, but Weasel continued. "Runs Fast caught me." Weasel looked quickly away.

A murmur went through the lodge, and their eyes turned to Runs Fast.

"But Runs Fast did not say this. He did not bring you in. How is this true, Weasel?" Gray Owl demanded.

"He had me where I could not get away. He said I could go free if I said where Sky Eyes had gone," explained Weasel. A hush had fallen.

"I told Runs Fast it did not matter that I was caught—that I should return with him, as is the way of our people. Runs Fast said that since he had not laid hands on me, it was my choice. I could say where Sky Eyes was, or I could return with him still a boy. I chose to say where I last saw Sky Eyes and complete my journey, but my heart was empty."

Another murmur went through the lodge. Runs Fast had deceived Weasel.

"But yet you came back?" inquired Gray Owl. "Explain this if Runs Fast did not lay hands on you."

Weasel was silent a moment. He glanced at Runs Fast who gazed steadily ahead. He looked back to Gray Owl. "Inside I knew I had failed … whether Runs Fast said I was caught or not. My people trusted me to be true. I could not deceive my people. I certainly could not deceive my heart. I knew, and that's what was true."

The council was silent. Runs Fast didn't attempt an explanation. He knew the truth, as did all the Sheepeaters.

Gray Owl spoke. "You speak bravely, Weasel, and for this I am proud. This is a sad day for the Twisted River Band. Each man is free to decide and live his own life, but this is against the people. One does not decide to live against the people."

Gray Owl again offered the pipe around and gave each man a turn to speak. Each murmured his agreement, except Runs Fast who remained silent.

"I have given the words of Free Hawk and Badger great thought. I have heard the words of this boy, Weasel. I am disturbed that one among us would go against the wishes of the Great Mystery. As such, we will look for Sky Eyes before we name the new men."

At these words, Runs Fast stood and left. No one attempted to rise to stop him, but a sadness filled Gray Owl's lodge. Another Sheepeater was lost to the Twisted River Band. Just as his father had left with the white boy's horse, now the son had left, perhaps also having caused the loss of the white boy.

***

Erik woke to the crack of thunder and pelting rain. His head throbbed terribly as he tried to sit up and orient himself.

Gingerly, he checked himself. No bones were sticking out. Blood, however, streaked his body, and his hand found an angry, swollen gash on his head. He tried to stand and, shakily, managed to get to his feet. He nearly toppled forward when he tried to put weight on his left foot. He now saw where he had bled freely on the rocks. He wondered about the amount, like a deer killed by a mountain lion. Like his father had bled. Suddenly he felt frightened. He felt weak. He tried to walk. His ankle was not broken, but waves of dizziness hit him, and he sat down heavily. Above lay the ridgeline and the rocks from where he had fallen. Rain washed over him. He touched it to his lips and sucked the drops from the grass.

He studied the sky. This rain would pass. He guessed it was late afternoon, almost evening of the fifth day. Now the Twisted River Band would believe he walked the sky trails. He felt the urgency to get back—to show them he was all right. The drops of rain didn't quench his thirst. He tried to lap water from the rock depressions, but the rain was only a spatter. He had to have water. He had no choice but to head downward away from the ridge, back to find water.

Stumbling downward through the strewn boulders and tufts of white-star flowers, he paused at a snow bank. Water trickled from beneath. Scooping a depression for it to collect, he watched as it filled. At last, he was able to drink deeply of the icy water. But now he was

251

tired—very tired. Half aware of what was happening, he curled up in the grass and slept.

***

The four watchers and three youths left the star-grass camp shortly after the council broke. A short thunderstorm caught them halfway to the basin where the vision seekers had begun their journeys. Runs Fast hadn't returned.

By late afternoon, they reached the basin and the small pool of water where they had painted on the sacred clay. There they rested and considered their plans for searching.

"We should follow Sky Eyes's tracks," Free Hawk stated.

"That will take a long time," commented Sees Far. "If he is in trouble, we might not have time. We should decide where he could be and go there to look."

The men were silent, considering the options.

"I know this," Badger stated. "He headed toward the same peak as I did. Then I saw him head to where the sun sets, toward the notch." Badger pointed. "That is the direction Runs Fast moved when I saw him," he added. "That should be the direction we go."

The others murmured in surprise.

"If Sky Eyes has gone into the country beyond the notch, I fear for him," explained Stands Alone. "Few men have traveled that country."

Whistling Elk agreed. "That land goes to River of No Return. A man can walk for days before reaching the river. And if he should go into the canyon, it would be many days before he could get back."

Others were silent. All wondered why Badger and Sky Eyes would choose this most difficult direction.

"We shall go in the direction Badger saw him go," declared Free Hawk.

When they reached the notch, they discovered Erik's tracks and where it looked as if Runs Fast had followed. When they reached the far side of the alpine basin, they saw the broken rock and knew with certainty that Sky Eyes had headed down into River of No Return canyon. But now there was no light to see a trail. They decided to camp.

***

Erik woke early the sixth day to the morning chill. He felt stronger. The throbbing and dizziness had lessened. Encouraged, he drank again from the seep. Hunger stabbed at him. All he had had for the past days were the onions and two trout. He found a few glacier lilies and dug and ate them—bulbs, leaves, and flowers. He also gouged out more onions.

Gaining his feet, Erik stumbled upward a few steps at a time. His head spun and ankle throbbed. He wanted to rest but knew he could not. No one would find him here. It was up to him and the Great Mystery to see him home. He thought of the star-grass meadows and the welcome he would receive. With new encouragement, he moved on.

Wearily he set his sights on the ridge crest and walked toward it. Steadily, he climbed, closing the distance. His strength continued to return, and the throbbing subsided to a tolerable level.

At last, he reached the ridgeline, and at last, he recognized familiar country beyond. Far in the distance were the familiar trees and hills surrounding the summer hunting camp. Continuing downward, he walked until he reached cover of some trees. Now exhausted, he dozed for a while.

He woke, his head pounding, his thirst had returned. He now felt hot, like on fire, although the sun was not strong. Something was terribly wrong. He wanted to sleep. His head and ankle throbbed. He fought to remain awake. To sleep now might be his last. He knew there was water back at the basin where he began his journey. He knew in which direction it lay and that with each passing step he grew closer. Those thoughts and the increasingly familiar terrain encouraged him onward. He caught himself dizzy, waking up as if he were asleep on his feet—like before his vision. This scared him, and he woke enough to lurch forward.

Now above him rose the mountain where Badger had sought his vision. To the south lay the saddle where he had headed westward. He thought he saw a flash above the saddle, some movement, but then his eyes blurred.

He had nearly come full circle, he realized, but his thirst burned, and his head had become light. A fuzziness filled his eyes. Now the world spun before him in a brilliant light, and he felt himself falling into a warm nothingness.

***

On the morning of the sixth day, the men split up. The four headed east to see if Sky Eyes had returned from that direction. Free Hawk, Whistling Elk, and Badger continued toward River of No Return canyon. They climbed the peak to the south and searched a broken maze of cliffs and draws nearby. Had Sky Eyes been there, there was no sign. They returned to where the tracks emerged onto the black cliff.

In the day's full light, Free Hawk stopped and kneeled, pointing to the marks. "You see the blood on the broken stone. Sky Eyes has gone this way."

He followed the sign, Badger and Whistling Elk close behind.

"Here you can see where Runs Fast has followed. See the spacing? Sky Eyes runs recklessly."

Free Hawk now felt a deep anger toward Runs Fast. *It is good for Runs Fast that he has left the Twisted River Band,* he thought bitterly.

He reached the cliff face and saw the marks. Free Hawk paused, studying his son, Badger, and Whistling Elk. He knew Whistling Elk could read the signs. He hoped Badger couldn't. It was unlikely Sky Eyes had survived. He wanted to go below the black cliffs, but with Badger, he knew he could not. Badger would insist on following. Anyone could slip. He could not bear to lose Badger.

"My brother friend," he addressed Whistling Elk, looking into his eyes, hoping he wouldn't say anything to Badger, "the trail disappears. We should return to see if Sky Eyes went another direction." Another day he would return with Whistling Elk to find another route down into the canyon where he reasoned his son's body now lay.

Whistling Elk understood. "Come Badger, I agree. We shall find the direction Sky Eyes came out."

Badger hesitated, but when both men turned toward the ridge, he did likewise.

With a heavy heart, Free Hawk retraced his steps and climbed back toward the notch. No one spoke.

Badger reached the notch first. Suddenly he let out a cry of joy and leaped up onto a rock, pointing. "It is Sky Eyes. He is below us. He heads to the place where we started."

Free Hawk reached the notch and glanced in the direction Badger pointed. His heart soared. "Sky Eyes!" he shouted. He began running toward his son, Badger and Whistling Elk closely following.

At the basin, he paused. Something was wrong. Sky Eyes struggled to walk. Dread seeped in. *He does not look strong. How will he make it back to the basin? He must in order to finish his vision seeking.*

They watched. Once they saw him fall. He stayed fallen for a long moment. When Free Hawk was about to go to him, Sky Eyes rose again and came toward them. Now they could read the expression on his face—not like the people's expression—the white boy smiled. He would have said something they were certain, but then he had not yet completed his journey.

Free Hawk searched his son's face. Where was the sign he had received his vision? Surely he had. Sky Eyes smiled and nodded; Free Hawk knew it must be so.

Erik was a few yards away. Dried blood showed on his shoulders and streaked his torso. Now he was a few steps away. His eyes moved between Free Hawk's and Badger's. They said all was well.

Joy filled Erik and gave him the strength he needed to make it to the basin. "I have returned," he managed to say as he came into their company. He scooped water and drank and then bathed his face and shoulders, washing away some of the blood.

The men relaxed. They wanted to ask about his journey, but knew they could not until he had spoken to Gray Owl. Instead, they expressed their joy. "We thought you were lost, but now you have returned."

The trilling was nearly deafening as the people spotted Sky Eyes and the others coming toward them. They formed a dancing line as he walked proudly between them until he reached and entered Gray Owl's lodge. The people celebrated. The strange little white boy would now become a Sheepeater man.

CHAPTER 40

ERIK FELT NERVOUS ABOUT visiting Gray Owl. Although he knew the language well, and he could accurately relate his vision, what he had witnessed had seemed too personal and somewhat silly. He feared that Gray Owl would think so as well. During the walk back, he relived the details, but try as he might, he could not recall the pika's song—not a single word.

When he entered the lodge, Erik greeted Gray Owl in the custom of the Sheepeaters and waited until motioned to be seated.

Gray Owl made the cleansing ceremony with the sage and juniper. Silently he lit the pipe, the tobacco a mixture of kinnikinnick and willow, and took several puffs. He passed it to Erik, recognizing his new status. Erik inhaled and felt the acrid smoke burn. He held the smoke, trying not to cough, and allowed it to escape. He took two more short puffs, as was proper, and returned the pipe to Gray Owl. Gray Owl set it down and lifted his eyes. Erik knew it was his time to speak. He knew only truth would be spoken, for having taken of the pipe, to utter a falsehood would commit one's life to misfortune—probably death.

Nervously, he began. He hoped Gray Owl wouldn't laugh. He watched his eyes; they remained focused on his every word and every sign. Never was there a hint of anything but respect. Erik repeated everything in detail. He talked of the night cat and her message to him. He spoke of the fighting elk and Quickly Smiles. Finally, he talked of the pika and his beautiful song story. As he began, the words and melody came back. Erik found himself choking—it was all he could do to keep back his tears—it was his mother's song. It was the soft lullaby of the Swedish hills and forests. It was a prayer to God that his angels would watch over him. But the pika had sung more words. Now Erik heard them plainly. He sang of a boy with courage who had struggled and survived. It was a song of hope that the boy would be reunited with his family. Only after he had finished relating the story and recalled the tune, a high, lonely, wavering tone, like the breezes through the trees, like the wolf calling, only then did Erik realize the pika's song had been about him.

Silence filled the lodge. Gray Owl stared quietly at the smoldering embers. Finally, he spoke. "You speak well of your vision, Sky Eyes, but perhaps you overlook something." He wondered if Sky Eyes knew of his helping spirit.

Erik was bewildered. He shook his head. "No, I have shared everything." He adjusted his position. He knew it was important to relate everything. He remembered his vision, but Gray Owl's question caused him to become uncertain, like somehow he had failed.

"Perhaps it is not of your vision."

Immediately Erik realized to what he referred. "Yes ... there is something more." He wondered how Gray Owl could know. Carefully Erik related hearing the soft whistle and feeling the presence.

"But you did not see this spirit?"

"No." How could he tell him about before, about his father, about his mother?

Gray Owl could see the boy struggle. He remained silent. It would be Sky Eyes's decision to say more.

"But ... but before, I-I did see the spirit. When I was bringing my father through the snow ..." Recalling the terrible ordeal, the falling snow, dragging his father to the cabin, he felt the ache return, and he struggled for words to explain.

He also spoke of the second time, when he was bringing his mother to the canyon, but shortly, he could no longer speak. The ache in his chest was too great. The pain and memories he had tried to bury came back, overwhelming him. He had never shared his ordeal. He rocked forward and back, shaking.

Gray Owl was silent. He was humbled by what Sky Eyes said—humbled by his strength and courage. No man should experience what this boy had experienced.

Gray Owl tried to find the right words. He could see the boy's pain. "It is not for us to understand the ways of the Great Mystery, Sky Eyes. Just know that you did as you should. You showed you are a true man."

Gray Owl paused. "I do not know all the ways of the Great Mystery. No man does," Gray Owl tried to explain. "Perhaps the spirit from the trees—Sohobinewe Tso'ape—was sent, not for your parents, but for you."

"I don't understand," Erik replied, searching Gray Owl's eyes, hands kneading his knees.

"This spirit was your helper while you were a boy. It was sent to bring you to the people."

Erik was troubled over the thought. *The spirit—the angel—was not sent to help my parents but was sent for me. But why?* He didn't understand why God would work this way.

"And now you are of the people and have received your vision," Gray Owl said, satisfaction in his voice.

He brought forth several bundles and unwrapped them, revealing some feathers, bones, hair, and bundles of pigment. "This is a proud day for you and for the people, Sky Eyes. Today you will leave this lodge a true man." Carefully he arranged the items in front of himself, all the time praying in his soft, hushed voice. One by one, he picked through them, selecting several and setting them aside on a square of sheepskin: a sky blue stone, an elk tooth, some red earth. He placed some sage and grass on the coals and, as the smoke curled, passed each item through the smoke, examining it carefully, praying softly.

But he was not satisfied and searched for another bundle. He now knew with certainty that Sky Eyes was meant by the Great Mystery to come to the people. How else could all this be explained? Yet he was saddened by what Sky Eyes's vision revealed—for Sky Eyes and for all the people. He found the bundle and pulled from it a mountain lion's tooth. Even he hesitated at bringing it into the light. What would the others say about a young man having his helper be the night cat? A night cat almost never came to a boy in a vision.

"Never has one returned as you have with a vision of three helpers. You are indeed blessed by the Great Mystery, Sky Eyes. Your trail ahead will be blessed, but it will also be difficult. Things I cannot say."

Gray Owl picked up the elk tooth, rubbed its tawny enamel. "You came to the people and were awkward at first. You were the young elk pushed around by the older, wiser elk. Now the shaggy-neck elk will give you his speed and strength for battle."

He took the blue pebble. "The blue pebble will remind you of when you were known as Sky Eyes. It is for the pika, the bringer of joy and song. Like the pika, you bring joy and song."

Finally, he touched the mountain lion's tooth. He wondered about presenting it. "The night cat brings many things: strength, power, wisdom, courage. But like the night cat hiding in the night, sometimes you will have these things, sometimes you will not. Sometimes you will be weak, silly, and scared."

He paused. "And the night cat brings fear. It brings fear because the people do not understand the night cat. They do not know when it will show itself and when it will not.

"Understand this, Sky Eyes; sometimes people will honor you, and sometimes they will fear you. Sometimes you will lead them, and sometimes they will turn from you.

"Now you are of the people, but like the night cat, one day you will be alone again."

Erik was shaken by Gray Owl's words. He felt the people had accepted and respected him. Never could he imagine they would fear him, that he could drive them away, that one day he would be alone again. *It's just an old man's words,* he told himself. *I am now a true man of the people. I can remain with the people. This is a good life.*

Gray Owl wrapped the items in a leather square and placed them into a small pouch on a leather cord. He beckoned for Erik to lean forward and slipped the cord and pouch over his head.

"You now leave as a true man, Sky Eyes. Pray always to the Great Mystery that these helpers will walk with you the rest of your days."

Erik rose and walked from the lodge, humbled. What Gray Owl said about his vision brought pride yet also concern. Could all this be? He clung to the melody of the pika's song. Gray Owl said it wouldn't be one to sing, but it was his very own, and he should protect it for his life.

Gray Owl remained seated for a long while after Erik left, pondering. He had always thought the Great Mystery brought Sky Eyes to the people and had always sensed he had a spirit helper. He had guessed it was Sohobinehwe Tso'ape and had worried that the spirit also brought some bad things, because this spirit could work in backward ways. Runs Fast had thought this and told him one day. Some had left the people, and the one who killed the bear walked the sky trails. But now that he knew of Sky Eyes's ordeal, he knew the spirit had not brought things bad. The Great Mystery wanted the boy to live and sent the spirit to watch over him, so he could be of the people. Now the boy was a man.

CHAPTER 41

THE PEOPLE GATHERED AT a council fire in the meadow, away from the lodges. There the night canopy of stars stretched above. Both boys and girls brought wood for a large fire. It would be a fire for songs and dancing. The women brought bowls of food. The children played and chased each other in the night. This was a good time for the people.

Gray Owl gathered the watchers and the new men around. He prayed to the Great Mystery, "O, Maker of all, we thank you for this night. We thank you for this season, for the good hunts, for the new children. But tonight, we give special thanks. We thank you for the true men who have returned from their vision journeys. Tonight they will be given new names.

"I would ask Free Hawk to bring forth Coyote and speak of him."

Free Hawk and Coyote rose. Free Hawk addressed the people. "I have been watcher for Coyote for but a short while, since Fighting Bear left the people, but Coyote has shown us that he is a strong hunter. He hunts the sheep and catches them when the arrows fail."

The people laughed. They remembered the story of Weasel and Coyote when Coyote tackled the sheep Weasel had wounded. The ram nearly carried him into the river.

"He shows he is strong. He can run with the fleetest and the strongest. He shows his heart is for the people. He will take his place as a strong hunter and provider. The people are blessed to have Coyote return from his vision journey.

"We have decided. Coyote will no longer be known as Coyote. His true man's name is now Holds the Sheep."

The people murmured their agreement, and Holds the Sheep was accepted as a true man of the people.

Gray Owl stood up. "We are blessed with a second boy who has returned from his vision journey. I ask his watcher, Sees Far, to bring him forward. What do you say about Badger, Sees Far?"

Sees Far stood and brought Badger into the firelight. "I can say many things about this boy we call Badger. I have been honored to be his watcher for many seasons. Although some thought he should wait a season before seeking a vision, I thought differently, and tonight the people can see he has done well.

"Badger is also a strong hunter. He can run down the sheep that Weasel and Holds the Sheep must shoot with arrows."

Again the people laughed.

"Badger showed us where the elk were, and the hunters brought back two.

"Although he lost a true brother, he has shown his heart is big and has become brother to Sky Eyes. It is good that he puts others first. That is the mark of a leader.

"I have talked to Gray Owl. We have wondered at Badger's vision, for he saw an eagle coming from the white clouds of the sky. Badger will become a leader of the people. The young women must watch themselves now. He is Badger no more. His man's name is White Eagle."

The people murmured, amazed. It was unusual for a first vision to be of an eagle. The eagle was the mightiest of birds and messenger to the Great Mystery. It was even more unusual to suggest a new man would become a leader of the people. But the people had watched White Eagle when he was a boy, and they knew he stood strong. He stood for what was right. Yes, one day he would lead the people.

Gray Owl addressed the people a third time. "The third vision seeker nearly did not return. Already the women were wailing their mourning. When he did return, another left the Twisted River Band. But we know it was not because Sky Eyes came to us that Runs Fast left; it was because Runs Fast's spirit helper failed him. It is four seasons since he returned from his own vision journey. He failed to recall the lessons he had learned. Where White Eagle has shown us it is a good thing to accept a new brother, Runs Fast showed us he did not have the true spirit to do what was right. I have spoken."

The people murmured their agreement. Gray Owl had thought long about the words he would say for Sky Eyes. He knew some blamed Sky Eyes for the loss of two men from the people. Yet, had either man not forgotten the ways of the people, neither would have been lost.

"Let Whistling Elk bring Sky Eyes forth and speak of him."

Whistling Elk came forward, standing Erik before him.

"Just as Sees Far could say many things for White Eagle, I can say many things for Sky Eyes.

"My heart is heavy this night, for though I can present Sky Eyes to the people and to his father, Free Hawk cannot present my own son, the one who killed the bear, for now he walks the sky trails. Let us recall, however, I was watcher for my brother friend's son. I failed him, for the one who hunts the elk also walks the sky trails. We should remember those who walk the sky trails this night as we name these new men. Let us remember this as part of the great circle." He spread his hands to the people.

"So it is a good thing I can present his new son as a man." He placed his hands on Erik's shoulders then turned him to face the people.

"We all know of what Sky Eyes has done. Even though he came to us a boy, he showed us he was like a true man. He gave up everything to be of the people.

"He swims like an otter and is fast like the night cat. He was able to bring back White Eagle from the water spirits.

"He shows us to be friend to all and to help all.

"He causes the cold spirits to visit to create new life in the people.

"He shows us to be strong like the badger and the shaggy-neck elk and never gives up his spirit.

"Truly Sky Eyes has brought blessings to the people.

"Gray Owl shares this with me as well. Three helpers came to Sky Eyes during his vision journey—the little pika, a bringer of song; the night cat, the bringer of courage; and the shaggy-neck elk, the bringer of strength. From today on, Sky Eyes is no more. Before you is the true man we shall call Two Elks Fighting."

Erik felt humbled by the words and his new name. He thought about receiving a new name. Maybe this would be a good practice for his people as well.

***

A few days after the naming ceremony, Whistling Elk visited Free Hawk. "It is ready," he told his brother friend.

Free Hawk rose and addressed his two sons. "White Eagle and Two Elks Fighting, you shall come with us this morning."

They walked for a short distance to where the sweat lodges were. There Whistling Elk brought forth two bundles, one he handed to Free Hawk.

Free Hawk spoke. "Our hearts are proud that you are both new men for the people. It is fitting that each of you owns a bow with which to hunt the deer and shaggy-neck elk, and even to hunt the hump-back grizzly."

Solemnly, Free Hawk pulled forth a brightly decorated sheep-horn bow, the one he had demonstrated to the boys, and presented it to his son, White Eagle. Similarly, Whistling Elk pulled forth an equally fine bow and presented it to Two Elks Fighting.

"You have watched us over the season as we built these bows," said Whistling Elk. "It is fitting for each of you to have one. You are true men now."

Neither White Eagle nor Erik could speak. How could they express their thanks for such fine weapons? A sheep-horn bow was the most cherished possession a Sheepeater could own. It had power enough to drive an arrow nearly through an elk. It was sought by all the Indians of the different tribes and would bring ten ponies if traded on the plains.

It was with great restraint that White Eagle and Erik refrained from trying the bows immediately. When they returned carrying their new bows, all eyes of the camp turned.

Entering their lodge, as proper, they proudly presented their new bows to Shining Water.

"Yes, I see you have men's bows." She smiled. "That is good. But White Eagle and Two Elks Fighting, you grow too fast."

Puzzled, Erik wondered what she meant. Yes, he had grown, but why would she say this? He saw her eyes flick toward their bedding, and following her gaze, he immediately spied the two shirts neatly laid out. His was decorated with two rows of carefully stitched red and green dyed porcupine quills, and White Eagle's was stitched with two rows of yellow and white quills.

Pride and joy flooded him as he picked it up and pulled it on. It fit perfectly, comfortably. How she figured his size correctly, Erik didn't know. He only knew this was a precious gift, a gift almost as precious as his horn bow. He felt his eyes mist. He couldn't keep himself from hugging Shining Water, not a Sheepeater custom. "Thank you, Mother," he choked. "I will cherish this forever."

***

As the ripening-berry moon approached, Weasel decided again to try for a vision. Gray Owl said he should because Runs Fast had not been truthful. Weasel prepared as he did in the days before. He was led to the sweat lodge again. Stands Alone painted his body with the sacred white clay. Gray Owl purified him in the smoke of the sage and juniper. Weasel returned to the high basin and, alone, headed toward his vision place.

Erik, White Eagle, and Holds the Sheep accompanied him to the preparation place, but they didn't offer to chase. Instead, Black Legs did so as before. He looked hard for Weasel, but this time Weasel had gone a different route, and by the time Black Legs guessed where the boy had gone, it was late.

Weasel returned on the third evening. The people feared he had not succeeded, for it was soon, but this was not the case. He had received a vision. They held a naming ceremony later that night. He was named Seeks Twice.

***

The seasons were changing. Erik and White Eagle again hunted elk, only this day, with their horn bows. They camped near timberline, built a small fire against the chill, and watched the sun set.

White Eagle nudged Erik. "I share this with you, Two Elks Fighting." He removed his medicine pouch.

"While seeking my vision, I journeyed past the peak where you last saw me. I found a high ledge. On the third night, I received my vision. The fourth morning, I climbed down into a basin and searched for food.

"I found this." He handed Erik a piece of bright yellow metal.

Immediately Erik recognized the gold.

"Many of these stones lay about. Some were white with only bits of yellow. Some were yellow. I brought this yellow one back."

Erik couldn't speak. White Eagle had found a fortune.

"Gray Owl told me I should keep it in my medicine pouch."

Erik turned the piece. Small bits of white quartz adhered to a nearly solid gold nugget. "White Eagle," he finally managed. "You have found *guld.*" Erik used the Swedish word.

White Eagle laughed. He remembered the word for the glowing lake. "How can this be water?" he asked.

"Not water," Erik tried to explain. "It's a rock we call *guld.* From it we make many beautiful things. It is precious." Erik found the thought strange. Here it meant nothing. Only its beauty had value. "I agree with Gray Owl," Erik continued, handing it back. "You should keep this with you. It is very special."

PART THREE

TWO ELKS FIGHTING

"I HAVE GIVEN MY SACRED WORD"

CHAPTER 42

SNOW CAME TO THE high country, and the people began their journey back to their winter camps. They followed Twisted River downstream to Thunder Noise River and turned upstream, continuing for another day past Bird Calls Creek.

There the river narrowed and cascaded white through the canyon, sometimes spreading itself out in narrow meadows, other times pooling into deep holes. Mostly it ran white and turbulent, squeezed between the tall, narrow volcanic cliffs.

As the trail gained elevation, the canyon broadened, and the volcanic cliffs became less steep. Dense black timber covered both sides until the trail broke out onto some narrow benches. There the south-facing knolls and cliffs were grassy and open. There the mountain sheep and mule deer came to winter—where the snow was less deep and the winds blew and swept clear the grass.

Partially dilapidated winter lodges stood scattered among sheltering trees below the open knolls. Immediately the people began repairing and reconstructing them.

Erik wondered, now that he was considered a true man, if it was not proper for him to build his own lodge, but none of the other new men seemed to be interested in doing so. Free Hawk didn't appear concerned either. He selected a large lodge from a previous winter, a conical log structure that remained largely intact, and instructed his sons to bring slabs of bark to help him recover the frame.

Erik dragged some to the lodge while White Eagle stripped more from some large, dead trees below the bench where the lodges were being built.

Free Hawk must have considered what Erik would be thinking. "Although you and White Eagle have completed your vision seeking, Shining Water and I would hope you remain with us." He hefted one of the slabs onto the side of the lodge. "You and White Eagle should become fine hunters or craftsmen, then perhaps in a season or so, you will court a woman, and it will be proper for me to help you build a lodge."

Erik handed another slab to Free Hawk. "Thank you, Father," Erik replied. "I should like to stay with you and Mother and Singing Bird. And with my new bow, I will soon be a fine hunter."

Free Hawk locked the slab into place and nodded. "Sooner than Shining Water would like," he said somewhat softly.

Erik was touched. His parents didn't wish to see him leave—not like some, as he understood. White Eagle said that was why Runs Fast built a young man's lodge.

When they finished the lodge, Erik was amazed at its size. It was the largest yet and the sturdiest. Certainly it was roomier and warmer than the cabin. But he tried not to think of the cabin. He didn't allow himself to think of his parents or of Katrine anymore. Now fifteen, he immersed himself in the people's life.

Evening fell, and the people gathered at the council fire. Gray Owl gave thanks for their safe journey and for their successful hunts. Chipmunk, who had carried the fire horn, came forward, and Porcupine Woman lit the council fire. As before, young girls carried the new fire to their lodges. Shortly, the odor of roasting meat and bubbling stews drifted on the evening air.

***

Soon the camp was buried in deep snow. Erik realized it was higher in elevation than the other winter camps and wondered why the elders came to this area.

One evening he visited Gray Owl; he enjoyed hearing his stories. "So why do the people camp here on Thunder Noise River?" he asked. "It seems to me the snows are very deep and not many redfish came."

Gray Owl cocked an eye at Two Elks Fighting. He wondered if already he didn't prepare for when he might be the one to whom the people turned.

"You should answer your own question, Two Elks Fighting," Gray Owl countered.

Erik was taken aback but soon realized that Gray Owl was sincere.

"I see many curved-horns on the barren hills above us, and there are many small fur animals. And although the snow is deep, the winds don't rattle through the canyon and break the lodges. Deep snow is warmer than the ice where we were last winter."

Erik paused a moment, thinking. "Also, the women gathered the shell animals from the river before it became stopped in ice. Now they make the shells into necklaces and ladles, but those are all the reasons I would say."

"Very good," Gray Owl nodded. "You should also remember the stone bowls. This is near the place where the stone can be cut."

Erik nodded. He remembered Shining Water now worked on carving out a bowl. She used his steel knife, and the work progressed rapidly.

***

Neither Erik nor White Eagle any longer asked for the permission of Free Hawk or their watchers to go hunting. They were free to decide what was right for each of them. This new feeling of responsibility humbled Erik. The men now looked upon him as an equal—not as a boy. He was trusted to do what was right.

"Shall we hunt today, Two Elks Fighting?" White Eagle asked, his arrows slung over his shoulder and bow already in his hands.

"As we always do, White Eagle," Erik replied, quickly pulling down his own weapons.

All fall and winter, they had hunted as often as possible. Both wanted to get fur animals: fox, coyote, and mink. There was already talk that this summer they would go to a place where Broken Blade would come to trade.

"Today we should go to a new place to hunt the curved-horns," White Eagle explained. "With a long winter, you and I should learn to make a new horn bow."

"Yes, we could trade just one horn bow and get more for it than all the fur animals we hunt," replied Erik.

They headed south to where a long ridge climbed high above the canyon. Unusual columns of volcanic tuff towered near its base. One, Erik guessed, stood seventy feet tall and supported a large boulder on its top. Other smaller monuments, similarly capped, rose eerily from the surrounding trees.

"This is the place where spirits become lost," White Eagle explained. "This is near Mountain That Cries. It cries because the spirits are lost. This is not a good place. We should hunt here for only a short time."

Erik could understand why White Eagle felt uncomfortable. Even he had difficulty understanding how large boulders could end up perched many feet up in the air on top of sheer, rock columns. It was as if some giant had carved the spires and, as an afterthought, for his amusement, carefully balanced round boulders on their tips.

A sound, much like a rifle shot, echoed through the canyon. Erik stood puzzled.

It came again. White Eagle grinned. "The curved-horns are fighting," he explained.

Erik remained perplexed.

"We shall soon see this. Perhaps this is good. The curved-horns will not be watching for hunters. We should get one."

Erik and White Eagle traversed the hillside, angling upward toward the sound. Rounding the edge, they came upon a large band of mountain sheep. The ewes were scattered, some bedded down, some pulling at tufts of grass where the wind had swept away the snow. Two rams, massive, curling horns that swept back and then curved upward to above their eyes, stood facing each other about thirty feet apart.

"Now you watch," breathed White Eagle.

The rams stood, eyeing each other. Suddenly they raced toward each other, heads lowered. Their heads came together, making an ear-splitting crack. Both rams were pushed upward by the force. One broke away and shook his head, dazed. The ewes paid no attention.

"The stronger curved-horn wins and can then have all the females," explained White Eagle.

Again, the rams faced off, and again, they smashed into each other. The sharp crack—bone hitting bone—echoed throughout the canyon.

They watched for a while, mesmerized by the display of power.

Erik remembered the first time he and his father had seen the mountain sheep. He remembered how his father had missed, how he had slipped and fallen … how he died.

He fingered his sheep-horn bow. Suddenly he no longer wanted to hunt. He tried to explain to White Eagle but could not.

White Eagle sensed something was amiss. "It is a long way to camp to carry a big curved-horn anyhow," White Eagle said simply.

Chapter 43

THE NEW-SHEEP MOON ARRIVED. The Twisted River Band journeyed south to a place near Mountain That Cries for their summer hunting camp. The star-grass moon arrived, but there were no camas. The meadows were small and scattered. Instead, the men hunted. Hunting was good. Several mountain sheep and mule deer were taken. Many smaller fur-bearing animals were also trapped and taken. The women remained busy dressing skins.

The flashing-sky moon came, but no young men went to seek a vision—Chipmunk was but thirteen winters. Now the moon of ripening berries came and grew long.

Shining Water and Moccasin Woman worked together as they often did when their husbands hunted. Moccasin Woman's daughter, Tiny Bird, often played with Singing Bird, making it easier for the two women to attend their work.

Shining Water pounded meat with her stone cobble and added a few dried serviceberries. "We do not find enough berries, Moccasin Woman," she said, as she began kneading together the berries with some fat and the dried meat.

"No. I fear we will not have enough pemmican for the snow seasons," Moccasin Woman agreed. "And there are no star-grass bulbs in these meadows."

"Meat is good, but the people will be thin and sick before the snow-eater moon arrives," muttered Shining Water. "It is the pemmican and star-grass bulbs that keep the deep-snow sickness away. If we don't find berries, Porcupine Woman will be boiling spruce needles for all the people." She made a bitter face and shuddered.

"Perhaps we should not have come to this camp. This is near where the spirits wander and the mountain thunders," offered Moccasin Woman. She wrapped the pemmican she had been making into a small skin. "The spirits hide the berries so that we will go away and leave them alone."

"Yes, I do not like this place either," agreed Shining Water. "We should talk to our husbands so they ask Gray Owl about a new camp."

***

Soon after, the Twisted River Band moved its summer camp toward the east to a large meadow, far from the Mountain That Cries. Almost immediately, a hunter discovered a draw where many chokecherries ripened.

Joyously, the women scooped up their children and baskets and hurried toward the draw, a short distance beyond the camp. Chipmunk and Squirrel were among the young boys who went to help the women. When Shining Water packed up Singing Bird, Erik quickly decided he would go as well. He remembered gathering chokecherries along the Snake River with his mother and little sister. They had made chokecherry syrup.

"Come on, White Eagle. Let us go to pick berries as well. We will help Mother get many for us," he said.

White Eagle decided Two Elks Fighting was being silly. Picking berries was women's work. They were true men now. But he didn't say this to Two Elks Fighting. He had long recognized that his brother thought it proper to help his adoptive mother. It was his way. He recalled a time when he had joined in with the other boys and teased him about doing women's work. Now he respected Two Elks Fighting for his choice. "Yes," he nodded. "I will go as well. Perhaps we will see some grouse to hunt."

Erik knew that saying they might hunt grouse was White Eagle's way of saving face. They took their sheep-horn bows and good arrows.

At the draw, Erik was amazed at the huge quantities of purple black berries. The branches bent heavily toward the ground. He selected a tall shrub and immediately began stripping the berries onto a robe. White Eagle joined and picked for a short while, but Erik sensed his heart wasn't in it. Out of respect and friendship to him, he kept him company.

"Perhaps now we should go to hunt grouse?" White Eagle soon asked, clearly impatient.

"No, White Eagle, if you wish to hunt grouse, you may. I would like to gather many berries," he replied. "Perhaps after a while, I will join you." Erik planned to make syrup although he didn't know how he would sweeten it.

"Then I shall get a fat grouse, Two Elks Fighting. Mother will be pleased when I bring one back."

Erik nodded and returned to pulling the clusters of chokecherries from the branches. His fingers were already stained red and purple.

As the women and children worked, they gradually moved up the draw toward the rock outcrops. Suddenly, a loud, terrifying cry filled the draw. Mothers and children screamed and ran terror-stricken past Erik, crying. A small girl tripped, spilling her basket. She scrambled back up, running, shrieking, "Bear! There's a bear!"

Erik heard the bushes splinter as he looked up to where they swayed. The animal growled. Erik felt rooted to the spot, unable to move, uncertain of what to do. Crying and wailing filled the draw as the women and young children continued to run past toward camp.

Moccasin Woman ran past, dragging Tiny Bird, shrieking the wailing cry. "It has killed my Chipmunk. My Chipmunk is dead."

Fear then anger flooded Erik. He thought of Whistling Elk losing his son. Grabbing his bow, he bolted uphill, running toward the bear. Whistling Elk had been Erik's second father—his watcher. He could not endure the thought of him losing Chipmunk.

"Get out of here!" he yelled, shaking with anger. He waved his bow and beat the brush. "Get out of here!"

He broke into an open area and froze at the sight. Near the rock outcrops, a massive bear swung at something on the ground. *A grizzly!* Erik felt his hair stand as an icy cold crawled down his back.

He saw the bleeding mass, hardly recognizable. It was Chipmunk. Erik's stomach churned; he felt dizzy. For certain, Chipmunk was dead. Anger raced through him, replacing his fear. He wanted to strike the bear. "Get out of here, bear!" He waved his arms and bow. "Get!"

The animal turned toward him. With a deep huff, popping its teeth, it rose on its hind legs, sniffing, investigating. It dropped back down, wagging its head. It turned its attention back to Chipmunk and batted him to the side then pawed at him like a camp dog paws at a mouse to see if it still lives.

Erik was stunned by the bear's size. He realized it could kill him—*easily* kill him. He wanted to run, to save his own life, but he was torn by the sight of Chipmunk bleeding in a heap in the bushes. Chipmunk began weakly moving, trying to get to his knees to crawl away. *He isn't dead! He's badly hurt. Maybe dying. I've got to do something!*

Erik notched an arrow and drew back, his fingers sweaty, shaking, aiming past Chipmunk toward the creature's neck. The bear opened its jaws and teased with Chipmunk's head. In horror, Erik realized that if it bit down, Chipmunk would die.

"Hey, bear!" he yelled, heart hammering, trying to get the animal to again focus on him. "Hey, bear!" The animal turned, took a couple quick bluffing steps toward him, and then stopped, wagging its head, popping its teeth.

This is suicide, Erik thought, heart pounding. He loosed the arrow. It went wildly off mark and clattered, splintering into the rocks.

"Hey, bear!" It was White Eagle, on top of the rocks above the bear. He threw a rock. The grizzly instantly turned toward him.

"Run, Two Elks Fighting," he shouted. He loosed an arrow. It buried itself deep in the animal's back. Instantly, the grizzly went mad with rage. It charged the rocks, lunging, smashing with its great paws, madly raking, trying to get at the man above him. White Eagle backed away, notching another arrow.

Erik could see that the bear wouldn't miss on its next lunge. He notched an arrow and brought it back at full draw, shaking. *Dear God, let me shoot straight. Don't let me hit White Eagle.* A calm settled his hand, and he released. The arrow went true and buried itself deep in the animal's neck.

The bear slashed at the air, roared, and turned around, looking for the arrow's source. It turned back toward White Eagle and lunged ineffectively. It turned again toward Erik, wagging its head, spilling bloody drool, and charged. Erik ran.

White Eagle immediately released another arrow, again striking the animal. The bear paused for a moment but resumed its charge. Erik had nowhere to go. Icy fear flooded him, he felt his body going numb as he desperately tried to reach some rocks to the side. His hair on his neck crawled. In a few yards, the bear would be on him. He braced himself, imagining the impending blow.

Suddenly, Erik heard the unmistakable flight of arrows whistling past; he heard the thud as they drove into the animal, and he heard the voices of the yelling men. Vaguely he realized he had heard them earlier.

The bear stopped, confused by all the men. It rose up, slashed the air, then stumbled. It struggled up, hatred in its eyes, and lunged. More arrows found home. The animal paused, staggered again. Erik drew and released another arrow but realized it was unnecessary. The animal collapsed, its massive ribcage wheezed, blood gushed from its great jaws. It did not struggle to rise. With eyes still fixed on Erik, it shuddered and died.

Erik was on his knees, shaking, holding himself up with his bow.

Whistling Elk ran to Chipmunk, covered in blood, barely moving. With a cry, he scooped his son into his arms and headed toward camp.

Free Hawk and Sees Far cautiously approached the bear and made certain it was dead. Otherwise, no one attended to the animal, rather they returned to camp to see about Chipmunk. Already women wailed.

Whistling Elk carried his son to Gray Owl's lodge where Porcupine Woman waited. He laid Chipmunk on a pallet of elk hides. Porcupine Woman poured water and began to wash and bind his wounds.

Erik couldn't believe the boy didn't cry out. He could see long red gashes across his chest.

Chipmunk was awake, moving his arms, writhing in pain. "I ... I am sorry, Father," he spoke weakly. "I had only my hands."

Whistling Elk tried to quiet his son, but Chipmunk continued. "H-he was after Mother … a-and Tiny Bird … I tried to play dead." Chipmunk squeezed his eyes, clenched his teeth, and shuddered in pain.

Whistling Elk held him. The boy had lost much blood.

Already the people knew and were whispering. The boy had attacked the bear with nothing but a stick and his fists in an effort to keep it away from his family. The bear had turned and swatted him like a bug into the shrubs. Chipmunk had shown true courage.

***

Porcupine Woman dabbed at his wounds, all the while softly chanting. Chipmunk's mother offered Porcupine Woman the healing moss. She took pieces and carefully packed them into Chipmunk's wounds, stopping up the blood.

A small fire was kindled. Porcupine Woman burned sweet sage, sang, and chanted softly, looking to the sky.

"Great Mystery, this boy is sorry he caused the death of a great hump-back brother. Do not blame him. He is just a boy. Just as you designed for all creatures, the boy tried to protect his family. Please let the spirit of the great bear walk satisfied. Do not let the bear spirit take this boy's spirit as his companion to walk the sky trails. Let the boy's spirit return to him yet for a while."

Erik silently said his own prayer. *Oh, God, please don't let Chipmunk die. He is a good son to Whistling Elk and Moccasin Woman. They have already lost Raven. They need their son. Please heal him. Put your spirit in him. Let him live.* Erik felt an ache in his chest. He had seen too much death.

He thought about his own life. He realized that had White Eagle not come back, had the hunters not come quickly, he would surely be dead. Without question, he knew at this very moment, he would be dead. He wondered if the people would have buried him like he had buried his mother or if they would have left his bones on the rocks like White Eagle said they did with Otter's body. He didn't want to die.

Porcupine Woman continued chanting and waving smoking sages over Chipmunk. She moistened his lips with water, but he didn't drink. Chipmunk appeared in deep sleep.

Erik knew this was good. How could anyone endure the pain of having his flesh flayed from his body?

***

The men returned to the bear's carcass where they gave thanks to the Great Mystery and asked him to allow the bear's spirit to walk the sky trails untroubled. They too assured the Maker that they didn't blame the bear, for it was doing what it had to do. They were thankful for the hide and meat and prayed the bear spirit wouldn't mind if they used them.

They butchered the animal and hauled it to camp. They would roast the meat and render the fat into tallow. They used bear fat to moisten skin and to keep away insects, to waterproof and preserve their hunting weapons, and to help cure skins. Carefully they removed the claws. These would soon be sewn onto shirts or made into necklaces for two young men and a boy. A hump-back grizzly claw was strong medicine.

***

Morning came. Chipmunk woke. He drank and ate. The people were overjoyed. They praised Porcupine Woman. Although Chipmunk would forever wear the white scars where the bear's claws had slashed him, soon to be marks of honor, he would live. Few people lived after being struck by a grizzly. It was fortunate this grizzly was young, at best in its second summer. Nevertheless, Chipmunk surely had powerful spirit helpers and strong medicine. The Great Mystery had protected him.

***

Gray Owl called for a gathering of the people. He thought about the young men, Two Elks Fighting and White Eagle. In his heart, he knew that the Great Mystery had brought them to be brothers. Soon they would be the ones to whom the people turned. Never had he witnessed something as wonderful as this given to them by the Great Mystery.

He turned to the people. "We have seen a boy put his life before his mother's and sister's by turning away a great hump-back grizzly with a stick and his fists. He has shown what true courage is. Let us sing praises for Chipmunk."

The people joyously voiced their praises.

"We have also seen two young men stand fearless against this mighty creature and bring it down," said Gray Owl. "Two Elks Fighting and White Eagle shall be in the songs of the people for having stood against the most dangerous and mightiest of animals.

"Let us sing praise of Two Elks Fighting. He faced down the great hump-back grizzly. He was first to draw the bear away from Chipmunk. He sent an arrow true into the great hump-back grizzly. Surely the Great Mystery has favored this young white man. Two Elks Fighting must surely have powerful spirit helpers."

The people broke into a high trill.

"Let us now sing praise of White Eagle, for White Eagle sent the first arrow true. He risked his life to draw the bear away from Chipmunk and Two Elks Fighting. Had White Eagle not done so, both would surely walk the sky trails. Surely White Eagle has favor with the Great Mystery. Surely he has powerful spirit helpers. White Eagle showed the way a true man should be."

The people again chanted a high trill of approval.

Soon they feasted and danced. They danced in honor of the bear's spirit. They danced in honor of Chipmunk. And they danced in honor of White Eagle and Two Elks Fighting. They sang a song in honor of White Eagle and Two Elks Fighting.

CHAPTER 44

BROKEN BLADE VISITED TO trade with the people shortly after the great bear was killed. He traveled in the company of a helper, Cries to the Wind, also a trader. The people hoped Cries to the Wind would fall in love with Sweet Grass or Quickly Smiles. Maybe he, like Black Legs, would marry and stay with the people. The people needed another good hunter. But Cries to the Wind already complained that he didn't like the journey to the broken-mountain land. This was a long journey and a lonesome journey.

Broken Blade traded for some of the fox, marten, and mink the young hunters had killed and the women had tanned. He had brought several dogs with him to drag travois piled with skins the Sheepeaters provided. It was a long distance to carry furs, but he knew the value of a well-tanned and dressed skin from the Sheepeaters. He would easily double their value trading them among other Indians or the whites.

Broken Blade had other reasons to come to the Sheepeaters. He was pleased to visit with his son, Black Legs, and his family. A grandfather should have young children to whom he could tell stories.

One evening, Erik observed the brush pulled in front of Sees Far's lodge.

"Why is there brush before Sees Far's lodge?" wondered Erik. "Sees Far visits with Gray Owl."

White Eagle laughed. "You should know. Magpie must have a visitor."

Erik was puzzled. Magpie was Sees Far's second wife, his young wife.

"Two Elks Fighting, it is a far journey from the burning-rock land for Broken Blade. Sees Far has given Magpie as a gift."

Erik shook his head in disbelief.

"Perhaps Sees Far did not have enough robes to trade," said White Eagle, laughing. "Swift Swallow and Magpie don't have three hunters as Shining Water does. Maybe Sees Far wishes to get his wives a good kettle for cooking."

Erik thought about Shining Water and Free Hawk. Although infrequent, whenever brush was in front of their lodge, he and White Eagle visited with Holds the Sheep or Seeks Twice. He was of an age that it made him uncomfortable.

Trading was good. Free Hawk was able to trade for an iron kettle, but Broken Blade no longer had steel knives to trade. Instead, Free Hawk traded for blankets and glass beads. Erik was amazed by the beads, blue and white. Shining Water was especially pleased and already planned to work on a new shirt for Free Hawk.

Both Erik and White Eagle successfully traded for some obsidian points. Erik remembered that Whistling Elk taught that the black-glass points were to be used only by true hunters. He was pleased he now owned some. Both he and White Eagle wished Broken Blade had traded with them earlier—before they had to kill the grizzly. The black-glass tips cut deep and swift.

***

The fattening-animal moon came. Soon it would be time to return to the winter camps. The hunting had been good; the great bear provided much fat; they had prepared a good amount of dried meat; they had found berries for pemmican; and the trading had been good. It was almost too much to carry to the winter camp. But the people looked forward to the winter camps where the days would be lazy and they could visit with relatives.

One day before leaving, Sees Far brought Little Fox to Porcupine Woman. Little Fox couldn't keep his food. Everything passed through him. His young mother, Magpie, cared for him, but Little Fox grew weak and still couldn't eat.

Erik watched Porcupine Woman prepare her things. He remembered how his own mother had been sick—how he tried to help her, to get her to eat—to drink. He remembered how Porcupine Woman had tried to help her—how she died anyway. Now he found himself troubled and prayed for Little Fox.

Erik listened as Porcupine Woman prayed to the spirits. He understood the prayers were meant to chase off the spirit that had entered Little Fox and made him sick. The smoke was meant to pull out the spirit—to cleanse him—much like the sweat bath and the purification ceremony he experienced.

Erik remembered the sickness that came to the wagon train. He remembered one youngster who had diarrhea but survived. They were near a place where kinnikinnick grew under the pines. He recalled one of the mothers seeped the bark and leaves in steaming water for the boy to drink. In a day, he was better. He was the only one who survived the sickness, but Erik figured it was a different illness. Now he wondered if kinnikinnick would work for Little Fox. He quickly gathered some and brought it to Porcupine Woman. He explained the best he could what happened to the wagon-train boy and began boiling water to seep the leaves.

Porcupine Woman respected Two Elks Fighting. Although the red-berry plant was for tobacco, she knew it also held strong medicine. She knew the young white man had helped Shining Water and Moccasin Woman collect plants when he was a boy. They had told her. She knew he had strong spirits that protected him—that the Great Mystery had brought him to the people. She decided to use the young white man's medicine he made from the red-berry plant.

Porcupine Woman gave Little Fox sips of the tisane. She said more prayers and burnt more sage and juniper. Erik listened to the prayers. She asked the Great Mystery to allow Two Elks Fighting's medicine to work.

Magpie's baby boy slept. By morning, he kept his food down.

The people murmured praises for Porcupine Woman's medicine. They murmured praises for Two Elks Fighting's medicine.

"Perhaps Two Elks Fighting will become a holy man," White Eagle said, bemused.

"No, White Eagle," replied Erik. "I know some things about plants, but I will not be a holy man. I prefer to hunt and bring home meat—not plants."

"Ah, Two Elks Fighting, you *are* growing older. I remember when you couldn't hunt and you gathered many plants with Mother."

"Yes. I could help her then in that manner."

"It is sad for me that you don't become a holy man."

Erik was surprised. "Why is this?"

"If you should, I would marry Quickly Smiles. A holy man does not marry."

Erik's heart quickened. He never thought of White Eagle marrying Quickly Smiles; now he realized his brother could take her from him. His stomach knotted.

CHAPTER 45

THE TWISTED RIVER BAND returned to the canyons for the winter season. This season, Free Hawk and Whistling Elk led the people west upstream along Twisted River across a high divide and down into a narrow, steep gorge.

The small stream they followed down from the mountain pass ran tumbling and broken among scattered boulders and through narrow clefts. In places, the people struggled to make their way along the steep cliffs. When at last they reached the canyon floor, they came to Sandy Water River. It flowed broadly through tall pines and gentle, grassy benches. The canyon reached upward of a quarter mile wide, and the river, in places, was nearly eighty yards wide. It flowed deep and quiet toward the north.

They turned upriver and continued for several miles. In a few areas, black basalt outcropped, some brightly stained yellow and green. Several hot springs bubbled near them, spreading outward from their bases, building brightly colored clay fans—yellows, ochers, reds.

Remains of lodges from past winters stood scattered across the benches. Most had small pits dug beneath them and stones piled up, forming foundations that supported the lodge poles. On average, they were as large as the conical log structures from the previous winter. Returning to their former homes, the people uncovered their soapstone bowls, baskets, and snagging poles from where they were stored. They quickly cleaned out the pits and repaired the walls with new brush and hides until each lodge was again weatherproof.

Once more, Erik and White Eagle chose to remain with their parents and Singing Bird, but Erik wondered if it was not now the proper time for him and White Eagle to build a young man's lodge. But neither he nor White Eagle could imagine moving into their own lodge. They were not prepared to make clothing, cook meals, tend a fire, carry water—the work women did for their men—what Shining Water did for him and White Eagle.

"What grandmother would want to move in with us and care for us?" Erik exclaimed. "Porcupine Woman? She already lodges with Gray Owl."

"Perhaps Yellow Flower," suggested White Eagle.

"But she has no teeth," replied Erik. "We would have to chew her food for her."

White Eagle laughed. "You can chew her food, Two Elks Fighting. I think I shall wait a while to build a young man's lodge."

Erik kept Shining Water company, talking to her, helping her gather wood and bring in water. Singing Bird no longer needed close watching; instead she tagged along, helping Erik as he helped her mother. They were often seen together, gathering wood and carrying it to their lodge. People recognized her as Two Elks Fighting's little sister.

In a few days, some families from the White Licks Band came and joined them. They dwelled in the canyons farther west, where Snake River and River of No Return came together, near the white licks frequented by the mountain sheep. A young man, Coyote Runs, showed interest in Sweet Grass. People talked. Perhaps Coyote Runs would come to live with the Twisted River Band. Erik was glad he wasn't interested in Quickly Smiles.

***

After a heavy snow when again the weather warmed, Erik decided to go with White Eagle and scout for elk, to kill one if possible, but mostly to determine if the elk were migrating toward the canyons to get out of the deepening snows in the high country.

The air was chilly and brisk when they trotted downriver, carrying their rabbit-skin robes and best arrows, some now tipped with obsidian points. Erik wanted to hunt a side canyon where a large stream entered Sandy Water River. While hunting mule deer, he had seen the white peaks showing through the gaps in the hills of the side canyon. He wondered if the elk were moving down from those peaks.

Late morning, they reached where the side stream spilled into Sandy Water River. They crossed where Sandy Water River broadened and spread itself shallow in white riffles. A faint game trail turned up the side stream. Erik thought he could see horse prints but was uncertain until White Eagle pointed them out in a damp place that had frozen.

"A white man has come this way."

Erik was surprised by the quick chill he felt. He could see the tracks pointing upriver. "How far from here does Sandy Water River empty into River of No Return?" he asked, gazing downstream, wondering if whites were nearby.

"At least a day's journey, but I don't know if our people have gone there. They go up this river. It is Black Rock River."

Erik felt dumbfounded. Rivers cut in every direction imaginable across this land, forming deep, inhospitable canyons. The canyons had isolated the Sheepeaters into a world lost but to themselves. But then he wondered about this as well. Perhaps this was what they wished. They didn't have horses, and they didn't seem to desire them. If they acquired them, as had Fighting Bear, they left the canyons. The Sheepeaters didn't often leave the canyons to trade. Persons who wanted the Sheepeaters' furs and skins, like Broken Blade did, came to the canyons to trade with them. The traders brought the steel knives, obsidian tips, and cooking kettles. The Sheepeaters were in want of little else.

"How mighty is River of No Return?" Erik asked.

"I have never seen the river, but the old ones say it is the size of three Twisted Rivers."

Erik was astounded. He calculated the river must be well over a hundred yards wide. "Does the water travel slow or is it fast like Twisted River?"

"In places it is slow. In other places, it is angry like Twisted River. The old ones say it goes to the place where the land ends in the great water. But I do not know more than this."

Erik tried to make sense of what he knew and what he had learned since coming to the Sheepeaters. Their train had followed the Snake, which flowed west. Eventually they would have reached a river that flowed in from the north, emptying the high valley they had intended to farm. These rivers, where the Sheepeaters lived, all emptied into the River of No Return. Erik reasoned that it had to be a separate river basin far to the north of the Snake. Erik shivered, an emptiness filling him. He knew that if he were ever to leave this country, to ever seek his sister, somehow he would have to find his way back south to the Snake River drainage, a terribly long distance away. He suddenly felt small, alone, and very far from his old cabin.

He stood and shivered, then turned up Black Rock River, following the faint game trail. It climbed through the cliffs and led out onto the sheer walls above the river. Coming around a corner, they spooked some mountain sheep including a couple good rams. Had they not been elk hunting, they might have decided to take a ram.

They studied the descending snowline above the yet barren, south-facing slopes. There should be elk if they had begun to come down. They began a downward traverse, past the steep sides, toward some aspen groves scattered along the fringe of fir and spruce, pausing frequently to scan for elk. Often, elk bedded down in the aspens during the day. The aspen now stood naked and stark.

Erik abruptly paused. "Smoke," he hissed.

White Eagle nodded. "There must be man, maybe the next draw."

Erik's heart quickened, his senses came on edge. He wondered if he was the white man with the shod horse.

"We must learn if this man is an enemy," White Eagle continued. "The people must know."

Cautiously they worked their way toward the camp smells. This was not a game they played this day. Both clutched their bows with arrows at the ready.

They eased around the edge of a rock outcrop where they could peer into the draw. Below them, a solitary man stooped at the edge of a small stream, swirling a large pan in the water. He wore a turned-up hat, revealing his face, weathered, sporting whitening whiskers.

A prospector, Erik realized.

Suddenly overcome, Erik jumped up and shouted. "*Hej!*" He started down toward the man.

White Eagle cried to him. "Two Elks Fighting, stop! That is a white man. Two Elks Fighting!"

Pushing well down the hill, Erik called again, "*Hej.*" He noticed a mule tethered near a gray canvas tent.

Hearing Erik, the man turned and, in two quick steps, grabbed and leveled a rifle at his middle.

Startled, Erik almost dropped his bow.

"Don't shoot. I'm a friend. I'm white." Slowly, he set down his bow and raised his hand, giving the sign for peace.

The man hollered back, but Erik didn't understand. The man spoke English. Erik spoke Swedish.

"I'm a friend," Erik repeated and signed, *friend.*

The man lowered his rifle, but then quickly raised it again, aiming past Erik.

Erik turned. White Eagle approached, an arrow notched.

"Don't, White Eagle. Don't shoot. Hold your bow out and set it down. Let the man know we are friends."

White Eagle did neither, but came forward slowly behind Erik. Erik felt he had no choice but to proceed forward.

"I'm a friend," Erik repeated, trying desperately to remember the English words for friend. Suddenly, he said, "Thank you," some of the English words, he remembered.

The man lowered his rifle. "Why, you *are* white. I seen your hair, but you sure look Injun. I'll be damned." He laughed. "Come here, son. You're dressed like an Injun." The man extended his hand.

Erik reached the man, understanding little of his talk but understanding the offered hand. He shook it and grinned. "*Hej,*" he said.

"Welcome."

The man squinted at White Eagle. "Your friend is certainly Injun. Sheepeater, I'd say. No one hardly ever sees them." He motioned for White Eagle to come down.

White Eagle picked up the bows and cautiously approached. He stood a protective distance behind Erik, not speaking, but extended the sign for peace.

The man returned the sign and addressed Erik. "I'm guessing you're Swedish. *Svenska?*"

Erik nodded jubilantly. *"Jag heter, Erik Larsson. Jag har bott med Tukudeka familj i tre år. Mina föräldrar är döda—"* He was saying, "I'm Erik Larson. I've lived with the Tukudeka for three years. My parents have died. I—"

"Now hold on, son," the prospector interrupted. His eyes were set deep beneath thick, graying, almost white brows. He pulled at his whiskers. "I didn't understand a thing you just said, 'cept 'Erik Larson.' I don't speak Swedish." He paused. "No *Svenska*," he said, shaking his head.

Erik felt his hopes shatter.

"I'm Hank Hailey," he said, dark eyes glinting. He was somewhat short, about Erik's height, but solidly built. The elements had etched his face and hands. He turned toward the mule, pointing. "The mule there's Jennifer. And that's home ... for the time being." He waved at the tent.

"Who's your Injun friend?" he questioned, pointing.

Erik understood Hailey's gestures. "White Eagle," he replied, signing.

Hank recognized the signing, and signed back. "Welcome, White Eagle," he said and stuck out his hand.

White Eagle stared at the hand. Erik motioned for him to shake. Finally, he did, and replied, "Hank ... Hai-ley." Then he turned back toward Erik, rapidly signing and said, "This is my brother, Two Elks Fighting, *not* Er-ik Lar-son." He frowned at Erik.

Erik smiled and signed. "Yes. My Tukudeka name is Two Elks Fighting."

Hailey appeared confused for a moment, but then addressed them. "White Eagle." He nodded toward White Eagle and then to Erik. "Two Elks Fightin'." They nodded.

"Mighty good to have you," he signed and said. "Gets pretty lonesome out here." He gestured for them to sit. "Don't have much to offer, but you're welcome to what I have."

He turned toward his tent.

White Eagle asked, "Is he a friend, Two Elks Fighting?"

"Yes. He won't harm us," replied Erik, but he wasn't entirely certain.

Hailey came back with a pot and two tin cups. Into each cup, he poured hot, steaming coffee.

Erik smelled and tasted it. It was strong, sweetened, rich coffee. His eyes misted as memories flooded back. The last time he had had coffee was before his father died—over three years ago. He thought of his parents. He choked back the ache welling within him.

"You okay, son?" Hailey asked. "You look mighty shook."

Erik didn't understand. He simply replied, "Thank you."

White Eagle didn't touch the coffee until Erik had sampled his. Then, carefully, he tasted the liquid. He smiled and drank more. The sweetness was pleasant. He drained the cup and handed it back to Hailey, smiling.

"Guess you like coffee," Hailey chuckled. "So, some of Two Elks Fightin's Swedish rubbed off on you. I'd offer you more, but it's pretty scarce in these parts. Got to last me through the winter."

Erik savored his coffee, sipping slowly. It had brought back a flood of painful memories, but he couldn't turn back time. Instead, he now saw an opportunity. This man knew where civilization was. He knew how to get back. Perhaps he could go with this man.

"I can't believe it," Hailey said. "I haven't seen hide nor hair of a human being in these canyons since I begun comin' down here over a year ago. Now I run into an Injun and a Swede. Neither one can speak a lick of English." Again, he chuckled.

He looked at Erik and said more seriously, "What am I going to do with you, son?"

White Eagle turned to Erik and signed, *What does he say?*

Erik signed back, *Don't know. Not Swedish.*

"Well, that I can understand," replied Hailey, signing, apologizing. "If I'm going to talk, I need to sign."

Erik no longer wanted to scout elk. He wanted to talk. He had so much to say—so much to ask. Erik recalled more and more English words as they did, but he spoke the people's language so White Eagle could understand.

Although White Eagle was cautious of the white man, he respected Two Elks Fighting's wish to talk. He wanted to learn about the white man as well. He was curious as to why the white man was digging in the creek and washing the gravel. He listened carefully, watching them sign.

"Why do you come here?" Erik signed and asked.

"I been prospectin' the Salmon River for nigh on four years. Heard of a strike up near Florence, a fur piece north of here, across the Salmon," he said waving to the north and signing. "Then some guys hit another'n at Warren's diggin's. Didn't want to be bothered, so I come down here and begun walkin' the river, prospectin' all the side streams and sandbars."

Erik turned his cup, looking to see if anything remained.

"Aw, hell," Hailey said, rising. "Got to have some more coffee." He returned to the tent and brought out the pot. Erik almost shook, holding out his cup. White Eagle beamed. "First time I've had company in months. This is worth celebratin'."

Hailey didn't sign, so Erik didn't understand, but he raised his cup. "Thank you."

Hailey reseated himself with his own cup of coffee. "A few months ago, I hit a rich spot up the hillside aways and got some coarse gold— some nuggets—and took 'em in to Russell City. That kept me goin' until now." He signed roughly but enough that Erik understood.

"Some good gold here, but I don't think it's the mother lode." He shook his head. "Probably be spendin' the winter here, though. At least 'til the gold runs out or I find where it's comin' from." He leaned back and pointed toward a distant peak. "Might be that's where it's at. But won't go there 'til spring."

He paused, studying Erik, then shook his head.

Erik wondered why.

"Don't know how exactly you come to this country, son," he said, signing. "I 'bout didn't make it here. Crossed the South Fork in the spring. Jennifer was swept off her feet. Dang near lost her and my gear, but she just rolled over and swum to the other side like nothin' had happened. Grabbed a branch with her teeth and held on 'til she got her feet under her." He laughed. "If I hadn't seen it with my own eyes, I wouldn't hardly have believed it.

"Point is, you wouldn't cross that river to this side in the spring. This river don't even have a name. At least not on the maps I've seen. That's why I 'spect no one else has been here either." He leaned forward, signing, trying to help Erik understand. "If there's gold in this country, this is where it's at." He pressed his finger into his palm. "I can feel it in my bones."

***

Hailey wondered what to do with Erik. From what he could gather, the kid's parents were dead. As near as he could tell, they had tried to settle on the south rim, over a hundred miles by crow flight from where he now was, but that hadn't been their intended destination. The kid, who called himself Two Elks Fighting, couldn't describe where they were headed. Hailey knew settlers were moving into the Oregon Territory, but nowhere near the Salmon River drainage.

From all appearances—his animal skin clothing, his weapons, his mannerisms—the kid had been adopted by the Sheepeaters. Hailey thought he couldn't have run into Indians who were any poorer. They looked ragged, albeit they wore excellent furs. They had no horses. They lived in brush piles. They avoided humans. The boy was likely to starve to death. Yet he couldn't take on the responsibility of this kid. He hadn't come right out and said he wanted to leave, but the boy asked a lot of questions regarding when he thought he might go back to a town and where he came from, where Warren's and Florence were. Maybe, if the boy wanted to leave, he could walk out with him when he went for supplies. It was a long travel down the main Salmon River to the nearest mining camp where there was contact with supply trains.

***

Evening approached. Erik didn't want to leave, yet knew he must. At last, he stood.

"Thank you for the coffee," he said and signed, offering back his cup. "Perhaps I will return soon?"

"Anytime, son." Hailey replied, picking up his pan and turning back toward his work.

"So what does the white man do with his pan in the stream?" asked White Eagle.

"He can probably show you." Without thinking, Erik turned to Hailey. "Show White Eagle some of the yellow rock." He signed and said.

Hailey brought up the pan, which held several specks scattered throughout some black sand.

"There," pointed Erik, to the small gold nuggets.

White Eagle's eyes grew large. "They look like my yellow stone, only tiny." He fumbled his piece from his medicine bag and held it close for comparison.

Hailey let out a low whistle. "Damn! Look at that!" He took the nugget, carefully examining it. "That's a mighty rich piece of ore," he said, sputtering, hefting it. "Where the hell'd you find it?" he gestured wildly.

Grinning, White Eagle signed and replied, "Many days east, far above the star-grass meadows." He pointed in the vague direction of his vision quest ledge.

Erik realized too late they should have left White Eagle's nugget hidden.

"Deep under snow right about now," breathed Hailey. "I don't 'spect you'd take me there next summer, now would you?"

But he didn't sign and neither Erik nor White Eagle understood.

"I didn't think so." Hailey answered his own question. "Well, maybe I'll take my prospectin' up that-a way." He wondered how he'd get White Eagle to take him to the spot. He doubted he ever would. He didn't expect other Sheepeaters would welcome his presence. He wondered if the boy could even find it again. From personal experience, it was near impossible to return to any given spot in this God-forsaken land, especially if it hadn't been carefully marked.

White Eagle understood that Hailey admired his stone. Impulsively, he offered it to him. "Trade?"

Hailey recognized what White Eagle intended. Nodding vigorously, he held up his hand. "Just you wait a minute. I believe I've got somethin'." He brought out one of the tin cups. White Eagle glanced at it but shook his head. Instead he pointed to Hailey's skinning knife.

"Oh, no." Hailey shook his head. "Mighty important to have a knife in this country."

White Eagle made the motions of taking back the gold but kept his eyes on the knife.

Hailey was silent. "Show me where you found the nugget?" he questioned, signing.

White Eagle nodded. "After the cold season." He gestured toward the mountains.

Hailey unbuckled the knife and handed it to White Eagle. White Eagle handed over the nugget. They both nodded. Hailey held out his hand to shake. White Eagle took it. *A funny custom,* he thought.

Walking away, Erik could hardly contain himself. "That was a really fine trade, White Eagle."

"Yes," replied White Eagle, "just for a yellow rock."

***

Upon their return, as customary, the Sheepeaters held a council to discuss the white man.

"He digs in the dirt and washes it for yellow rock," White Eagle explained. "I traded my yellow rock for his steel knife." White Eagle passed the knife around for the men to admire.

"I have heard of the yellow rock," Black Legs spoke. "The white man comes to my father's land and digs everywhere. It is no good. They hunt and kill all the game. They kill some of my people. Now there is only war. We should kill this white man, so more will not come."

Erik couldn't bear the thought. "I know the white men," Erik began. "I don't think this man will harm us. He was friend to White Eagle and to me."

"Yes," White Eagle agreed. "He gave us a sweet drink, and he and Two Elks Fighting talked a long while. He will not harm us."

"Perhaps not this white man," Stands Alone added. "But more will come. Some will be bad. They will harm the people."

The men murmured their agreement with Stands Alone.

"He only finds tiny specks of the yellow rock," Erik offered. "I don't think he will stay if that's all he finds." But he knew better. He knew Hailey would keep looking as long as there was a spot untouched.

"No. Stands Alone is correct," said Black Legs. "More white men will come to look for the yellow rock. They will build their lodges in the canyons. They will drive away the game. We will have to find new places for our lodges and new places to hunt."

Free Hawk pulled his robe more tightly. "If they find the yellow rock on Black Rock River, I think they will stay there." He didn't like the white man living so near, but he didn't like the idea of killing the white man. His son was white.

"Yes, they will stay there," agreed Gray Owl. "We will go back to Twisted River or River That Cries. When the white men leave, as they always do, we will come back to Sandy Water River. Now we should leave this man alone and watch.

"But hear this. If we kill this white man, more will come, and in turn, they will kill the people. That is the way of the white man. Even Black Legs says his people now fight the white man."

Erik looked away, troubled. It hurt to realize the people believed this. Hailey was a good man.

Gray Owl must have sensed Erik's feelings. He addressed the council. "I do not speak of Two Elks Fighting," he said quietly. "When Sky Eyes came to the people, he gave away all he owned so he could become one of the people. He is no longer like the white man. He is Two Elks Fighting."

Erik nodded. Although he knew those were not entirely his intentions when he gave away his belongings and burned his clothes, he didn't contest what Gray Owl said. Instead he carefully weighed all that was said. He couldn't bring himself to say that someday he would leave the Twisted River Band and go back to the white world. He didn't say that Hailey might now be his way back.

Chapter 46

Between storms, Erik and White Eagle hunted—more so than Holds the Sheep and Seeks Twice. Erik and White Eagle were becoming known as fine hunters. True, they both had exceptional bows, but they never tired of hunting. They truly enjoyed hunting with each other, and they shared all they saw and did.

Many days they hunted together along the river bottoms, searching out new places, stalking game. Rarely would a few days pass without them getting meat. Some days, it would be a mule deer. Other days, they hunted sheep. But some days it would be coyote, fox, or even otter. Infrequently, they spotted elk but hadn't been successful in killing one.

One day Erik and White Eagle had gone upriver to hunt. They looked for bighorn sheep as was usual. Both wanted to make a second hunting bow. They hiked past one of the hot springs and headed toward the cliffs beyond, to a place where the mountain sheep came down to the river to lick the clay. Seeps that formed the clay steamed warmly, keeping the area free of snow.

Once, Holds the Sheep and Seeks Twice had come here with the dogs and killed a fine ram. They let the dogs chase the mountain sheep while they hid behind the rocks the people had piled into a wall. The mountain sheep always made a big circle and came back to where they started. The people had learned this and built blinds from which to hunt. However, Erik and White Eagle didn't like to sit behind blinds and let the dogs chase the sheep.

Erik noticed the clouds scudding in, appearing as if more snow would come. By late afternoon, the weather had turned, and wet snow began to fall. If the sheep had been down at the licks, they had now returned to the ridges to bed down and get out of the snow. Erik studied the roiling, black water of Sandy Water River. He watched as it gobbled up the snowflakes softly landing. It was no longer good to be hunting.

"We should head back, White Eagle," he suggested. "The curved-horns now seek shelter, and my clothes are getting wet."

"Yes, that is true. Mine are as well," replied White Eagle. "In the morning, we shall come back if the snows don't continue."

The two turned and headed back toward camp. At the hot pools, the steam billowed upward into the swirling snow. Both Erik and White Eagle generally avoided them because of the sulfur smell, but now they appeared inviting.

"Let us bathe," suggested White Eagle. "After a long walk, it will feel good on the shoulders."

"Yes," replied Erik. "It will feel warm as well. I am cold and beginning to shake in my clothes."

They set aside their weapons and clothes and lay back in the warm water against the smooth river rocks. The rocks were somewhat warm, but only below water. The wind, whistling downriver, froze the water above, coating the rocks in ice.

Erik's hair froze, and he occasionally ducked under to melt the ice. He bobbed back up, relaxing in the warmth. One spot was particularly warm—where the water bubbled from the bank, steaming in a billowing cloud into the sky.

Erik realized how tired he had been, and the warmth sapped his strength even more, but it also eased the ache from his muscles. He lay back, floating, watching the snow come down in swirling clouds, melting on contact with the steaming water.

"This is good," said White Eagle. "Even though this is a stinky place, it is good to bathe here. My body feels the strength of the hot water."

"This is why the winter camp is here?"

"Yes. The waters are good."

Both could have fallen asleep, but that, a hunter would never do. But they didn't hear the women coming until they came to the rocks directly above them. It was Quickly Smiles and Sweet Grass.

Erik's heart skipped as he quickly sat up.

The young women giggled. Erik noticed it took Quickly Smiles longer than was proper to avert her eyes. A strange feeling came to him as he realized Quickly Smiles had gazed upon him.

"You should say when you are near," protested White Eagle.

"Good hunters should never be surprised," Sweet Grass replied.

"A woman should not be so bold," White Eagle scolded. "My ears were beneath the water."

The young women giggled and walked from sight.

Both Erik and White Eagle climbed out and dressed. Erik didn't know what to think. He knew this was not proper, but then he remembered another time.

"We are even," he said to White Eagle. "We saw them at the meadows, and now they have seen us."

"They better not tell the old grandmothers," replied White Eagle. "It is not proper when girls and boys are of age to be seen without clothes by each other—not unless they are married. The grandmothers will tell stories to every woman in camp and will cackle behind our backs."

The two headed toward the village. On the way, they passed the women returning to the hot springs. "You should hope we do not show poor manners and come back and watch you bathe," White Eagle said.

Again, they giggled, but this time they averted their eyes.

***

At night, in his robes, Erik found himself thinking of Quickly Smiles. All he had to do was recognize her presence and ask Stands Alone for his permission. He thought of being married, of having a child. He thought of Quickly Smiles in the robes, warm beside him in his own lodge. The feelings stirred him. Quickly Smiles, the beautiful girl he had watched grow into a beautiful woman—she could be his wife. But he knew this could never be. He intended somehow to leave the Twisted River Band. He felt strongly that Hailey was now his answer. He had a mule. He knew how to get out of the canyons. Perhaps in spring he would go with him.

Erik rolled over in his robes. He ached for Quickly Smiles's touch, the touch he knew he would never know. He allowed himself to drift asleep, the thought of her embrace firmly held.

***

One day, during the snow-eater moon, they returned to the clay lick and killed a bighorn sheep with large horns. When Free Hawk inspected it, he thought it was a good curved-horn and began to help them prepare the horns for a new bow.

"We should hunt the elk again," suggested White Eagle. "Mother could use a new elk hide. Actually, you could use a new one. Your bed has become ripe."

Erik felt embarrassed. "We all could. We are all ripe."

White Eagle laughed. "Soon the snow-eater winds will blow, and we can bathe where the water is not stinky."

"Yes," Erik shuddered, remembering the sulfurous waters. "But that will be a while. But it will be good to hang the robes in the warm winds."

"If the camp dogs don't eat them," added White Eagle, again laughing.

Erik gazed towards the hillsides beyond where they rose above the river.

White Eagle knew he was thinking.

"I wish to return to visit Hailey," stated Erik. He knew spring would soon come. As difficult as the decision was, he needed to make, he had to do it.

"Yes," replied White Eagle. "Perhaps he will have some more sweet drink."

Erik lit up at the thought of the hot, sweetened coffee. "That alone would be worth the journey."

***

It was decided. As the two had done many times now, they packed their robes and food and informed Free Hawk and Shining Water.

"My hunters seek more elk?" she asked.

"Perhaps. Perhaps not. Maybe we'll just come home with owl feathers for our arrows," replied Erik.

Free Hawk suspected what his adopted son was thinking. He had struggled with knowing that some day he might leave the people although he never spoke of it.

***

They traveled as they had before. By day's end, they had found no sign of the prospector—only the stones where the fire had been. Where the mule had grazed, the grass was trampled and the ground was barren.

Erik was amazed at how much Hailey had dug along the creek. Surely he had found much gold. He wondered if he had headed up to the high country toward where White Eagle had found his gold. He couldn't be sure, because tracks led to and from the campsite in many directions. He sat thinking.

White Eagle sat with him. "The white man who digs in the dirt has gone, Two Elks Fighting."

"Perhaps, White Eagle," replied Erik.

"I think he was too weak for this country. I do not see many pieces of dead animals—no hides. Maybe he starved."

"I don't think he starved." Erik knew the prospector had to balance his time between mining and hunting. Additionally, he had to care for the mule. But Hailey was capable. "He may have just moved on."

"But to where? He finds the yellow rock here."

"You indicated where you found your yellow rock, White Eagle. Perhaps he goes there to look for more."

White Eagle laughed. "Hah, the high country still has snow. Besides, that is very big country. How can he find a tiny speck of rock on a mountain so big?"

Erik thought about trying to explain that Hailey knew how to read the rocks. Only certain rocks would have gold. It was not terribly difficult to search for the likely places. He decided not to explain. "Yes, you are right, White Eagle. He must have gone."

The significance set in. Hailey had left the country, perhaps never to return. And what were his chances of ever finding him again if he did return? An empty, hopeless feeling seeped in, filling him.

"What is wrong with my brother?" whispered White Eagle. He sensed Erik's struggle.

Erik looked at White Eagle. Even if he found a way out, how could he leave White Eagle who had truly become his brother? Could he give up a sister for White Eagle? He shook his head miserably. Perhaps it was good that this decision was taken from him for at least a little while longer.

"Sometimes I think of my other family, White Eagle. That is all. I hope they are happy."

"I understand. I think of the one who hunts the elk as well, but I am happy you came to be one of us."

***

They slept that night near Hailey's camp. Erik woke to hear wolves howling, something that was rare. He wondered why there were so few in the canyons. He shook White Eagle, "Hear the wolves talk?" But White Eagle was already awake, listening. Silently, they sat for a while. They could hear the lonely drawn-out call of the adults and, almost humorously, the yap of the younger wolves trying to join in. At last the chorus ended with a wavering, lonesome howl dissipating into silence.

"Do you suppose they are also calling to their lost ones?" asked Erik. "It sounds as if they do."

"The people say they do. They are very much like the people."

CHAPTER 47

THE TWISTED RIVER BAND headed east from Sandy Water River back toward the Twisted River drainage and set up their summer hunting camp near the divide between both rivers. They camped near a series of mountain meadows, some interconnected by small streams, others separated by low ridges. It was not difficult to travel from one series of meadows to another. Whistling Elk and Free Hawk said there should be more game. This area had very few camas, however.

One day Erik and White Eagle killed a mule deer, its horns shrouded in velvet. Both worked on skinning the animal and preparing the meat to haul back to camp.

"When are you going to marry Quickly Smiles and start your family?" White Eagle asked.

Erik stopped work, stunned. "What?"

"You hear well, Two Elks Fighting, what I ask."

"I won't, White Eagle." He shrugged and resumed cutting apart the meat, but he felt a flutter in his stomach.

"But her heart is for you, you know this. Everyone in camp knows this. Stands Alone just waits for you to ask."

"You are not truthful," Erik said, the feeling moving upward, his heart quickening. He piled the meat on the hide and carefully cleaned and put away his knife. He wiped his hands in the grass.

White Eagle laughed. "I am." He shoved Erik onto his back and wrestled with him until he sat astride, pinning him.

"If I had a woman looking at me like Quickly Smiles does you, I would marry her now," he said, panting. "You are silly not to."

Erik was beside himself. How did White Eagle know his feelings? "That is something I must decide for myself, White Eagle," he protested. But the picture of Quickly Smiles at his side with a young child, perhaps his son, filled him. A strange, wonderful feeling flooded him as he pictured himself a father.

"I would if I could," Erik whispered.

"Ha, *if* you could. You *can!*" White Eagle replied. "If I had a woman who loved me, I would no longer wait to share my robes." He got off Erik with a push. "I thought you had quit being a silly white boy." He sat a short distance apart, now studying his brother.

Erik sat up. "Why don't *you* marry her, White Eagle? It would make my heart glad as well to have my brother marry the one I care for," replied Erik.

"But she has eyes for you," White Eagle replied loudly. "If I asked, she would, but that wouldn't be right. It is you she sneaks her looks to, not to me."

"She looks at you, too," replied Erik, brushing himself off.

"Only because I am with you."

"That is not true."

"Ha." White Eagle got up and lifted the buck's front-quarters to his shoulders. "She is yours, Two Elks Fighting. We shall speak no more of this." He headed back toward camp.

Erik stood, hoisted up the remaining meat, and slowly followed, thinking.

***

Erik couldn't shake White Eagle's comments. One morning he decided to wait by the trail where Quickly Smiles walked to get water. Boldly, he took the water bag, filled it, and carried it for a distance. Before he came to within eyesight of the camp, however, he set it down. Quickly Smiles allowed him to do this and briefly glanced into his eyes. That was enough.

A few nights later, Erik coughed at the lodge of Stands Alone and Ripe Berry. He was calling on Quickly Smiles. As customary among the people, he addressed Stands Alone. "I would visit with your daughter this night."

Erik saw both women steal a glance his way. Stands Alone rose, took Erik by the shoulder, and stepped from the lodge. He led him to a place away from other eyes and ears and sat.

"It honors me and Quickly Smiles that you cherish her. You are a fine hunter, Two Elks Fighting. I know you can provide well for my daughter, but my heart is troubled. I have known for two seasons your desire for Quickly Smiles. I have also known for two seasons her desire for you. Again, I am honored by this. But is this what Two Elks Fighting really wishes?"

Erik sat, unprepared for the question. Since White Eagle had mentioned it, he had spent every moment thinking. To marry Quickly Smiles would mean he would remain with the people. Had Hailey not gone, he would not have even considered staying. Now he no longer knew when he would leave the Sheepeaters, if even he could. He had allowed himself to believe his sister was lost. Otherwise God would have helped him leave. God's angel had brought him here. It now seemed the right decision to stay.

He looked at Stands Alone, "Yes, this is what I wish."

"Then it shall be, and I shall call you Son." He embraced Erik.

In those words, all that needed to be said was said.

"I will be at the council rock, Father." He didn't look back. He knew that if Ripe Berry didn't object, Quickly Smiles would visit him. If they were right for each other, they would marry.

***

Heart beating as it never had, strange feelings flooding him, stirring him, his mouth dry, Erik stood at the rock with his robes. *What if she doesn't come? What if White Eagle is wrong about Quickly Smiles? Perhaps I am a foolish white boy and did not see her looking when I was bathing or when I carried the water. Perhaps she has simply decided she doesn't want me.*

He need not have worried. He felt and heard the soft pads behind him, and he turned quickly to embrace Quickly Smiles. He pulled the robe over them from prying eyes. Incredible feelings flooded him. Here was this most beautiful woman in his arms. The woman he had watched, thought about, even dreamed about. Quickly Smiles was *really* here, her warmth against his, pressing against him. He pressed back, feeling the tightness. He wanted to hold her forever. He touched his nose softly to hers, brushing it, then to her cheeks … to her lips. Then he allowed his lips to touch hers. She pressed back. The sensation was overwhelming. His heart raced. How could this be? He had often kissed his mother, but these feelings, *these* feelings, were different. Here was a warm, loving person, giving herself to him—to Two Elks Fighting. Here was a person he suddenly wanted to be with forever, a person with whom he wanted to share everything—here was Quickly Smiles.

***

The meeting had been good. Two Elks Fighting signaled his intentions by presenting Stands Alone his steel knife. The talk was soon all over camp, and the people were in high spirits. Two Elks Fighting and Quickly Smiles were to marry. Gray Owl had said this would be a good thing. Even Porcupine Woman agreed this would be good for the people.

The men constructed a lodge for the couple a distance away, beyond the sight of camp, near the rocks, where no eyes could pry, where no one could hear. This was proper so Two Elks Fighting could know his wife. The couple would share a few days together before returning to the people where they would be recognized as man and wife.

Erik led Quickly Smiles away from her lodge and to the new lodge. The women had spread many robes so they would be comfortable, and already, the grandmothers had brought food and water.

Erik sat, not sure of what to do—of what was customary—for this was something of which one did not ask. Quickly Smiles stood and let her robe fall. Erik felt stunned. Prickles ran across his back and neck—across his face. He felt himself flooded with awe for this beautiful woman, a woman soon to be his wife. This woman was his to touch, to hold, to love.

She stepped to him, pulled him to his feet, embraced him. He caressed her lightly, held her tightly, felt his heart beating with hers, felt her breath on his cheek, felt her body meld into his.

Gently, he pulled her to the robes. There he looked deep into her eyes, flooded with feelings for this woman. He kissed her and lightly touched her. In the moonlight, he watched her breathing, her chest rising and falling. He would not rush this thing.

A cough sounded. Erik sat up. Instantly, cold raced down his spine. He knew the sound. A fear he had almost forgotten flooded back. *A night cat!* But then his fear passed. The night cat was his helper. The night cat was no danger to him. He sat reflecting on his vision, what it meant. A mountain lion was outside his wedding lodge, possibly hunting. Maybe it smelled meat in the camp and was bold enough to sneak around the outskirts to find a piece.

Quickly Smiles sat up and held close to Erik, eyes worried, "What has disturbed Two Elks Fighting?"

"Sh-h-h-h," he whispered and touched her lips. "It is the cough of a night cat."

Fear flooded Quickly Smiles's eyes, and she grabbed for her robe, pulling it about herself.

"It's all right," Erik whispered. "The night cat will not harm us. She hunts for easy food."

Erik stared into the night through the gaps at the bright moonlight filtering across the meadows and scattered trees, but he couldn't see the lion. The moonlight reminded him of another night when he searched for another lion.

With an icy jolt, the pain, the ache hit him. The night of the lion attack came back. He could see the crouching shadows and Red. He could see the mountain lion as he fired at it and missed and as it bounded away downstream. He could feel his mother's worry. "Katrine," he whispered.

And then the ache overwhelmed him, and he began to shake. "This … this cannot be, Quickly Smiles." In a flash, his vision helper had revealed to him who he really was. There was no question. The mountain lion had come this night for a reason. Erik believed it with every fiber of his body.

"I'm … so … so sorry, Quickly Smiles," he choked.

Quickly Smiles frowned, a scared look on her face while she clutched her robe tightly about her. "Two Elks Fighting scares me. What is wrong?"

Erik pulled her tight. "Do not be frightened, Quickly Smiles. I truly do love you."

She smiled but uneasily. She tried to pull him back to the robes, but he refused.

Instead, Erik held her tightly and tried to explain. "Quickly Smiles, I do love you. I always have. I am so honored you love me as well. I would love to share my life with you, but I cannot. I cannot be your husband."

Erik felt her stiffen, and she began to shake. Erik knew that for a woman to be turned away by a man was disgraceful, humiliating. Likewise, although he knew what must be done, he risked Stands Alone's anger, possibly even death.

"Don't, Quickly Smiles," Erik continued. "I cannot be your husband. I made a promise many seasons ago, of which the night cat reminded me. Someday I will leave the people. I have a sister. I promised her I would find her, no matter what. I promised my mother and father that I would. I have given my sacred word, which I cannot break. I do not know when I will go, or if I will be back."

Quickly Smiles continued to shake. Erik continued, trying to sooth her. "You made my heart glad, Quickly Smiles. More than I can say and more than you will ever know."

She turned to him. "Then do not leave, Two Elks Fighting. You are my hunter. I would have you for my husband. My heart wants you as well. I do not want to become an old grandmother like Yellow Flower. Instead, I will kill myself."

Erik sat stunned. "*No!* ... No, Quickly Smiles. You must not think like that or say things like that." He held her tightly, stroked her hair, looked into her frightened eyes. "No, Quickly Smiles. Do not think that."

Already Quickly Smiles knew she had said more than what was proper.

"Quickly Smiles, I *must* go away. The Great Mystery has revealed this to me."

"Then I will go with you."

"You cannot. It's not possible. It's … it's just not." He sat back. Erik knew it would be difficult to explain.

"I will."

"You cannot, for you would have to leave the people," Erik tried to explain. "Too many have left the people because I came." Abruptly Erik stopped, then turned to her.

"There is another who loves you, Quickly Smiles. He would have you for his wife."

Quickly Smiles stiffened and stared hard at Erik. "This is not true. Only you have had eyes for me."

Erik shook his head firmly, smiling. "No. This other has had eyes for you. I know. He is a good hunter, so you could not see. A good hunter keeps hidden."

Quickly Smiles sat, bewildered.

"He loves you as much as I, perhaps even more."

Quickly Smiles shook her head. "No. This man has not shown himself to me. You have. You carried the water."

"He would not. He would not say to you his love, for he honors me. He is my brother, and I am the older, so he would not say."

"White Eagle," Quickly Smiles breathed quietly, nodding.

"Yes. White Eagle," answered Erik. "We have talked. He would have you. He loves you, as I do, Quickly Smiles."

"But how can you be certain? Maybe he jokes, as do all men about women. All men want women."

Erik smiled to himself. "Yes. We do. But he has told me this, and White Eagle always speaks true. And I have seen it in his eyes. He cannot hide this from his brother."

Quickly Smiles embraced Erik. "Your ways are truly strange, Two Elks Fighting," she whispered. "My father did tell me."

With that, Erik took his robes and left the shelter. He sat quietly, his robe about him, watching the stars slowly spin in the night sky until light streaked the sky.

***

Quickly Smiles was not disgraced. Erik had left the brush across the front of the door. The people accepted his words as truth.

Gray Owl considered Two Elks Fighting's words. He knew the customs of the white man were different. Although Two Elks Fighting was of the people, he did not understand all the ways of the people. Never had something like this happened among the people. Something this implausible had to be true.

White Eagle and Quickly Smiles were married a few days later. White Eagle presented Hailey's knife to Stands Alone. Stands Alone returned Erik's knife. Erik thought about giving it to White Eagle as a wedding present but instead gave him some of his finest arrows. His father's knife was all he had of his father's. Besides, White Eagle was accustomed to using a stone knife; he wasn't.

The people rejoiced when White Eagle and Quickly Smiles returned from their wedding lodge. A new man and a new wife had come to the Twisted River Band.

A short time later, the two brothers found themselves building a real lodge. "You surprise me, Two Elks Fighting. I was certain I would be helping you build your own lodge."

"Perhaps someday you will." But Erik was thinking of a different world.

***

The summer grew long. Erik found Free Hawk's and Shining Water's lodge surprisingly empty. He could sense Shining Water and Singing Bird both missed White Eagle. They rejoiced at the marriage. It was good. It was part of the circle of life.

He couldn't sleep. He rose from his robes, and carrying one about his shoulders as he often did, he wandered into the meadow and sat looking back at the village. Overhead, the brilliant stars filled the black canopy. He could just make out the lodges against the skyline.

Erik reflected on his vision journey. *Two summers ago.* He was a man in the eyes of the people. He smiled to himself. He was nearly married to Quickly Smiles. A stab of sorrow filled him. Maybe he had made a mistake. He glanced toward White Eagle's lodge. He envied his brother and his wife. *This is my brother's world. In a year or two, he'll be a father. He'll have a son. The people will talk of him and make songs for him. I'll be an uncle to a nephew I'll never know.* The ache filling his heart was nearly unbearable.

CHAPTER 48

"I GOT SOME TRACKS here, Frank," spat Ed Blaine, a stocky, short man with dirty blond hair. "Can't tell if they's shod or not. 'Spect they are. Don't know of any Indians in these parts got horses. Got to be him."

Frank Gibbs, dark hair matted, leaned his lanky frame from the saddle of the gray mare, peering down at the tracks. "Think you're right, Ed. Some moccasin tracks, as well. Maybe, we're too late and those tracks won't be comin' back out."

"If they're Sheepeater moccasins, that old sourdough don't have a thing to worry about," replied Blaine. "They're too timid to even come out from under their brush piles."

Gibbs straightened up. "That's what folks say, but I know stories about more'n one poor bastard that just ended up disappeared in this country."

"Can't say it was Sheepeaters," countered Blaine, kicking the red roan to urge him up over some rocks.

"Can't say 'tweren't, either." Gibbs nudged the mare to follow.

They drifted along the trail, keeping their eyes scanning for sign. They were now certain the prospector was somewhere ahead. They had checked everywhere else nearby where they had lost sight of him a few weeks back. It wouldn't be long until they found him again.

"Might not be a bad thing to have those tracks followin' this guy," mused Blaine. "If things git outta hand, might be good to have a few renegades 'round to blame."

"You got a point, Ed."

***

Blaine and Gibbs had watched the prospector leave town and then tracked him down the Salmon River. Tracking him was difficult. He was good at making tracks disappear. The sourdough was also good at watching his back trail. Twice they had spotted him in the rocks, just watching. He knew they would be trying to follow. Blaine and Gibbs figured all of Russell City would empty and stampede for the river, following the prospector.

"Guess we were wrong about the camp emptyin' and followin'," mused Blaine.

"The old-timer kept things quiet. Probably offered the assayer a cut to keep quiet as well," replied Gibbs. "Maybe they won't be comin' this way anyhows."

"How's that, Frank?"

"They got a new strike up by Florence."

"Maybe so, you're right then," replied Blaine. "Russell City's about done for anyhow. Haven't found any lode gold, and now the placers have dried up. There's more leavin' than comin' in. Ain't too many folks that like this canyon country anyhow."

"That's 'cause no one's findin' anything here," Gibbs retorted. "And it's too damn rugged."

Blaine dismounted and began leading the roan across broken talus beside the river. "Findin' this guy had better pay off," he muttered. "I ain't used to workin' this hard."

Gibbs laughed sarcastically. "Neither of us are. Not since we worked for that skinflint up near Deadwood, runnin' his sluice."

Blaine scowled, remembering. "Ya shouldn't have got caught, Frank," he spat. "We coulda snatched a lot more gold."

"Yeah, well I ain't a miner," replied Gibbs. "Too damned much work. Seein' those nuggets in that sluice, well … I just couldn't let them lie around sparklin' in the sun like that. Some other bastard would have grabbed them if I hadn't."

313

"And they'd be huntin' that poor bastard, lookin' to stretch his neck instead of ours," snapped Blaine.

Gibbs muttered to himself. "He got what he deserved, Ed. Didn't pay us worth squat."

"Well, we sure as hell made up for it," Blaine retorted. "'Bout all we didn't take of his was his mule."

"And takin' is a damn sight easier than mining," muttered Gibbs.

They remounted. A game trail now ascended toward distant peaks. The horse prints were more distinct.

"Got to be him," affirmed Blaine, pointing. "Good thing we showed up in Russell City when we did, or we wouldn't have chanced on him."

"I think our luck's about to change, Frank." Blaine spurred on the roan.

***

After being run out of Deadwood, Blaine and Gibbs had headed east toward the Salmon River mines, which were just opening. They intended to snoop around the mining camps until they found some easy gold for the taking. They weren't disappointed. Someone had recognized a prospector who had come back into town. He had been in town before with several ounces of gold, good, coarse gold. Most gold coming out of the Salmon River country was flour gold, hardly worth the time to pan it. Those who knew the river figured the prospector was near a lode, probably along a tributary above the canyon.

Blaine and Gibbs had chanced on him as he was leaving the assay tent. Seeing the opportunity, they walked in. Visible gold in chunks of white quartz lay strewn on the counter before the assayer could clear it off. Without a doubt, the prospector had found lode gold.

From the hills outside the town, they tried to keep an eye on him, but he slipped past them. They had floundered around the canyons for weeks with no luck at finding him. Low on supplies, clothes tattered and caked with mud, ready to give up, they chanced on hearing a gunshot up a side canyon. They had avoided the canyon because of the sheer cliffs and the fact that they'd need to ford the river to get to it. But now on the opposite side, the tracks were clear. The prospector had to be near.

CHAPTER 49

ERIK AND WHITE EAGLE headed east toward a tributary of Twisted River. The peaks where Erik sought his vision were visible in the distance farther to the northeast. As they drew near the canyon rim, Erik's thoughts turned back to Hailey. White Eagle had indicated to Hailey in what direction the gold was. Now he wondered if Hailey was nearby, searching.

Erik was greatly troubled. He had decided to leave the Twisted River Band. He would go before the winter snows. He had been surprised when White Eagle approached him a few weeks after he had married. They had been hunting, had no luck, and were walking back toward the summer hunting camp.

White Eagle had asked him if he ever thought of Quickly Smiles.

Of course he thought of her, he had told him, but he was proud she was wife to White Eagle. He asked White Eagle if she cooked well, but that had been a stupid thing to ask. Of course Erik knew she cooked well. Often he was at their lodge. But whenever there, Quickly Smiles politely avoided his eyes. He knew the hurt it caused. It was as if nothing had ever existed between them.

Then White Eagle said he wanted him to have Quickly Smiles. Erik was stunned. At first he thought he was throwing her away. He had protested. He knew they loved each other very much.

White Eagle had laughed. Erik remembered his words: "No, Two Elks Fighting—I am not throwing her away. I am offering her as a gift to my brother."

Erik couldn't comprehend the request. He would never have considered such a thing. He told White Eagle he could not. "It is not my way."

And they had argued. White Eagle had insisted. Quickly Smiles had been his first before she came to him. Erik reminded him they had not come together, they had not become man and wife, but White Eagle said it didn't matter; it was the same thing.

Then White Eagle told him, "Besides, Two Elks Fighting, this is something *I* decide, not you. I understand you have strange ways, but you must understand. This would honor me. Quickly Smiles agrees. This would honor her."

And Erik had felt wretched because he began thinking about being with Quickly Smiles, and he knew he wanted her. He could no longer argue. He knew it was wrong, but his being ached for her. She wanted this. He knew he wanted this. But how could he allow this? He also knew that he couldn't refuse. His throat dry, he replied, "If it would please my brother." And, miserably, he remembered his heart racing.

Soon after, Erik shared his robes with Quickly Smiles. Although it was good, very good, it also deeply troubled him. He remembered lying next to her, her soft touch, her smile, and his heart ached. She would have had him. They could have been together. Although White Eagle had insisted, he couldn't shake his troubling thoughts. It had been wrong.

***

Erik gazed toward the canyon. *I have tried to be of the people; however, this troubles me too deeply. I can no longer do this.* He knew he couldn't refuse White Eagle's gift—he wouldn't have the strength to refuse Quickly Smiles's love. He wondered if he could walk the many miles out of this land, back to his white world on his own.

For a long while, he had wrestled with leaving. He always told himself it was too far—he would never survive—but in his heart, he knew he had already faced worse, much worse. He could survive. It was the people he didn't wish to leave; it was White Eagle; it was Quickly Smiles. In truth, he was now torn between the two worlds. But for this reason, for Quickly Smiles, he knew he must leave—soon, before the deep snows came.

They paused on the rim, the broken draws descending before them. Finally, Erik turned to White Eagle. "I have to know if Hailey is near. Perhaps he is looking for your gold near your vision ledge," Erik said. "If I seek him, will you come with me?"

White Eagle studied the broken country in front of them. He knew it would mean a difficult climb down into the canyon and another back up toward his mountain. It would mean several days from camp. "If my brother must go, then I will go."

For some reason, Erik felt Hailey was somewhere north of them. That country was closer to River of No Return. If they got close, perhaps they could smell his campfire.

It took a day and most of the next to descend to Twisted River and climb back to the canyon rim beyond. Now they turned west, crossing through the alpine meadows between the drainages, heading toward River of No Return canyon. Erik began to doubt his hunch. They hadn't seen tracks on either side of Twisted River. Now they stood on a high ridge from which they could see the canyon. The river lay hidden beneath the folding hills.

One basin remained between them and River of No Return. Erik decided that if he didn't find Hailey, he would make a loop west and return to their summer hunting camp. They dropped into the basin, skirted a small alpine lake, and dropped across the next ridge. Below them, two draws merged into a rock outcrop. Immediately Erik recognized Hailey's camp and smelled the smoke.

Elated, Erik started in a trot toward the camp. White Eagle followed.

Erik hollered to the tent but received no reply. He thought perhaps that Hailey was working near the rock outcrop; he saw broken white rock strewn about. Hank had found a lode, he guessed.

Suddenly, the canvas was thrown back and Hailey emerged, followed by two men. Both men, armed, brought their weapons into view.

"I thought I heard somethin'," a tall, black-haired man said. Thinly smiling, Gibbs studied Erik and White Eagle.

"*Hej*," Erik called, nervously smiling, searching Hailey's face.

Hailey's expression went from joy to sudden concern. "Hello." He signed for him to leave.

The men shouldered past Hailey. "Well, well, looks like we got some Injuns for company now too."

Hailey was clearly stressed, but Erik, intent on finding the man for so long, overlooked the warning signs. He realized too late, it was a bad situation.

"You know these Injuns?" Gibbs asked.

Hailey didn't reply.

The stockier man with lighter hair waved his pistol at Erik. "Well I'll be damned. Looks like one of 'em is white."

Erik backed up, showing his hands and giving the sign for peace as he did.

"Musta got himself captured by the Injuns," speculated Gibbs, then he added. "I'd put those bows down 'fore somebody gets hurt." He motioned with his rifle.

Erik and White Eagle stood, confused.

"They don't understand English," Hailey explained.

Erik and White Eagle stood warily out of reach, eyeing the weapons.

"What'd happen? He get captured when he was a littl'n?" asked Blaine.

Hailey didn't reply. He tried to sign *not good, leave.*

Erik wasn't sure what to do. Instead, he signed back asking who the men were.

Signing, *evil men,* Hailey tried again to tell them to get away.

They turned then to leave, but the tall black-haired man leveled his rifle. "I wouldn't go nowheres boys," Gibbs said coolly. "Now shed them weapons."

They froze. They understood having the rifle aimed in their direction and slowly put down their bows. Both showed their hands.

"We was just havin' a friendly chat with your friend here. Admiring his gold, you might say," offered Blaine. "Especially this purdy piece." He showed the rock to Erik and White Eagle. "Said he traded for it from an Indian. Couldn't be you, could it?" He eyed White Eagle.

"I said they don't understand English," Hailey said, desperately trying to turn their attention from the gold.

But Blaine noticed the flash of recognition in White Eagle's eyes.

"Well, I'll be damned. That young buck don't need to understand English." He smiled. "Looks like he recognizes that gold rock, all right." Blaine passed it in front of him again. "This was yours, wasn't it? Sure is purdy. Where'd you find it?" He threatened with his pistol, cocking the hammer.

White Eagle stood, eyes steady, unflinching.

"*Don't!* I told you, he doesn't understand," protested Hailey.

"You stay outta this, old-timer." He turned and waved the pistol toward Hailey.

"It *wasn't* his," continued Hailey. "Told you I got it from one of those Bannock traders. Now I think your welcome's wore off. You got my gold. It's time to git."

"We was aimin' to do just that." Blaine leveled the pistol and pulled the trigger. The ball ripped through Hailey's stomach. "You're right, old-timer. We got your gold. Don't need you no more."

Hailey stumbled, then collapsed, blood soaking his shirt. Writhing in agony, gut shot, he tried to sit up.

Erik screamed and jumped on Blaine's back, flailing him with his fists. Blaine spun, trying to dislodge him.

White Eagle drew his knife and tried to reach Blaine but couldn't because of Erik.

Gibbs swung his rifle butt down with a dull thud across Erik's head. Erik dropped limp, blood welling through matted hair.

White Eagle slashed at Blaine, catching his arm, spilling blood.

Blaine cried out, spun away and fired past White Eagle. "Bastard!"

"Don't kill him," shouted Gibbs, stepping forward to stop Blaine. "He knows where the gold is."

White Eagle spun around, balancing his knife.

"Don't aim to, unless I have no choice," Blaine said, eyeing White Eagle, examining his cut arm.

White Eagle glanced toward Two Elks Fighting, then back at the two men. Both the rifle and pistol were aimed at him. He didn't know if Two Elks Fighting was dead or not.

Cautiously, Gibbs approached White Eagle. "Drop the knife, Injun."

White Eagle stood, balanced on his toes, ready to lunge. He knew he could quickly kill the tall one, but the stocky man would get him before he could get them both. Two Elks Fighting's life depended on him. He didn't care about his own life—it would be good to kill this man—but he did care about Two Elks Fighting.

He relaxed and tossed his knife next to his bow and signed for peace. Gibbs gathered the weapons and threw them out of reach.

"Now *sit down!*" Keeping his pistol on White Eagle, Blaine shoved him so his knees buckled. "Tie his hands, Frank."

Blaine wrapped his own arm and then stepped over to examine Erik. "Looks like you damn near killed him, you idiot. Damn near crushed his skull."

"Thanks, friend," muttered Gibbs as he finished tying White Eagle. "Guess I shoulda just let him slit your throat."

"Hell, I could handle him. He's just a damn kid."

"You didn't get a good look at the knife he's wearin' did ya?"

Blaine looked and was silent for a moment. "Yeah, good thing he seems to have forgot about it. Wonder how he got to be an Indian anyhow."

"Probably got stole, like you said. Them Injun's take younguns and raise them as their own. This one don't even know English, so he probably got stole when he was real young."

"Unfortunate bastard." Blaine eyed Erik lying in a heap. "Guess we'll never know. Come on, Frank. Get our stuff so we can go after that gold. I'm gonna talk to this young buck." He turned toward White Eagle. "Sure is a scrawny, poor-looking bastard, don't you think?"

"They both are," agreed Gibbs. "Sorriest lookin' Injuns, I ever saw."

"Well, it probably doesn't matter how sorry lookin' they are. When these two don't show up from their happy huntin' trip, we might have some company. Their kin ain't gonna take kindly to them not comin' home."

"Hell, Ed, maybe you're right, maybe we should just head out. We already got the old-timer's gold," Gibbs said. "That Injun's gold could've come from anywhere. Besides what makes you think that buck's going to take us to it, anyhow?"

Blaine laughed sarcastically. "Use your head, Frank. We just killed a man …" He looked in Hailey's direction.

Hailey was slumped, still gasping.

"B-bastards," Hailey managed. He worked his mouth and spat blood. "Rot in hell." Pain flashed across his face as he tried to sit up.

"After you, friend." Blaine stepped over, put his boot on Hailey's chest, and pushed him down. "By the way, thanks for runnin' your mouth. Otherwise I'd never have known about the Indian's gold."

Hailey cursed, words unintelligible. He lay slumped, blood soaking his shirt and trousers.

Blaine turned back to Gibbs, waving the gold. "Look at it, Frank. This piece of rock is damn near pure gold. Probably got an ounce in it if it's got any. We find it, I figure we can scoop out enough in less than a day to make us rich."

"Yeah, we'll be lucky to get a day with the whole damn Sheepeater tribe on our tails, not to mention miners coming in from—"

"Hell, Frank," Blaine replied, now irritated. "You don't think much. No one alive is gonna track us in these canyons. *No one.* Not even them damn Sheepeaters. When they realize these two ain't comin' back, we'll be across the main Salmon, halfway to Canada."

Blaine approached White Eagle. "Where'd you find this, boy?" He waved his arm in an arc toward the peaks. "*Where?*"

White Eagle pretended ignorance. He shrugged, speaking rapidly. *"Mehwe gizhaande daiboo'. Mehwe nuun gai yeyenkah. Ne deegai-mehwe deasen wase mehwe."* He told them, "You are bad men. You do not deserve to live. I will hunt you and kill you, because you no longer have a right to live." He spoke proudly, confidently. They understood nothing.

"Maybe he don't understand, Ed."

Blaine laughed. "Oh, he understands all right. He understands I just killed a guy for that rock and now I wanna know where it came from."

"Yes, but what makes ya think he's stupid enough to just get up and take us there?"

"This!" Blaine jerked Erik up and put a knife to his throat. He looked directly at White Eagle, "Where'd you find the damn rock?" He held up the gold and repeated his gesture of scanning. He knew from the brief sharp look in White Eagle's eyes that he had communicated.

He laughed cruelly. "So you two are pretty good friends, huh? That'll make it real easy. You'll do as we like or your friend dies."

White Eagle understood the knife at Two Elks Fighting's throat. He nodded at the rock, then toward the peaks to the northeast. He stood and faced the peaks, nodding with his head.

"Ha!" Blaine exclaimed. "Told you he understands. Get the horses and bring the kid. I'll follow the Indian."

***

Gibbs jerked Erik up and slung him across the saddle on the gray mare. He swung up behind him and propped him up. "What if the buck takes us to his camp?"

Blaine was silent. "I suppose he might. But I'd wager their camp ain't up in them rocks. It's gotta be farther south, maybe in the meadows. If he values his hide like he does his friend's, he'll take us there all right." Blaine mounted the roan and shoved White Eagle in the direction of the peaks.

White Eagle knew his hope lay in Two Elks Fighting's recovery. He worried that he might be badly hurt. He knew the black-haired man had hit him hard. Together they would stand a chance against these men. Alone … he would wait and see.

***

White Eagle led them east. He picked the easiest route he could. It would take at least a day to get back to the star-grass meadows where the summer hunting camps had been and then another day to reach his vision seeking area.

He picked out the general direction toward his vision ledge and began a slow traverse upward. He was not going to hurry. He wanted to give Two Elks Fighting a chance to recover. Already it was late afternoon.

White Eagle kept a close watch on Two Elks Fighting. He appeared more dead than alive. He decided that if Two Elks Fighting died, he would kill these men. He tried to get close to check on him. When he did, it irritated the shorter man.

"Stallin' ain't gonna make it easier on you, Indian." Blaine rode up and shoved him. "Keep movin'."

Erik began to come around when they were about halfway to the old summer hunting camps. White Eagle tried to catch his eye. Erik's head bobbed and flopped around. White Eagle could tell he was unable to hold himself steady. He could also see where blood had trickled down his shirt and clotted in his hair.

Finally, he got his chance when they reached the next stream. He stopped. "We need water," he said loudly and motioned to Blaine.

"Guess we can stop a minute," Blaine said. "Let the horses get some water as well."

White Eagle offered his hands to him. "Untie," he demanded.

Blaine recognized the gesture. "All right, but no funny business." He untied his hands and pulled his pistol, making certain White Eagle understood.

That was what White Eagle wanted. He could go all day without water. It was for Two Elks Fighting. He needed the water. Nevertheless, he drank deeply, knowing it would be foolish not to.

Erik stirred. White Eagle scooped some water and carried it to him.

"Two Elks Fighting," he whispered. "You got hit hard. You need to wake up now. You need to drink."

Erik tried to say something but dropped his head again. White Eagle could see the injury was bad.

White Eagle continued to talk to him. Blaine hit his hands, spilling the water.

"No talking." Roughly, he jerked White Eagle's hands back and retied them. He shoved him in the direction of the peak. "It's time to find that gold."

Evening approached. White Eagle purposefully angled along the canyon breaks toward a rock face. He had to talk to Two Elks Fighting, and he needed his hands to do so. When they reached the rock face, White Eagle again stopped and motioned for the stocky man to untie his hands. "Untie." He nodded his head at the rocks.

"Where the hell's he leading us now? This don't seem like the best route to the top," muttered Blaine.

"I say he's leading us on a wild goose chase," Gibbs answered. "I say we dump 'em both and head out with what we got."

"Where's the damn gold?" Blaine shouted.

White Eagle looked at him and nodded over his shoulder. "Untie." He raised his hands again.

When Blaine realized White Eagle wouldn't traverse the rocks while tied, he dismounted and untied him. "Go, and make it quick."

White Eagle tried to help Two Elks Fighting walk while the men led the horses. He whispered to him.

"I said no talking!" Blaine knocked White Eagle in the head.

White Eagle glared.

"And if you try running, I'll kill your friend." He gestured this with his pistol, unmistakable to White Eagle.

White Eagle quit talking, but when the men weren't watching, his hands untied, he signed all that he had been thinking. Erik signed back his understanding.

"How far, Indian?" asked Blaine. He tried to communicate this by walking his fingers and shrugging, pointing in the direction they were headed.

White Eagle pretended he didn't understand; he indicated only the next ridgeline by pointing, and then he kept glancing back toward the canyon below. When he noticed the men looking, he quickly gazed away. His game worked. He noticed the men snatching glances along their back trail as well. Carefully, he continued the game until nightfall.

Neither he nor Two Elks Fighting were tied again until White Eagle decided the place to camp. He walked to some trees bordered by rock, where a seep emerged, and sat down. He waved to the sky. "Night is here. We shall camp." He didn't want to start a fire. If the two men suffered, it would be better for him and Two Elks Fighting.

Gibbs began to wonder what was going on. He had seen the Indian trying to sign talk to the white kid. Ed didn't seem to worry about other Sheepeaters, but he wasn't so sure. He was glad they had stopped for the night. Come tomorrow, if they didn't quickly find the gold, he'd leave Ed and head out on his own.

"Whatcha lookin' for, Injun?" he demanded. "I seen you lookin' back the way we come."

White Eagle stared at him, unblinking.

"Damn Injun. He's up to something, Ed," he muttered and pulled out some jerked meat and sat eating noisily while glaring at White Eagle.

White Eagle rose, scooped water, and offered it to Two Elks Fighting. "Come on, brother. Have some water," he whispered. Erik finally drank.

"No talking."

White Eagle signed instead. They sat quietly. White Eagle hoped they wouldn't retie his hands. He figured Two Elks Fighting was pretending to be more out of it than awake. White Eagle had that to his advantage. They didn't know his thoughts, and now time was on his side.

***

"That white boy ain't comin' 'round like he oughta, Ed," Gibbs observed.

"Now how do you go about explainin' that? You damn near killed him. He's lucky to be comin' 'round at all."

"Well, if he don't improve, that Injun ain't going to bother to take us to his gold," replied Gibbs. "That Injun won't care two licks about leavin' him if he's dead."

"Good point," replied Blaine. He stood. "Guess it's time to tie 'em back up."

Blaine kept his pistol readied while Gibbs began to retie White Eagle.

"By the way, Frank, what do you make of him always eyein' the back trail? Think someone's followin', or does he just want us to think so?"

"Not sure," replied Gibbs. "I've been watching. Haven't seen a thing. Best be on our guard either way, though." He finished tying White Eagle. "What do you want me to do with the white kid? Think I need to tie him? He's still out of it."

"Might be he comes to in the middle of the night. We don't want to wake up with our throats slit."

325

Gibbs got more rawhide and tied Erik's hands. Erik's head bobbed. He didn't resist.

"I think he's sleepin'. Probably he'll be better in the mornin'," offered Gibbs. He finished with Erik and returned to sit with Blaine.

"Reckon that Injun is still takin' us to the gold, or is he just leadin' us on? I can't believe it's this high up."

"I think he's headin' us in the right direction all right," said Blaine. "He hasn't wavered from his heading. But we'll know, come mornin'." Blaine leaned back, gazing at the night sky. "If he's leadin' us on, or if the white kid dies, we'll make short work of him and head on outta here."

"Sooner than later, I take it."

"Yeah, I'm beginnin' to think so," mused Blaine. "But remember, that prospector figured it was up here. Least that's what he was tellin' us when he was still talkative. Otherwise, I'd for sure have figured that young buck was just leadin' us around."

"Reckon you're right," Gibbs recalled. "He sure was happy to have company there for a while. Even suggested there was room across the draw if we wanted our own diggings. Almost got me to thinkin' I could take him up on his offer and make an honest livin' for a change." He guffawed. "Too bad he didn't check our credentials 'fore invitin' us in.

"Then he had to go and show off those rocks of his, includin' the Injun's. Mighty peculiar what the high lonesome can do to a feller. He shoulda knowed better than to go and gab. He just plumb made the takin' a lot easier than the mining."

"For a fact," agreed Blaine, stretching.

Erik was awake, listening, trying hard to understand what they said. He understood a few words—not that it much mattered. Erik figured that if they were openly talking, they didn't intend to leave any witnesses.

"You think they'll try to make a break for it tonight?" asked Gibbs.

"Not as long as one of 'em is still near dead," replied Blaine. "You been watching that Indian? He sure is protective of that white kid. He ain't about to leave him, and that white kid ain't in no condition to go nowhere. So if we keep 'em tied up nice and snug, I don't think they'll go anywhere."

"Just the same, I think we should take turns watchin'," suggested Gibbs. "Got that back trail to worry about some too."

"Sounds fair." Blaine stood. "Come on, Frank, let's get these guys taken care of."

They moved them to where they could secure them to a tree. Then almost as an afterthought, they tied their legs.

"Mornin' we best find that ledge, Indian." Blaine showed the gold again and gestured enough to communicate morning. "If not, you *both* die." He sliced across his neck and looked sharply into White Eagle's eyes. "Sleep tight."

Erik and White Eagle nodded their understanding to each other and drew down as comfortable as possible. Although their hands and legs were bound, they slept quite well, much better than the two who held them captive. They knew they weren't going to try anything that night, but their captors didn't. As a result, Blaine and Gibbs stayed awake, watching their two captives as well as their back trail. White Eagle's constant searching toward the rear had them convinced something was amiss. At night, the possible grew to nagging reality.

CHAPTER 50

GIBBS KICKED HIS CAPTIVES' feet. "Time to get a move on." He untied them.

When Gibbs shook Erik, he shuddered and rolled his eyes. When his hands were untied, he moaned and crawled into a fetal position. It spooked Gibbs.

"I think the white kid's had it. He ain't any better," he whispered to Blaine. "He's still actin' goofy."

"Don't let on to the Indian," hissed Blaine. "If somethin' happens to that kid, the Indian will likely turn on us."

"That's what I was sayin' yesterday, Ed."

"Well then we best get a move on 'fore somethin' does happen."

Blaine walked over to Erik and pulled him to his feet. White Eagle watched keenly. "Come on, kid," said Blaine. "You're not hurt that bad. If you are, I'm a figurin' on leavin' you for coyote bait, so if you know what's good for you, you'll get a move on." Erik stood, wavering.

Blaine continued in a softer tone. "You can do this, kid. Look, it's a good day." He turned Erik to face the sun and waved.

Erik decided not to overdo it and allowed himself a crooked smile.

White Eagle watched Two Elks Fighting and also glanced to the sun. Inwardly, he smiled. Two Elks Fighting was fooling even him, except that they had been whispering earlier, quite coherently.

***

They mounted up, Gibbs propping up Erik. They didn't think it necessary to tie him. He was using his hands some and helping keep himself in the saddle. Blaine took the lead as before behind White Eagle who again walked. White Eagle angled toward a rocky peak.

Erik wobbled in the saddle, and every time he did, Gibbs had to prop him up to keep him from tumbling. "Kid, you better not give out on us," he muttered. "You do, I'll slit your throat and leave you right here." Erik understood some of the English, but didn't let on. He knew what his acting communicated.

They came to a rocky slope, and White Eagle paused, turning to indicate he wanted his hands untied so he could climb.

Blaine dismounted and approached him. "How far?" he gestured. This time he threatened with the knife. He was getting tired of the chase.

White Eagle replied, speaking rapidly in Sheepeater, knowing they couldn't understand. "That rock is where the gold is. Untie me so I can climb up and show you." He pointed with his head and tried to sign, making it obvious he couldn't communicate. "Untie," he repeated.

"I ain't untyin' you—not just yet," Blaine muttered. "Don't trust you no more."

White Eagle seemed not to care. He turned again and excitedly nodded toward the peak.

"I think we're about there, Frank. The Indian's acting excited about that peak up ahead."

"'Bout damn time," muttered Frank. "I'm more'n ready to toss this sack of flour over the edge and get out of here."

They began working their way along a narrow, rocky ridge. Ahead, it came to a sharp edge. White Eagle tried to communicate excitement. "Here, here!" He acted as if he wanted to run ahead.

"That Injun's acting pretty sure we're near. He keeps nodding at that rock ledge. Man, Ed, I can't wait to see that gold. I think this place is about as good as any to dump these two and climb on up there."

"Hold a minute, Frank. Maybe he isn't 'memberin' right. Don't kill the goose yet," he said. He eyed the sheer rocks ahead. "I'm thinkin' we better hoof it from here, though. These horses ain't gonna be able to get us up there." They had reached a few limber pines growing in a narrow saddle that fell steeply to both sides. "Might as well tie 'em here."

They dismounted. When Gibbs tried to help Erik down, Erik held tightly, as if he feared getting off the horse. He shuddered and mumbled words. Only these were Sheepeater words meant for White Eagle. The moment Erik's feet touched ground, he came alive, pulled Gibbs toward him, squatted, rolled backward, and pulled the man from his feet, throwing him over the side. Gibbs shrieked as he tumbled. Erik didn't pause to look. He grabbed a rock and headed toward Blaine who had turned toward him, pistol in hand.

He saw the muzzle flash and heard the explosion. The ball ripped past. White Eagle charged the man from behind, butting him with his shoulder. The pistol flew as Blaine stumbled. Blaine grabbed for his knife and turned toward White Eagle, trying to slash him as he came at him again. Erik closed instantly and brought the rock smashing down with a hollow crunch. The man stumbled. Erik smashed the rock down again as Blaine turned and tried to fend off the blow. The second blow glanced from the man's protecting arms, knocking the knife free. Erik raised the rock again and brought it down, this time finding his forehead. Blaine convulsed, a wheezing and gurgling noise shuddering from within, blood pooling.

Erik grabbed the pistol and ran back to where he had thrown Gibbs. White Eagle desperately fought his bonds. Erik spotted Gibbs, nearly back to the saddle, coming toward him, knife in hand, shrieking. He leveled the pistol, cocked it, and fired, but missed. Memories of missing the snowshoes came to him. Shaking now, not allowing himself to think, he aimed and fired again. Gibbs pitched backward, blood staining his shirt. He fell onto a rock and rolled to the ground, eyes staring sightless at the sky.

Erik sat heavily, shaking, letting the pistol slip from his hand. His head throbbed. He noticed White Eagle still wrestling with his bonds. Struggling to stand, Erik picked up a knife and cut them. He allowed White Eagle to take the knife, knowing what he intended.

White Eagle approached Blaine and, without pause, drove the knife to its hilt into his stomach. The moan reaching their ears told them he was not yet dead. Now he would know death the way Hailey had. White Eagle plunged the knife again and watched as the blood flowed across his hands. He sat back, nodding. He knew this man would die an agonizing death. White Eagle wiped the blood from his hands onto the grass and took the knife for his own.

Neither Erik nor White Eagle spoke. They left the bodies, staring sightless toward the sky where they had fallen. Flies already buzzed around the blackening blood.

Erik collected the men's weapons and caught up the two horses. Leading them, he headed back down the ridge.

Finally, he spoke. "We were right in what we did, were we not, White Eagle? They were bad men; they deserved to die."

"Yes, Two Elks Fighting. They were bad men," White Eagle finally said. "But it did not feel good to kill them."

"No."

"It was not like taking the spirit from an animal so we might eat," White Eagle continued. "It was not like killing a night cat that attacks you. They were like worms. They were not worth death."

"Yes. It was like … nothing I would ever want to do but had to do," agreed Erik.

The two continued, finally stopping for water.

Erik stood near while White Eagle mounted the roan and rode in circles, getting used to ridding. After he knew White Eagle could handle the horse, Erik mounted the mare and turned her downhill. He knew the roan would follow. Even so, he picked an easy route to allow White Eagle more time to learn how to handle the horse. But already he knew White Eagle would become an excellent horseman. It struck him then that White Eagle's world would now be changed—changed forever. He could only hope it was for the better.

It was late afternoon when they reached Hailey's camp.

Erik found Hank. He had crawled into the tent, still barely alive. Erik brought him water and got him to drink. His eyes focused, so Erik knew he recognized what was taking place. Hailey took some water and mouthed the words, *Thank you*. Erik signed back, *Thank you*.

White Eagle started a fire. He was mystified the man still lived. Something inside him did not allow him to die.

They sat, trying to explain in signs what had happened. White Eagle showed him the blood on his hands. Hailey finally realized the two men were dead—killed by these two boys who now tried to keep him alive. But it was all right now. It was finished. He closed his eyes and breathed his last.

***

Morning came.

"We must head home to the camp, soon, Two Elks Fighting," White Eagle said. "The people expect us back, maybe three days gone at most. Perhaps even now they come to seek us."

"Yes, White Eagle." Erik nodded. "But I have something I must do for Hailey."

He found the pick and shovel and began digging the grave. White Eagle mostly watched, but helped pull some of the rocks from the hole. After Erik rolled in the body and filled the grave, he piled on rocks and cut a cross, placing it at the head.

"Why do you put the man who digs in the dirt in a hole and not on the rocks?" asked White Eagle, pointing to a cliff above them. "In the hole, his spirit will not find its way to the sky trails. On the rocks, it can find its way."

"This is a white man custom, White Eagle," Erik tried to explain. "Only his body remains. His spirit has already departed for the sky trails. I bury his body to keep animals from eating it, to be respectful to the man who digs in the dirt."

White Eagle nodded but still looked confused.

For a short time, they remained at the camp. Hailey had left some venison hanging, and they now sat around a smoky fire, enjoying roasted meat. Both had gone without food for much of the time they had been captives.

"Are many white men like the two we killed?" asked White Eagle, suddenly quiet.

Erik was surprised. Never had he given this any thought. "No," he answered. "At least not those I've met."

"That is good," replied White Eagle. "Some of the people say that all the white men do is kill each other and kill the people. That is why some of us fear them. Stands Alone says they will come someday and kill us all."

Erik felt sadness. *How can the people think this way?* "That's not why my family and I came here."

"No," replied White Eagle quickly. "You have a good heart. You wanted to be of the people. You are a true man, Two Elks Fighting."

Erik weighed the words carefully. White Eagle called him a true man—a Sheepeater.

White Eagle continued. "At first I did not think so. I thought you were silly and stupid. I did not want you for a brother."

Erik was startled by White Eagle's talk. That was past three winters ago. Suddenly, he felt saddened. Why would White Eagle mention this now if he had not considered it for a long time—if it had not bothered him? "That is all right, White Eagle …" But the look in White Eagle's eyes caused him to quiet.

"Yesterday, you gave me my life back a second time, my brother. Forever, I am grateful."

Erik looked away. He realized White Eagle felt indebted. "No, Brother. Yesterday you gave me *my* life back, just as you did before when the hump-back grizzly attacked. No, we did for each other what was needed." He paused, then softly spoke, "You have also given me my life in ways I cannot say."

They sat quietly for a moment longer. Erik wondered about the men's belongings. He half wanted to pile everything inside Hailey's tent and set it on fire. Hank had good cooking utensils, a good rifle, an ax, a mule. The horses they had taken from the dead men and their weapons were possessions of which any Sheepeater would be envious. But possessions might cause another to leave the band. Erik didn't wish to see that happen.

"Although the white-man things are good, perhaps it would be better to leave them here, White Eagle," stated Erik.

"I would have the rifle," quickly replied White Eagle. "Perhaps Mother would like one of the man who digs in the dirt's kettles. He has no use for them anymore."

"I am thinking if other white men come and find the people with these things, they will blame the people for the man who digs in the dirt's death."

"You can tell the white men what happened, Two Elks Fighting," replied White Eagle. "You are white; they will accept your words."

"Perhaps." But Erik was thinking other thoughts. Finally they decided on a few items. Erik couldn't dissuade White Eagle otherwise.

Leading the mule, they headed toward Twisted River. Pausing for water, they crossed and then began the long traverse up the canyon toward the summer hunting camp. As they grew near, Erik wondered what the people would say when they rode into camp on horses. He worried that it was not a good thing.

They rode up to Gray Owl's lodge. The people gathered, wonder on their faces.

Erik couldn't help but scan the people to find Quickly Smiles. When his eyes finally met hers, she glanced away. Without question, her eyes had been upon him. That was not good. Now she quickly looked to her husband and ran to his side. Erik feared what others would think if ever they saw his eyes seek her out. This was not right. But he felt proud, how she now reached up to White Eagle.

The men met in council. Gray Owl took the news quietly as did the others. Erik feared what Stands Alone would say, that the whites would come to kill the people. He didn't speak. None did for a long while.

"Gray Owl," Erik addressed him. "Was it good to kill these men? Should we have not tried to sneak away at night?"

Gray Owl studied him. "You wonder because they are of your own kind, perhaps?"

"Perhaps."

"You did what a true man must do, Two Elks Fighting," he said. "They took a man's life without reason. They stole from another man. It is never good to kill a man. But people who do evil are no longer men."

This was what White Eagle had said. Erik found himself wanting to believe it.

At last, Stands Alone spoke, "What the people ask is now that our young men return with horses, will they leave for the Lemhis, like Fighting Bear?"

Both glanced at each other. "No," White Eagle quickly replied. Erik remained silent. On the return trip, he realized what having the horse meant.

White Eagle looked at him, stunned. "Two Elks Fighting, where ..."

Erik sat too troubled to look at him. Finally, he spoke. "I have a sister I must someday seek."

White Eagle looked frantic and stood. "Two Elks Fighting ..."

Erik finally looked up at him and signed, unable to speak. *I must, White Eagle, I made a promise. I gave my sacred word.*

White Eagle turned and left the lodge.

The men considered White Eagle's actions. Perhaps too much had happened. But they knew he had already lost one brother; Two Elks Fighting had also become his brother. It would be hard to lose a second.

Stands Alone spoke, "Perhaps it would be good for Two Elks Fighting to leave the people. He should take the horses. When the white men discover their dead, they will blame the people."

Each man pondered what Stands Alone said. They knew his words to be true.

"If Two Elks Fighting remains with the people, he can speak the truth for us," insisted Free Hawk. "Surely they will listen to one of their own." The thought of Two Elks Fighting leaving brought him pain. He had just witnessed White Eagle's pain. He too did not understand how he could lose a son twice. He wondered what the Great Mystery planned.

"It will be Two Elks Fighting's decision," replied Gray Owl. He said it with a heavy heart. "Each man must choose for himself what he must do."

***

The ripening-berry moon arrived. In a few weeks, the people would leave for the winter camps. Erik knew he would not. White Eagle had not offered Quickly Smiles to him. Erik prayed he would not. He did not know how he would respond when next he would. He knew what his heart and his being wanted.

White Eagle didn't talk of his leaving. They hunted as if nothing had happened. Now they rode the horses out and easily reached game where no one could before. The young boys gathered around. Already they were learning how to care for the animals. Already they were beginning to ride. Something inside Erik said this too wasn't right. This wasn't right for the Twisted River Band.

Then White Eagle again offered Quickly Smiles. Erik felt the dread seep in. How could he tell White Eagle that he loved Quickly Smiles? He wanted her but not as a gift. He loved her, and he knew she loved him.

With great difficulty, he spoke. "Before, White Eagle, when you offered Quickly Smiles, you said it would honor you. It would honor Quickly Smiles," Erik said softly. "I shared the robes with Quickly Smiles, and it was good, White Eagle. But I cannot do this again.

"Now I ask you, please honor me; take away this gift." He remembered his vision. The elk said he would fight for Quickly Smiles. He knew now the elk spoke of White Eagle. He could not do this. Perhaps not now, but one day this would cause him to go against his brother. An ache welled within his chest.

White Eagle sat confused. He tried to understand what Two Elks Fighting was saying. A sadness came to him. "Though my heart hurts, I respect your wishes, Two Elks Fighting. I wish to honor you," he whispered. "We will no longer speak of this."

Alone with his adoptive parents several nights later, he heard the wolves howl. He rose with his robe and wandered to the meadow, listening. He missed his family. He wondered about his sister.

He stood feeling the unusual warmth of the evening. After the last cold rain, it had warmed again like summer. *Ah, the fool's time,* he remembered. *The summer warmth to fool the hunter before the cold spirits returned.*

He noticed the brush pulled in front of White Eagle's lodge. *This is a very good thing*, he thought, and a gladness came to him.

He walked to the shore of the small lake and watched the moonlight dance from the tiny waves. Impulsively, he dropped the elk robe and dove into the crisp water. He swam a few strokes and then lay floating in the water, staring at the night sky, at peace.

Shortly, he grabbed his robe and dried himself. Now he could smell the change in the weather. He returned to his own quiet lodge and slept.

CHAPTER 51

THE STORM ERIK HAD sensed came the next evening. The rain ended in snow, leaving an inch on the meadows, but it soon melted in the sun. The leaves in the high country were changing. It was the moon of the fattening animals. Soon the men would hunt again for elk and, in a few days, return to the winter camps. Erik would not make this journey with them.

Erik slowly made the rounds of the camp. He explained to Gray Owl that he would tell no one of the Sheepeaters. He would pray to the Great Mystery that the white men would leave the people alone. He could not deny that more whites would come into the canyon, just as he and his family had done, looking for land to settle or looking for gold. They would probably not settle in the canyons—it wasn't suitable to farm—but they would come near enough that they would soon enter this country.

He met with Free Hawk and Shining Water. At this point, Erik found it difficult to speak. He took both of Shining Water's hands in his and looked into her eyes. *"Nean Bia', Aishenda'qa. Aishenda'qa nean mukua.* My mother, thank you. Thank you for my life," he said. "I shall remember you as Mother for this part of my life, forever. I will speak of pride to others about you. Your name will be kept alive with me."

Shining Water bowed her head and reached around Erik, pulling him to her, whispering, "My little Sky Eyes, you are the man that I saw you would become. I will think always of you. And perhaps when you have found your sister, you will bring her to your mother so we can tell stories." Erik realized she believed he would return. "You shall take this with you for your sister." Carefully she pulled the necklace of mussel shells from about her neck and placed it upon Erik's.

He addressed Free Hawk. "Thank you, Father. You gave me life when mine was finished. You shall walk with me each day, for it was you who took and made me his own. I shall speak with pride of you always." He unbuckled his father's knife. "This I gave to you before I became your son. You gave it to me when you took me in. But once more, this is yours."

Free Hawk grasped the knife, tracing its outline, studying it. Erik couldn't help but notice how weathered his hands had become. Even his hair now showed streaks of gray.

He embraced Erik. "The people wondered if you were a gift from the Great Mystery. Some said you were not, that you brought some things bad. I believed you were a gift. This day, you should know you were a gift to me, more than I can say. I will always call you my son."

To Singing Bird, he said, "You shall always be my littlest sister. You never hesitated to share with me what was yours. Of you I will also speak with pride."

Singing Bird reached up and hugged him. "Someday you shall come back, and I will be your wife." Erik hugged her back, laughing, thankful for the child's perspective on life.

Finally, he turned to White Eagle and Quickly Smiles. He was hardly able to speak. "Quickly Smiles, I thank you for what you have given me. I thank you for being wife to White Eagle. You will have fine children. You will be a fine mother."

Quickly Smiles looked down. Erik knew she wouldn't show her feelings—it was not proper. But he knew her heart.

"White Eagle, you are my true brother. Brothers do not need to share words. They know each other's heart. White Eagle, you know mine. You too I will keep alive in my heart forever."

White Eagle stood, not speaking, not moving. Only his dark eyes showed his thoughts.

He turned to face the people who had gathered. "To all of you, I will not say *adjö.*" He spoke the Swedish word for good-bye; there was no word in the people's tongue. "Instead, I will tell you, my brothers and sisters, I take far more from you than what I have given, and for this, I thank you from my heart.

"Two Elks Fighting goes to find his sister and return to the white man's world. I gave my sacred word to my sister that I would come to find her. You can understand this. I can now keep my word. You will all remain in my heart forever. *Aishenda'qa.*"

Erik turned the mare, and striking her, he raced from the meadow. "*Flytta på dig häst!* Move, you bastard!" he exclaimed. "Get me out of here."

Erik heard pounding hooves behind him. He turned to see White Eagle.

He slowed to let him catch up.

"Stop, Two Elks Fighting. I shall ride with you."

Erik didn't protest. It only made it harder, but he knew White Eagle could decide for himself what to do.

"Then come with me for a while, Brother," Erik replied.

They turned the horses for the canyon. In the background, Erik could hear the wailing of the women, for one who has left to climb the sky trails. It hurt his heart.

Erik traveled hard and descended into Twisted River canyon. White Eagle followed. He made long traverses to keep the mare from stumbling and falling. Still he almost lost the horse. Erik didn't want to second-guess his decision. Now that he was leaving, he wanted to put miles between him and his memories. He reached the river and slowed down for White Eagle to catch up. They camped that evening at the former winter camp on Twisted River.

Morning came. They journeyed on to the mouth of Twisted River where it joined Thunder Noise River. Erik hesitated. He could turn south, head upstream along Thunder Noise River, and try to go over the mountains, or he could continue downstream to River of No Return.

"I have always asked you about River of No Return, White Eagle. You say it is but a day from here. With horses it would be much less," Erik said. "I know River That Cries must lead into River of No Return.

If we go to River of No Return, would you recognize when we come to River That Cries?"

"Yes. We can follow River of No Return to River That Cries. It is much shorter to walk over the mountain where you first came to us. But here, there is a good trail along River of No Return."

Satisfied, Erik headed north along Thunder Noise River. This was good. He knew the horses would have had difficulty traveling over the mountains. By midday, they reached the great river.

Erik dismounted and stood on the bluffs above the river. Very few trees grew along the walls, only in clumps in the draws. The river was well over a hundred yards wide, about twice the width of Thunder Noise River. At last, he stood on the banks of the river of which he had heard so much. He marveled at the power, at the deep, swift, green waters sliding past.

They continued a distance upstream before they camped for the night. Neither he nor White Eagle spoke much. How could they, knowing they would soon part. He tried not to think of the coming days.

All the next day and the next, they followed the mighty river upstream. They arced southeast, then south, and at last, southwest. Streams entered frequently from both sides. Slowly the great river diminished in size. When they turned southwest, Erik realized they were finally drawing closer to his cabin. His eyes misted as he thought of the days that had passed.

They turned up River That Cries, now not much smaller than the main branch of River of No Return. Late afternoon they reached the site of the first winter camp when Erik had come to the Sheepeaters. Memories flooded back. He wondered when the people would return here for another winter. Perhaps it would be this winter.

Erik couldn't continue. He paused to remember his life in this spot. He remembered where his shelter had been, now only some broken poles. He remembered where Free Hawk's lodge had stood. He went to the painted rock and examined the figures, where his spirit had been painted.

White Eagle also came to the rock. He found where the one who hunts the elk had been painted. However, this he did not tell Two Elks Fighting.

Erik gazed at the place where they had fished and swum. "Come on, White Eagle, it is not too late." Erik walked to the old swimming place. "We can enjoy a swim together." He set aside his clothes and dove in.

Like young boys, they swam. Erik floated in the current, remembering how it had been. They swam across the river and back. When they climbed out and dried off, Erik turned to the setting sun. "Remember, I pray to God at night."

White Eagle stood with him facing the orange sky showing above the notch in the canyon to the west.

"Great Mystery, we stand before you as brothers this night. You have given us much. You have given us life. You have given White Eagle a wife and, hopefully soon, a child. Keep us safe, always. Amen."

White Eagle repeated, "Amen," and turned to Erik. "You say a good prayer, Two Elks Fighting. When I have a son, I shall name him Sky Eyes."

Taken aback, Erik first felt a flash of pride, then a stab of dread. "B-but he will have your eyes, White Eagle, brown eyes." Already Erik couldn't help but wonder if he would have blue eyes.

"And if he has eyes of blue, then I know he shall be my brother's son, and he will honor his father, just as you have honored me and Quickly Smiles."

Erik was baffled. He would never know, he realized sadly, but he would always wonder if a part of him remained there.

They slept in their robes next to the painted rock. Erik felt comfort having his brother beside him again as they had been for many nights during the past years.

***

By late afternoon the next day, they reached Erik's old cabin.

Erik gazed in silence around him.

White Eagle did not speak; his brother's silence and gaze told him he was remembering. He had wondered how he would feel when at last he himself gazed on the place from where his brother came.

Erik studied his former home, memories flooding back. Four years ago, he had come to this valley, this same season. He had still been twelve. It seemed a lifetime ago.

The corral still stood, although the stock roof had caved. The pond was as it had always been. The wagon had tall grass and shrubs growing up around it. It would never move again. The cabin roof, never completely finished, was now home to swallows and sparrows. Small torn shreds of canvas still slapped in the wind. He spotted the crosses on the hill, nearly obscured by the tall grass and rosebushes—the bushes from which he had gathered rosehips for tea. The aspens had turned golden and leaves fluttered down. *This is a good place to sleep,* he thought.

He walked to the graves. White Eagle watched, quiet and sullen.

"*Mamma, Pappa, det är jag, Erik.* Mama, Papa, it's me, Erik." His Swedish words sounded strange. "I came to say good-bye and to tell you that I am going to find Katrine as I promised.

"I have finished my life with the Tukudeka. They are good people, Mama, Papa. They believe in God. It's just different from us, that's all. They loved me. I loved them. They were my family when God took you from me. Now they will always be part of me." He choked on his words.

"Now I am going to find Katrine so I can tell her what has happened, and so I can care for her. You can be sure I will find her. Maybe someday I will return and show Katrine where you are.

"You can sleep now. This is a good place. Do not worry for me. Thank you for my life. Farewell. You will live in my heart forever."

Erik turned and entered the cabin. White Eagle followed. He found the old clothes chest and pushed the fallen roof poles from it. He opened the lid. The clothes were much the way he had left them. He unwrapped and pulled out the Bible. Then he rummaged through and pulled out one of his father's shirts and a pair of his trousers. Carefully removing his Sheepeater clothing, he dressed in his father's clothes. They were slightly large but not by much. Their strangeness hit him. He didn't remove his medicine pouch but tucked it inside his shirt. He also kept on his moccasins.

Carefully he rolled the clothes Shining Water had made for him into a bundle. These he would take as well as his bow. That's when he noticed a cartridge in the corner of the trunk. He had forgotten. He reached in and felt around the bottom. He found six good cartridges. He laughed to himself. These he needed years ago, not now.

Remembering, he reached under the rocks near the hearth and pulled out the rifle, turning it in his hands. It was dry and in good shape. It showed a little rust but would most likely fire.

He noticed the blue and yellow vase on its side, a spider web inside. He picked it up, rubbed off some of the dirt, and carefully wrapped it within his clothes. Katrine would want this. It had been Grandma Anderson's.

White Eagle looked at him. "You scare me now, Two Elks Fighting. You really do look like a white man."

Erik smiled. "Yes."

He swung up onto the mare and tied his Sheepeater belongings behind the saddle. These he would never part with.

It was evening.

White Eagle sat astride the roan, watching.

"It is time, White Eagle," Erik signed and spoke. "I must leave now. You have your life with Quickly Smiles and the people. I must find my own family."

White Eagle didn't speak. His dark eyes simply studied Erik. They showed understanding but also pain.

"I know you never say *adjö*. You do not know the meaning. I think that is a good thing. Too often it means forever. Perhaps I shall return one day. Perhaps not. To the people, life is a hoop. You always return.

"I won't say *adjö* to you either, White Eagle. You are my brother, my true brother."

White Eagle reached out to him and clasped his arm. "My brother, my heart cries."

Erik had never seen White Eagle cry, not even when he knew him as Badger. Now he saw tears.

"My heart hurts more than it has ever hurt," White Eagle whispered.

"My heart hurts too," replied Erik. He studied his brother. "I must go, White Eagle. You will be in my heart with me forever. I will pray always to the Great Mystery that he smiles with favor on you and Quickly Smiles and the people."

Erik hit the flanks of the gray mare and headed south toward the old wagon trail and the burning-rock land. He did not look around; he could not.

"Er-ik Lar-son, my brother," White Eagle whispered, speaking to the empty prairie. "I will remember you forever."

EPILOGUE

CIRCLE OF LIFE

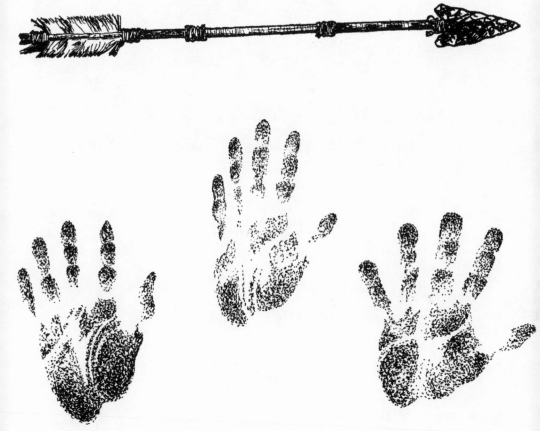

Epilogue

ERIK JOURNEYED SOUTH TOWARD the Snake River until he again intersected Jeffrey's Cutoff. From there, he journeyed on to Fort Boise following the wagon tracks, remembering his own days along the trail. But it was no longer like it had been. Many wagons had now come this way. He stopped to hunt sage hens and mule deer and found, surprisingly, that he favored his bow and arrows to his rifle and ammunition.

Riding into Fort Boise, a new fort, he learned, he found a settlement teaming with emigrants and miners. Some were wintering. Others awaited soldier escort. The country was now embroiled in civil war, and because there were fewer soldiers available to protect the settlers, Indian attacks all along the Snake River route had increased. Settlers once approached Erik, asking if he could guide them through to the Oregon Territory. Now seventeen, he regarded the question a compliment. He realized something about him had changed in order for others to suspect he had the experience for such an undertaking.

Instead, Erik made the rounds, and with difficulty in broken English and sign language, he asked about the possibilities of his parents' train coming through four years earlier. The answers, when he could understand them, were always the same. For the few who could have remembered, too many wagons had been through. Swedes didn't stick out any more than Germans, Irish, or Yanks. Men had come and gone in both directions because of the war. No one knew of any particular valleys being settled—at least not in Idaho Territory. True, some people were traveling north to the Idaho goldfields, but just as many were traveling to other mining camps in the Dakotas or the Nevada Territory.

Striking out on his own, Erik spent weeks riding west and north out of Fort Boise checking all the trails leading into the Oregon Territory and then searching along all the side trails.

Frustration set in. He came to a ridge where the trail he was following descended into a barren canyon. *None of this country matches Adolphson's descriptions. It's desolate and barren like the broken-rock prairies along the Snake.* He gazed north. The edges of forested mountains peeked above the desolate hills, but no trails, at least no major trails, led toward them. He remembered his promise to his sister and felt the ache boil within.

Winter turned to spring, and the rivers ran high with the melting snow. He thought of his days with the people. They would call this the greening-grass moon. Perhaps they would be fishing for steelhead or salmon. Soon they would strike their winter camps and head for the high country to follow the game and gather camas. Perhaps White Eagle and Quickly Smiles would soon have a child. A pang of sorrow washed him. He remembered her embrace and knew his heart still ached for her. And he missed his brother—his true brother. He sat studying the far peaks, wondering where the people would be at this time.

"Hey, son, you wanna give us a hand?"

Two men struggled with a large wheel, trying to load it onto a wagon. Erik knew from the man's tone and gestures what he needed.

Immediately he jumped up and grabbed a hold. Wrestling it up, the three of them managed to slide it into the bed. They fell back, breathing hard.

The man who had asked turned to him. "Thanks, son."

"You're welcome," Erik managed, and out of habit, he signed the words.

The man chuckled. "You appear to know signing pretty well." He also signed as he spoke.

Erik nodded, thankful he could communicate.

"What?" he pointed to the wheel.

"Not rightly sure. Some mining company up north wants us to freight it in. Got about six more like it," the man replied.

"Where do you go?" he signed and asked. Erik was pleased with his English. After arriving at Fort Boise, he had no choice but to learn. The words were quickly coming to him.

"Some place on the Salmon." The man used the unmistakable signs for River of No Return.

Erik grew attentive. "River of No Return?" He spoke the people's language.

"Sounds like you know some Indian as well. I thought you acted a bit strange. You've been around them."

But the man didn't sign, and Erik only partially understood.

"Hey, kid, you want a job?" he signed and asked. "You want to go with us, maybe be an interpreter?"

Erik understood. He also realized that somewhere north, probably between here and the Salmon River, was the high mountain valley he sought. He shook his head excitedly. "Yes, please."

***

When it came time for Quickly Smiles's baby to come, White Eagle told himself repeatedly, *This is a good time. My baby will not be winter born. The grandmothers will not say to leave him in the snow.*

He worried because of the stories Shining Water had told him. But this was the snow-eater moon, and soon the greening-grass moon would arrive. The people had a good winter. They still had food. So why did he worry?

Quickly Smiles came to the lodge, and White Eagle scrambled to his feet. She looked tired but couldn't hide the emotions she felt. She showed the small fox-fur bundle to White Eagle. Her eyes sparkled from tears of joy. "We are parents, White Eagle," she breathed, "of a new baby boy."

White Eagle's heart raced. The joy he felt was unmatched by any memory. Trembling, he took the bundle and looked upon the face of his new son. He felt deeply humbled. "We shall thank the Great Mystery, always, for our new child," he finally managed. "Quickly Smiles, my words cannot express my feelings for you and for our son."

Carefully, he set the bundle down and drew Quickly Smiles to him and held her tightly. "We are now a family. We will be a good family for the Twisted River Band. The people shall sing songs of us and of our new son."

They sat, unable to comprehend this happening, watching their son. The baby's eyes focused on White Eagle; he smiled, and his face crinkled.

White Eagle suddenly looked at Quickly Smiles. She nodded.

"If you look closely, you can see by his eyes."

"Then I am truly honored," breathed White Eagle.

"Yes," replied Quickly Smiles. "He is your brother's son."

White Eagle sat quietly for a moment, unsure, unable to speak.

"He is our son, Quickly Smiles."

"Yes," she replied and carefully picked the baby up. She placed him to her breast. He suckled, his small hands opening and closing into tiny fists. White Eagle touched his little finger against one of his son's hands. The baby opened his fist and grasped the finger. White Eagle smiled and, with his other hand, brushed Quickly Smiles's hair, then brushed his nose against hers.

He sat back and then, at length, spoke quietly. "Gray Owl always said Two Elks Fighting was a gift from the Great Mystery. I always believed this. And then when Two Elks Fighting went away, I could not understand how Gray Owl could be wrong. Why would the Great Mystery do this? Now I see Gray Owl was not wrong."

He reached to touch the baby's cheek.

"A summer ago, I offered you. He honored me, and he honored you. And later, when I offered again, he asked instead that I honor him. I did not understand. But he said he could not. It was not his way."

Quickly Smiles looked away. She had always wondered. But it wouldn't have been right to ask. She felt hurt that Two Elks Fighting had never come to her again. Now she understood. Two Elks Fighting truly loved her, and he truly loved his brother. She looked down at her nursing son—Two Elks Fighting's son.

White Eagle continued, "Two Elks Fighting has given us a greater gift. He has given us his son."